I0610511

The Return of Judex

The Return of Judex

by
Arthur Bernède
&
Louis Feuillade

translated, annotated and introduced by
Rick Lai

A Black Coat Press Book

English adaptation and articles Copyright © 2013 by Rick Lai
Cover illustration: René Cresté as Judex in the 1917 film.

Visit our website at www.blackcoatpress.com

ISBN 978-1-61227-159-0. First Printing. April 2013. Published by Black Coat Press, an imprint of Hollywood Comics.com, LLC, P.O. Box 17270, Encino, CA 91416. All rights reserved. Except for review purposes, no part of this book may be reproduced or transmitted in any form or by any means, electronic or mechanical, including photocopying, recording, or by any information storage and retrieval system, without permission in writing from the publisher. The stories and characters depicted in this novel are entirely fictional. Printed in the United States of America.

TABLE OF CONTENTS

Arthur Bernède in his office.

Introduction

Judex was a movie hero fashioned by director Louis Feuillade and writer Arthur Bernède. The character appeared in two movie serials, *Judex* (1916) and *La Nouvelle Mission de Judex* (1918). The novelization of the screenplay of the first serial was translated and published by Black Coat Press in 2012. This is the translation of the novelization of the second serial. Although the serial's title literally translates as "Judex's New Mission," this translation bears the more appropriate title of *The Return of Judex*.

When translating the first novelization, I had the advantage of being able to see the serial on DVD to resolve any ambiguities in the text. Unfortunately, *La Nouvelle Mission de Judex* is not available for viewing. Apparently only the first nine of the twelve chapters have survived. However, the French edition of the novelization available to me was amply illustrated with stills from the serial.

I have used the French terms for all titles of nobility. A Count is a Comte, a Baroness is a Baronne, etc. Although I normally use the French terms of formal address (e. g. "Monsieur" instead of "Mister"), the novelization had a lengthy conversation between two American characters, James Milton and Wilbur Osborn. In translating that passage, I had those characters use English terms such as "Mister." Milton had an adopted daughter whom he gave the name of "Primerose" in the original French. Since Milton was an American. I have rendered his adopted daughter's name into the English equivalent, Primrose.

Judex's origin story is the following: As a young boy, Jacques de Trémeuse saw his father driven to suicide by Maurice-Ernest Favraux, a powerful banker. Favraux's motivation for this persecution resulted from his romantic advances being rebuffed by Judex's mother. As a young boy of fourteen,

Jacques was forced to swear an oath of vengeance by his mother.

Upon reaching adulthood, Jacques adopted the identity of Judex (Latin for "judge"). Also known as the "Mysterious Shadow," because he wore a black hat and cloak, Judex abducted Favraux by faking the plutocrat's death with a catalepsy-inducing drug. The vigilante tormented the banker in a subterranean cell where his movements were constantly monitored by an early form of television. Judex also transmitted messages that appeared as fiery letters on the wall of Favraux's cell. However, his resolve weakened when he fell in love with Jacqueline, Favraux's daughter. A widow with a five-year old child named Jean, Jacqueline was the embodiment of self-sacrifice. Learning of her father's corrupt business dealing, she signed away her inheritance. Eventually Judex decided to release Favraux from his prison, but his decision was vetoed by his formidable mother.

Judex's operations were also challenged by Diana Monti, a seductive swindler with designs on the banker's fortune. The battle between Judex and a criminal gang led by Diana comprised most of the storyline of the serial. When this conflict ended, the agreement of Judex's mother to the merciful treatment of Favraux removed all obstacles to the marriage of her son and the banker's daughter. A remorseful Favraux agreed to live in seclusion since the entire world believed him dead.

Assisting Judex in his first adventure were his younger brother, Roger, Pierre Kerjean, an ex-convict who had been made a scapegoat by Favraux, and Prosper Cocantin, a bungling private detective. Cocantin's main role in the serial was to provide comic relief. Cocantin married a formidable American athlete, Daisy Torp. The couple adopted a street urchin, the Licorice Kid, as their son.

In my translation of the first novelization, I had an afterword discussing whether Judex influenced The Shadow. My conclusion was that the primary writer, Walter Gibson, probably wasn't influenced by Feuillade. However, the backup writer, Theodore Tinsley, had written a novel, *The Prince of*

Evil (April 15, 1940), which contained some similarities to Judex's first adventure. In order to confirm the theory that Tinsley was familiar with the French hero, it needed to be determined whether the *Judex* serials were ever shown in the United States. My findings were then inconclusive. Since that time, I discovered new evidence indicating that the serials weren't marketed in the United States. However, there was another way for Tinsley to have been exposed to them. Tinsley was an American soldier in France during World War I. He could have seen the *Judex* serials during his wartime service.

There is another literary character whom the Judex serials may have influenced. In any series with a recurring hero, it becomes important to create a memorable villain. Once the hero is established, only a worthy antagonist can make the story noteworthy. Feuillade and Bernède needed to create a master criminal to combat Judex.

Feuillade was no stranger to criminal masterminds. He had directed five films based on Fantômas, the murderous fiend created by Pierre Souvestre and Marcel Allain: *Fantômas – À l'ombre de la Guillotine* (*Fantômas: In the Shadow of the Guillotine*,1913), *Juve contre Fantômas* (*Juve vs. Fantômas*, 1913), *Le Mort Qui Tue* (*The Murderous Corpse*, 1913), *Fantômas contre Fantômas (Fantômas vs. Fantômas*, 1914), and *Le Faux Magistrat* (*The False Magistrate*, 1914). When Feuillade lost the rights to Fantômas, he created a gang of similar criminals in his classic serial, *Les Vampires* (*The Vampires*, 1915-16). The most memorable member of that gang was Irma Vep, a cat burglar who wore black skintight garments.

La Nouvelle Mission de Judex borrowed from both Fantômas and Irma Vep in fashioning two memorable evildoers, *N'a-qu'un-Chasse* and Baronne d'Apremont. Like Fantômas, *N'a-qu'un-Chasse* was a master of disguise. This new master criminal also headed a gang similar to the Vampires, *La Rafle aux Secrets*, which literally means "The Raid to the Secrets." I have taken the liberty of translating this organization's name as the Secret Raiders.

N'a-qu'un-Chasse possessed an ability that was absent in Fantômas, an almost supernatural power of hypnotism. Feuillade and Bernède probably got this idea from Alexandre Dumas's novels of the French Revolution. Dumas had taken an historical confidence trickster, Joseph Balsamo, who had played a minor role in a sensational swindle of the 18th century, and transformed him into a master mesmerist manipulating the destiny of France. By combining Fantômas and Balsamo in the character of *N'a-qu'un-Chasse*, Feuillade and Bernède had anticipated Dr. Mabuse, the German master criminal created by Norbert Jacques. Mabuse became the central character in three films directed by Fritz Lang.

N'a-qu'un-Chasse was described rather cleverly in the original French as "le mauvais genie," a phrase which could be translated as either "the evil genius" or "the evil genie" (although "evil spirit" would be more accurate). Therefore, the arch-villain could be viewed as both a human mastermind and a supernatural force. I have translated this phrase as "the evil genius" or "the evil spirit," depending on its proper context in the novel.

The chief assistant of *N'a-qu'un-Chasse*, Baronne d'Apremont, was a femme fatale in the tradition of Irma Vep. The Baronne even wore the same cat suit as Irma. In the novelization, the Baronne was a woman under 30. However, the movie stills reveal that she was portrayed by Juana Borguese, an actress clearly over 40. The reason for this discrepancy is suggested by a careful reading of the text. In the storyline, *N'a-qu'un-Chasse* was assisted in a kidnapping sixteen years earlier by a woman named Elsa Rhener. In the novelization, the Baronne and Elsa were different people. In the movie serial, Elsa Rhener probably assumed the alias of Baronne d'Apremont.

The novelization utilized a false legend about a French queen, Marguerite de Bourgogne (1290-1315), also known as Margaret of Burgundy. In 1314, she was accused of adultery (probably falsely) by her husband, Louis X. A year later, she died in prison under mysterious circumstances. The tragic story of this French queen was totally twisted into a wild tale in which she became a serial killer who strangled lovers after making love to them. These murders allegedly transpired in a fortress called the Tower of Nesle. In this bizarre perversion of fact, Marguerite's crimes were supposedly witnessed by a famous philosopher, Jean Buridan. Listed among Marguerite's victims was a totally fictional character named Philippe d'Aulnay. This libelous story was popularized in a play, *Le Tour de Nesle* (1832), written by Alexandre Dumas and Theodore Frédéric Gaillardet.

Rick Lai

THE RETURN OF JUDEX

Part One: The Mysteries of a Summer Night

I. The House of Bliss

The La Frondaie estate, located on the Seine, near Fontainebleau, was certainly one of the most beautiful and lavish
residences in France. This vast Norman mansion of modern
construction had three quarters of its surface decorated by a
mass of wisterias and roses. Flower beds harmoniously punctuated the green lawns alongside tress as forceful and majestic
as those of the neighboring forest. A network of ivy-covered
walls surrounded a park of several acres whose natural vegeta-
tion remained unsullied by human hands. A stream flowing
through the park was a torrent in miniature that spun an eternal
song of eddies and cascades. The trilling of blackbirds, night-
ingales, warblers and finches enhanced the fragrant atmosphere of the countryside.

This aura of pure beauty served as a constant invitation
to the blissful joys of life. Nevertheless, for many years, this
area had remained deserted and ignored. This had been a soli-
tary part of the forest until an army of laborers under the direction of a skilled architect transformed this isolated park into an
Eden of delights.

The owners of this angelic realm appeared. The tall husband had an aristocratic profile conveying an energetic vision
of nobility. The infinitely graceful wife had kind eyes and a
gentle smile. She was accompanied by a six-year old child.
This blond boy was as handsome as the angels that filled the

immortal frescoes of the Italian painters of the Renaissance era.

No one in this area had known the family prior to their arrival. These new lords of the manor evoked both curiosity and sympathy from the local inhabitants. In fact, they tactfully displaced a discreet generosity that quickly disarmed any envy normally directed against those whom fortune favors. The Comte and Comtesse de Trémeuse quickly earned the respect of their neighbors and were embraced with admiration and friendship. Their intense love for each other was exempt from the materialistic worries that hold happiness hostage. When one saw them with their gently linked arms and radiant faces, their harmony represented the tranquility that every human being craves.

On a lovely mid-summer afternoon, the Comte and Comtesse de Trémeuse sat on a bench near a shadowy passage leading to the entrance of the park. Despite leaning lovingly towards her husband, the Comtesse appeared lost in deep thought, her smile gradually disappeared. A melancholy expression crept across her features. A small tear ran down her cheek, Already sensing the anxiety of his spouse, Jacques de Trémeuse seized her hand and spoke in a soothing voice.

"Jacqueline, what's wrong?"

Raising her head, she shivered slightly as she sought consolation in the bright, clear eyes of her husband.

"Jacques, I'm afraid. "

"Afraid... My love, why?"

"I'm afraid of being too happy!"

The Comte replied with deep emotion. "Why question the bliss that unites us? Haven't we paid for it in advance? I'm reluctant to remind you of past events which should be exiled from our memories. Since you're overwhelmed by an inexplicable anguish, I have no choice but to evoke the tragic circumstances of our courtship.

"A terrible oath sworn to my mother bound me to conduct a vendetta against your criminal father. My destiny was to be an implacable avenger. My mission was to strike without mercy. Then suddenly my resolve weakened. Jacqueline, you entered my life with your grace in the face of misfortune, I was captivated by the allure of your exquisite soul. Your charm and beauty disrupted my commitment to vengeance. From the moment I saw you, I was in love. My heart belonged to you."

"My lover!" murmured Comtesse de Trémeuse resting her head on her husband's shoulder.

"It was then," continued the Comte, "that both of us learned the true extent of human suffering. To condemn your father was to lose you eternally. How could I grant absolution? My honor was bound by my promise to my mother. Our love prevailed over this frightful dilemma. Our love instilled pity in the heart of my mother. Our love caused tears of remorse to flow from your guilty father. Our love destroyed all the misery separating us. Our love permitted us to be one in marriage by hurling into oblivion the family secrets separating us."

The Comte lowered his voice to a whisper. "Today, the world believes that the banker Favraux rests in the cemetery of Les Sablons. Silence has descended forever on the memories of his misdeeds. You, his daughter, are consoled by the knowledge that he still lives consecrated to a life of atonement."

"You speak the truth, my love!"

"Haven't we earned the right to be happy! Jacqueline, our happiness wasn't wrongfully attained! My love, look at me with your clear eyes, show me the radiance of your being. Be attentive to our joys. The bad days are finished. Judex has disappeared. There is only the man that loves you."

"Jacques, I love you," she declared with all the romantic vibrancy of her emotions. "Your words have dispersed the vague impression of anguish disturbing our bliss. We have ample reason to forget our past sufferings, but don't force me to forget Judex. On the contrary, let me always remember that fearless and irreproachable hero, that Knight of Justice who appeared when I was near death. You were so handsome! You were so profoundly noble that immediately I loved you without knowing the truth! It was from that moment that my heart became the sanctum of your spirit. Don't destroy my memories of the first time you enraptured me."

"Jacqueline!" Comte de Trémeuse's lips tenderly touched those of his wife.

She responded fervently. "You weren't satisfied to remain the hero that I'll always admire. You not only rescued a woman, you loved her son as if he was your own. This small child now truly has a father. Jacques, you know how much I love you, but you never realize how much I revere you!"

"How could I not love our Jean? Didn't he melt my mother's heart? Didn't he inspire the forgiveness that permitted our love? He's so full of goodness. It thrills me that he returns my affection. In a word, I want him close to me as recognition of the eternal debt that I owe him."

Jacqueline was full of maternal pride. "Speaking of our little angel, he has just returned from visiting your mother's."

A luxurious automobile stopped in front of the gate of La Frondaie. Followed by a young gentleman in an elegant suit, a charming boy ran with outstretched arms towards his smiling parents.

"*Bonjour*, Mama. *Bonjour*, Papa. Grandmother de Trémeuse wanted to keep me longer. Isn't that true, Uncle Roger?"

"It's true," confirmed Judex's brother.

Jacqueline took Roger's hand. "Thank you for driving my son. How is your mother's doing?"

"Very well!"

Hugging and kissing his mother, Jean overwhelmed her with the account of his stay at his adopted grandmother. Inexhaustibly babbling, the lad asked for news of his pony Lutin and his two dogs, Flip and Bobby.

Under the golden light of a superb sun, they all walked towards the house. The family marched in a joyful unity that seemed capable of withstanding any assault. Shortly thereafter, the two brothers conferred in a luxurious living room whose wide bay windows allowed the clear daylight to illuminate this happy home.

Roger affectionately embraced his brother. "Jacques, you're so happy!" Then as he was invaded by bitterness, Roger collapsed into an armchair. "But I suffer!"

Jacques looked at his brother with concern. "Why didn't you tell me the truth earlier?"

"Forgive me for keeping secrets from you. Before I confided in anyone, I wanted to be sure my dream wasn't impossible. I hoped that my love would be returned!"

Jacques smiled. "And if I bring you, not hope, but certainty that your dream will come true?"

"Brother!"

"You shall see! The older brother calmly talked into a telephone. "Operator, please connect me to 0-17?"

"The Chateau d'Arbois," emphasized Roger becoming pale.

"Exactly, the Chateau d'Arbois," repeated the Comte, absolute master of the situation.

"Jacques," interrupted a deeply troubled Roger.

"Wait a minute. Hello, my dear Primrose. It's Jacques de Trémeuse... As I promised this morning, I'm calling to let you know Jean and Roger are back at La Frondaie... Understood... Perfect... My regards to Monsieur Milton... See you soon."

Turning towards a bewildered Roger, the master of La Frondaie cheerfully addressed him. "It's my pleasure to inform you that Primrose will be here in five minutes. I hope that you are now happy."

"I don't understand. I'm afraid to understand! It's as if a blindfold had been removed from his eyes. Then... Primrose?"

"Primrose has feelings for you as deep and pure as those she inspired. Do you believe that I would break your heart by fostering an illusion?"

"Did she say anything to you?"

"Nothing! It wasn't necessary. For months, both of you betrayed your feelings for each other. Like you, she hesitated. Like you, she was blinded by uncertainty caused by your shyness and her purity. You never noticed how she reddened while talking to you. She couldn't realize how you trembled while looking at her. She shall come. Without fear, you will be able to fulfill the divine promise already engraved in your heart. The words are just waiting to flow out of your lips. Go to her. Tell her. She will reply. "

"Jacques," shouted Roger falling in the arms of his brother. "I no longer envy your happiness."

An ecstatic Roger ran outside.

II. Primrose

Some years earlier, a rich American, James Milton, had settled in Chateau d'Arbois, the estate adjacent to La Frondaie. The reclusive Milton never revealed his activities or the reasons why he left his native land. Shunning his neighbors, he devoted himself to long trips and scientific experiments conducted in secret. The only person privy to Milton's endeavors was his devoted secretary, Wilbur Osborn.

The local inhabitants were suspicious of this wealthy foreigner. Their mistrust evolved into hostility that his haughty indifference did nothing to disperse. Absurd and contradictory rumors circulated in the neighborhood.

Some claimed Milton was a madman. Other said that he was a criminal. To the surprise of all, there arrived at the castle an extremely beautiful woman with enchanting brown hair, distinct velvet eyes and the smile of a Madonna. Her name was Primrose. She was James Milton's daughter. After graduating from a prominent French boarding school, she moved in with her father. Gossip circulated that the eccentric American would now end his rigid isolation. That didn't happened. His doors remained stubbornly closed. Other than some Paris professors engaged to complete Primrose's education, no one crossed James Milton's threshold. The young lady didn't seem to suffer. She appeared to love her father as much as he loved her. The honest joy on both their faces made this evident.

A visit by Jacques de Trémeuse, their neighbor, on the minor matter of a joint wall, had the consequence of altering the habits of the residents of the Chateau d'Arbois.

Monsieur de Trémeuse expected to encounter an arrogant eccentric. Instead, he discovered a well-mannered gentleman and a brilliant scholar. The two men immediately developed a cordial relationship.

Possessing similar intellectual interests, they enjoyed each other company. Their relationship was discreet at first, but James Milton eventually discerned the noble character of his neighbor. Accepting Monsieur de Trémeuse as a close friend, the American related his past.

Despite being the heir to an immense fortune, he desired to make money by his own hard work. By the age of 30, his genius as an inventor had already made him famous in the United States. With a loving wife and daughter, his life couldn't be happier. Then catastrophe struck. An extra edition of a major New York newspaper reported that his wife and child had perished in a railway accident. Hours later, he was present at the scene of the tragedy. He identified his loved ones among the charred and disfigured corpses.

In order to avoid being driven insane by the tragedy, James Milton took refuge in France. His gnawing grief might have overwhelmed him if not for a decision to take a stroll in the forest around Fontainebleau. He heard plaintive cries arising from bushes along the road. Responding immediately, he discovered an abandoned infant, no more than 15 months old, crying from fear and hunger.

James Milton's initial intent was to turn over his discovery to the police. As soon as he took the child in his arms, she stopped crying. Instinctively her hands reached out in a gesture of love. Her head pressed against her savior's chest. Her lips formed a smile that reflected a prayer from a lost soul. To this touching display of affection, words flowed from the American's mouth. "I'll keep you!" It was at that instance that he christened the child Primrose.

James Milton instantly felt an attachment to his adopted child. As she grew, he gave her all the love which his heart could bestow. Due to the child's exquisite and affectionate nature, she gave him a new goal in life. Similarly his love molded her.

Primrose viewed her foster father more as a god rather than a benefactor. When Milton insisted that she forego sharing his life of isolation to seek the natural company desired by a girl of her age, she refused.

"No! I live only for you. Just as you live only for me!"

This the story that James Milton told Monsieur de Trémeuse. This nobleman developed a deep regard for the American. Without needless sentences, both men exchanged a firm handshake that traditionally seals true friendships. The next day, James Milton and Primrose visited La Frondaie. Not only did Primrose charm Jacqueline, she conquered Jean. Within a week, the young boy went from calling her his "girl-friend" to referring her as his "big sister." Then fate intervened. Prince Charming appeared to Primrose in the person of Roger de Trémeuse. Love consumed her. It was the exquisite romance that could only bloom in the heart of a 17 year-old girl.

Near the gate separating the two properties, Roger waited in ecstasy. Jean was playing next to him. Suddenly they gave a cry of joy. Walking very softly, Primrose appeared. Who would she greet first? Roger or Jean? It was Roger whom she approached. She hesitated as her face reddened from embarrassment. With his hat in his hand, Roger cautiously moved towards her. He opened the gate.

"*Bonjour*, Primrose!"

"*Bonjour*, Roger!"

Silence followed, but it was a charming silence which united their souls. When their eyes met, any words became unnecessary. Roger eventually spoke the song playing in their hearts.

"We love each other!"

"Yes, Roger, We love each other!"

The lips of Jacques's brother skimmed Primrose's forehead before she interrupted.

"Now, I understand the joy that I felt in your presence, and the sadness that I felt when you left. It was love."

"Yes, Primrose. As early as today, if you consent, my brother as my proxy will ask Monsieur Milton for your hand."

She paused before resuming. "You bear an illustrious name. I am a foundling."

"That isn't important in my eyes. I love you."

"A mystery surrounds my birth. Monsieur Milton was unable to discover any clues to my true origins."

"We live in an era where the only important alliance is that of the heart. When a man loves a woman, it's unimportant what her past is. I can never love you enough. I want you to be the companion of all my days --- the good angel of my life."

"I also want this with all my soul!" admitted James Milton's foster daughter. "At the same moment that I am drawn to you by an irresistible force, a fear embraces me."

"What?"

"I may be unable to make you happy."

"What are you trying to tell me?"

"I don't want to cause any worry, but I must reveal something that I have hidden from my father."

"Speak."

"Roger, I'm plagued by strange sensations. At certain times, especially during evenings when I'm alone, my soul seems suddenly to leave my body. I become nothing more than an inert mass whose spirit floats in the air. Then there is another feeling... even more painful. I feel the presence of an evil shadow, a harmful ghost that seeks to rob me of all I love... my father... you. .. It pushes me towards an unfathomable abyss. At this moment, the most frightening thing happens. Everything freezes inside me. It's as if I was abducted by an invincible force. I'm in a state of living death. I depart... but I don't know where! It's horrible!"

"Primrose!"

"I wonder if this haunting isn't an emanation from my unknown past! Perhaps it wants to possess me to perform some vengeance of which I will both be the instrument and the victim!"

"My beloved," assured Roger, "rid your mind of these delusions. Our love will suffice to exorcise this dark spectre. You shall no longer be haunted by these visions. They were only the fleeting symbols of the anxieties surrounding our courtship. Trust in me. Nothing shall separate us. I'm here to protect you... to love you, Primrose. No one can foresee their fate. No one can predict the next day. We live in an era where human passions cause us to imagine precipices that lead to a maelstrom of catastrophe. What's important is that our hearts are united. No barrier separates us! Primrose, we are privileged to live in a time when only love matters!"

"Roger! I believe you!" shouted Primrose. "You have just reassured me completely. Yes, it was only a bad dream. I'm yours forever!"

Jacques's brother repeated those two words that Primrose had said from the depths of her soul.

"Yours forever! Yours forever!"

Suddenly the girl staggered and became pale. As if the evil spirit of her fears spread its wings over the park, she repeated the words voiced earlier by Jacqueline de Trémeuse:

"I'm afraid... Yes, I 'm afraid of being too happy!"

III. The Secret Raiders

"Gentlemen," declared the Comte de Trémeuse to his guests, "I have a wonderful announcement."

Silence immediately gripped the parlor of La Frondaie. Looking at James Milton kindly, the host made his revelation

"My friend and neighbor, in honoring the betrothal of his daughter to my brother Roger, will donate to France his invention that will revolutionize naval navigation."

A smattering of applause circulated among the audience. An elegantly dressed man with snow white hair spoke.

"Monsieur Milton, is this your automatic propeller?"

"Yes, Doctor," confirmed Primrose's foster father. "After countless years, I have realized my dream. My coastal experiments have succeeded beyond my wildest hopes. In a few days, I hope to deliver my patent to the Minister of the Navy."

"This is a spectacular gift," affirmed the Comte. "I'm convinced that all France shall recognize this fact."

As the applause grew louder, the inventor interrupted humbly.

"I wish only that my modest gift illuminates the happiness of the lovely young couple who will soon marry."

"Thank you!" stated the Comte as he shook his friend's hand.

"Monsieur Milton," said the white-haired man, "you stated earlier your intention to deliver your remarkable invention to the Naval Ministry."

"Exactly, Doctor, I expect to be summoned, at any moment to the Rue Royale."

"Of course, but don't you fear a theft?" Some other attendees visibly objected to that remark. "Wait, my colleagues!" shouted the doctor. "It's always wise to take precautions."

"Doubtless," confirmed Comte de Trémeuse. "Are you alluding to the criminals, known as the Secret Raiders, who are currently committing burglaries in Paris?"

"Yes," noted the doctor. His sonorous voice contained a slight American accent. "Everyone is aware of the fantastic crimes committed by these perpetrators against the most prominent families and renowned scientists of France. Not only do they respect nothing, but they have easily plundered the most closely fortified residences."

"Hopefully," observed the Comte, "the police will soon put an end to their crimes."

"I'm skeptical," replied the doctor. "The Secret Raiders closely resembles another gang that ran rampant in the United States. None of them was ever caught. I fear that French police will fare no better than their American colleagues. That's why, Monsieur Milton, I counsel caution."

"My dear Howey," stated the inventor. "I recognize fully the wisdom of your advice, but I'm totally at ease concerning the plans of my propeller. They rest in a hiding place that my talented secretary, Wilbur Osborn, has constructed. Only the Comte, Wilbur and myself, know the secret location. I challenge the world to search for it."

"Wonderful!" concluded the doctor. "It would be tragic if the fruits of your genius fell into the wrong hands just when you're going to grant it to the French government."

Beautiful musical arrangements played on the piano could be heard in the background. "Gentlemen," proposed the Comte, "let's abandon the sinister subject of the Secret Raiders and rejoin the ladies."

"Gladly," concurred Milton placing his arm over his host's shoulder.

While the lord of La Frondaie and his friends moved into a vast hall filled with the fragrance of the rarest flowers, Dr. Howey lingered in the parlor. Seated in an armchair, he appeared lost in thought.

Dr. Howey was a man of indeterminable age. His snow white hair contrasted sharply with the freshness of his unwrinkled face. His features radiated youthful enthusiasm. The slanting corners of his mouth implied a slight disenchantment.

After being a Professor of Aesthetics for several years in Washington, he had moved to Paris. His dignified manners and charming wit had quickly made him a welcome guest in the highest echelons of society.

His renowned health regimen, which combined regular exercise with the basic principles of classical aesthetics, had quickly earned him a large and wealthy clientele. James Milton had entrusted Howey with the artistic education of his foster daughter while the Comte de Trémeuse, a man very careful in choosing friends, had hired the health specialist to supervise the physical training of his stepson, Jean. The doctor appeared to be a man of high morals who was beyond material concerns.

Dr. Howey seemed to be savoring life as a blissful smile wandered on his lips. His contentment was symbolized by the bluish vapors escaping from his nearly exhausted cigar. Suddenly he quivered upon hearing a series of long coughs. Rising from the chair, Howey slowly walked a few steps before stopping. He noticed a man of medium height buried inside a vast leather armchair. The fellow had a large forehead, an immense nose and the distraught air of someone confused by life.

"Monsieur Cocantin!" exclaimed the professor. "I didn't notice you."

"I'm here more or less," said a gloomy voice.

"Exquisite evening!" commented Howey.

"Quite," said the hollow voice.

"Mademoiselle Primrose is a charming lady."

"Truly."

"Roger is a true gentleman."

"The best."

"They make an adorable couple."

"Indisputable."

"The Trémeuse family is lovely. Have you known them long?"

Upon hearing a direct question, Cocantin regained his composure.

"Why are you asking?"

"Isn't the Comtesse the daughter of a banker named Favraux?"

"I believe so," said Cocantin in a lugubrious tone.

"Didn't Monsieur Favraux die a year ago in mysterious circumstances?"

"I don't know," vigorously replied the man with the colossal nose.

Taking a seat next to his fellow guest, Dr. Howey continued to ask cordially.

"Comte de Trémeuse told me that you're the head of an important detective bureau -- the Céléritas Agency. Don't you conduct investigations for prominent families?"

"Well... I..," mumbled Cocantin nervously. Suddenly he became angry. "Doctor, don't ask me about such matters!"

"Pardon me." Howey smiled benevolently. "You're usually so loquacious. Why are you so morose tonight?"

The private detective rolled his bulging eyes. "Because I'm depressed."

"Depressed!" replied the professor who seemed more entertained than worried.

"For eight days I have been dispirited," divulged Cocantin. "It's horrible."

"Was your depression caused by sorrow?"

"More by contrariness. My darling wife, Daisy, went to America to claim an inheritance. Our delightful son, nicknamed the Licorice Kid, is attending an English boarding school. I feel lonely and unhappy."

"Why don't you seek a diversion?"

"I tried in vain. " Cocantin's eyes widen. "While taking the train to La Frondaie this morning, I met an ingratiating woman, Baronne d'Apremont. We talked for a long while. She's very sweet. Do you know her, Doctor?"

"Thank God, I don't."

"That's the worse for you. She's extremely beautiful. She's the Italian ideal, a combination of Mona Lisa and La Tosca. She invited me to tea at her place! I felt that my moodiness had been healed. You must have noticed that I was in a good mood when I arrived at La Frondaie."

"You sparkled during dinner!"

"Upon leaving the table, I was consumed by melancholy. Neither the smiling ladies nor the witty conversation, nor even Jean's jests, could raise my spirits. In order to avoid disrupting the jovial mood, I hid in a corner. Doctor, I'm very ill."

"No, Monsieur Cocantin, you aren't ill."

"Then what's wrong with me?"

"You're suffering from a hypersensitive hysterotomy."

"What's that?"

"A rather unusual form of inertia."

"Is it serious?"

"Not at all -- provided you take proper care of yourself."

"What must I do?"

"You must perform special exercises. For example, you must walk in wet grass preferably in the moonlight. Then there's the slithering."

"The slithering?"

"You must crawl on the ground performing rhythmic movements that I shall teach you."

"And afterwards?"

"I recommend ritual dances in leotards. Try this prescribed treatment, and in less than eight days your depression will fly away as it evolves into a beautiful butterfly."

"You're sure?" asked Cocantin skeptically.

"I guarantee it."

"Then, Doctor, I'll try it. If it works, I promise to remember you in my prayers!"

From the lobby came a young woman's voice accompanied by the melodies of Debussy.

"Come listen to Mademoiselle's Primrose's singing," advised Howey. "It should do you a lot of good."

"You're probably right."

Getting out of his chair, Cocantin went into the hall followed by the professor. Stopping at the threshold, Howey watched the director of the Céléritas Agency slip behind the piano. The doctor was puzzled. *How could an intelligent man like the Comte de Trémeuse be a friend of such a simpleton?*

As the Comtesse played on the piano, Primrose seemed to sing only for Roger. Her words of love were deified by Jacqueline's musical genius. Roger's face formed an indefinable expression as he murmured between his teeth: "My sweet dear!"

That evening Primrose fell into a deep sleep. Never had she been so happy. She felt enraptured in a lovely dream.

When she closed her eyes, endless joy filled her being. She no longer feared the astounding nightmares that had plagued her. She was convinced that those disturbing shadows had been permanently exorcised. Only the fulfillment of her most ardent hopes seemed to lie in the future.

Primrose rested calmly, but gradually she felt signs of unease. While her eyes stubbornly remained closed, her breathing became irregular. Long sighs followed by exclamations of fright escaped from her lips. Opening her eyes, she raised her arms upward. Seeing a vision that shook her very soul, she finally spoke.

"The evil spirit! I see him... He's here... I'm afraid... Roger, help me!"

Feeling as if she had been ruthlessly seized by an invisible hand, she dropped her arms. Primrose became totally inert. Then slowly she arose with dazed eyes. Getting out of bed, she robotically put on her dressing gown. With a somnambulist's gait, she left the room. A mysterious occult force had supplanted her will. Primrose walked through the dark house. Descending the large stairway, she crossed through the room without bumping into any furnishings. Her steps were as silent as a ghost. It was as if a spirit from beyond had returned to stalk the material world.

Primrose entered James Milton's study. In the obscure moonlight, she walked to a corner of the room. Halting in front of a vast library of books, her arm touched the wall. Her fingers groped for something Near a portrait, she found a groove hidden in the wall panel. She opened a secret compartment that contained shelves filled with folders.

Without the least hesitation, Primrose removed a bulky yellow envelope inscribed with these words: "Automatic Propeller Plans."

With a frightening serenity, she closed the secret panel. Still moving in a trance, Primrose returned to her room. Opening the door to her balcony, she walked into the open air. She dropped the envelope over the railing. The precious documents fell to the earth. A man had been hiding behind a clump of trees. Grabbing the envelope, he disappeared into the night.

Closing the door to the balcony, Primrose calmly returned to her bed. As she closed her eyes, she exhaled a deep breath. It was as if Primrose was expelling a sinister demon that had possessed her.

She returned to the sound slumber that had been interrupted by her sleepwalking. With a clear conscience, Primrose slept. Her angelic mouth uttered these words: "Roger... I love you."

IV. The Terrible Enigma

After receiving the complimentary farewells of their guests, the Comte and Comtesse de Trémeuse joyfully retreated to the confines of their chambers.

While Jacqueline delivered a goodnight kiss on the forehead of her son Jean, Jacques entered his private study illuminated by Venetian crystal. He was examining the papers on his desk when a cry of surprise burst from his lips. A large yellow envelope had attracted his attention. Written on the surface were large characters in red ink: TO JUDEX.

Recovering from his shock, Jacques de Trémeuse opened the envelope. It contained the following message in bold handwriting:

At a time when so many people are driven to despair, when criminals brazenly commit their atrocities, why doesn't Judex resume his mission of Justice and Redemption. Why doesn't he rescue the victimized? Is Judex too happy?

The message was unsigned. Reclining in his armchair, Jacques reflected on the message.

Who could have written this letter? It invites me to reassume the role of a champion of justice against these Secret Raiders whom Dr. Howey warned about. The mysterious correspondent must be someone involved in the terrible drama of last year.

Let's consider the possible suspects. It couldn't be one of my enemies. I have nothing to fear from Diana Monti, nor Moralès, nor Amaury de la Rochefontaine since they paid for their crimes and took my secret to their graves. Even if one of their former criminal accomplices uncovered my identity, he would hardly challenge me to combat an association of thieves and assassins. More likely, he would seek to blackmail me.

Could it be someone else involved in my earlier investigations? Favraux? Kerjean? Both of them live in retirement, and only want to finish their days forgotten by the world. Therefore, outside of Jacqueline, Roger and Cocantin, no one knows that the Comte de Trémeuse is Judex. Jacqueline is too desirous to preserve our happiness so dearly purchased. Roger is too enamored with Primrose. Cocantin currently seems unwilling to engage in a great adventure. This is bewildering!

Unconsciously, but irresistibly, he recalled the past. Draped in his black cape, he had decreed a pitiless verdict against the wretch responsible for his father's suicide and the destruction of his mother's happiness. He relived dispatching his pack of bloodhounds against those opposed to the cause of justice. He remembered how a young woman and her child, innocent victims of his quest for retribution, had evoked the Angel of Mercy to halt the merciless execution of his righteous vengeance. His mission of implacable hate had been transformed into one of divine forgiveness.

How unforgettable had been those experiences! They had awakened in a modern gentleman of the 20th century the flame of the legendary paladins of the feudal era. These memories had made Jacques de Trémeuse feel once more a champion of limitless bravery and indomitable will. Despite his reluctance, a thought entered his brain.

Yes, it would indeed be a glorious task to war against these elusive outlaws and frustrate their infernal designs. As my anonymous correspondent wrote, their victims demand justice. It is always righteous to assist those who suffer.

But why should I supersede those officially charged with punishing criminals? Do I have the right or the strength? I am now encumbered with responsibilities. Can I neglect my duties to my wife and child? They are my life as I am theirs.

No, Judex's mission is finished. My sole mission in life is to provide for the family that is the very core of my being!

Jacques then realized who wrote the letter. It could only be his mother! She had trained him to become the living embodiment of justice. There were at least two servants in the household who were strongly loyal to her. One of them must have slipped the letter among his papers. His mother had romantic notions of retribution instilled during her childhood in Corsica. Those notions had dominated his early life, but no more! A year ago, Jacques had a fantastic idea of continuing his dual life as a vigilante once he returned from his honeymoon. The harmonious ecstasy of married life had rapidly driven that plan from his mind. No use in asking his mother about the letter. If she wrote it, she would still deny it.

He was about to destroy the letter when the door opened. It was his brother Roger, visibly distressed.

"Jacques! I have just witnessed something horrible!"

"What happened?" questioned the Comte sharply.

"Primrose has betrayed me!"

"That's impossible!"

"She betrayed me! I tell you! I saw it with my own eyes!"

Roger stumbled irrationally towards his brother.

Jacques responded with affectionate authority. "Calm down and tell me the truth."

Roger responded in a quavering voice. "About half an hour ago, I looked out the window. In this lovely summer night, I looked for my fiancée's house. In the middle of the lawn that leads to the Seine, I glimpsed the figure of a man behaving strangely. Avoiding the possibility of an unnecessary alarm, I went outside to investigate. I discovered the mysterious individual to be our friend Cocantin. He explained that his quirky movements were exercises prescribed by Dr. Howey.

"Satisfied with this explanation, I was about to return to the house. Then I heard a car motor near the side of the road.

Approaching the gate, we spied a luxurious vehicle driving fast with its headlights extinguished. It parked near the fence separating the Chateau d'Arbois and La Frondaie. A man got out if the car and vanished into the night. I feared that he was trespassing on Milton's property. What I saw was horrible!"

"Continue," insisted Jacques.

"Cocantin and I followed him. We heard a noise inside our neighbor's grounds. We wondered if several burglars were trying to commit a robbery. We didn't hesitate. We climbed over the fence. There were no lights on in the house. The window of Primrose's room opened. She appeared. I moved forward, then I halted. Primrose leaned on the balcony as if she waited for someone. Then she let a letter drop to the earth. Appearing from behind a tree, an individual retrieved the letter. As Primrose left the balcony, the intruder bolted into the darkness. We pursued him, but he outran us. When we got back over the wall, the car was gone.

"Brother, we must face facts. Primrose is having an affair. She played me for a fool. She doesn't love me. She never loved me. How she must have secretly laughed at me when she lied about those hellish visions."

"What did she tell you?" asked Jacques.

"A ghost supposedly possessed her! She claimed it stole her will power. She must have been mocking me!"

"Finish your story."

"I'm finished. Now you know how I suffer!"

Maintaining his self-control, Jacques responded gravely. "All isn't lost. Don't despair."

"Brother, what are you saying?"

"Let me ask you some questions."

"Ask."

"Describe the man who retrieved the envelope."

"I could barely see him, but he looked more like a criminal than a gentleman."

"Was the letter in a large envelope?"

"It seemed rather thick. Its weight wasn't light because it fell to earth very swiftly. "

"That's all I need to know," asserted Jacques. "I'm convinced this wasn't a love affair. Listen very carefully. The plans of James Milton's invention have just been stolen by the Secret Raiders!"

"Milton's invention!" repeated Roger. "Then Primrose is the accomplice of notorious thieves. She betrayed her foster father -- the man to whom she owes everything! She seemed to love him with all her soul! Then she has committed a more abominable act than betraying me! No, Jacques! It's impossible."

"It's the truth," declared the Comte authoritatively.

"I know your powers of deduction," acknowledged Roger, "but how can Primrose act like such a hypocritical monster!"

"What if she's innocent?"

"Innocent!"

"Why not? She confided to you about her hallucinations. She claimed to be dominated by a will that annihilated her own."

"Yes."

"If this girl obeyed a criminal suggestion implanted in her mind, would she be responsible for her actions?"

"You're right, Jacques! She is innocent! An angel like her can't be a demon!"

"I hope I'm right, but I must be sure."

"How can you prove your theory?"

"I shall act!" promised the Comte de Trémeuse full of vibrant energy. I have just received an anonymous message wondering when people are being victimized, why Judex doesn't continue his mission of justice and redemption.

"To ensure your happiness, brother, I'm willing to sacrifice mine. I shall solve the mystery that has intruded upon this summer night. Even if I confront more fearful opponents and greater dangers than those of the past, I shall fulfill this mission imposed by brotherly love. I will restore your shattered love. Your happiness shall equal mine. I swear it!"

"Brother, I love you more than life!" replied the younger of the two siblings.

"Not a word in front of Jacqueline!"

"I promise!" Roger grasped his brother's hands. "I shall wait."

"As you wait, also hope."

Part Two: Farewell to Bliss

I. Innocent

Following his daily morning routine, James Milton entered around 9 o'clock his spacious study on the ground floor of the Chateau d'Arbois. Examining a pile of letters on his desk, he was noting in the margins whether they required any replies. Suddenly the telephone rang. Answering it, his head nodded in approval as he replied to the caller.

"Yes, Minister, Rue Royale, 3 o'clock this afternoon. I'll arrive at the Rue Royale with the propeller plans. Thank you."

Hanging up the phone, Milton pressed twice the button activating an electric bell. Soon the door opened. It admitted a man whose age was between 35 to 40. Perfectly attired, he had a somber demeanor.

"Wilbur, I have good news," announced the inventor. "We'll be going this afternoon to the Ministry of the Navy."

"Congratulations." declared the secretary as he sincerely shook his employer's hand. Believe me, sir, I'm happy for your success."

"Our success. I owe you a great deal."

"Thank you, Mr. Milton."

"You deserve it, my friend. Your assistance was invaluable. Every day you demonstrated unwavering devotion and gave intelligent advice. I shall never forget your contributions. You shall share in my honors."

"The only reward that I desire, Mr. Milton, is your friendship."

"You have it!"

"That's glory enough for me."

The two men exchanged a vigorous handshake.

Regaining his composure, Milton gave instructions to his secretary. "We should review the propeller plans one last time before surrendering them to the Minister."

"Shall I get them?"

"Yes, please."

Going to the secret wall panel, Wilbur opened it. After examining the shelves, he was perplexed.

"It's strange."

"What's wrong?" interrupted the inventor.

"Weren't the plans in a yellow envelope."

"Yes," confirmed Primrose's foster father. "You put them back on the upper shelf yesterday morning."

"That's what I remembered."

"Well?"

Wilbur Osborn became pale. "They aren't here!"

"What are you saying?" The inventor joined his secretary near the secret compartment.

The two men examined the piles of documents in the vain hope that the plans had gotten stuck between a pair of dossiers. They found nothing. The automatic propeller plans had disappeared.

Remembering Dr. Howey's warning from last evening, Milton trembled. "Could the Secret Raiders have done this? It's impossible. There aren't any signs of burglary. No one could break into a house like this without awakening the owners or the servants. Finally..."

Milton paused. His eyes grew wide with terror. A huge pain seemed to rip through his trusting nature. His gaze focused on his secretary. Wilbur's shoulders became hunched as he sensed the monstrous accusation that then erupted from his employer's lips.

"Wilbur, only three men knew the secret of this hiding place: the Comte de Trémeuse, myself and you."

Hearing these words, Wilbur raised his head to exclaim from colorless lips. "Sir!"

Milton implacably pointed at his secretary. "I have no motive. The Comte is above suspicion. That leaves only you!"

"Me?"

"The thief has to be you!"

"Mr. Milton!"

Milton became consumed by anger. "I lavished on you praise and affection! You betrayed me! It was for money! Wasn't it, Wilbur? If you needed more than your salary could provide, why didn't you ask me? I never refused you anything! I could kill you! You wretch!"

Seizing Osborn by the collar, Milton shook him.

"What did you do with the plans? Answer me! What did you do with them?"

Milton released his hold. The miserable secretary fell into an armchair.

"I swear to you, sir. I'm innocent!"

"I don't believe you!"

"For 10 years, I've loyally served you!"

"No more lies!" shouted the furious inventor. "Stop trying to fool me!"

"What about the Secret Raiders?" sobbed Wilbur.

"Don't use the Secret Raiders as your scapegoats! Only you could have stolen those documents!"

Nearly fainting under the burden of this false accusation. Osborn tried a last ditch effort to reason with his employer. The secretary defended himself with dignity.

"Mr. Milton, I admit that circumstances are against me, but you condemn me without letting me defend myself. You seek to crush me with your contemptuous anger, but listen carefully. Sooner or later, the full truth shall become known and the real guilty party will be unmasked. Then you'll shed blood-filled tears over sacrificing a loyal servant who would gladly have given his life for you!"

Ignoring his secretary's words, Milton grabbed the telephone and gave the operator a number. "Maître Desreiux, have a gendarme come immediately to the Chateau d'Arbois. I'll explain when he arrives... Thank you."

Scarcely had the receiver been replaced when a harmonious female voice interrupted. "Father, why are you summoning the police?" It was Primrose speaking from the study's doorway.

Milton pointed at his secretary. "You want to know why the police are coming? It's to arrest this thief!"

"Arrest Wilbur! Father, you must be wrong!"

She silently contrasted her father's harshness with Osborn's anguish. "What has Osborn supposedly stolen?"

"He stole the propeller plans!" answered Milton.

"That's impossible!" Primrose replied.

"I want to believe that," Milton gravely stated, "but I can't."

Wilbur's hands covered his face in despair.

Primrose felt deep compassion for the secretary. "Wilbur, you can't be guilty."

The secretary fell on his knees in front of Primrose. Suddenly a glimmer of hope irrationally rose within him.

"Miss Primrose, you know that I'm innocent!"

II. Guilty

There was a knock on the door. A footman announced that Roger de Trémeuse and Prosper Cocantin requested to speak to James Milton on an urgent matter.

"I'll see them," said the surprised American inventor. The two visitors came into the study. "Gentlemen, I didn't want to keep you waiting outside, but I can't hide the crisis erupting around me."

Roger and Cocantin exchanged a knowing glance between themselves.

"I can't keep the truth from you, Roger," said Milton restraining his anger. "I've just discovered that my secretary has stolen the propeller plans."

"What?" said Roger.

"Wilbur Osborn is a miserable traitor who shall be turned over to the police."

Roger coolly controlled his emotions.

"Monsieur Milton, before impeaching your secretary, do I have your permission to ask Mademoiselle Primrose some questions?"

Milton was troubled by the agitated manner of both his visitors. "Primrose? Why?"

Roger was reluctant to reply, but the director of the Céléritas Agency intervened.

"Monsieur Milton, please grant us two minutes of your time. I believe everything will sort itself out."

"Everything will sort itself out..." repeated the American inventor.

While Wilbur Osborn looked hopefully at the two men whom he believed to be his saviors, Primrose was seized by a premonition of dread. Sensing her distress, Roger took her hand. They walked out of the study towards a big bay window that looked out on the courtyard illuminated by the burning June sun. Primrose's heart was beating faster than normal.

"Roger, I need reassurance. The evil spirit of which I spoke earlier hovers over me. The theft of these plans and the accusation against Wilbur disturbs me greatly. When you appeared, I felt my joy restored. However, you're speaking to me with a strange tone and tearful eyes. Roger, we're in love! Last night, you were so tender. Today you act as if a withering breath has poisoned the flower of our love. Roger, tell me again that you love me!"

"My love has never been greater than it is at this moment!"

Upon hearing Roger's words, Primrose's became radiant with joy. The two lovers embraced.

"Primrose, in the name of our love, you must not allow an innocent to be accused."

"What are you saying?"

"Last night, a theft was committed in Monsieur Milton's study!"

"I know."

"Your father has accused Wilbur Osborn. He isn't the perpetrator."

"I'm greatly relieved to hear that."

Roger sighed. "He isn't the culprit. You are!"

"Me!"

"Yes... You!"

An ashen Primrose suddenly froze. She gave no cry of protest. She made no angry gesture. She merely gazed at her fiancé with shock.

The young man stroked the hands of his betrothed. They were as cold as a corpse's.

Primrose stood in silence.

"Listen carefully to me," said Roger. "Last night, I saw you appear on the balcony of your room. You threw an envelope outside to a stranger."

"It's impossible!" yelled Primrose returning to reality.

"Primrose!"

"I swear that I didn't leave my bed. "

"And I swear that I saw you. If I was alone, I could be persuaded that I hallucinated. But there was someone with me."

"Who?"

"Monsieur Cocantin."

"Did he also see me?"

"He saw you."

"I repeat, Roger, that I never left my bed. I dreamt about you all night"

"But I saw you deliver the plans to an intruder."

"This is madness!" shouted Primrose. "How can you believe me guilty of such a crime!" Raising her hands to her forehead, she ran back into the study towards James Milton.

"I'm accused of having stolen your plans. And who accuses me? Roger, the man I love!" Primrose fainted into her foster father's arms.

Milton confronted Roger. "How dare you accuse my daughter?"

"Monsieur Milton," interrupted Roger, "we're here to solve a mystery that threatens us all. I'm a man of honor faced with a terrible dilemma. I must either allow an innocent man

41

to be condemned or accuse the woman for whom I would gladly sacrifice my life a hundred times. Imagine what I am suffering. I can prove my claims."

"Speak!" ordered Milton.

Roger turned towards the private detective. "Cocantin, relate what we saw. I no longer have the strength."

Cocantin narrated his experiences last night with Roger. As he spoke, Milton's face became convoluted with shock. Still in her foster father's arms, Primrose beckoned with her arms towards her fiancé.

"Tell him that it isn't true!"

"I swear that Cocantin spoke the truth!" said Roger.

Wilbur Osborn exhaled a deep breath as he had awoken from a nightmare.

"Primrose, is this true?" asked Milton

She protested her innocence. "No! No!" There followed a deadly silence that seemed to last an eternity. Primrose finally broke the stalemate.

"Now I understand! It was the evil spirit!"

"Yes!" shouted Roger feverishly. He underwent a transformation from pitiless accuser to passionate defender. "I am here to vindicate two innocent souls. For I believe Primrose to be no more guilty than Wilbur. If she committed the infamous act that I witnessed, it was because an invisible force made her a blind instrument. I believe you, Primrose, to be the purest of women. I call upon your father, so painfully wounded, and Wilbur Osborn, so unfairly libeled, to help us expose the true source of this tragedy."

Roger advanced toward his fiancée with outstretched hands.

Primrose's eyes glimmered brutally. "It's hopeless. Leave me." She moved towards the doorway. "I know what I must do," she said grimly.

Milton blocked her exit. "Are you guilty?"

"Monsieur Milton!" interrupted Roger.

The American spoke bitterly. "Roger, after accusing your fiancée in the name of honor, you proved your love by defending her. You acted like the perfect gentleman, and I thank you. No matter now this bitter ordeal has broken me, I still must respond to your revelations. I'm unfortunately too realistic to have any faith in the pseudo-science of a superior will magically controlling another human being. I have always dismissed the phenomenon of hypnotism. If Primrose performed this shameful act instead of Wilbur, she did so voluntarily. I know what needs to be done!"

To this horrible indictment, Primrose responded only with a sigh. Repressing her tears, she moved backward slowly. She saw implacable punishment in the face of her foster father. Cocantin looked at her with a combination of tragic sadness and benign understanding. Wilbur Osborn was bewildered. Roger loyally tried to embrace Primrose, but she rebuffed him.

"Roger don't follow me. My fears have become reality. The malign influences that I feel make it impossible for us to be together. I would tempt you into the abyss that engulfs me. That must not be. Farewell, Roger. Farewell, forever!"

She ran tearfully outside. Roger tried to follow her, but Milton stopped him.

"Forget her, my friend. She is guilty. If she was innocent, she would have collapsed into your arms."

"If she was guilty," argued Roger, "she would have dropped on her knees."

"And who dares say Primrose is guilty?" proclaimed a solemn voice.

"Brother!" shouted Roger.

Jacques de Trémeuse crossed the threshold. He scanned the faces of Roger, Milton, Cocantin and Wilbur Osborn. He was no longer the Comte de Trémeuse He was a judge who radiated supreme authority. He was Judex!

"And now, gentlemen, let's talk!"

III. The Evil Spirit

The Baronne d'Apremont, the widow of a wealthy owner of tin mines in Indochina, had moved to an unusual abode following the demise of her husband. Situated on the Rue de Mussert in the far end of Auteuil, the house's exterior looked more like the home of a modest member of the middle class rather than the residence of an elegant aristocrat. Nevertheless, after crossing a small garden and ascending a flight of steps, a visitor would be escorted by a smiling maid into a luxurious antechamber. Filled with statues and paintings done by the old Masters, the parlor revealed the owner to be a true connoisseur. A splendid tapestry of Beauvais hid the door to a special room. This chamber was neither an elegant dining room or a stylish boudoir, but a vast office. Its tables were cluttered with diagrams, dossiers, books, typewriters, telephones, and train schedules.

After flipping through a voluminous file, a woman rapidly pressed the keys of an Underwood typewriter. She barked orders into an acoustic tube or one of the numerous telephones. These commands to her mysterious correspondents would seem unintelligible to the casual observer. This was a typical day in the life of the enticing Baronne d'Apremont.

No one in the neighborhood ever questioned the reclusive life of the worldly woman endowed with singular beauty, a title of nobility and a large bank account. There were several reasons for this lack of interest. She received very few visitors. She rarely spoke to anybody. She paid the local merchants promptly and tipped generously. Her domestic staff from the chauffeur to the chambermaid were totally discreet. Thus, she avoided becoming the subject of gossip while shrouding her life under a veil of discretion.

Rising at an early hour, the dark-haired Baronne d'Apremont, dressed in a provocative robe, was already at work sealing a large yellow envelope with wax. A telephone rang close to her. Placing the receiver against her ear, the Baronne spoke into the tube.

"Is that you, Belles-Mirettes? I'm waiting."

Some moments later, a young woman in the attire of a foreign student appeared. Carrying a briefcase, a cigarette dangled from her lips. Her nickname of Belles-Mirettes meant "Beautiful Peepers." This alias originated from black eyes that radiated intelligence and determination.

Squeezing brutally the hand offered by the Baronne, she spoke harshly.

'"Do you have Milton's plans?"

The Baronne extended the sealed envelope. "They're inside."

"Perfect!" said Belles-Mirettes. She took the envelope and placed it inside her briefcase.

Another telephone in the office rang with an extremely loud intensity. The Baronne lifted the receiver and listened.

"That is excellent," she simply said into the phone before hanging up. The Baronne turned towards her companion. "*He* is waiting for us over there."

"Again!" complained Belles-Mirettes.

"You're well aware that he moves swiftly," retorted the Baronne. "My car is outside. As soon as I'm properly dressed, we'll leave."

Shortly thereafter, the two women sat in the back of a superb limousine with a 24 horsepower engine. The skilled chauffeur drove swiftly along the road from Paris to Fontainebleau. Upon entering the forest, the Baronne gave the driver detailed directions. After following the main road for 15 kilometers, he made a series of turns that led him to an isolated intersection. There he parked near a stone pylon covered with moss and lichen.

The Baronne and Belles-Mirettes left the car and proceeded rapidly to a narrow path. Before they had advanced a short distance, a weird figure appeared in front of them. Wearing a wide cap, the individual had a hairy beard. His left eye was concealed by a black patch that covered half his face. The two women weren't frightened by this intruder. He spoke with a sarcastic tone.

"I, Bébert, alias *N'a-qu'un-Chasse*, sincerely regret disturbing you once more. Ladies, the matter is urgent. Listen carefully. James Milton has discovered the theft of his plans. Accusing his secretary, Wilbur Osborn, he was about to have him arrested when Roger de Trémeuse, accompanied by a certain Cocantin--"

"I know him," stated Baronne d'Apremont with an ironic smile.

"--arrived at the Chateau d'Arbois. They related having seen Mademoiselle Primrose, Milton's adopted daughter, throw a large sealed envelope from the window of her room to a man in the courtyard. Primrose fled in tears. Then Roger's brother, Comte Jacques de Trémeuse, a formidable individual whose history shall be related later, appeared. A large discussion then transpired between Milton, the Trémeuse brothers and Osborn. They agreed to embark on a campaign with two goals: first, the unveiling of the truth about Primrose and second, the recovery of the propeller plans."

"How do you know all this?" ask Belles-Mirettes.

"I have only one eye," replied Bébert authoritatively, "but I see all. Milton's footman secretly owes allegiance to me. He was able to secretly overhear the conspirators united against us. I'm not aware of the exact means these men will employ to pursue their goals, but they must be forestalled. No one interferes with our schemes. You, Jacques de Trémeuse alias Judex, dare to attack the Secret Raiders! You will soon feel the wrath of the man known as *N'a-qu'un-Chasse*."

A whistle sounded.

"The signal," noted Bébert. "Come with me, my dears... The comedy will begin." Docilely followed by the Baronne and Belles-Mirettes, Bébert hid in the woods.

Who was this mocking personage who declared war on Judex? His nickname of *N'a-qu'un-Chasse* was French slang for "Only Has One Eye." Was he the chief of the Secret Raiders? Was he the evil spirit that terrorized Primrose during her terrible nightmares?

Fleeing her foster father's study, Primrose confined herself in her room. Dropping on a divan, she gave full reign to her tears. The weight of the catastrophe overwhelmed her for a long period before she summoned all her willpower to face reality. Accused of an abominable crime by the man she loved, she needed to confront the evidence. Roger couldn't be mistaken. Unconsciously, she must have thrown the envelope to the intruder. She must have betrayed her benefactor under the domination of a will not her own. Despite her sincere claims of innocence, her father gave no credence to her protestations. She feared that Roger, even though he fervently defended her, still harbored doubts. It was more than the poor child could bear. A terrible depression descended on her.

She now was certain that some dark power of evil had cursed her at birth. Was she destined to be the herald of tragedy until she died? The evil spirit seemed to lurk very close to her. Rather than endure such a terrible curse, she resolved to end her life. Resolute in this decision, she sat behind a Louis XV table adorned with crystal vases containing flowers. There she wrote a brief note. Once she had finished, she sealed the letter inside an envelope addressed to her foster father.

There was an emergency stairway located in her bathroom. It was to be used only in case of fire. Using the exit, Primrose went outside. Traversing a deserted pathway to the fence, she opened a small gate that led to the Seine. As she walked along the bank of the river, the sunlight was reflected in its waters.

Suddenly a young boy made a cry. "Big sister!" Primrose was startled. Vibrating with joy, Jean approached her. He hugged her.

"What are you doing here darling?" asked the young lady.

"I'm taking a walk with Juliette," said the child pointing to a chambermaid some distance behind him. "And why are you here?"

Primrose became pale. "I'm also taking a walk."

"Can I walk with you?"

"No, my dear, not today. I need to be alone. Because I'm sad. Very sad."

"My poor sister!"

Tears gushed down Primrose's cheeks.

"Are you crying?" asked Jean.

Removing herself from the youngster's embrace, she ran. "Farewell!" she shouted. "You won't see me again!"

The child wanted to follow her. Juliette, who had heard nothing, gently took Jean's hand.

"You must leave Mademoiselle Primrose, Jean. It's time to go home. I don't want to be scolded by the Comtesse."

Although disturbed by Primrose's behavior, the child felt compelled to obey the servant. He took a last look at his "big sister" as she disappeared behind a hedge.

Primrose ran until she reached a dam that crossed part of the Seine. Advancing to the middle of the dyke, she contemplated the water that flowed through the sluices.

"My body will disappear quickly. It's for the best. I'll die quickly."

She knelt down, but not to pray. She feared that by evoking God, she might receive his order to live. She envisioned the shroud that nature would wrap around her body. The water would become a tomb where she would lie under mystical clarity of the evening stars. She would return to float along the currents as a modern Ophelia with clasped hands and an improvised crown constructed from flowers. She imagined the image of Roger in the water. She dreamt of an eternity with him locked in his arms. Yielding to this exquisite hallucination, Primrose prepared to throw herself into the river.

Yet a subtle terror caused her to pause. Over on the shore, between the leaves of the trees shined a luminous apparition that apparently followed her. Primrose feared the spectre of light was here to devour her soul. Falling over backward into the river, Primrose's face froze in terror.

"The evil spirit!" she screamed.

IV. Judex!

"Monsieur Jacques, tell your brother not to despair," said Cocantin.

While the Comte de Trémeuse worked at his desk, a distraught Roger pouted in the corner. The director of the Céléritas Agency continued to speak. "Do you know what he said to me while we walked back to La Frondaie. He wondered if Primrose was innocent."

"You still have doubts?" asked Jacques.

"I no longer know!" said Roger.

"My dear Cocantin," stated the older sibling, "please leave us for a moment. I need to talk to my brother."

"Gladly," consented the sleuth. "I'll practice the exercises prescribed by Dr. Howey."

After their friend left, the two brothers stared at each other in silence. Rising from his desk, Jacques walked towards his brother.

"The battle has scarcely begun, and you're really to admit defeat," reproached Judex affectionately.

"I suffer!"

"Your suffering should motivate rather than decimate."

"What's happening is monstrous!"

"I know. I felt the same way when my love for Jacqueline appeared hopeless. Get a grip on yourself. You shall need all your strength and intellect. The more that I reflect on the problem, the more I'm resolved to solve it. I have no doubts about Primrose's innocence. I say this not to console you, but because it's my deep conviction. The important thing is to promptly expose the people behind this crime."

"Do you have any clues?"

"Perhaps."

"Tell me."

"Not yet. I want to deal in firm facts not speculations."

"Nevertheless, you hope for success?"

"I do more than hope. I act!"

"Brother!"

"Be quiet! Someone's coming."

A disheveled James Milton entered the room.

"What's wrong?" asked Jacques

"Read!" replied the American extending a crumpled letter.

Grabbing it, Judex read the letter aloud.

Father,

I'm innocent, but you believe me guilty. I have left. If you hear of my death, know that I departed blessing you.

PRIMROSE

Upon hearing these words, Roger screamed in agony. Always master of the situation, Judex questioned the American.

"When did you find this letter?"

"Once you left," explained Milton, "I followed your advice to seek out Primrose. I found her door close. I knocked. When she didn't answer, I opened the door to see that she was alright. The room was empty! She must have left by the stairway in her bathroom. Then I found the letter. After reading it, I immediately went outside. I looked for her in vain. She had disappeared.

"I came to your home hoping desperately to find her here. This letter is a sincere cry of despair. Once I read it, all my doubts disappeared. I now believe in this evil spirit. Why did I accuse her so harshly? Roger, I should have listened to you! I may have driven her to her death!"

"Don't blame yourself!" interrupted Judex. "There isn't a moment to lose! We must find Primrose! We may still have time to save her!"

The trio ran down the stairs. Outside they met a tearful Jean being led towards the house by the chambermaid.

"What's wrong?" asked the Comte.

"He's upset," explained the servant, "because I wouldn't let him take a walk with Mademoiselle Primrose."

"Where?" shouted Judex.

"She was near the dyke, Papa. She didn't want me to go with her. She said I would never see her again."

Judex didn't need to hear anymore. Followed by Milton and Roger, he ran towards the Seine. The lord of La Frondaie owned a motorized dinghy anchored near his home. Jumping into the boat with his two companions, he immediately turned on the motor. The boat zoomed towards where Jean had met Primrose. When they arrived, the dyke was deserted. Had they failed to avert the tragedy?

Without any of its occupants uttering a word, the dinghy followed the current. Suddenly they spied a white form caught on a log adrift in the river. They quickly approached the debris. They found a human body totally wrapped in a blanket that hid its features. Bringing the flotsam aboard. Milton Roger and Judex fearfully raised the veil. Judex opened the shroud.

"It's not her!" exclaimed Roger.

It was actually Cocantin in a lamentable state. Pale and half-suffocated, he was dressed in a soaked leotard that stuck to his frozen flesh. Judex and the others hurried to revive the detective.

Cocantin opened his eyes.

"Did you see Primrose?" asked Judex.

"Prim... Primrose?" stammered the shivering sleuth. As Judex piloted the dinghy to explore the river further down. Cocantin related his recent ordeal in sentences punctuated by hiccups.

"I was exercising by the water when I saw a small butterfly drowning in the river. I can't allow a beast to suffer, not even an insect. I belong to the Society for the Protection of Animals. Since the water might be cold, I wrapped my blanket around me. From the shore, I reached over to rescue the endangered bug. I lost by footing and fell into the river."

"During your exercises, did you see anything?" asked Roger.

He never had a chance to answer. A voice yelled from the shore. "Monsieur de Trémeuse!"

Judex immediately directed his boat towards the bank. As the dinghy approached, a bargeman shouted joyfully.

"Thank god, it's you and Monsieur Milton."

"What's happened?"

"Are you looking for the girl from the Chateau d'Arbois?"

"Yes."

"Was she wearing a pink dress and a ribbon in her hair?"

"That's her!" exclaimed Roger. "Speak quickly in Heaven's name!"

"Don't worry," assured the bargeman. "The young girl is safe."

"My God, where is she?" demanded the American.

"Sirs, I don't know," said the seaman calmly. "I can only tell what I witnessed. I was trimming the reeds a little further down the river. I saw the girl rushed to the edge of the dyke. She fell on her knees. Fearful that she might drown herself, I was about to rush to her assistance. Before I could act, a big stranger appeared in a burst of blinding light like a genie from a bottle. After blowing on a whistle, he grabbed the girl as she fell into the river. Then he ran away with her. I yelled at him, but he didn't answer. I chased after him. He led me to a car where two ladies were waiting. One woman was very elegant with earrings as large as coins. The other wore masculine attire like a foreign student.

"With the girl in the car, they drove swiftly in the direction of the Repentir crossroad. The driver would been ticketed for speeding if a policeman had seen him."

Anxiety appeared on the faces of the two brothers and Milton as the bargeman concluded his story.

"I'm not sure who those people were, but the girl could now be back at the Chateau d'Arbois."

Roger and Milton were going to ask more questions, but Judex's eyes indicated that they remain silent. He placed some money in the hands of the bargeman.

"Thank you for your helpful information. Our fears have been allayed."

As the bargeman said farewell, Judex and the others got back into the dinghy where Cocantin awaited them.

"Come my friends," said Jacques de Trémeuse. "We can only return home."

The boat arrived at La Frondaie.

"Well, brother? asked Roger.

"What just happened?" said Milton.

"It appears, my dear Milton, that the Secret Raiders weren't satisfied to steal your plans. That blinding flash that accompanied the appearance of the stranger is an old stage magician's trick. The man who grabbed Primrose must be a member of the Raiders. They have kidnapped your daughter."

"Jacques!" cried Roger while Milton stifled a sob.

"Rest assured!" asserted Judex solemnly. "We shall find Primrose and the plans. I shall follow these outlaws even to their lair. Justice will be done. I promise!"

That same evening, around 9 o'clock, Jacques was about to put Jean to bed when the door was opened by his wife. She couldn't repress an emotional cry of surprise. Her husband was no longer Comte Jacques de Trémeuse. The elegant gentleman was Judex wearing his black cape and felt hat. Long riding boots extended up to his knees. The Comte looked as he appeared to her in old Kerjean's mill.

Her face became intensely pale. "My love..."

"My inspiration..." muttered Jacques gently. "Let me apologize in advance for the distress that I'm about to cause you, but you'll approve of my actions. Once you know the facts, you'll condone the new mission of justice that I must undertake."

"You frighten me," said the daughter of the banker Favraux.

"Jacqueline, you won't tremble once I explain."

"Speak!"

"A series of tragic mysteries have unfolded in the Chateau d'Arbois since last night."

"Poor Primrose!"

"And poor Roger!"

"You have sound reasons for your decision, You must help them."

"Thank you, Jacqueline! You've always been compassionate and courageous. I should never have doubted your support for an instant."

"Tell me more, my love."

"Yesterday, I received an anonymous letter. It questioned why I didn't resume the mantle of Judex to combat the misery caused by the Secret Raiders. I have no clues to who wrote this. Perhaps it was my mother. Perhaps not. The letter ended with this sentence: 'Is Judex too happy?' It was true. You said it yourself. We were too happy! Enraptured by my joy, I refused to obey this strange injunction. In retrospect, it was a warning of the terrible events about to unfold. Primrose was accused of a crime of which she was superficially guilty but morally innocent. Her foster father, perhaps our best friend, has been thrown into a deep depression. Our beloved brother is so crushed by sorrow that I fear for his sanity. Could I remain inactive in face of so much misfortune? Could I allow the happiness of people we cherish to be destroyed? If I remained neutral, you would be the first to reproach me for your selfishness. I would no longer be the Judex you once revered. I must fight the malevolent forces around us. I must once more deliver justice to the wicked!"

Roger then entered the room. Comte de Trémeuse directed his gaze towards him.

"Brother, I entrust you with Jacqueline and my son. Tonight, I embark on a new campaign. May Heaven preserve you all!"

Magnificent in her noble resignation, Madame de Trémeuse embraced her husband.

"Yes, go. Go, my hero, my god, my lord! I won't say a word to restrain you. Our love is invulnerable. Wherever you go, I shall be with you!"

Grabbing her son in her arms, she presented him to her husband.

"Kiss our Jean and bless him. Kiss this radiant angel. He will be the talisman that will both protect you and ensure your victory!"

Jacques embraced the woman and child that was his life.

Some minutes later, a powerful car driven by a loyal chauffeur rapidly transported this modern knight to an unknown destination. After following the Paris road, it veered left by an intersection towards Versailles and crossed through Mantes. After passing through this beautiful city, the car drove up to the top of a steep hill where moonlight illuminated the imposing ruins of a majestic feudal castle.

Nimbly leaving the car, Jacques de Trémeuse signaled his driver to leave him. The Comte climbed a path into the ruins. He disappeared behind a huge pillar that rose from the middle of a heap of flagstones. The hoot of an owl ominously sound in the darkness.

The eagle was once more in his aerie. Judex had returned to the Chateau Rouge!

45 Centimes. Tous les Jeudis.

LA
NOUVELLE MISSION
DE
JUDEX

Par ARTHUR BERNÈDE et Louis FEUILLADE

L'ENSORCELÉE

Part Three: The Bewitched

I. A Family Secret

"Has the Comte returned?"

"No, Comtesse."

Dismissing the footman who had answered her questions, Jacqueline de Trémeuse remained alone in the vast hall of La Frondaie. Then she gave voice to her fears.

"I hope that he's safe. Poor Roger! Poor Primrose!"

She gazed through a bay window that allowed a view of the courtyard. Her face became calm. She had just sighted her son on the lawn. He was receiving his lesson in aesthetic culture from Dr. Howey. With graceful agility, Jean executed the regulated rhythmically movements taught him by his instructor. The teacher and student got along fabulously. Jacqueline could hear Dr. Howey's complimentary praise of Jean's movements

"Excellent. Perfect."

Jacqueline was watching the joyful reaction of her son when a footstep on the sumptuous rug caused her to turn around. It was her brother-in-law. He held a finger against his mouth to indicate that they must communicate in whispers.

" Jacques?" asked Jacqueline.

"He just telephoned me that all was well," reassured Roger.

Jacqueline breathed a sigh of relief.

"Kerjean is here," added Roger. "He brings a message from your father."

Roger raised a curtain that concealed the door through which he had entered. An old man, simply clothed, walked towards Jacqueline. She extended her hand which he grasped with respect. Taking a letter out of his jacket, Kerjean presented it. The Comtesse unsealed it.

My dear daughter,

For some time, I feared my retirement was discovered. Suspicious strangers prowl around my house. I read a report in Le Petit Parisien *about the Secret Raiders. I'm nervous. If the world learns that I'm alive, what new ordeals will you suffer because of me? What should I do? I entrusted Kerjean to personally deliver this letter in order to prevent it from falling into criminal hands. Give my love to my grandson. My warmest affection to your husband.*

F.

"Kerjean, did you know about my father's worries?" asked Jacqueline.

"Yes, Comtesse. Since your father and I live in voluntary exile together, we confide in one another."

"Do you agree with my father?"

"I consider Monsieur Favraux's fears well-founded. In our remote refuge, I have noticed two strangers. Their presence was even more disturbing due to their inspection of our villa. Of course, I would defend our sanctuary if it was attacked. But I'm no longer a young man in good health. The same is true of your father. Weak men like us could only mount a futile resistance to determined invaders. Monsieur Favraux promised not to venture outside during my brief trip. I only agreed to leave him alone because I felt it was vital for your safety as well as our own."

"You have done well, my brave Kerjean," approved Jacqueline, "but don't be frightened. Monsieur de Trémeuse watches over both you and your father. Therefore, you have nothing to worry about.

"I thank you for your consoling words," replied Kerjean, "but I have another commission."

"Speak, my friend."

"Monsieur Favraux wants me to kiss your grandson for him."

"I'll call Jean," said the Comtesse.

"Are you sure?" asked Roger.

"An indiscretion," noted the Comtesse. "As you're aware, my friends, it was impossible to conceal from Jean his grandfather's existence. A minor lapse or a moment of forgetfulness on my son's part was feared. Here's what Jacques and I decided to safeguard this family secret. We told our darling: 'If you told anyone that your Grandpa is alive, you'll cause him to die.' As you probably guessed, Jean gave us his word not to tell a living soul. You know his big heart."

Roger left to fetch the young child. Making his excuses to Dr. Howey, Roger took charge of his nephew. While the instructor sat on a bench outside the house, Judex's brother escorted Jean inside. Seeing Kerjean, the boy ran towards him.

"Hello, Monsieur Kerjean."

Favraux's companion took the small child in his arms. "I deliver a kiss from your grandfather. You will tell no one. Isn't that right?"

The boy answered firmly. "Rather than let Grandpa die, I would allow myself to be chopped into little pieces like in *Puss in Boots*."

After his lips kissed Jean's forehead, Kerjean released the child.

"Can I continue my lesson?" asked Jean as soon as his feet touched the ground.

"Yes my dear," said Jacqueline. "You can go."

The boy ran outside to where his teacher waited.

"Comtesse," said Kerjean, "I must depart."

"*Au revoir*, Monsieur Kerjean. Roger will escort you. Tell my father that he has nothing to fear. We watch over him!"

"*Au revoir*, Madame."

Kerjean left with Roger. Alone Jacqueline felt all her anxieties explode inside. She was convinced that danger threatened her loved ones. Her eyes filled with tears. Sobs erupted from her chest. Soon her sighs evolved into words.

"I was too happy."

"Jacqueline!"

"You!" exclaimed the young woman as she fell into Judex's arms.

Her composure restored by her husband's arrival, she summarized what recently happened.

"I've just received a visit."

"Yes, from Kerjean. I saw him outside."

"He brought me a letter from my father." She showed him the letter.

Judex perused the document. "Don't worry. I'll protect him."

"I told Kerjean that, but I'm still worried. I fear that your new enemies are even more formidable than those you defeated in the past."

"That may be true," conceded Judex. "Last time I pursued vengeance. Now I defend our happiness. That fact makes me stronger than ever. Already during my investigation, I have unearthed certain clues."

"Monsieur James Milton wishes to speak with the Comte," announced a servant.

"Perfect! Did you conduct him to my study?"

"Yes, Monsieur le Comte."

"I shall join him there. Is Monsieur Cocantin here."

"He's performing his exercises in the woods."

"As soon as he returns, tell him that I want to see him."

While the servant left, Judex kissed his wife.

"Have no fear, my darling. The Secret Raiders shall not steal our happiness. I shall steal theirs!"

II. The Two Letters

The prior day's events had taken their toll on James Milton. He looked several years older than his actual age. When Judex entered, James Milton brandished an unsealed letter. "I just received this. Read it."

Father,

I'm guilty. I wasn't able to withstand the passion that entranced me. I'm leaving with the man whom I truly love. You shall never see me again. Forgive me.

PRIMROSE

"This is driving me mad," claimed the unhappy inventor.

Judex replied immediately. "My friend, do you have Primrose's first letter."

Milton withdrew a paper from his wallet.

Father,

I'm innocent, but you believe me guilty. I have left. If you hear of my death, know that I departed blessing you.

PRIMROSE

Judex closely examined the two letters. "I'm guilty! I'm innocent! What a contradiction! Nevertheless, the handwriting is identical. The same hand wrote both letters."

"So?" asked Milton.

"It was fortunate that you carried the earlier letter. It confirms the earlier hypothesis that I formulated at the start of this adventure. Primrose was hypnotized by one of these criminals to commit the robbery."

"Do you think she's still alive?"

"Absolutely!"

" In the hands of these miscreants?"

"There's no shadow of a doubt."

"How do we rescue her?"

"It isn't my custom to fill my friends with false hopes. We must look at the situation realistically. I need time. Be patient for the next 24 hours. I shall not delay."

"I put my trust in you."

The footman announced that Cocantin had arrived.

"Hopefully he will bring proof of my deductions," added Judex. "Julien, have Monsieur Cocantin join us."

The director of the Céléritas Agency, who has just concluded his physical exercises, entered with his head proudly raised. He seemed totally cured of the depression that had overwhelmed him so painfully. After shaking the hands, Cocantin loudly addressed his friends.

"Comte, do you have some news for me?"

"'Not yet, my dear friend, but I expect to have news soon."

"I'm not surprised."

"It all depends on you."

"On me?"

"Or rather," clarified Judex, "on your answers to certain questions."

"My dear Comte, I'm all ears."

"Let's begin. The other day, during your journey to La Frondaie, you traveled with a young lady."

"She was a captivating companion."

"Describe her."

"A tall brunette. Very fashionable and attractive."

"Was she wearing large golden earrings?"

"Yes."

"What was her name?"

"Baronne d'Apremont."

"Her address?"

"The Rue Musset in Auteuil. She even invited me to have tea with her at 5 o'clock on Tuesday."

"Did you tell her who you are?"

"Yes."

"Did you mention that you would be staying at La Frondaie?"

"Why would I keep that hidden?"

"Did she ask detailed questions about me?"

"She barely discussed you. She was more interested in the Chateau d'Arbois. Her family knew the former owners."

"Really?"

"She even asked me if the small gate in the fence still led to the Seine, and if --"

"My dear Cocantin, you don't need to say anything more. Today is Tuesday."

"Yes."

"It's 2 o'clock. My chauffeur will drive you to the house of the Baronne. You have time to accept her invitation for a cup of tea."

"Of course. I'll go."

"Let me explain why I want you to visit the Baronne."

"Excuse me!"

Judex spoke precisely. "I need to know everything about this lady --- her relations, her habits, the layout of her house. That's very important Cocantin. The layout of her house, as detailed as possible... the furniture, the windows, the doors. In short, a complete floor plan."

"That will be child's play," proudly proclaimed the detective.

"On one condition," said Judex smiling, "don't allow yourself to be seduced by her."

"Have no fear, my dear Comte." asserted Cocantin reddening with embarrassment. "I shall be a man of bronze, or at least marble. Besides, you've seen me work. You know what I'm capable of."

"Precisely because I know that," declared Judex politely. "I have entrusted you with this delicate task. I recommend you to be prudent, my gallant firebrand."

"I shall transform myself into a torch of justice."

"It's time. You must leave now. My car awaits outside. Baptiste has all my instructions."

"*Au revoir*, my dear Comte!"

"*Au revoir*, my dear Cocantin!"

Judex accompanied the detective to the antechamber. When the Comte returned, he cordially asked Milton a question.

"What do you think about that?"

"I don't understand anything."

"Look straight into my eyes. You'll see that I'm calmer than usual. Come back tomorrow at 10 o'clock. I shall have good news for you."

The inventor shook the nobleman's hands.

"Let me borrow Primrose's two letters," said the Comte. "I need to study them again. Until tomorrow, my friend."

"Until tomorrow, and thanks!"

Once he was alone, Judex continued to examine the two letters. His eyes lit up as he tried to fathom their mysterious secret. Soon he engaged in a soliloquy.

"Now I understand. I've deduced everything. The first letter declaring her innocence is the cry of her heart. This is the truth. Her feverish writing indicated a desolation without bounds. The second note is a transcribed in symmetrical letters, words evenly spaced, and scrupulous punctuated. It's written in the formal style of a schoolgirl replying remorselessly to a charge of bad conduct. And that sentence: 'I'm leaving with the man whom I truly love.' She loves Roger and no one else. This second letter is an abominable lie! She wrote it under the mental domination of a stronger will. My original conclusions were correct. I'm on the right trail. If Cocantin succeeds in his mission, I'm convinced that we'll soon rescue Primrose!"

III. Madame Potiphar

Readers of Judex's earlier exploit will undoubtedly recall that Prosper Cocantin wasn't a professional detective. Inheriting the Céléritas Agency from his uncle Ribaudet, he was ill-suited for a career as an investigator. His main assets were loyalty and determination, but he was lacking in the intellectual gifts necessary to practice the art of scientific deduction. Thrown by chance into the extraordinary Judex case, he had initially blundered badly before courageously acquitting himself. Cocantin had developed an unlimited admiration for the Comte de Trémeuse, whom he worshipped as his hero. Cocantin was neither a fool nor a sleuth capable of sensational triumphs, but an effective and devoted agent when supervised by a higher intelligence.

He understood immediately the commission entrusted to him. Extremely flattered by the confidence placed in him by the man he deemed his master, Prosper Cocantin was determined to prove himself worthy of such trust. As the car transported him towards Paris, he had, according to a favorite expression, "returned to his sanctum." In other words, he had entered into a state of deep meditation.

Throughout his life, Cocantin had demonstrated a deep reverence for Napoléon Bonaparte. Whenever faced with an important decision, the detective drew inspiration from the Emperor's career. He wondered what Napoléon would have done in his place. Cocantin searched his mind for an analogous situation from his idol's military campaigns. When he arrived at the Rue Musset, not only were the detective's eyes full of excitement, but his immense nose shook with anticipation.

After crossing the small courtyard, he ascended the steps of the porch, and rang the doorbell. He imagined himself a gallant knight paying a visit on a lady of quality. The door immediately opened revealing a pretty face. It was Belles-Mirettes. She had abandoned her garb of a foreign student to wear the outfit of a chambermaid.

"Is Baronne d'Apremont at home?" inquired Cocantin.

"She's here, Monsieur."

"Could you deliver my card to her?"

"Enter," replied Belles-Mirettes acting under orders. She showed Cocantin into an elegant parlor. "I will inform Madame." She smiled obliquely at the director of the Céléritas Agency just before departing.

The detective had just begun to make his reconnaissance when the chambermaid returned. Cocantin feared that he was about to be dismissed.

"The Baronne sends her regrets," said the false chambermaid. "She is very busy at the moment. If you wait a while, she will be delighted to receive you."

Cocantin's nose twitched. "I'm quite willing to wait." He was delighted to have more time to examine the house. As soon as the chambermaid exited, he embarked upon his task. Cocantin took an investigative tour in which he counted the windows and doors, noted the furnishings, and labeled the pictures.

He was briefly startled. Resting on a Louis XV table, a mirror reflected his image. Always very meticulous about his appearance, Cocantin just noted a misplaced hair on his thinning scalp. Instinctively pulling out a grooming kit from his pocket, he removed a comb and brush to fix his hair. As Cocantin was correcting his hairstyle, he observed a notepad on the table. The sleuth was able to recognize the tracing of several words. He clearly could decipher a name.

"Primrose," he muttered in shock. A close examination revealed that that Primrose's second letter could be deciphered in the notepad.

Father,
I'm guilty. I wasn't able to withstand the passion that entranced me. I'm leaving with the man whom I truly love. You shall never see me again. Forgive me.
PRIMROSE

Cocantin understood the full ramifications of his discovery. Removing the top leaf on the notepad, he shoved it into his wallet. No sooner had he performed this action, then the door opened.

It was the Baronne. She had never looked more stunning. She combined all the artifices that a siren would use to entice a mariner in her nets. She was wearing a enticing dress that accentuated her splendid neckline and incomparable complexion. Her black eyes were full of magnetic fire. Her crimson lips formed a smile capable of sending Lucifer to a second damnation.

Before the splendid image of this enticing temptress, Cocantin feared that he would succumb to her charms. Then he remembered his promise to Judex. *I promised to be marble. I shall be ice!* Now like Joseph in the Bible, he could resist Potiphar's wife.

"Monsieur Cocantin," said the Baronne. "Forgive me for forcing you to wait. I would have been extremely upset if you left. Please sit down."

However, Cocantin had only one desire. He wanted to flee this seductress as quickly as possible and inform Judex of the evidence concerning Primrose's presence in this house.

"Baronne. I'm extremely embarrassed. I've forgotten an important business appointment."

"Please, Monsieur Cocantin, remain for a few minutes."

"Unfortunately, that's impossible." As he stroked the Baronne's hand, he felt a shiver down his spine that seemed a prediction of his inevitable capitulation.

"Please don't be unkind," scolded the adventuress. She didn't suspect that Cocantin's visit had an ulterior motive, but she merely wanted to have some fun at her guest's expense. At the very least, it was an opportunity to test her powers of seduction.

Trying to maneuver himself towards the door, Cocantin continued to protest. "It's impossible. I'm so sorry. I'll return next Tuesday. I promise."

Madame d'Apremont refused to be beaten. Seizing Cocantin's arm, she induced him towards a couch covered with cushions.

"Come rest. Our conversation on the train was so sweet."

"Baronne!"

"You can be late for your appointment. Remain here a little longer."

This isn't a Baronne, thought Cocantin, *this is a volcano.*

Fortunately, the gallant Prosper did not succumb. At the moment when he was close to surrender, a particle of dust flew into his nostrils. The prodigious sneeze that resulted had the effect of causing the Baronne to move away from him. Taking advantage of the siren's retreat. Cocantin leapt from the couch and ran fort the door. Reaching the outside, he jumped into the car.

"Return to La Frondaie at full speed," yelled Cocantin at Judex's chauffeur.

Peering from a window, an astonished Baronne watched the car's departure.

"I don't know his reason for coming here," murmured the Baronne.

An electronic beep came from her office --or rather the office that she maintained for her enigmatic superior. Madame d'Apremont hurried to pick up the receiver.

"Yes... I understand... It shall be done." Before hanging up, she spoke further.

"I've just received a visit from Cocantin. He acted very oddly. No sooner had he arrived than he left... You think he's a fool? Then the matter won't be discussed any further. Until tonight!"

The Baronne opened a door concealed behind a screen. She walked into a simple but comfortable room. Prostrate in an armchair was a young woman in a death-like trance.

Judex has not been deceived by his enemies.

Primrose was in the power of the Secret Raiders!

IV. I'm Watching

Prosper Cocantin arrived at La Frondaie, around 8 o'clock in the evening. Immediately he was ushered into Judex's study.

"Was your visit fruitful?" asked the lord of the manor

"Very fruitful," acknowledged Cocantin.

"Did you gather any clues?"

"Better than that?"

"What?"

Very solemnly, Cocantin extracted the piece of paper and gave it to Judex.

"My dear Comte, hold this paper in front of the lamp."

The nobleman did so, and recognized Primrose's second message, To Cocantin's disappointment, Judex was not surprised.

"You found this at the Baronne's house?"

"Yes, Comte."

"I suspected that Primrose was in this woman's house. This note paper is absolute proof. Let's go."

At that moment, Judex noted a look of disappointment on the face of the detective. "I forgot to congratulate you. You did extremely well. You have confirmed my theory."

Cocantin couldn't ask for anything more. He shook Judex's hand.

"Believe me, my dear Comte, I constantly strive to prove myself worthy of the trust you put in me."

"I recognize that fact, and I shall never hesitate to employ your services."

"Again and again, I hope."

"I won't hide from you that your next mission will be more difficult."

"So much the better!"

"The task is so delicate that you must honestly evaluate it to determine whether you're qualified for it."

"Tell me, and I shall give you a frank appraisal."

"What kind of woman is Baronne d'Apremont?"

"Now I studied her closely, I can label her more of a courtesan than a socialite."

"Could you romance her?"

Proper Cocantin reddened somewhat. "I would be lying if I didn't admit that her romantic conquest already seems an accomplished fact."

"My congratulations, my dear Cocantin. I know you're a formidable seducer."

"I must add in my haste to bring you the notepaper, I had to flee like Joseph from Madame Potiphar."

"Again my congratulations! Nevertheless, extreme caution must be exercised when dealing with a woman like the Baronne."

"I did so," affirmed Cocantin.

Judex laughed with a combination of benevolence and irony.

"It's possible that you aroused such lust in this woman that she's incapable of concealing it!"

"Quite true," commented naively the Céléritas Agency's director.

"But it's also true that you're confronted with an accomplished adventuress! You could be engaged in battle with a woman whose sole motive is to lead you into a trap."

"That fact is somewhat damaging to my self-esteem," cheerfully admitted the detective, "but I must accept it to ensure my safety."

"Then you feel you can resist this temptress?"

"Yes."

"Tomorrow morning, you will send the Baronne a bouquet of flowers with a message regretting your abrupt departure and requesting permission to see her in the afternoon to personally tender your apologies."

"What if she doesn't reply?"

"She shall reply. To put it bluntly, she wants to play you like a fiddle. She won't hesitate to summon you. You must turn the tables on her."

"I shall be inspired by your words and the example of my idol, Napoléon."

"Listen to me, Cocantin, I haven't finished. Once you have penetrated her house, you must take full advantage of the situation."

"My dear friend..."

"Tomorrow evening, you must persuade the Baronne d'Apremont to have dinner with you away from her home and give her servants the night off," said Judex authoritatively. "I need to search her house."

"I shall do what you ask. I swear it."

"How will I know that you succeeded?"

Cocantin scratched his nose before answering. "I'll telephone you at your apartment in Paris around 7 o'clock. Once I leave with the Baronne, you'll be free to conduct your search. Until tomorrow, my dear Comte. I'll leave for Paris at the crack of dawn."

"I can rely on you?"

"Absolutely."

Pausing for a moment, Judex put on his hat and cloak. Leaving his study, he walked alone into the large hall that filled the first floor. He went into the parlor where Jacqueline had been entertaining Roger and Dr. Howey. She was alone. Roger was driving Howey to the station in order for him to catch the Paris train.

Jacqueline appeared languid. When her husband entered the room, she didn't respond to his presence. Jacques de Trémeuse was deeply troubled. This was the second time today that he found his wife yielding to dark reflections. Earlier in the morning, she had seemed lost in a similar trance. He approached very slowly.

Jacqueline gradually became aware of his presence. As in the morning, her eyes became filled with glimmers of joy.

"You're here," she whispered.

"Yes, my beloved," replied Jacques. He tenderly held her hands. "Jacqueline, what's wrong? You were once so brave. You gave me the strength to undertake my new mission."

"My beloved," said Jacqueline passionately embracing her husband. "Don't imagine for an instance that I doubt you. I know you're capable of overcoming any obstacle. I don't want to hinder you but assist you in your task. I admire your decision to relieve the suffering of others by sacrificing our own bliss. Besides, any happiness that becomes selfish ceases to be true happiness! I am proud to be your companion on this road of honor."

"Thank you," said Judex before depositing a long kiss on Jacqueline's feverish hands.

"You don't see a woman easily frightened. I'm not intimidated by the tangible dangers threatening us. I support your noble battle against these criminals. It's the crusade of the honest knight against shadowy assassins. However, I've had a premonition since this morning that an evil spirit has invaded our home."

"You're afraid?"

"Yes, as Primrose was. Like her. I sense an invisible emissary of darkness overpowering me. It threatens you, our son, my father, Primrose... All my love ones seem endangered by an infernal whirlwind."

"Jacqueline, I'm here."

"I shall always want you near me. In your presence, I no longer fear this omen of terror and death. It's like it was three days ago when we thought our happiness was limitless."

"Jacqueline, go to the room of our precious Jean. Kiss him on the forehead. Then go to your bedroom and enjoy the sleep of a pure angel. This night, I shall not leave La Frondaie, and I shall soon join you. Leave your door open. If you feel threatened by any danger, call my name. I shall hear you. I'm watching over you."

Jacqueline yielded to the entreaties of her husband. After she left, Judex prepared to ring for a servant, but then his brother appeared.

"I've just driven the doctor to the station."

"Listen, Roger. When all the servants have gone to bed, you must remove the keys from my office drawer. You will unlock all the gates outside. Upon your return, you must be vigilant. Extraordinary things will happen tonight, and I must be able to enter La Frondaie freely."

"Brother, what are you saying?"

'"Know only that all is well, and do simply what I ask."

"No matter what you hear, stay here unless you hear three whistles. Then you'll know that I'm in danger."

"You can count on me."

"By tomorrow morning, Roger, we shall be closer to solving this mystery."

As Roger prepared to execute his brother's order, Judex went outside. He vanished into the night.

V. The Knight of Justice and the Spirit of Evil

Obeying Jacques's reassuring orders, Jacqueline purged herself of all the gloomy thoughts clouding her mind. She ascended the stairs to her son's room. Not wishing to disturb the child, she listened carefully to make sure he was asleep. Hearing his gentle breathing, she gently opened the door. The room was lit by the glimmer of an electric lamp. Seated close to the bed, Juliette the chambermaid dozed. She didn't hear the Comtesse approach the child.

The little boy was sound asleep. His head rested on the soft lace pillow. His sleeves could be glimpsed at the tip of the blanket. His mouth expressed an innocent ecstasy. He breathed regularly lost in the endless joy of a dream.

Madame de Trémeuse was reluctant to disrupt, even with a kiss, this tranquil evocation of heavenly bliss. However, she couldn't resist her maternal instincts. She leaned forward and kissed her son. The boy opened his eyes slightly to view the lovely vision of his mother.

"Mama!" he murmured before closing his eyes again. The child returned to a heavenly slumber.

Stifling a yawn, the chambermaid had arisen.

"You can leave, Juliette," said Jacqueline.

"Does the Comtesse need my services."

"No, my girl, you can retire."

After Juliette left, Jacqueline gave a final look at Jean. She then retreated to her bedroom which was directed connected to her son's. Removing her father's letter which she had hidden in her blouse, she placed it in the table drawer next to her bed. After undressing, she looked at her son's photo.

"I'm watching over you," she said before going to bed. For two hours, she calmly rested as if the tutelary protection of Judex guarded her. Then she became agitated. Her arms spread forward as if they were repelling a nightmarish intruder. Her breathing became sporadic. Long sighs escaped her lungs. Her hands reached for the light switch.

Jacqueline's face was illuminated. Her dazed eyes stared out of an immobilized face. She looked like Primrose had during the night James Milton's plans had been delivered to the Secret Raiders.

Jacqueline opened the drawer of the night table. She removed Favraux's letter. Walking into the hall, she stopped before a curtain. The curtain parted revealing a girl's white hand. Extending itself toward Jacqueline, the hand seized the letter.

As the hand withdrew, Judex revealed himself to be hiding before a vast armchair. Seizing the wrist of the thief, he pulled her from behind the curtain. The burglar was Primrose. She made no effort to resist. Primrose was clearly in an hypnotic trance.

Unconscious of the extraordinary scene that had unfolded in front of her, an impassive Jacqueline returned to her bed where she fell into a heavy sleep. Judex calmly observed Jacqueline's actions. He didn't remove the letter from Primrose's grasp. He permitted Milton's foster daughter to retain possession. His intention was to follow her.

She walked down a servant's stairway that led to the ground floor. While exiting the house, Judex noticed Primrose retrieve a skeleton key from a door to the outside. It wasn't necessary to have Roger leave all the doors unlocked. The criminals manipulating Primrose had taken their own precautions.

Judex wondered how this unknown mastermind had breached the security of his home in order to make mesmerized slaves of his wife and Roger's fiancée.

He continued to follow the bewitched Primrose. She stopped before a gate that led into the forest. The gate was open. In the moonlight, he saw Primrose retrieve another skeleton key from the lock. The Secret Raiders had planned everything to the last detail.

Primrose was now in the forest. Judex needed to know where she would deliver this letter proving Favraux still lived. Hiding behind a tree, Judex noticed Primrose approaching a small red light. Judex pulled out his gun. Standing visibly against the clear summer night was a large automobile. Only its rear taillights were lit. The chauffeur opened the passenger door.

As Primrose prepared to enter the vehicle, Judex leaped on the chauffeur. Instead of using his gun, Judex immobilized his adversary with a jujitsu flip. Oblivious to what was transpiring around her, Primrose took her seat in the back.

Terrified by this apparently superhuman apparition, the driver immediately surrendered. Joining his prisoner in the front seat, Judex issued his commands.

"You will drive this girl to the place that your superiors designated."

The conquered criminal followed Judex's instructions. He drove to an intersection where stood a rock pylon. He stopped the car.

"Monsieur," muttered the chauffeur fearfully, "this is where I was supposed to transport Mademoiselle."

Judex realized that the driver must be telling the truth. Still staring mindlessly into a void, Primrose got out of the car. She walked towards the pylon. As Judex followed her, the chauffeur fled the car. Running into the forest, he found two women hidden behind a tree.

"All is lost!" yelled the chauffeur.

"Yes, I saw," replied the Baronne d'Apremont. She led her accomplices back to the car. As the automobile quickly left, The Baronne raised her fist in Judex's direction.

"That man! He's an obstacle to our plans! I recognize him. He's Comte Jacques de Trémeuse. Judex!"

"Judex?" repeated Belles-Mirettes.

"Yes, Judex! Tonight he has proven stronger than us. I shall have my revenge. I'll kill him."

Ignoring the chauffeur completely, Judex had trailed Primrose. Stopping near the pylon, she extended the letter in front of her. Gently Judex grabbed the letter and placed it in his wallet. At that moment, the girl awoke from her trance.

Her features moved. Her eyes expressed intelligence. Exhaling a deep breath, she beheld Judex in the moonlight.

"Monsieur Jacques! What happened?"

Suddenly she gave a cry of agony. She remembered her attempted suicide.

"*Mon Dieu*! How am I alive?"

"Primrose," said Judex benevolently, "the mystery surrounding you is now clear. I always knew you were innocent."

A glimmer of hope illuminated the girl's face.

"Come with me," declared Judex. "Be reunited with those who love you... your father, my little Jean and your Roger. Your happiness will again bloom."

"Yes, Monsieur Jacques. Take me to them." She seized his protective arm. "I don't know what happened. I don't understand. Everything's confused. But I'm not afraid because you're with me."

"Primrose, you were enslaved by an occult power. I have just liberated you from it. Between the evil spirit and myself, there is now a merciless war. You have nothing to fear. I'll protect you!"

Part Four: The Prison Chamber

I. Family

"Primrose, now that you're safe and sound," said Jacques de Trémeuse, "tell us what you saw."

The light of the beautiful morning sun flooded the lobby of La Frondaie. Seated in a large armchair, Primrose looked kindly upon the faces of the Comte and the Comtesse de Trémeuse.

"I'm trying to muster my memories. It's impossible to see clearly. Sometimes there's a glimmer of light, but then darkness obscures everything. I want to answer your questions. I'm haunted by my father's rejection. I remember Roger's protestations of love. I want to disperse all their suspicions!"

"Primrose," reassured Jacqueline, "be calm. My husband has talked to your foster father and Roger in private. Both of them still love you. They'll be here soon. If we delayed your reunion with them, it's because we didn't want you to suffer too much emotional stress."

"I don't blame them for doubting me. Appearances were against me." Primrose grabbed Judex's hand. "It's over. Isn't it? The evil spirit won't return. You'll defend me. Tell me that you'll always be there to defend me."

"Yes, my child."

"Monsieur Jacques, if not for you, where would I be? Confined somewhere far away, even in a foreign country. Rescue me from this nightmare. Exorcise this evil spirit. Save me!"

"Primrose," answered Jacques, "you're totally under my protection. Listen well. I shall not rest until I totally solve this troubling mystery. I need to ask you some questions."

79

"I thirst for the truth, Monsieur Jacques. I shall answer as best I can."

"First, there is the matter of this letter." Jacques gave Primrose the first letter in which she protested her innocence.

"I wrote this," admitted Primrose.

"And this?" The Comte showed her the second letter.

Roger's fiancée began to read the letter aloud. "*I'm guilty...* I swear that I never wrote this!"

"Nevertheless," emphasized Judex, "this is your handwriting."

"Yes, this is my handwriting."

"You don't remember?"

"From the moment that I fainted on the dyke in the Seine until I beheld you in the forest, Monsieur Jacques, I remember nothing. It was as if I died."

"Last night," said Jacqueline, "I felt the icy sensation of the void. It was horrible!"

Jacques contemplated Jacqueline and Primrose. Both displayed an aura of terror. He had dreaded that the evil spirit had not been checkmated, but continued to prowl his estate. Did it threatened his soul as well? Did it intend to prey further on these two women? Finally he began to understand the full danger represented by this supernatural force.

I accept your challenge, my monstrous foe, thought Judex. *It's not enough to defend against you. I must also attack you. Primrose has christened you the "evil spirit." You have crossed the thresholds of both the Chateau d'Arbois and La Frondaie. You have cowardly violated the souls of Jacqueline and Primrose. I shall crush you. I shall defeat you in the name of justice and honor!*

This splendid resolution spread across his handsome face. His indomitable energy was instantly communicated to the two women, who seconds earlier had been consumed by anguish.

"Why do you tremble, Primrose," said Jacqueline. She pointed at Judex. "He's here. You don't know, as I do, what he's capable of. We are both under his protection. Believe in him as I do. He's my husband and your future brother-n-law. Courage! Primrose! Courage!"

"Yes, Jacqueline," declared Judex moved by his wife's words. "Depend on me absolutely. Just as our love, Jacqueline, overcame all obstacles, so will the love of Primrose and my brother Roger."

The silhouettes of Milton and Roger appeared on the terrace. Judex opened the door. "Enter, my friends. Welcome back Primrose."

It was a moment of intense emotion. Primrose's face radiated joy. Her hands joined together to thank the Lord God. Milton and Roger came forward. The former looked at her with paternal devotion while the latter's face displayed intense love. Milton embraced Primrose. Controlling his emotions, Milton turned towards Roger.

"My friend, her heart now belongs to you! Only you had faith in her."

Resting her head on her fiancé's shoulder, Primrose replied in a heavenly voice.

"Father, don't speak that way. The pain that I felt when you thought me guilty is erased by the joy of being restored to my family. Our love has passed a difficult test." She gazed at Judex. "We owe everything to the Comte. Thanks to him, I can smile again!"

"I know our debt to the Comte," admitted Milton, "and I shall never forget it. I'm about to take a business trip for a couple of weeks. I asked our friend to guard you here during that time. He agreed unconditionally."

"And with the greatest pleasure," added Judex.

Milton placed his foster daughter's hands in Roger's. "When I return, we shall celebrate the union of these children."

"Return quickly, Father!"

"As soon as possible!" Milton winked at Judex.

Jacques de Trémeuse later conferred with Roger in private.

"Roger, I must leave La Frondaie for several hours. I shall deliver an assault tonight on the Secret Raiders that won't be my last. However, if I'm not deluding myself, it will be decisive. During my brief absence, you must watch over Jacqueline and Primrose. Be discreet in your surveillance, but don't let them leave your sight for an instant!"

"You can rely on me!" said Roger.

"You shall be guarding both your happiness and mine!"

"Do you fear for them?"

"I fear everything, and I fear nothing," said Judex. His eyes glowed as if they were lit by a divine flame.

II. The Revenge of Joseph

Around 11 o'clock in the morning, Baronne d'Apremont received a splendid bouquet of flowers. Attached to it was a note.

My Charming Friend,

I departed yesterday with the greatest reluctance. I was so overwhelmed by regret that I couldn't sleep. Please accept these modest flowers as symbols of my tearful sorrow. May their subtle perfume placate your legitimate anger, and persuade you to allow me today to personally deposit at your feet my humble excuses combined with the burning desire of my boundless admiration. A telephone call from you shall make me the happiest of mortal men. Your devoted slave until death,

Prosper Cocantin
52 Rue Milton,
Telephone: Louvre 72-97

Baronne d'Apremont had returned to her home at 4 o'clock in the morning following the eventful night in the forest of Fontainebleau. She was in a bad mood. Her initial reaction was to throw Cocantin's love letter in the trash, but then she changed her mind.

"This fool's visit comes at an opportune time. A vicious smile formed on her lips. A wicked gleam appeared in her eyes. "These people think I'm an idiot." Grabbing the phone, she talked to the operator: "Hello! Mademoiselle, please give me Louvre 72-97." She altered her voice. "Is this Monsieur Cocantin?"

The director of the Céléritas Agency replied politely. "Yes, Mademoiselle. Whom am I speaking to?"

"I'm the maid of Baronne d'Apremont," began the adventuress.

"Delighted to meet you."

"The Baronne thanks you profusely for the flowers."

"Oh! It was only a small gesture of appreciation."

"She has instructed me to contact you... Hello, did you hear me?"

"I do more than hear you, Mademoiselle. I'm absorbing every word you say."

"The Baronne instructs me to inform you that she will be at her home at 2 o'clock. She would be very happy to receive you at that hour."

"Tell the Baronne. I'll be there even if I have to walk on my hands... You say it would be better to take a taxi. You're correct. I'll be there promptly. Tell the Baronne that I'll always worship her!"

Cocantin hung up. "I hope Judex will be happy with me."

After lunch, the Baronne made a telephone call to her mysterious chief, Bébert alias *N'a-qu'un-Chasse*. They formulated a plan on how to deal with the detective.

At 2 o'clock, Prosper Cocantin arrived at the residence of the Baronne. This time she didn't force him to wait.

"There you are, you naughty boy." She stretched out to the private detective a deliciously languid hand. Cocantin deposited a long kiss on her fine and silky skin. A romantic sensation immediately seized him, but then he remembered his promise to be a man of marble.

Joseph had returned to see Madame Potiphar, but with a cool and level head. Nonetheless, he had to give the Baronne the impression that she had bewitched him. He gave a long sigh, and then pleaded sadly.

"Forgive me, Baronne. Yesterday I was..."

"There's no need to speak about that. Sit next to me on the couch."

By Jove, thought Cocantin, *she's beautiful.* His eyes feasted on this siren who hoped to make him her puppet. Determined to play his role to the hilt, Cocantin pretended to be totally enraptured by the female Raider.

The Baronne smiled. "Monsieur Cocantin, I can't hide how much you attract me."

"Oh Madame!"

"I've always been horrified by handsome men. Most of them are stupid braggarts. How much I prefer someone, who though lacking the physical beauty of an Adonis or a Hercules, has your qualities. You have the tasteful elegance of a gentleman belonging to the intellectual elite of our country."

While hearing those compliments, Cocantin drank milk. He gulped it down because his self-esteem was tickled by the praise of his hostess which he sincerely believed. *What a charmer I am,* he thought. *Judex never guessed how skillfully I would pretend to succumb to these feminine wiles.*

"My dear Monsieur Cocantin," continued the adventuress. "I hope to see you often."

"How often, Baronne?"

"Perhaps a strong bond of friendship could unite us."

"Certainly."

"You must realize what I am."

"You are the..."

"Wait, I haven't finished. First, my personality is a little eccentric."

"Mine also."

"I could go days, even weeks, without seeing you."

"Really?"

"But I can then behave unexpectedly," added the Baronne mysteriously. She lowered her eyes.

"Speak," implored Cocantin.

"I'm capricious. If I summoned you abruptly, would you come?"

"I would desert everything for you."

"Even your Daisy."

"She isn't here now."

"And when she returns from America?"

"I would leave Daisy!" shouted Cocantin.

"You're the most gallant man I've ever met."

"You complete me!" Cocantin gripped the hand of the adventuress.

"Now that I reveal my flaws," she replied, "let me reveal my strengths."

"It isn't necessary, Baronne, I discern them. You have beauty, charm and grace! You are *the* woman! The *only* woman! Baronne, I love you!"

The moment he made that statement, he regretted it. Perhaps he was coming on too strong. Had he blundered?

The Baronne provocatively winked at him. "I shall make allowance for you, Prosper, but I can't spend any more time with you today!"

"Baronne!" exclaimed Cocantin falling to his knees .

"Get up! You're acting like a child!" commanded the adventuress.

Cocantin remained prostrate. "Baronne, listen to me. Don't refuse this favor! I want to be with you! I want to shower you with kisses! A kiss is like a wonderful flower. Don't refuse me! I'll feel crushed!"

"Courage!" replied the Baronne.

Clasping his hands, Cocantin rolled his bulging eyes. "Please do me the honor of dining with me tonight at a restaurant of your own choice!"

"My dear friend, I accept your invitation. Pick me up tonight between 7 and 7:30."

"Which restaurant do you want to go to?"

"I'll let you choose."

"Perfect! Didn't you tell me on the train that you're a gourmet?"

"I love rare delicacies."

"You will be satisfied. Baronne, I know a small exclusive restaurant that caters to connoisseurs."

"I shall be indebted to you."

"I'll see you at 7."

"I'll be ready."

"Thank you." Cocantin was satisfied with his success. As he prepared to depart, Cocantin realized that he was negligent in one detail. In order for Judex to conduct his search, it was necessary to arrange not only for the absence of the mistress of the house, but also the servants.

Belles-Mirettes, clothed as a chambermaid, was preparing to open the door.

"Did you talk to me this morning on the telephone?"

"Yes, that was me," lied Belles-Mirettes.

"You performed your assignment very well."

"Thank you, Monsieur."

"I would like to reward you." He handed her 5 francs.

"Do you like the cinema?"

"Yes, Monsieur. A lot."

"Do you go often?"

"Not often. I rarely get time off, and it's expensive."

"What your name?"

"Louise."

"Well, Louise, I'll be dining in the city with the Baronne. You have the night free. When I return to pick up Madame, I'll bring you tickets for the cinema."

"Monsieur is very kind."

"How many employees work here?"

"There is the cook, the chauffeur and me."

"I'll bring you four tickets. This way you can take your fellow workers and a boyfriend."

"Monsieur, you're very generous."

"Opening a door, Belles-Mirettes called the other servants. "Justin... Mariette." There appeared a muscular man in a servant's vest and a stout woman in an apron.

"Madame will be dining out this evening," explained the false Louise. "This gentlemen will supply us with tickets to the cinema."

"You should leave early to get good seats," added Cocantin.

Both servants thanked Cocantin profusely. Leaving the small house in Auteuil, the detective tried to choose a comparable victory in the life of Napoléon that matched the apparently successful conclusion of his mission for Judex. Cocantin's mind was divided between the battle of Marengo and the overthrow of the Directory.

After Cocantin's departure, Belles-Mirettes immediately conferred with the Baronne in her office.

"Do you have a dinner engagement with Cocantin this evening?"

"Yes," confirmed the Baronne.

"He bringing me four cinema tickets. They're for me, Mariette, Justin and my boyfriend. Movies really have very little interest for me. I'll let Justin and Mariette go alone."

"No," commanded the Baronne. "You shall go with them."

"Why?"

"It's necessary that the house be empty tonight."

"I'm curious to know--"

Not giving Belles-Mirettes the opportunity to finish her sentence, the Baronne broke out in a feverish rant. "Cocantin came here with a precise goal. It was child's play for me to see through his tomfoolery. He wanted to cause my house to be deserted tonight. His trickery with the movie tickets confirms my suspicion. It is quite likely that my home will be burglarized a half hour after our departure. I know the name of the burglar. He's the man who frustrated our plans by rescuing Primrose last evening."

"Comte de Trémeuse?" asked Belles-Mirettes.

"Yes, the sworn enemy of the Secret Raiders."

"Why aren't we staying here."

"Be quiet!" retorted the Baronne. "We have good reason not to be here. I've prepared a surprise reception for our visitor."

III. The Trap

As early as 6:30 in the evening, a limousine with drawn curtains entered the Rue Musset. It parked two houses down from the residence of the Baronne. Placing his eye against a hole in the rear curtain of the car, Judex could observe all the movement outside the house of the Baronne. He saw Cocantin arrive in a car hired from an auto club. The detective cut a dashing figure as he entered the house. Within minutes, he escorted the Baronne to the vehicle. It quickly departed to take them to dinner. The servants then left the house.

After whispering some brief instructions to Baptiste the loyal chauffeur, Judex left the limousine. The street was deserted. Judex proceeded to search the house.

Judex had been somewhat reluctant to undertake this mission. In fact, he had to overcome his conscience. Being a true gentleman, he felt it unseemly to break into a woman's home even in the cause of truth and justice. If there had been any other means to gain the desired information, Judex would have pursued it. However, this was the only practical strategy. Therefore, he overcame his qualms to protect his loved ones from the Secret Raiders.

Judex suspected that the Raiders had proof that Favraux was still alive. He had to act quickly to avoid the scandal that would result if the authorities discover his father-in-law's empty coffin at the cemetery of Les Sablons. Besides the publicity that would adversely affect Jacqueline, an exhumation could make Judex himself liable to criminal prosecution.

Judex had to chose whether to conquer or surrender to his moral qualms. Surrender would deliver Jacqueline and Primrose into a terrifying power of darkness. Judex couldn't allow his happiness, as well as his brother's, to be irreparably damaged. If the Raiders triumphed, then their campaign of plunder and murder would be as successful as their American exploits described by Dr. Howey.

Swayed by these arguments, Judex found a path to justify his actions. *To look for an alternative would be cowardice,* he thought. *One couldn't behave chivalrously with criminal swine like the Baronne d'Apremont. A hunter had ever right to violate the den of a predatory beast. Forward!*

Having overcome his doubts, Judex no longer hesitated. His hands steadfastly removed a batch of skeleton keys from one of the pockets in his pants. Examining these thin instruments, he chose a long one with a steel hook at the end. Introducing the implement into the lock of the front gate, he easily opened it. Closing the gate behind him, he walked through the garden to the front door. Using a different skeleton key, he was able to gain entry into the antechamber of the house. Since turning on the lights would attract the unwanted attention of the neighbors, he used an electric lamp. Having been given a floor plan by Cocantin, Judex began his exploration. He started with the large parlor. Since all the parlor windows were boarded up, Judex turned on a light switch. The clarity of the electric lights made Judex's mission easier to accomplish.

He immediately entered the public office of the Baronne. There was the notepad from which Cocantin had taken a leaf. Examining it, Judex found nothing significant. There was a locked drawer in the desk. Since the key was still in the lock, Judex didn't bother to open it. After quietly lighting a cigarette, he opened another door that led into a small corridor. The passageway led him into the Baronne's secret office.

There Judex expected to reap a fruitful harvest. He slowly and methodically scrutinized the room. There was a single door, his initial point of entry. A lone window looked out on the garden. The furniture then attracted his attention. He planned to minutely examine them.

Suddenly the ringing of a telephone filled the air. Expecting to learn something of vital importance, Judex seized the receiver. Scarcely had he placed it against his ear, two metallic barriers slammed down on either side of him. His access to the window and door were cut off. A female voice erupted from the telephone.

"*Bonsoir*, Comte de Trémeuse. It's Baronne d'Apremont. How do you feel? Hello! You hear me, Comte."

"I feel very well."

"I'm being treated to an excellent dinner by your friend Cocantin."

"*Bon appétit,* Madame."

Judex maintained a dramatic flair even when his life was imperiled. The sarcastic remark exasperated the adventuress. She giggled maliciously.

"You interfered in matters that you should have avoided. The Secret Raiders will grant you no quarter!" The Baronne hung up the phone.

Maintaining his self-confidence, Judex continued to calmly smoke his cigarette. Examining the iron walls that had imprisoned him, he couldn't find a way to cause them to retract. Returning to the desk, he inhaled the final fumes of his cigarette.

"My dear friend, please forgive me," said Baronne d'Apremont returning to the private dining room of the establishment where Cocantin had driven her. She was dressed in an elegantly suggestive gown with a low neckline. "The telephone operator had difficulty making the connection."

"In restaurants, it's very difficult to have a telephone conversation."

"Or for the other party on the line to hear you."

"Did your conversation go well?"

"Admirably," said the Baronne with an ironic smile. "Let's order."

"Let 's order," concurred Cocantin. Although he wasn't wealthy, the private detective was a gourmet of very refined tastes.

The menu constituted a true masterpiece. After being shown the selections by an impassive headwaiter, the eyes of the Baronne widened with desire. Her reaction flooded Prosper Cocantin's soul with pleasure. Falsely believing that he had successfully deceived Judex's enemies. he felt now that he had the added compensation of having a fabulous meal with a dazzling woman. Once the headwaiter departed with their orders, the detective planted a passionate kiss on the shoulder of this fascinating beauty. Taking advantage of Cocantin's absorption in his lengthy kiss, the Baronne opened a secret compartment in one of her rings. Inside the compartment was a colorless powder that she dropped into Cocantin's glass.

When the headwaiter returned, he diplomatically coughed in order to avoid an awkward situation. Brought back to reality, Cocantin ceased his amorous actions and slipped his spoon into the bowl of soup before him.

"Baronne," said Cocantin, "tell me I'm not dreaming!"

"You're like a big child!" exclaimed Baronne d'Apremont.

Acting as he was deaf to this exchange, the stoic headwaiter removed a bottle from an ice bucket. He filled the couple's glasses with expensive champagne.

The exquisite dinner continued to be served. While the Baronne became more animated, Cocantin's eloquence and fervor declined. He yawned several times. His vision became blurry. A creeping torpor enveloped him. He tried to fight his mysterious lethargy, but he inevitably had to admit defeat.

When he ceased laughing at her provocative jokes, the Baronne reacted. "Are you alright? Do you feel ill?"

"Not at all," disputed Prosper Cocantin. "It must be the lateness of the hour. I drank very moderately. This must only be a momentary dizziness. Maybe... it's the excitement of..."

"Or the lack of air. It's very hot in this room. I'll open a window."

"Don't... bother."

However, the Baronne had already left the table. When she returned, Cocantin had fallen unconscious. His face was resting against the half-eaten fish on his plate.

"Wonderful," said the Baronne. "I can leave." She summoned the headwaiter. "Bring me my cloak."

With the air of an outraged queen, she placed on her shoulders a superb satin cape from the House of Geneviève. She pointed to the slumbering Cocantin. "Let him rest. Give him the bill once he awakens."

Pretending to be as angry as Venus upon learning that Jupiter had deserted her to romance Amphitryon's wife, the Baronne left the restaurant. Jumping into the car that Cocantin had rented for the evening, she instructed the driver to take her back to the Rue Musset in Auteuil. She smugly reclined on the cushioned seat.

"And now for you, my dear Judex!"

IV. The Doctrines of Doctor Howey

While these events unfolded themselves between Auteuil and the Boulevard of La Madeleine, a peaceful calm seemed to reign in La Frondaie. Primrose had moved into the room adjacent to Jacqueline's. The two ladies had spent a charming three hours moving Primrose's possessions from the Chateau d'Arbois. Keeping the promise to his brother, Roger found reassuring pretexts to protectively observe his fiancée and his sister-in-law. Both women apparently had forgotten the sinister influence that dominated them.

Around 4 o'clock in the afternoon, Roger received a telephone call from Judex inquiring about the state of affairs at La Frondaie. This was before Judex undertook his expedition to the Rue Musset.

"All goes well," declared Primrose's fiancé.

"Any visitors?"

"None. How are you progressing?"

"I hope to have good news before midnight."

Shortly thereafter, Dr. Howey arrived to give his lesson of aesthetic culture to Jean. During the summer, Howey lived in a modest villa not far from La Frondaie. Jean was having a superb time. Seated on a bench, Jacqueline and Primrose watched the graceful frolics of the young boy. Roger joined the two ladies.

The lesson lasted about a half hour. Never before had the professor been more anxious to develop the natural gifts of his young student, nor had the pupil shown itself more willing to follow his mentor's instructions. It was an appealing spectacle to see the lad perform these artistic movements that climaxed in an amusing pirouette. The performance combined the classical with the modern. It was a combination of Greek, French and American styles that reflected the contemporary Parisian trends. When the lesson was over, Jacqueline, Primrose and Roger applauded the educator and his disciple. The inhabitants of La Frondaie felt that this celebration of physical beauty had dispersed any lingering traces of the evil spirit that had threatened them.

Jacqueline had delighted in seeing her son excel. She complimented Howey on the lesson.

"Doctor, you've brought great pleasure to our house. Although the Comte won't be here tonight, would you dine with us at La Frondaie."

"Oh! Please accept," added Primrose. "We're going to have a music recital. You play the piano very well, Doctor, and could accompany my singing. I just received a collection of old melodies. I love the old French songs. They have a unique flavor. We could interpret them together."

"I don't want to abuse your hospitality," said Howey.

"Doctor," interjected Roger, "don't deprive us of your artistic genius."

"My household staff expects me home for dinner," protested Howey.

"You're the master," argued Roger, "and the master has all the rights."

"That's true," replied Howey.

"You accept?" asked Jacqueline and Primrose together.

"With all my heart! Clearly I have passed the best hours of my life at La Frondaie."

Comtesse de Trémeuse and Primrose escorted Jean back to the house. Howey took Roger aside.

"Were you and your brother able to follow the dictates of your heart? It's too late for me! Arts and Science devoured the best years of my life. I worked so hard that I had no time for love. I deeply regret it. Now that I've made my fortune, I realize that the foundation of my existence was hollow selfishness rather than altruistic sacrifice. You chose the better path! I envy you!"

"Doctor, one can always recover lost time."

"At my age!"

"I don't know your year of birth, but you remain surprisingly youthful for a man with white hair."

"You're saying that I'm capable of romantic conquests?"

"And why not?"

"You're making fun of me!"

"Doctor, I would never be so mean!"

'"Then you're being too kind."

"Not at all. "You're strongly attractive to women."

"To women in general? No. To certain women, perhaps. Snobbish socialites are prompted by curiosity to converse with me, but their interest soon wanes as does mine. What do these flirts with their momentary liaisons have to do with true love? Nothing! They live an artificial existence that's a caricature of tenderness, a masquerade of sentiment. They are more like mannequins than women of flesh and blood. I want nothing to do with them. Realizing it's too late to obtain my heat's true desires, I must merely observe, without bitter jealousy, the happiness of my friends."

"A noble sentiment, Doctor. Your comments only increase my regard for you."

Howey was uncharacteristically exuberant. "I'm delighted then. You don't mind if I continue to confide in you."

"Please do."

"I take great pleasure in sharing a little of my old soul with your young heart."

"Doctor..."

"I have developed a special friendship for you and your brother. You're both exceptional human beings. We live in an era when few men have ideals, or few ideals have men. You can raise yourself above human prejudice and break resolutely with outdated traditions that imprison men's souls. What more beautiful exercise of moral independence! Forgive me for being so intimate."

"There's nothing to forgive."

"There's no better illustration of your brother's noble character than his courageous decision to marry the daughter of the banker Favraux. He had ample reason to choose her for a wife. The Comtesse is a charming and perfect creature. For the Comte, ideals overcame bias. This is a perfect example of what I have christened the Modern Duty, the ability to judge people solely by their own merit. This completely contradicts the dangerous and immoral doctrine of atavism which I have always condemned."

"Yes, my compassionate brother has been well-rewarded by his wife."

"As you will be by the lady that you have chosen to marry. Your sister-in-law is a sublime living refutation to all the theories of heredity. If I may be so bold, I have observed her rather carefully. I couldn't distinguish the least trace of any fraternal traits. She radiates frankness and integrity. In a word, she's the very opposite of her father. I knew Favraux. To be precise, I had some business dealings with him."

"Really?"

"Yes. He was a frightening man full of bitterness and incomparable brutality. The rumor is that when he died, he was suffering from extreme ennui. They say he committed suicide."

Roger shrugged evasively.

"That's unimportant," concluded Howey. "The important thing is that he died before he could ruin forever his daughter's life. Forgive my bluntness, but the main point of this conversation was to demonstrate the accuracy of my doctrines against the outdated theories of moral heredity. How unfair is that stupid adage: 'Like father, like son.' Of course, I'm talking about a daughter in this case."

When the two men returned to the entrance of the house, Jacqueline and Primrose descended from the veranda. "We're gathering roses," said the Comtesse.

"May I accompany you," asked Roger.

"With pleasure," replied his fiancée.

"And you, Doctor?" inquired the Comtesse.

"I need to telephone my villa that I'll be having dinner here."

"Certainly," acknowledged Judex's wife.

"Excuse me, ladies." The Professor of Aesthetic Culture entered the lobby. Approaching the telephone on a corner shelf, he noticed Jean. With his back towards the doctor, the lad was seated at a table. Busy writing a letter, he was oblivious to the doctor's presence. Gently Howey walked over and looked over the boy's shoulder.

The youngster had traced on an envelope two words: "Monsieur Favraux." At this point, Jean spied the image of his tutor in a wall mirror. He continued to write. The address read like this when it was finished:

Monsieur Favraux
With the Good Lord
In Paradise

The doctor tapped him affectionately on the shoulder. The child lied to protect his family's secret.

"Doctor, every Wednesday, I write a letter to my grandfather. When I go to sleep, I leave it in my room for an angel to find."

V. The Demon in the House

Jacques de Trémeuse had finished his cigarette as nonchalantly as if he was in his study at La Frondaie rather than trapped by the Baronne. His hat and cloak rested on a chair.

"Ah! You believe that Judex is captured. You may be a formidable opponent, but Judex is your match!"

Methodically he examined the walls of his prison. Locating a wooden panel on one of the regular walls of the room, he pulled a case from his pocket. Inside were tools that resembled surgical instruments. Choosing a drill, he created in the panel a hole that was half a centimeter wide and nearly six centimeters deep.

Noticing a large wooden chest on the floor, he opened it. The empty interior was large enough to accommodate a human body. Satisfied that it was empty, he returned to the small hole in the wall. From his bag of tools, he pulled out a sort of miniature torpedo. Attached to this torpedo-like advice was a winding mechanism like a clock. After turning the timing mechanism, he placed the device in the hole that he had drilled. Lying down in the chest, he closed the lid. Some seconds after, a loud explosion occurred. Debris splattered through the chamber. The unique explosive had punched a wide gap in the wall. Once the smoke and dust settled, Judex got out of the chest. The hole in the wall was large enough for him to pass through.

"Time to leave," he muttered through his teeth. "Even though I've barely lifted the veil hiding the operations of the Secret Raiders, it's not safe to linger."

Retrieving his hat and cloak, he passed through the massive hole into a corridor. Making his way to the front of the house, he opened the door to the courtyard.

Instantly a cry of rage resounded from Baronne d'Apremont who had just entered the courtyard. With the courteous gesture of a gentleman, Judex removed his hat. He behaved formally.

"Madame, I had to damage part of your house. Please accept my apologies." He exited the doorway and moved to the side of the porch. "You're now free to enter your abode. It's too late to have a lengthy conversation. Perhaps another time, Baronne."

Judex's biting irony had been as brutal to the Baronne as a whip to the face. Leaping like a panther into her house, she shook her fist at Judex from the doorway

"Then it's war!" she hissed.

"Yes, it's war!" Judex's piercing gaze was like a knife in the Baronne's side.

"Well! Denounce me to the police! Brand me as a thief! Your victory will be complete!"

"No," said Count de Trémeuse with a certainty that froze the temptress. "I render my own justice!"

After uttering an obscene blasphemy, the Baronne slammed the door.

Inside his car, Judex issued commands to the loyal Baptiste.

"Quickly take me back to La Frondaie. The entire evening wasn't wasted. What the blazes has Cocantin been doing during all this time!"

Leaving the Rue de Musset around 8:30, Judex returned to La Frondaie at 11 o'clock. Seeing the lit windows of his villa, he was relieved to be back among the loved ones he had sworn to protect. As soon as he exited the car, a cry of despair sounded from the veranda. It came from the Comtesse.

"My son! My child!"

Judex rushed to his wife. "Jacqueline! What's happened!"

"Jean and Primrose have disappeared," said the Comtesse before she fainted.

Falling into her husband's arms, she was taken in to the library and deposited on a couch.

"Be calm, my beloved," implored Judex, "and explain what happened."

The young mother only replied with sobs. "My child!"

A distraught Roger appeared. He was followed by Dr. Howey, whose face displayed signs of deep concern, and several servants. The panic-ridden utterances of the household staff created an atmosphere of severe confusion.

"Leave us!" barked Comte de Trémeuse at servants. The nobleman was left alone with his wife, his brother and the doctor.

"Roger, tell me what happened," demanded the Comte.

"Speak. Doctor," said Roger. "I don't have the courage."

"Here's what happened," explained Howey. "The Comtesse was kind enough to invite me to dinner. Right after the meal, Jean was tucked into bed. I was alone with Roger, Primrose and the Comtesse. We began to perform a musical piece. I accompanied Primrose on the piano as she sang. She went to her room to retrieve a collection of old songs. After a half hour, she hadn't returned. The Comtesse became worried."

Jacqueline interrupted. "When I went to Primrose's room, I found it empty. I decided to check Jean's room. I found Juliette asleep in a chair. Jean's bed was empty. I tried to awaken Juliette, but she slept like a log. I summoned the servants. They searched the house and the grounds. It was all in vain."

"Jacques, I beg you in the name of our love, in the name of the little child whom we both love, find our Jean!"

"Jacqueline, I swear to you that I shall not rest until I've found Jean and Primrose. As for the monster who abducted our son, I'll strangle him with my bare hands!"

"Brother," implored Roger, "forgive my failure to protect this house!"

"I don't have to forgive you," said the older brother. "Don't blame yourself. There's a demon in this house. I feel his presence. He hides in the shadows. I must expose his hideous face to the light of day. I already know his servitors. I most discover his infamous secret."

"And we will be there to help you," volunteered Howey.

Part Five: The Haunted Forest

I. The Hanging Tree

Nothing is more beautiful than a restful forest during a clear summer night. No breeze shakes the leaves of the large trees or the shrubs of the groves. No wing rustles. No bird cries. The silent serenity is only disrupted at rare intervals by the galloping onslaught of deer or the roar of a wild boar.

Under the cover of these dark arches, the forest gives the impression of an immense cathedral illuminated only by the stars, those small lamps lit by the invisible hand that rules all. You may initially be terrified by a mysterious aura of the unknown, but soon you feel protected by the large trees that serve as motionless sentinels. You will want to walk slowly though the avenues of this poetic dreamlike landscape.

On a night like this, around 11 o'clock, there walked a child whose hand was held by a young woman. The girl walked slowly and unevenly. The child had no choice but to follow her meandering course. Nevertheless, he questioned their odyssey.

"Big sister, must we take such a long walk."

Primrose replied ominously. "You must come with me."

Jean docilely followed her. Primrose was once more under the hypnotic influence of an unknown force. She proceeded deeply into the forest. As time progressed, the boy started to succumb to fatigue.

"Not so fast, big sister! Not so fast!"

Without replying to the child's pleas, Roger's fiancée accelerated her pace. The boy became fearful.

"Why don't you talk to me, big sister? Are you angry?"

It was becoming difficult for Jean to follow his bewitched companion. His feet rubbed against plant roots. He almost fell several times, but Primrose's hand steadied him.

She held him in a grip of steel. A cry of despair erupted from the child's trembling lips.

"Mama! Mama!"

Deaf to this appeal, Primrose continued on her route. Suddenly she stopped in front of a gigantic tree. It was one of the most splendid oaks in the forest of Fontainebleau. All the other neighboring trees were dwarfed by it. This colossus of nature had a sinister name. It was called "The Hanging Tree."

Twenty years earlier, the park rangers had found the corpse of a vagrant suspended from one of the oak's branches. Since that time, the inhabitants made the sign of the cross whenever they passed the tree. The children never played near the oak.

Yielding doubtless to the dark influence that manipulated her, Primrose knelt at the foot of the oak. Inside her frozen soul, there was a vague awakening of kindness and mercy. Rebelling against the secret instructions that had conquered her brain, she hugged Jean and kissed him on her forehead. She then spread herself on the ground. Jacqueline's son, physically and mentally exhausted, collapsed next to her. His head resting on Primrose's shoulder, Jean slept.

What had happened earlier at La Frondaie? When Primrose had gone to her room to search for her collection of old French songs, she was in such good spirits that Roger never considered following her. Scarcely had she arrived at the foot of the staircase when she raised her hands to her forehead, Primrose shook as if she was fighting an invisible opponent.

Finally conquered by this mysterious force, she ascended the steps in a trance. Reaching the upper floor, she went straight to Jean's room. The child was still awake. He looked at Juliette, who had fallen into a deep sleep after placing the boy in his bed. The repeated cries of Jean failed to stir the chambermaid. Jean didn't know whether he should be worried or amused. He was about to press a button which would ring a bell to summon a servant. Then Primrose appeared.

"Juliette won't wake up," said Jean. "Shake her a little, big sister!"

Primrose placed a finger over her lips. The boy worshipped the young woman. He had absolute trust in her. He would never disobey her.

Not paying any attention to the motionless chambermaid, Primrose pointed to Jean's clothes. "Dress!"

Not at all frightened by the presence of "his big sister," Jean imagined that he was going to assist her in a joke involving either his mother or his uncle. He put on his clothes. Taking him by the hand, Primrose led the boy into the outside corridor. She took the boy down a service stairway into the courtyard. Still under the illusion that he was participating in a prank, Jean didn't protest when Primrose directed him through a gate into the forest. Normally that gate was locked. Tonight it inexplicably wasn't.

Once they entered the forest, the child became anxious. "Where are we going, big sister?"

Primrose didn't answer, but the moonlight shined on her face and created the illusion that she smiled. Jean's qualms were momentarily soothed. He would follow Primrose to the ends of the earth. Instead she led him to the Hanging Tree.

The two wayfarers had rested near the oak for a long time when Primrose began to show signs of life. Letting Jean's head fall gently on the ground, she rose up. Her eyes stared into the night. She trembled slightly as she moved. Ignoring the sleeping child, she disappeared into the depths of the forest.

Jean slept for another hour before opening his eyes. Initially surprised not to find himself in his soft bed, the boy wondered if he was still dreaming. He rubbed is eyes. Seeing the forest around him, Jean remembered how he got there.

"Primrose!" he yelled. There was no reply. He continued to vainly shout her name. Primrose's disappearance threw the boy into despair. His pitiful screams resumed.

Eventually his panic dissipated. He remembered the story of Tom Thumb. When the fairy tale hero found himself lost in a forest, he climbed a tree to scan the area for a light that would show the path out of the woods

"To find the right path, I only have to climb a tree!"

Jean was extremely flexible and agile. Dr. Howey's physical exercises had not disciplined Jean's natural brazenness but given him a extreme nimbleness. To Jacqueline's fright, he had already successfully ascended several trees in the grounds of La Frondaie. Therefore, Jean was not afraid to risk it. Repressing his tears, he was ready to mount the Hanging Tree.

First, he calmly inspected the huge trunk. To scale this behemoth, he needed a plan of attack. A shout of joy issued from the boy. The centuries helped by rain and the burrowing of insects had dug a natural stairway in the wood. This route would allow him to reach the closest branches. Without a moment's hesitation, his hands and feet positioned themselves on the wooden surface. It was then that he recognized that his task was harder than he initially imagined. Worm-eaten wood crumbled under the pressure of his feet. The boy couldn't ascend easily. Jean had scarcely advanced before he was forced to retreat.

However, Jean was tenacious. His perseverance was rewarded. He found sufficient support to move steadily towards his goal. Despite scraped hands, bruised knees and torn clothing, he was able to straddle a strong branch. After catching his breath, he carefully continued his ascent. Having tested the sturdiness of each branch, he declined to reach the summit of the oak. Instead, he attained the extremity of a very stout branch that could act as an excellent observation post.

In the clarity of the moon, Jean glimpsed an ocean of foliage that extended infinitely. Besides the stars shining brightly in the sky, there were no other lights on the horizon. There was nothing to indicate a house which could provide sanctuary. The boy felt as he was attached to a mast in the middle of a big ocean.

Despondency overwhelmed the boy. What should he do? Climb back down? Where would he go? Although he had earlier displayed courage that would have been the envy of older boys, all the hope inside him crumbled.

Becoming dizzy, Jean had to steady himself on the branch that he straddled. Closing his eyes, he forced himself to climb even higher up the oak. At the crossroads of two branches, he found a safe haven. He no longer saw the jungle of leaves that had disheartened him. He no longer found himself suspended above an abyss. He felt a sense of serenity. Up in the heavens, a corner of the sky seemed to beckon him. No longer wishing to descend, Jean counted the stars.

II. The Heart of the Mystery

Accompanied by Dr. Howey, Judex searched vainly the grounds around La Frondaie. Under the light of the servants' lanterns, no corner of the vast estate was ignored. All the gates to the forest were found to be locked.

Judex lost himself in conjectures. Where did Primrose flee with this poor child? At 3 o'clock in the morning, he returned totally discouraged. Comtesse de Trémeuse had remained in the house with her brother-in-law. Several times she had wanted to assist with the search outside, but Roger prevailed upon her to desist. She felt that her only recourse was to pray.

Before her husband and Dr. Howey said anything, she could tell from their faces that they had been unsuccessful.

"Jacques." she said, "my child..." With her eyes closed, she lost her balance. The ordeal had taken its toll.

When Jacques and Roger prevented her from falling, Howey volunteered his medical opinion.

"The Comtesse is on the brink of a nervous breakdown, but she's not in danger. She only needs peace and quiet right now. There's medicine at the pharmacy in Fontainebleau to calm her nerves. I'll go get it."

"Do you want me to drive you?" asked Roger.

"No, I have my car here."

"Thank you, Doctor,'" said the Comte.

"I'm only doing my duty."

As Howey left, Jacques and Roger escorted Jacqueline to the bedroom. Lying on her bed, she regained her senses.

"Jacques, are you there?"

"Yes, my beloved."

"Continue the search for our Jean. You too, Roger. Summon Martine to stay with me. I'll be strong. I promise."

As Jacques remained at his wife's bedside, Roger went in search of Martine, a maid who had long been with the Trémeuse family. Leaving Jacqueline with their loyal retainer, the two brothers conferred.

"Roger, were you able to wake Juliette?"

"Yes. She knows nothing. I suspect that she was drugged. She had a cup of tea before putting Jean to bed."

"How much time passed between Primrose's departure from the music recital and the discovery of Jean's disappearance?"

"About 25 to 30 minutes."

"What was the time?"

"9:40 exactly."

"What did you and the others do?"

"While Jacqueline and some of the servants searched the house, the other servants went with Howey and me to check the grounds."

"Did you notice any gates unlocked?"

"No. I personally verified that they were all locked."

"This is very weird," declared Jacques. "We must have neglected some clue. It will be daylight soon, and that shall be a tremendous help. We must search again!"

Going outside, the brother stopped at the gate to the forest. This time, the gate was unlocked. Judex was perplexed. No key had been left in the lock.

"Come!" said Judex. "We must have a visitor."

Returning to the villa, Judex immediately led his brother up the stairway. In the corridor, they heard voices. In Primrose's room, two women were engaged in an loud conversation. The brothers listened outside.

"What did you do with my child?" shouted Jacqueline.

"I don't know!" replied Primrose.

"Answer me! Where is my child?"

"I swear to you that I don't know!"

"Speak! Tell the truth!"

"I remember nothing!"

"That's impossible!"

"I swear that it's the truth!"

"You're driving me to my grave!" screamed Jacqueline.

The last outburst was so strident that Judex and Roger felt compelled to enter the room.

Jacqueline ran into her husband's arms. "She returned alone! She doesn't know what happened to my son!"

Judex addressed Martine, who had accompanied her mistress into the room. "Please leave, but don't go far. I may need your services."

Not understanding the mysterious drama unfolding around her, the young servant departed. Judex turned his attention to Jacqueline.

"When did you realize that Primrose had returned?"

"I heard a door open. Despite Martine's objections, I left my room. I found Primrose in her room. She apparently could see me. Primrose had the aura of a sleepwalker with glazed eyes and a shambling gait. She screamed and collapsed on her bed. She remained prostrate in a frozen position. I feared that she was dead. She gradually started to move. Eventually rising, she stared at me for a long time before shouting my name. I questioned her."

"I heard her replies," said Judex compassionately looking at Primrose. "She really doesn't remember anything. She once more succumbed to the domination of the evil spirit. "

"Then my son is lost?" shouted the Comtesse.

"No," replied Judex. "I won't fool you with false promises, but we must recognize that the current crisis isn't hopeless. Our enemies are barbaric. Although they're capable of any crime, I'm convinced they kidnapped Jean not to harm him. They must want to use him as a hostage."

"My poor child! How he must be suffering!"

"Neither his pain nor yours shall be of long duration," predicted Judex. He pointed to Primrose's dress. It was covered with some twigs and a few dead lives. "This is a clue which may lead us to Jean."

Primrose finally spoke. She was hysterical. "I have brought misfortune into your house once more! I have delivered into the hands of these outlaws an innocent whom I deeply love! Madame, I'm the cause of your grief! You'll never be able to forgive me."

"Primrose," consoled Judex, "don't torment yourself. Someone else is responsible for all these misfortunes."

"Monsieur Jacques, confine me in a convent or a prison. The evil spirit is too powerful to fight."

"Listen to me, both of you. Now that I have a trail, I must go into the forest with Roger. I must ask you -- no, I must order you -- to both remain in this room during our brief absence. It's vital that neither of you come into contact with anyone else." Judex smiled. "You are now my prisoners. Martine will be your jailer. She'll make sure that no one approaches you. I have total faith in her. No one, not even an evil spirit, shall breach this chamber. This seclusion is essential for me to find Jean."

"My beloved," proclaimed Jacqueline, "Primrose and I would obey you absolutely."

"Absolutely!" repeated Roger's fiancée clasping her hands together as if she was fervently praying to God.

Judex embraced his wife in a long kiss that was a demonstration of their undying love.

"Kiss me, my darling," said Roger. Kissing Primrose, he gently stroked her forehead. "Our love will be eternal."

"Yes, eternal," confirmed Primrose as tears rolled down her cheeks.

"Come!" said Judex to his brother.

Leaving the room, the brothers encountered a very concerned Martine.

"Martine," said Comte de Trémeuse, "you have proved your loyalty in the past. I have complete confidence in you. Events threaten to overwhelm us. Jean has disappeared, and a danger hovers over the Comtesse and Mademoiselle Primrose. While my brother and I are out of the house, I want you to guard them. Take care of the ladies, but don't leave them unsupervised for a second. I shall instruct the other servants to follow your commands. With the exception of yourself, no person can enter the ladies' room. The ladies have been informed of these restrictions. This is not a punishment imposed on them, but a precaution. I have placed on you a heavy responsibility, but you have my trust. I needn't say anything more."

"Monsieur le Count, your orders will be faithfully executed."

"Thank you, Martine."'

While the capable young woman returned to Primrose's room, Judex and Roger went downstairs. There the other servants were informed of their temporary subordination to Martine. Once the servants were dismissed, Judex told Roger of his plan to locate Jean.

"We must act quickly. Brother, assemble the best bloodhounds from our kennels. We will use them to search the forest."

As soon as Roger turned around, Judex noticed the arrival of a new visitor. Prosper Cocantin was on the veranda. Jacques de Trémeuse opened the door.

"Ah, my friend," ironically said the lord of the manor, "why are you busy at such an early hour."

"Don't ask," moaned Cocantin as he came inside.

"You must explain what happened last night in Paris."

"I'm so ashamed."

"If this concerns your private life, perhaps this is none of my business. I f you have only committed a mistake, then it can be rectified. I need to know the truth. Your information can shed light on a dark chaos that has engulfed my house. Tell me quickly because I don't have a minute to lose."

"Comte, this is what happened. Yesterday, everything seemed to be going well. I had succeeded in persuading Baronne d'Apremont to have dinner at an expensive restaurant and sent her servants to the movies. In the middle of the meal, although I had only drunk moderately, I suffered a blackout. I awoke around 2 o'clock in the morning. I was on the couch of an office. The waiters told me that they had found me asleep with my face in my plate. As for my companion, she left this note before her departure."

The detective handed the message to Judex.

My dear Cocantin,
Your nose is large, but you can't follow the scent. No one outwits me. See you soon!

Baronne d'Apremont

"Fortunately the auto club car that I hired was waiting on the boulevard. This scheming Baronne had the decency to send it back for me after having been driven to her house. I returned to my apartment humiliated. After taking a bath and changing my clothes, I instructed the hired car to take me to the Baronne's house. I had to discover what happened. As sooner as my car reached the house, I saw the Baronne and her maid leaving it."

"That's interesting," observed Judex.

"The duo climbed into a limousine that departed at full speed. I ordered my driver to follow them. Unfortunately we lost them. Not knowing what to do next, I came here."

"You were right to come here. Jean disappeared last night."

"What? How did that happened?"

"The evil spirit possessed Primrose again. There's no doubt that this unfortunate girl delivered Jean to the Secret Raiders."

"That's monstrous."

"Monstrous, indeed. Once Roger has gathered the blood-hounds, we shall search the forest."

Suddenly a shocked Roger burst in the house.

"All the dogs are dead. The entire pack was poisoned."

III. Jean

The previous evening, Baronne d'Apremont had been in a state of indescribable fury. Convinced that Judex had fallen into her a snare during her dinner with Cocantin, she rejoiced at that the prospect of informing her superior, the enigmatic Bébert alias *N'a-qu'un-Chasse*, of their redoubtable enemy! Instead, she had to confess her shameful defeat. The recognition that she had been tricked was an unbearable burden on this proud woman.

When she discovered the damage done by the explosion, her only desire was to seek a terrible revenge. She was intelligent enough to realize that the fearsome association to which she belonged was now opposed by a formidable adversary. She had to be crafty and patient. The Secret Raiders generally practiced murder as a last resort. The instructions of *N'a-qu'un-Chasse* had been quite definite: "Only kill in a legitimate case of self-defense." Despite this restriction, the unabated hatred of the Baronne caused her to coldly sentence Judex to death.

It only remained to choose the method to execute her verdict. She realized that Judex's assassination wouldn't be easy. This man knew how to protect himself. A proper plan must be formulated. Meeting her subordinates in her undamaged parlor, she related the details of her recent defeat. During this gathering, there were no longer any distinctions between employer and servant. The conspirators conferred as criminals united by greed.

The Baronne talked in a blunt matter. All listened to her with the respect accorded to a colleague whose competence had proven her superior judgment.

"We have no choice. This base has been compromised. It must be abandoned before our enemy attacks again. Tomorrow, we move to the Rue Bergère."

Before she could say anything further, a ringing resounded from the antechamber. It was coming from a telephone. The Baronne laughed.

"Fortunately Judex didn't disrupt all our communication with the outside during his escape."

Answering the phone, she listened to the speaker on the other end. Her face first expressed astonishment and then admiration. Belles-Mirettes, the chauffeur and the cook observed in silence. Once the Baronne hung up, they awaited her words.

"That man is incredible!"

"Who?" asked Belles-Mirettes.

"*N'a-qu'un-Chasse*!" revealed the Baronne. "He knows everything that happened during the last three hours!"

The three other Raiders were dumbfounded.

"He knows that Judex escaped my trap and returned to La Frondaie," said the Baronne.

"He's phenomenal!" exclaimed Belles-Mirettes. The other two Raiders, who contributed more brawn than brains to their criminal gang, were still stunned.

"That's not all!" added the Baronne. "*N'a-qu'un-Chasse* wants me to go to the Roche-Grise to receive new instructions in the regular way. He promises to put an end to Judex and his accursed clique. We can't waste time." She looked at her chauffeur. "Get the car ready! We leave in ten minutes. Belles-Mirettes will accompany us." She pointed at the cook. "You must prepare our new headquarters in the Rue Bergère. This shall be a sleepless night for us, but no worse than any other night we have passed in the service of the Secret Raiders. This probably won't be the last such night."

No one questioned the instructions of the Baronne. They were all slaves to the infernal designs of their enigmatic one-eyed chieftain.

Cocantin had then seen the Baronne and her pseudo-maid leave in their car. Although their destination remained unknown to the private detective, they were headed for the forest of Fontainebleau. There dwelt the mysterious master of this French Camorra whose accomplishments had already surpassed the infamous secret societies of the past.

When the Baronne and Belles-Mirettes arrived at the sinister den of this elusive predator, dawn had awakened the forest. At the designated rendezvous, there existed a special mailbox that allowed this colossus of crime to correspond at any time with his underlings. Leaving the car, the women walked towards the stone pylon which they had visited on prior occasions. Constant rainfall had dug moss-hidden cavities inside the stone. This was the Roche-Grise (the "Grey Rock").

Belles-Mirettes reached inside a specific cavity that seemed to the naked eye indistinguishable from the others. She withdrew a leaf of paper folded twice. Belles-Mirettes spread it out. The paper was blank. Accompanied by the Baronne, she went to a small stream that flowed through the rocks. After soaking the paper in the water, Belles-Mirettes looked at it closely. Letters began to appear on the page.

The child was taken by Primrose to the Hanging Tree. Fetch him. You must force him to reveal the address of his supposedly deceased grandfather, Favraux. I won't be joining you just yet. You know why. I have another plan to execute while you follow my orders.

BÉBERT

While their chauffeur waited, the two women went in the direction of the Hanging Tree. They were extremely familiar with the topography of the forest. Instead of taking the main avenues which led to intersections with signposts, they navigated through side paths. Within 10 minutes, they reached the Hanging Tree. Neither Primrose or Jean could be seen. The Baronne and Belles-Mirettes futilely searched the areas adjacent to the oak to no avail.

They wondered if Bébert miscalculated. The child was nowhere to be found. They were about to return to the Roche-Grise when they heard a series of faint cries.

"Mama! Mama!"

Raising their heads, the women perceived a startling sight in the light of early morning. Perched on a fork formed by two connected branches was Jean. Weakened by fatigue, the boy was too frightened to descend. He called vainly for the one person whom he trusted more than anyone else in the world, his mother.

"It's him," whispered the Baronne to her accomplice. Modifying her voice to convey kindness, she shouted at Jean. "Is that you, darling?"

"I'm afraid! I climbed up here, but I can't get down."

"Why?" asked Belles-Mirettes. Despite her masculine attire, she seemed to feel genuine compassion for the child.

"Because the way down is full of twists!" replied Jean.

"Listen carefully," said the Baronne. "Are you facing the tree?"

"Yes."

"Find a place where you can put your foot. Then try to climb down."

"Be careful!" cautioned Belles-Mirettes.

Reassured by the presence of the two women and unaware of their true intentions, Jean regained his confidence. Executing the instructions of the Baronne and encouraged by Belles-Mirettes, the boy reached the beginning of the "stairway" in the oak. His natural boldness restored, he let himself fall in to the arms of the women waiting at the bottom.

"What were you doing up there?" asked the Baronne.

"I wanted to be like Tom Thumb," admitted the child. "I looked for a light, but I found only stars. Watching them, I fell asleep. When I woke up, the stars were gone. Did the wind take them away?"

Belles-Mirettes smiled. "Yes, it was the wind."

"I didn't know where I was," explained the child. "I called for my Mama."

"Where do you live?" asked the Baronne insidiously.

"La Frondaie."

"Do you want us to take you to your parents?"

"Yes, Madame. Please. Please." The boy jumped for joy. "Mama, Papa and Uncle Roger will scold me for leaving, but it isn't my fault. Primrose took me, and then left me alone. Do you know Primrose?"

"No, my child," said the Baronne.

"She's our neighbor's daughter. For my birthday, she gave me a beautiful white pony, Lutin. He's very sweet. He can do tricks like a circus horse. He likes me a lot. He eats sugar from the palm of my hand. He's better than my two fox-terriers, Flip and Bobby. They don't obey my commands. They do what they want."

Jean just noticed that he wasn't being taken towards La Frondaie, but deeply into the forest.

"Madame, where are you taking me?"

"Home," said the Baronne.

"This isn't the way."

"If you know the way home, why didn't you take it last night."

"Because it was dark, and I was scared."

"Be quiet and walk with us!" impatiently ordered the Baronne.

Jean became worried. He lost all his trust in the two women. They now frightened him. He hadn't seen either of them before. There was no kindness in their eyes, voices or gestures. The suspicion gradually grew inside him that they meant him harm.

Once again he recalled an episode from the story of Tom Thumb. The diminutive hero had marked his path with stones. Jean wanted to mimic the fairy tale hero, but the Baronne was watching him too closely. She spurred him to walk faster. Although Belles-Mirettes showed signs of reluctance, she anxiously looked behind them to make sure nobody was following. Jean quickly found a way to trick his captors.

In his pocket was a small bag of candy that his mother had given him yesterday. Slowly he dropped them on the road to leave a trail. Due to Jean's skillfulness, Belles-Mirettes didn't spot the boy's stratagem. By the time they reached an isolated clearing, the bag was empty.

The Baronne decided it was time to perform her primary mission of tricking Jean into revealing valuable information. She nodded to Belles-Mirettes to keep watch. Kneeling in front of the child, she gently stroked his hands.

"My darling, we didn't intend to rush you. Only we know that your grandfather, Monsieur Favraux, is alive."

"My grandfather is dead."

"You lie! Where is he?"

Lowering his head. The child remained silent.

The Baronne noticed that the boy had around his neck a small medallion depicting the Blessed Virgin. She grabbed it.

"Swear on this holy symbol that your grandfather is dead."

The child remained silent. The Baronne threw the boy on the ground.

"Since you won't tell the truth, all the ghosts of the forest will come to take you!"

Hearing these words, Jean suppressed a sob. With his hands held against his head, he remained motionless. Lying on the ground, he didn't dare cry. When he finally rose up, the two women had vanished. All alone in this isolated corner, he was petrified with terror. He didn't dare move because of the fear that the older woman's prediction would come true. An excessive fever seized him. The delirious boy envisioned the surrounding bushes as shrouded figures. These imaginary spectres formed a circle around him.

Clasping his hands, he repeated a prayer that he said with his mother every evening. "Our Father, who art in heaven..."

It seemed to the child that the holy words from his mouths had changed the menacing revenants into beautiful angels. He imagined the heavenly figures forming a protective circle that vigilantly guarded him against the bad ladies and the ghosts of the forest. No longer afraid, he smiled at the heavens above him as consciousness left him.

IV. Lutin

Upon learning that his bloodhounds had been poisoned, Judex, despite his extraordinary self-control, issued a cry of anger.

"How did this happen! To enter my kennels without awakening anyone or provoking the dogs requires an intimate familiarity with La Frondaie. This is very grave. Has one of my servants betrayed me? I can't imagine any of them capable of such an infamy. To expose the guilty, I must cast suspicion on the innocent!"

Cocantin and Roger listened attentively as Judex continued.

"It's imperative to find Jean. Primrose must have brought him into the forest in order to deliver him to the Secret Raiders. Those miscreants must then have taken the boy elsewhere. The loss of the bloodhounds prevents us from pursuing the Raiders' trail. Their deaths show that the criminal feared this eventuality. I have lost my trump card." Judex stopped for a few seconds. "I've found the solution!"

"Roger, take the car. You have an errand that must be accomplished without delay. You must telegraph our ally in Paris and inform him about Jean's abduction. If we fail to find Jean soon, the Secret Raiders will undoubtedly hide him in Paris. We'll need our friend's help if that happens. Once you've sent the telegram, meet me at the intersection of Repentir. As for you, Cocantin, do you know where Lutin's stable is?"

"Jean's pony?"

"Yes, he's also needed at the Repentir crossroad."

"Understood, my dear Comte."

"You must hurry, both of you. Time is of the essence."

After Roger and Cocantin left on their assignments. Judex went outside and greeted Dr. Howey.

"My dear Comte, I apologize for not returning earlier. My car broke down in the middle of the forest. It took me a half hour to fix it. The pharmacist also took his time in filling the prescription. How is the Comtesse?"

"She's calmer."

"Here's the medicine that will steady her nerves."

"Thank you."

"What about Primrose and Jean?"

"Primrose returned."

"With the child."

"Without him."

"What did she say?"

"Many extraordinary things have happened, Doctor. Come with me and I'll tell you everything. "

"And the medicine?"

"I'll send it to the Comtesse." Summoning a servant, Judex ordered him to take the medicine to Martine. Judex then directed the doctor towards the forest.

"Doctor, I need your professional advice."

"I'll be happy to oblige."

"It's not for me, but for someone whom I deeply care for. Through an amazing exercise of the power of suggestion, an unknown individual has transformed an innocent girl into a docile slave. The girl is Primrose. She has been forced to commit crimes that this man can't commit himself. These crimes include the theft of Milton's plans and Jean's abduction. Do you understand her malady?"

"Very well."

"Is there a scientific means to remove this girl from this harmful influence? Is there a way to protect her against this occult intrusion?"

Howey had listened without displaying any emotion. "My dear Comte, I must admit that your revelations take me by surprise. I have a superficial knowledge of hypnotism. It's a delicate matter about which there is much scholarly debate. Nevertheless, I accept the general principles. It may be possible to defy a hypnotic influence by imposing on the subject a will superior to the one that already dominates. Unfortunately, this is only an hypothesis with no firm scientific evidence to support it. I could give you better advice if you brief me thoroughly on Mademoiselle Primrose's case."

"Of course, my dear Doctor." With lighting rapidity, Judex then related a detailed narrative of the mystery surrounding Primrose's behavior. By the time he had finished, they had reached the Repentir intersection where Roger was waiting.

"My dear Comte, I appreciate you taking me into your confidence. In order to give you the correct advice, I need a little time to do some research. With proper reflection, I may be able to combat this malign influence that persecutes this charming girl"

"My friend," affirmed Judex. "I have total confidence in your judgment."

"As do I!" said Roger.

Considerable time expired, and Prosper Cocantin had not appeared with the pony. Judex became impatient.

"Where is Cocantin? After the poisoning of my dogs, Doctor, I had an idea. You know Lutin, the pony which the Miltons gave as a birthday gift to Jean?"

"He's a very intelligent animal who came from a circus."

"We saw him perform at Médrano. He was billed as the Pony Detective. Impressed by Lutin's various tricks, Jean begged my wife and I to buy the pony for him. We refused. Three days later. James Milton and his foster daughter, both of whom are very fond of Jean, purchased the horse for him as a birthday present. Jean quickly formed a bond with Lutin. They even played a game of hide and seek together. In place of my dogs, I hope to use Lutin to track his young master. "

"That might work."

"I'm very concerned that Cocantin..." A distant neigh interrupted Judex. "Listen!"

About 50 meters from Judex and his companions, there appeared a white pony gracefully running at breathtaking speed. He carried a large object in his teeth. Abandoning Howey, Judex ran towards him.

Following Judex's orders, Cocantin had gone to Lutin's stables. The detective intended to ride the pony to the Repentir intersection. Before he could saddle Lutin near the edge of the forest, the pony bolted for an unknown destination.

Cocantin tried to chase after the pony. His ambition exceeded his reach. The two-legged detective couldn't equal his four-legged counterpart. After a hundred steps, Cocantin was stalemated. His foot was caught in a poacher's trap. While the man debated how to escape the snare, the young horse faded in the distance. Lutin's name translates into English as "Goblin," and the former circus performer had the speed of a demon.

Drunk with the fresh air of liberty, Lutin ran without a firm destination. His trajectory disrupted hares and other forest animals. Suddenly Lutin halted. Stretching his nostrils, he smelt the wind. Lutin set off slowly in the other direction. Lowering his head to the ground, his teeth gasped a small object from the ground. It was one of the candies Jean had sowed on the ground. Fond of sweets, the pony ate it with visible pleasure. Lutin continued to eat the other candies until reaching the area where Jean had been apparently abandoned by the Baronne and Belles-Mirettes. Actually the child continued to be watched by the two women hidden behind a shrub. They still intended to coerce Favraux's whereabouts from his grandson. They had merely pretended to abandon the child in order to crush his spirit.

The two women never got the chance to retrieve the child. Lutin sensed danger. As if he perceived their criminal intent, it raced like an arrow at the two female Raiders. The Baronne and her associate leaped to the side in order to avoid being trampled.

Advancing towards his young master, the perceptive animal deduced that Jean had fainted. The pony gently rubbed his snout against the inert body. Seeing that the child wasn't awakening, the pony recalled one of the old circus tricks that he had performed with Antonio the Clown. Seizing Jean's belt in his powerful jaws, Lutin lifted him off the ground. The pony ran towards the nearest road. Unhinged by the pony's intervention, the two Raiders had allowed Jean to be rescued under their very noses.

Spotting Judex and Howey, Lutin advanced towards them. the brave beast deposited his precious burden into the arms of Comte de Trémeuse. Jean regained consciousness. His eyes beheld the image of his stepfather.

"I knew, Papa, that you would find me. The Good Lord told me."

Searching for Cocantin, Judex and his companions heard his hopeless cries. They delivered him from the poacher's snare. Although Cocantin was delighted with the outcome of the adventure, he was slightly dejected that his prestige as a detective had suffered. Still he congratulated his successful four-legged rival. The small procession returned to La Frondaie.

From the window of Primrose's room, Comtesse Jacqueline viewed Jean escorted on his pony by Jacques, Roger, Howey and Cocantin. Unleashing a shout of joy, she ran outside to greet the small caravan. An instant later, Jean was in her arms. This was a moment of spectacular emotion. Everyone burst into tears.

Later when she was alone with her spouse, Jacqueline effusively thanked him.

"I made you a solemn promise," said Judex. "Before all, I promised to return our child unharmed. Although I fulfill that pledge, we must remember that we are in the middle of a fight. My work is not yet finished, but I now know more about our enemy. I shall emerge the victor."

"I believe in you," fervently asserted Jacqueline. "Nevertheless this unfortunate Primrose is the cause of so many hardships. Should we have her move out of our house?"

"It would be a mistake to expel Primrose. She is the key to unmasking these criminals."

45 Centimes.   Tous les Jeudis.

LA
NOUVELLE MISSION
DE
JUDEX

Par ARTHUR BERNÈDE et Louis FEUILLADE

UNE LUEUR DANS LES TÉNÈBRES

Part Six: A Light in the Darkness

I. The Test

"Let me summarize," explained Judex to his brother. "As the unknown leader of the Secret Raiders has used Primrose against us, I shall use Primrose against him and his accomplices without her knowing it. She will unconsciously betray them just as she unconsciously acted against us!"

The brothers were seated on a vast Louis XIV couch in the lobby of La Frondaie. Roger de Trémeuse, had listened to his elder brother with full confidence in his ability to outwit their foes.

"Poor Primrose!" exclaimed her fiancé. "She's always the victim."

"Roger, Primrose is as sacred to me as she is to you. Above all else, I want to protect her. A frightful mystery surrounds her. I intend to solve it."

"I've reflected on the comments of our friend, Dr. Howey. Although he isn't a specialist in these matters, he speculates that another strong will can combat the malign influence manipulating your fiancée. Jean's abduction by these two women, one of whom is clearly Baronne d'Apremont, was committed to learn his grandfather's location. It's clear that these criminals aren't content to merely defend themselves. They're launching their own offensive against us. So far I've frustrated their plans, but the Secret Raiders will continue to seek vengeance on us. We must constantly be vigilant. We must act quickly."

"Brother," resumed Roger, "you know that I'll follow your commands to the letter. The events of last night proved that I can never let my guard down. This time, I won't fail in my duties."

"These are my orders," declared Comte de Trémeuse. "While Jacqueline and Jean remain under your constant surveillance, Primrose is to be allowed a relative degree of freedom."

Roger was shocked.

"I didn't intend to scare you," indicated Judex. "I said *relative degree*. In other words, her freedom will be partially restricted."

"Restricted by whom?"

"By you, Roger. You will carefully observe everyone who approaches Primrose. That includes the members of our household as well as outsiders. If someone wishes to speak to her in private, permit it. If you notice any unusual expressions on her face, it may be that she is under the control of the person she naively calls the 'evil spirit.' Then don't leave her alone for a second. Follow her."

"Your instructions will be scrupulously executed. I shall do it for her and for you!"

"I never doubted it for an instant!"

"But I'm a little confused, Jacques."

"Feel free to voice any doubts. In order to protect our loved ones, there must be no misunderstandings between us."

"Why am I giving Primrose this relative degree of freedom?"

"In order for her to lead us to our secret enemy."

"Yes, but..."

"Your confusion is understandable. The situation is complicated, and you're blinded by your love for Primrose."

"True."

"Let me explain more fully. It is evident that the Secret Raiders had infiltrated our home. If they've planted spies here, we must identify them. Your surveillance of Primrose should accomplish this goal. Someone in the Secret Raiders will contact Primrose to learn about our plans."

"Now I understand."

"I will tell your fiancée that I have to leave for ---"

Judex stopped. Primrose had just entered from the far end of the room.

"Not a word," whispered the Comte de Trémeuse. "It's for her own good."

"*Bonjour*," said Primrose. She shivered slightly. "Keep me close to you. The evil spirit may come again, but I won't fear it if you're nearby."

"The evil spirit won't come," said Roger.

"I'm not so sure," revealed the Comte. "I must leave for 48 hours."

"Why so long?" asked Primrose.

"Remember those old ruins that I own near Mantes?"

"The Chateau Rouge," said James Milton's foster daughter.

"I intend to restore that antique abode to its past splendor. I intend to reconstruct it into a true work of art. I have an appointment tomorrow morning with my architect. We're meeting at 11 o'clock in the Basket-Maker's Cabin, a shack near the foot of the Chateau Rouge. There we shall have an excellent view and be able to plan the necessary modifications."

Being of an artistic nature, Primrose was captivated. "It would be lovely to see the restoration of this fortress of the great feudal lords. Tell me it's history."

Judex smiled.

"The Chateau Rouge was an important fortress that the English used to defend Normandy from the French. It was built by Richard the Lion-Hearted. Some years later, after a siege that lasted nearly a year, it fell to the forces of King Philippe-Augustus of France. Briefly reoccupied twice by the English, it was eventually incorporated into the royal domains of the French monarchy. Henri IV finally ordered the fortress dismantled. Abandoned, it fell gradually into the state of decrepitude that I intend to overcome. I intend to surprise the Comtesse with this project at a later date. Therefore, no one else must know about my appointment at the Basket-Maker's Cabin."

"It shall be our secret," said Primrose. "You won't regret taking me into your confidence, Monsieur Jacques."

Jacqueline entered with Jean. The boy was reluctant to approach Primrose. Seeing the child sheepishly cling to his mother, Primrose was uneasy. Encouraged by the friendly demeanor of Roger and Jacques, Primrose knelt before the boy.

"My dear," she said softly, "you think that I tried to harm you. I won't explain everything now, but a day will come when you will know the truth. When that day arrives, you shall once more call me your 'big sister.' Ask your Papa, Mama or Uncle Roger. They will tell you that it's okay to like me."

Jean looked at his parents and his uncle. They all smiled kindly at Primrose. The boy didn't need anything more. He embraced the young woman kneeling in front of him.

"I'm very happy to know that you weren't being mean," he said with innocent sincerity.

While Jean and Primrose hugged each other under Roger's supervision. Judex took Jacqueline aside to a corner of the room.

"As I told you earlier," whispered the Comte, "I must provoke a confrontation. My absence should be brief. Roger shall watch over you until I return. If you feel assaulted by the lethargy that you experienced earlier, warn Roger immediately. He shall prevent you from doing anything harmful under the control of this malign influence. He's also entrusted with protecting Jean."

"And Primrose?" asked the Comtesse anxiously.

"Don't worry about her. As I mentioned earlier, she shall be our passport to the truth."

"God hears you," said Jacqueline meekly.

II. The Manicurist

Judex left La Frondaie in his car piloted by the faithful Baptiste. A half hour later, an elegant automobile with a 14 horsepower arrived at the gates of the estate. A middle-aged man with a distinguished air got out of the vehicle. After giving some orders to his driver, he entered the property. As soon as Howey crossed the threshold, he greeted a man in the courtyard. "Monsieur Cocantin!"

"Doctor Howey," replied Prosper Cocantin carrying a suitcase.

"Are you leaving?"

"Hush! I need to slip out. Something's not right at La Frondaie."

"Considering the theft of Milton's documents, the disappearances of Mademoiselle Primrose, and Jean's abduction, that's an understatement."

"You have a thorough knowledge of the current situation."

"Comte de Trémeuse hid nothing from me. He asked my professional opinion."

"You're very lucky."

"I'm merely a doctor."

"Well, I was his close friend. It may be an exaggeration to say that I was his right arm, but I was certainly his left. When I offered him my services this morning, the Comte replied that he had no need for them. Evidently, he feels that I bungled my recent missions. Only those that do nothing never make a mistake. It wasn't my fault that a drug was placed in my champagne. Yesterday, that cursed pony left me at the stables, and I have the misfortune to step into a deer trap. In any case, those events weren't sufficient ground to dismiss me."

"This isn't the proper time for the Comte to antagonize a friend whose profession is the unveilings of mysteries."

"You're quite right," said Cocantin swelling with conceit.

"Does the Comte intend to consult the police?"

"He would never do that."

"Why?"

"Because he can't." Cocantin gave the impression that he had been indiscreet. "But that's neither your affair nor mine. It's his."

"*Au revoir*, my friend," said Howey. "I hope this recent setback doesn't prevent you from employing your deductive skills."

"Oh! I have no intention of withdrawing from the battlefield," announced the disciple of Napoléon. "I intend to work independently in order to prove that I'm not a fool. I shall have my revenge!"

"Good luck, Monsieur Cocantin. Don't forget to do your exercises!"

"For now, I have other priorities. Thank you, anyway." Solemnly, the director of the Céléritas Agency made a prediction. "Mark my words. It won't be long before you hear from me."

Very proud of himself, Prosper Cocantin got ready to exit through the gates.

"Wait!" yelled Howey. "Do you intend to walk all the way to the train station carrying that suitcase?"

"Why not?"

"It's a distance of several kilometers."

"You recommended exercise."

"But in your agitated state, any physical exertion can be harmful." Howey turned to his chauffeur. "Adolphe, drive Monsieur Cocantin to the Fontainebleau train station. Then return for me."

"A thousand thanks," said Cocantin.

"I'm happy to oblige."

"Remember what I said, Doctor. Before long, the Secret Raiders will fall into my trap. For now, not a word to anyone."

"I promise."

Once Cocantin got inside, the car left for the station. Watching it fade in the distance, Howey made an ironic smile. He walked towards the house.

About 6 o'clock in the evening, a respectable lady rang Baronne d'Apremont's doorbell. The visitor was dressed in an old-fashioned dress that stank of mothballs. On the head of this personage was a wide hat. The figure was apparently a manicurist. There was a case of instruments belonging to that profession in the individual's hands.

There was no response from the residence in the Rue Musset. The manicurist pressed the doorbell again and again to no avail. Since all the windows were boarded up, the manicurist couldn't look inside. The manicurist finally noticed a sign outside the residence: *HOUSE FOR RENT*

The abode was uninhabited. Moving away from the empty house, the manicurist was greeted by a delivery boy carrying a box of pastries. His raised arms perched the box on his head.

"Hello, Monsieur Cocantin."

The detective was annoyed that his elaborate disguise had been penetrated. "How did you recognize me?"

"By your nose," said the youth. "Are you going to a masked ball?" The lad ran away to avoid the consequences of his sarcasm.

Prosper Cocantin froze for a moment, then pursued the young confectioner. "If I get my hands on you, I'll pull your ears off!" yelled the enraged sleuth. Besides the delivery boy's head start, Cocantin's speed was hampered by the skirt he was wearing. The boy was far ahead.

The phony manicurist was halted by a sturdy gendarme. He demanded an explanation of the comedy that just unfolded. Exhausted, Cocantin was about to explain everything to this representative of the law. Still holding the box on his head, the delivery boy returned. He screamed into the gendarme's ear.

"That's no lady! It's Cocantin!"

Unnerved by these words, the gendarme bumped into the delivery boy. The inevitable disaster ensued. The boy lost his grip of the box of pastries. Its contents spilled all over the policeman's head. Covered with an assortment of ice cakes, the gendarme released Cocantin and seized the delivery boy.

Taking advantage of the confusion, Cocantin ran into a nearby café. Dropping into a chair, Cocantin sighed. A waiter approached him.

"What are you ordering, Madame?"

Cocantin initially didn't reply. He had forgotten that he was disguised as a woman.

"Madame," pressed the employee, "what do you desire?"

"Ah! I'm a lady," mumbled Cocantin grasping the reality of the situation. "A cup of curacao, please."

"Weird lady..." muttered the waiter.

Cocantin was lost in his thoughts.

Mon Dieu! What can I do? This is not the first time my nose has betrayed me. Always when I'm disguised, someone recognizes me because of my nose. It's understandable, but it's always happened in neighborhoods where I'm known. This is the far end of Auteuil. I haven't been here more than four times in my life. This is disturbing. In seeking to trap the Baronne, have I trapped myself?

Her place was deserted. Where has she gone? My adversary is far more cunning than I initially suspected.

Forgetting that he was in a public café, the false manicurist struck the table three times with his fist while shouting "I shall have them!"

The waiter returned under the mistaken impression that he was being summoned.

"Yes, Madame?"

Prosper Cocantin regained his sense of reality. "How much do I owe you?"

"60 centimes."

"Here's a franc! Order me a car."

"A taxi?"

"As soon as possible."

Some minutes later, the taxi pulled up in front of the café. As he was entering the cab, the false manicurist was accosted by a young street hawker that was distributing leaflets. A cap covered the hawker's head.

"Here, Madame," said the hawker extending a leaflet to Cocantin. "This won't give you cholera, but will give me pleasure."

Anxious to return home, Cocantin refused to take it.

The hawker was angry. "Who do you think you are? An Empress?"

Without replying Cocantin got into the taxi and gave the driver an address. Its collapsible roof was down. This fact permitted the enraged hawker to throw a bunch of leaflets into the air. They rained on Cocantin as the taxi drove away from the curb.

Mechanically Cocantin picked up a leaflet and read it.

What do you want to know?
Ask the famous seer
LA BELLE FATHMA
139 RUE BERGÈRE
She knows all, sees all, tells all
Consultations between 2 and 7 o'clock on Sundays

"Well!" said the private detective stuffing the leaflet into his manicurist's case. "This might lead somewhere!"

Unknown to Cocantin, the street hawker was really Belles-Mirettes in disguise. The tip of the cap had shaded the upper portion of her face.

"Like a fish, my dear Monsieur Cocantin, you've been hooked," she gloated as the taxi sped away.

III. The Basket-Maker's Cabin

The next morning, around 10 o'clock, Judex's car, piloted by the loyal Baptiste, stopped in the middle of a forest that crossed the road of Bonnières to the Andelys.

"Wait here," said Judex. "I may need you. If you hear my whistle, rush quickly to the Basket-Maker's Cabin."

"I understand, Monsieur the Comte," replied Baptiste. "I may have the pleasure of rudely dealing with certain people."

In recognition of the confidence that his master placed in him, the chauffeur raised his two fists. Each was capable of knocking a man senseless. "The Comte can rely on me."

"I have no doubts on that score," answered Judex, "but intervene only if I summon you."

"Your orders will be obeyed, Monsieur the Comte. But if I see you fighting crooks, my hands will itch to smash them!"

"Temper your enthusiasm," advised Judex. "Your turn will come. All in good time, Baptiste."

A large muscular man, Baptiste was 35 years old. He had been born near Dreux. His parents had been tenant farmers in the service of the Trémeuse family. The Dowager Comtesse had developed an interest in him as a child. Since he had displayed a faccination with automobiles, she had him trained as a mechanic. He became her chauffeur. Baptiste's irreproachable conduct and superb driving skills was greatly appreciated by his patron and her two sons. After the marriage of her older son, the Dowager Countess moved to Paris. At that time, Jacques de Trémeuse asked that Baptiste be transferred to his service. To Baptiste's joy, Madame de Trémeuse accepted. He preferred to drive long distances on the beautiful roads of France rather than maneuvering the congested traffic of Paris. When the Comte revived his alter ego of Judex, he didn't hesitate to take this competent man who doubled as driver and mechanic into his confidence.

Upon his master's departure for the Basket-Maker's Cabin, Baptiste lit a cigarette. Pulling a newspaper out of his pocket, he proceeded to read it.

With the calm manner of a man taking a stroll, Judex had followed the road winding up the hill where rose the ruins of the Chateau Rouge. Shortly before reaching the old feudal abode, he forked to the right. Walking towards the middle of a large field, he approached a big wooden shack. This was the Basket-Maker's Cabin. Its name had been derived from an old peasant. Totally deaf and half blind, he had taking refuge there to etch out an existence by selling baskets made with his arthritic hands. When Judex had purchased the Chateau Rouge and the surrounding field, Prairie-aux-Girolles (which roughly translates into English as "Mushroom Meadow"), he had hospitalized the old hermit. Although the bulk of his life had been filled with misery, the recluse had spent his last days in some semblance of joy. Since that time, the Basket-Maker's Cabin had remained without a tenant.

Some peasants, perhaps having indulged too much in wine, claimed to have seen the light filtered through the cracks of the cabin at night. There was a legend that the spirit of Marguerite de Bourgogne returned there at night to celebrate the Black Sabbath. The Basket-Maker's Cabin was supposedly a sanctuary for ghosts of royal blood. This harmless legend established a sinister reputation that warded off explorations by the neighborhood children.

Years ago, Jacques de Trémeuse had padlocked the shack's door and barricaded the window with a shutter that could only be opened from the inside. Therefore, the aura of mystery surrounding the cabin lingered. In any case, the structure hadn't been entered for a long time. When Judex went to open the padlock, three-quarters of the key encountered a thick layer of rust. He had to push the key in several times in order to open the lock. Nevertheless, there was no foul odor inside the structure when Judex entered it. One could even imagine that the cabin had been well-ventilated during the morning or the preceding night. Judex opened the shutter. A wave of light penetrated the shack whose only furniture was a table and a stool. Looking outside, Judex perceived the ruins of the Chateau Rouge. Closing the window shutter and the door, Judex sat on the stool in front of the table as if he was awaiting the architect who was supposedly bringing the restoration plans for the old fortress.

A rather strange phenomenon occurred. Despite the lack of a breeze, the ferns on the far side of Prairie-aux-Girolles stirred as if they were swept by a windstorm. Two bodies crawled on their hands and feet away from the trees. They created the illusion of being human-sized reptiles. Creeping close to the shack, the individuals stood up. Each carried a gun.

As Judex had foreseen, Primrose had revealed his whereabouts. The Secret Raiders were about to strike, but Judex had chosen the field of battle. The criminals slowly opened the door. Judex couldn't have heard them because his back was to them. He appeared lost in reflection. The two outlaws leaped upon Judex and seized him by the throat.

Cries of disappointment and rage erupted from the attackers. It wasn't Judex whom they assaulted. It was a dummy dressed in identical clothes. The mannequin's impassive face tormented them.

"What just happened?" shouted one of the Raiders. "If he left the shack, we should have seen him."

"Let's look for him!" replied the other. "He couldn't have gone far."

Suddenly the door closed in front of them as controlled by a secret mechanism. they tried to open it, but their efforts were in vain.

"We're trapped, Louchard!" yelled the first intruder.

"How do we get out, Julot?" asked the second.

No sooner had Julot pronounced those words than a cloud of asphyxiating gas rose from the cabin's floor.

"They're smoking us out like badgers!" shouted Julot.

Louchard noticed that there was no padlock on the shutters. Running to the window, he opened it.

"Jump, Julot, or we're finished."

The two bandits leaped out of the window together. Hardly had their feet touched the ground, when the earth opened to swallow them. They had stepped on a trap door, about three meters in width, that was covered by a patch of fake daisies. As soon as they disappeared beneath the earth, the trap door swung back into place concealing the opening. Louchard and Julot were trapped in a snare like those used by hunters against Bengal tigers or the lions of the Atlas Mountains.

A cry of astonishment had erupted from two spectators who witnessed the capture of these human predators. Hidden behind an embankment, a woman in a dark coat and a younger companion in a cyclist's cap had seen everything. They were Baronne d'Apremont and Belles-Mirettes. The latter wore the masculine clothes that she had used to deceive Cocantin the day before.

"We can't stay here, Belles-Mirettes."

"You're right. This man has outwitted us. We must rejoin the others."

Leaving the embankment, they saw from a distance the parked car where Baptiste was smoking while reading the newspaper.

Belles-Mirettes pointed at the vehicle. "That must be Judex's car."

"Yes, with a driver," answered the Baronne. Her eyes flashed with ferocious delight. "We lost the first round, but we can win the second. Hide behind that tree. Don't let the chauffeur out of your sight. Wait till I return."

The Baronne walked through the wood to a clearing. There was her limousine and two men as husky as Louchard and Julot.

"All is lost at the Basket-Maker's Cabin," she announced, "but the battle isn't over yet. Come with me."

"Yes, Baronne," said a muscular brute.

"We obey," echoed a man of shorter stature. Although not as intimidating as his companion, this man was still a fearsome opponent.

They rejoined Belles-Mirettes. After a brief consultation with the Baronne, she put an unlit cigarette in her mouth and approached Baptiste. Absorbed in his newspaper, the chauffeur was totally oblivious to the plot that the Secret Raiders were weaving against him.

"Hey, can you give me a light?"

Raising his eyes from the newspaper, Baptiste perceived his interrogator. He couldn't tell if this grinning speaker was a man or a woman. Momentarily surprised, he wondered where this character came from. He didn't have time to reply to the request for a match. While Belles-Mirettes served as a distraction, her two male accomplices overpowered the chauffeur. The skilled assailants swiftly bound and gagged Baptiste. The man with the powerful fists had been easily subdued.

The Baronne complimented her male underlings. "Well done, Mimile and Maillochard. The big boss will be happy with you, my pretties."

"What do we do with this guy?" questioned the horrible Mimile, the shorter of the two ruffians. On his left hand was a tattoo representing a semi-circle intersected by an exclamation point. This symbol was the insignia of the Secret Raiders.

"Let kill him," cynically proposed the massive Maillochard, who was tattooed identically.

"You know very well that Bébert wouldn't want him killed." She looked at the rage-filled eyes of the gagged Baptiste. "Maillochard, take him into the woods and tie him against a tree.

Mimile, you're about the same height and weight as our prisoner. Put on his cap and goggles. You will sit in the driver's seat. When Judex returns, he won't notice our substitution. Drive him quickly to the Cateaux intersection near the Chemin Boulard and the Sentier Margot. Maillochard and I will be waiting there. Belles-Mirettes, you cling to the back of the car in order to spy on our target from behind. Luckily the roof of the car is down. If Judex begins to suspect our trap, use your scarf!"

Belles-Mirettes mumbled under her breath. She was clearly questioning the wisdom of her assignment.

The Baronne quickly quashed any challenge to her commands. "I've seen you work! I know that you're quite capable of following my orders."

"I would perform better if I knew that Judex's car would be given to me as a reward," stated Belles-Mirettes. "I relish the idea of driving a vehicle with a 24 horsepower engine."

"It shall be yours after our business is completed," promised the Baronne. "Mimile, I'm counting on you, Don't fail me. Both you and Belles-Mirettes are quite resourceful. If you need to immobilize Judex, don't damage him too much. Reserve that pleasure for me."

"I'll do my best, Baronne," laughed Mimile.

While Maillochard tied Baptiste to a tree, the Baronne smiled triumphantly.

"This time, Judex, you won't escape the Raiders!"

IV. The Mysteries of the Chateau Rouge

When Louchard and Julot had fallen into Judex's trap, they imagined themselves hurling into an abyss. In fact, they fell a distance of only three or four meters. Their descent had been cushioned by a mattress filled with sand. As a consequence. they didn't suffer any serious injuries. Surrounded by darkness, they were numbed by terror. Louchard was the first to break out of his stupor.

"Hey, Julot, are you there?"

A painful groan revealed the presence of his accomplice.

"Anything broken?" asked Louchard.

"I don't know," whined Julot. "What about you?"

"I can't tell in this darkness! I'm searching for you. I think you're close."

"I am." Julot tested his limbs to see if he could move freely. "Where are we?"

"We're in the bottom of a pit," answered Louchard.

"It's probably a gas pit! Don't light a match! Let's try to find an exit!"

The two criminals groped in the darkness. Julot cried out. He had bumped into something. The unknown object felt like it was made of metal. Suddenly the pit was filled with light. The Raider had inadvertently activated an electric lamp. He lifted it up.

"We have light!" exclaimed Julot. "All we need is heat."

"And a meal and a bath," added Louchard.

Consoled by light, the two ruffians examined their prison. It looked like an abandoned well. Plants and vines covered the walls. Looking up, they glimpsed the trap door through which they fell. Climbing on Louchard's shoulders, Julot tried to get a grip on the wall to climb up to the trap door. However, his hands and feet couldn't find a secure hold. The two criminals abandoned their efforts.

"We're acting like fools!" declared Louchard.

"Judex's playing a dirty trick on us!"

"How do we get out of here?"

"There's a door," said Julot.

"Where?"

Julot pointed to a corner of the well. There was the outline of a worm-eaten gate.

"You're probably right," concurred Louchard. "Let's see how strong it is." He delivered a vigorous kick that knocked the gate off its hinges into the ground. An opening was revealed.

"Wait!" yelled Julot. "We could get lost in there."

"It may be another of Judex's dirty tricks." said Louchard.

"If he wanted us to stay here," stated Julot, "he would have blocked this opening."

"You're right. But since we can't do anything else, let's go in there. We'll just have to be careful. "

Carrying the lamp, Julot went first followed by his partner. The two Raiders passed through an underground tunnel. Advancing cautiously, they walked 300 meters before reaching the bottom of a stone stairway.

"Should we climb it?" asked Julot.

"I'm wondering the same thing," replied Louchard.

"What's the risk?"

"With a guy like Judex, expect the unexpected. Like that lamp you found in the well. This looks bad, Julot."

"I agree, but we can't return to the pit. We must go forward. What do you think, Louchard?"

"Lead the way."

"I've just realized something. There's an old fortress here."

"The Chateau Rouge."

"Do you know its history, Louchard?"

"Enlighten me."

"In these old castles, there were an abundance of secret passageways."

"You're sure?"

"Yes. We could be in an underground passage of the Chateau Rouge."

"You're probably right."

"Then this passage leads into the ruins. We'll be able to escape."

"Let's hope so."

"Shall we climb the stairs?"

"Of course."

With Julot carrying the lamp, they ascended the narrow stairway that had been dug into the heart of the mountain. Julot was correct. They were in a secret passageway of the Chateau Rouge. However, it did not lead them to an open corridor of the feudal abode. After climbing the stairs for a considerable distance, the two Raiders found themselves in a dark vault.

"There's no way out!" shouted Julot. Behind them, a noise sounded. A metal barrier descended blocking their access to the stairs.

"What did I tell you?" grumbled Louchard. "We're trapped again."

Barely had the Raider pronounced those words, than a terrifying vision appeared. On the wall in front of them, letters of fire appeared. They were so radiant that they made the electric light look like the glimmer of a candle. The letters formed the following message:

You are prisoners. Throw away your weapons. Put your hands in the air.

JUDEX

"It's over," murmured Louchard.

"We've lost," sighed Julot.

Gnashing their teeth, they removed from their pockets all the weapons they carried. To be precise, their arsenal consisted of two pistols, two knives, a "sheep bone" club, and a knuckle-duster. They raised their hand in the air.

A concealed door in the wall opened revealing Judex. Upon seeing the man in the felt hat and the black cape, the two Raiders were gripped by fear. They awaited their enemy's verdict. They had abandoned all hope. They were convinced that this merciless judge was going to decree their deaths.

Judex calmly approached them. "Are you members of the Secret Raiders?"

"Yes," cravenly admitted Louchard and Julot.

"Who is your chief?" asked Comte de Trémeuse. His haughty, robotic voice sent shivers down the spines of the two ruffians.

This time they remained silent.

"Would you prefer," asked Judex, "to be imprisoned for the rest of your lives in the Chateau Rouge's dungeons?"

Still raising their hands, the sinister duo growled in protest. Louchard decided to tell all.

"Our chief only has a nickname. It's *N'a-qu'un-Chasse*."

"We know nothing about him," added Julot, "except that he pays well and demands much."

Judex realized that these men spoke the truth. "Why are you members of the Raiders?"

The two criminals lowered their heads in shame.

"It's useless to try to trick me," declared the Comte. "You're Louchard, an escaped convict from the penal colonies. You, Julot, was recently condemned in absentia to 20 years for armed robbery. Am I not well-informed?"

"Yes," said the two criminals

"I hold you," claimed Judex, "and I hold you tightly. You're in my power. No one can help you. Whether I keep you here or turn you over to the law, you're lost! Yet, there is a way for you to be spared those fates. You may eventually be punished, but it won't be by my hand."

"Tell us, Monsieur," begged Julot.

"Speak," implored Louchard.

"I want to be taken to your chief."

"To *N'a-qu'un-Chasse*?" asked Louchard.

"Precisely, to *N'a-qu'un-Chasse*."

The two criminals looked at each other. They hesitated to answer.

"Do you refuse?" pressed the Comte. "So much the worse for you. I give you two minutes to decide."

"Monsieur!" shouted Julot.

"Do you agree to my terms?"

"Yes," murmured the cowering Raiders.

"Julot, where does your employer live?"

"I don't know exactly. He hangs out in a Paris café near Les Buttes-Chaumont. You have to be lucky to find him there. He has no set hours. Sometimes he goes there. Other times, he telephones. "

"You shall take me to this café. For the moment, that's all that I demand from you. Once we're there, I'll have further orders. Louchard, you shall remain here as a hostage."

Pushing the servile Julot in front of him, Judex exited the cell. Closing the door on Louchard, the Comte secured it by bolting two locks.

"Come with me, scoundrel. Be warned. If you try to run away, you're a dead man."

Gasping Julot by the arm, Judex guided him through the maze of underground corridors in the Chateau Rouge. Some moment later, Judex and his hostage arrived at the car where the false chauffeur was waiting. Julot was ordered to sit next to the driver. Judex got into the back of the car.

"Baptiste, drive us to Paris."

Impersonating Judex's driver, Mimile drove away at a fast pace. Scarcely had the driver turned the wheel, than Julot had to suppress an outburst of surprise. On the hand of the silent chauffeur, Judex's prisoner recognized the tattooed emblem of the Secret Raiders. At the same time, Mimile indicated to Julot to look down at the car's floor. A gun rested there.

As Julot bent down to pick up the weapon, Judex became suspicious by the prisoner's sudden movement. Before he could intervene, another Raider struck.

In accordance with the Baronne's instructions, Belles-Mirettes hung on to the spare tire in the rear of the car. With incredible swiftness, she sprang on Judex from behind. Using her thick scarf, she threw it over Judex's head. As Judex was restrained by the scarf around his throat, Julot turned around and pointed the gun at his enemy.

"Hands up!" he yelled.

Breaking Belles-Mirettes's hold, Judex twisted the female raider around to use as a living shield against Julot's pistol. Afraid of wounding his female accomplice, Julot didn't fire.

"We'll be there in two minutes!" shouted Mimile.

Judex quickly grasped that his chauffeur had been replaced with an impostor. He deduced that his attackers were heading to a rendezvous where there would be reinforcements. The car was going too fast for Judex to jump out of it. He glimpsed ahead a large oak with a branch spread across the road. Throwing Bells-Mirettes against Julot, Judex leaped upward and grabbed the branch. As the car sped away, Judex hung from the branch. Displaying the skill of an acrobat, he swung into the tree and disappeared among the branches.

Momentarily stunned, Julot recovered in time to fire a series of shots in the direction of the tree. However, Judex had already vanished. Swinging from branch to branch, Judex reached another side road.

Mimile stopped the car. Getting out along with Belles-Mirettes and Julot, they were joined by the Baronne and Maillochard.

"Bah!" shouted the Baronne. "He escaped us again. Search for him. If you find him, give no quarter!"

The Secret Raiders searched the woods, but found nothing. It was as if Judex evaporated.

A further cry of rage erupted from the Baronne. She went to the elm where Maillochard had bound Baptiste an hour ago.

Judex's chauffeur was no longer there. The ropes that had bond him were resting on the ground.

"Back to the car quickly!" screamed the Baronne. "Judex will use it to escape."

The Baronne was correct. In their haste to find their enemy, the Secret Raiders had left Judex's car unguarded. Driven by Baptiste, the car transported a victorious Judex away.

That night, the Comte de Trémeuse arrived at La Frondaie.

An impatient Roger ran to greet his brother. "Did everything go well? Did you succeed?"

"Yes, but I had to fight and then retreat. These Secret Raiders are a tough bunch. At last, I learned information that will prove valuable in the future. My suspicions were verified. Primrose revealed my whereabouts. Before I tell you in detail what happened, I need to know something. Did Primrose speak to anybody after I left?"

"Besides me, she only talked to Dr. Howey."

"Was she alone with him?"

"For about 15 minutes."

"When did they meet?"

"Yesterday, shortly after you left La Frondaie."

"Were you present when Primrose was talking to the doctor?"

"No. Remember you wanted me to be discreet in my surveillance."

"After the doctor's visit, did Primrose behave strangely?"

"She became depressed and complained about a very painful headache."

"You're sure that she didn't talk to any other outsiders?"

"Absolutely."

Judex reflected in silence. His face darkened as if a shadow passed over it.

"Primrose's evil spirit must be Howey."

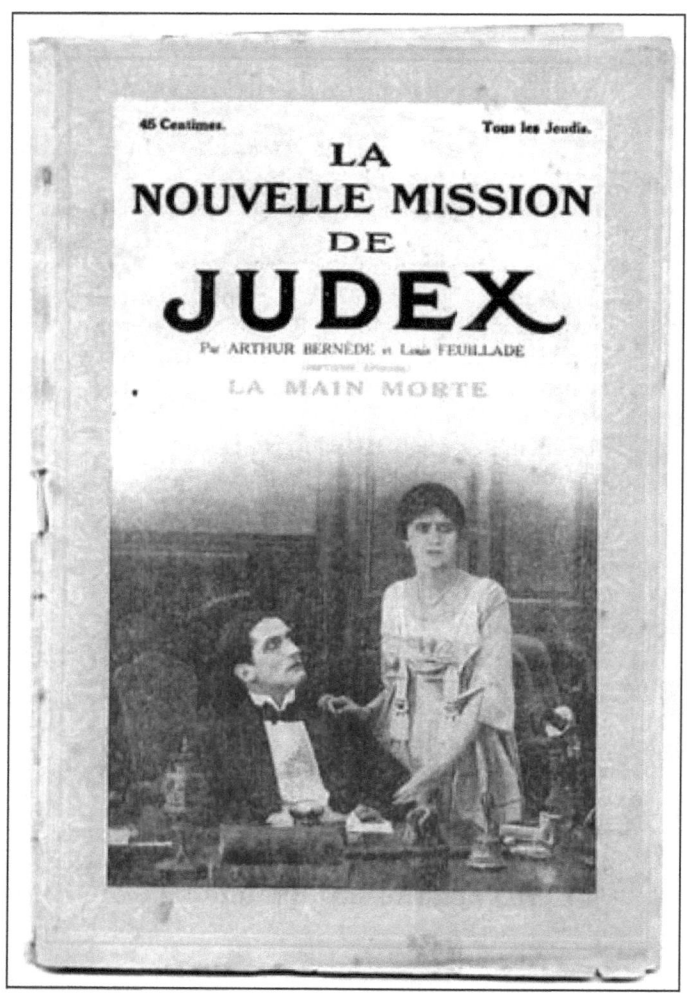

Part Seven: The Dead Hand

I. Cocantin's Great Idea

"Howey is the evil spirit?" questioned Roger de Trémeuse.

Seated at his work table, Judex responded with his habitual calm. "Perhaps I should refrain from being so sure. He's the last person whom I would have suspected."

"I feel the same way."

"Howey," explained the Count, "always produced an excellent impression on everyone who met him. He seemed a man of irreproachable dignity. He also had the proper attitude.

His conversations not only revealed a scientific spirit of the first order but also an exceptional moral conscience. Furthermore, his expenditures are rather modest. However, you're telling me that he was the only person alone with Primrose during my absence."

"The only one."

"Are you sure none of our servants had a private audience with your fiancée, even if it was brief?"

"I'm sure."

"That's very disturbing. Imagine the implications of Howey being affiliated with the Secret Raiders. He has access to both Jacqueline and Primrose. His scientific genius is a valuable asset to that association of malefactors. My theory about him seems to surpass all probability. Without firm proof of his complicity in this abominable infamy, I must give him the benefit of the doubt.

"Nevertheless, we must take precautions. Under the pretence of accompanying Jacqueline, Primrose and Jean to Paris, you shall actually drive them to the Chateau de Joyeuse which our mother has placed at our disposal. This luxurious abode has the advantage of being situated in the middle of the country, between Mantes and Saint-Germain. Our three loved ones shall be secure. No one else beside you and I shall know their location. Not even Cocantin. I told him to leave Fontainebleau in order for him to be ignorant of our plans. We can't afford a leak due to his unintentional blundering. Take Martine with you. Her loyalty is unquestionable.

"Once your charges are safe, you shall return to the Chateau Rouge. There, you will find in the isolation chamber a Raider I captured. His name is Louchard. Feed him and ignore any questions he asks. Then return to the Chateau de Joyeuse to await further instructions."

"I'm very confident, Roger. I think we're on the verge of capturing the sinister individual behind all our troubles."

"I have complete confidence in you, Jacques. What about Howey?"

"He remains an enigma. This is the most extraordinary mystery that I ever had to solve. Let's prepare for your departure. "

Leaving his study, Judex informed Jacqueline, Primrose and Jean of his precautions. They departed for the Chateau de Joyeuse the next day. Driving them to the train station, Judex advised his brother one final time to be careful. Upon his return to La Frondaie, Judex secluded himself in his study. He planned his new line of attack against the Raiders. Faith and fortitude shined through his eyes.

A telephone rang. After listening to the other person on the line, Judex replied.

"Everything's going well... No more need to communicate by telegraph with me and Roger. We're use the telephone... Perfect...Very skillfully played... That doesn't surprise me... Like you, I have the firm conviction that they'll come... Tomorrow at 3 o'clock, I'll be at your office... Things are going well... The Comtesse's doing fine... Primrose also... Don't worry... I've taken precautions... You have nothing to fear... Understood, my friend... Until tomorrow."

After Judex hung up. Prosper Cocantin knocked on the door. It was inevitable that he would return to Fontainebleau.

After Napoléon, he considered the lord of La Frondaie to be his master. The director of the Céléritas Agency desired a new mission to make amends for the clumsy execution of his previous assignments.

"Do you have a commission for me, dear friend?" asked Cocantin.

"Not today."

"In that case, I ask your permission to spend the next 24 hours in Paris. I have some small matter to tidy up there."

"Permission granted."

"I would like to pay my respect to the ladies before I go."

"The ladies aren't here," said the Comte simply.

"What? The ladies left"

"Yes. I needed to protect them from the threat of the evil spirit."

"You had ample reason to move them. Where are they?"

"I'm resolved not to reveal that to anyone."

"Even me."

"Even you."

"My dear Comte!"

"This must remain my secret."

"I'm a little shocked by your silence," said a visibly annoyed Cocantin. "Are you trying to insult me?"

"Of course not!"

"I also believe that I've given you enough proof of my loyalty to avoid the slightest suspicion of treason."

"Agreed."

"Then I don't understand why you're hiding your family from me."

"My dear Cocantin, not only do I esteem you highly, but I have an intense affection for you. No one in the world appreciates you better than me. You have intelligence plus a big heart. I don't want to hurt your feelings, but recently your impulsiveness has caused you to make irreparable mistakes."

"You are harsh, my dear Comte."

"I don't want to rub salt into the wound, but recall your recent misadventure with Baronne d'Apremont."

147

"I shall have my revenge!" shouted Cocantin.

Adopting a kindly tone, Judex resumed. "It is precisely because you're in such an agitated state that I wish to grant you a vacation. During that time, the performance of the exercises prescribed by Dr. Howey would restore the cerebral tranquility needed to perform great deeds."

"Thank you, my dear Comte, but I can't follow your advice."

"Why?"

"Because I have a great idea."

"About what?"

"The Secret Raiders."

"I repeat, Prosper, that it would be better for you to take a vacation."

"And I assure you, my dear Comte, that I have never felt more ready for a fight! Little Cocantin will amaze you unless you insist otherwise."

"I don't insist. But if your decision has dire results, I warn you that the blame shall fall on your head!"

"I'm confident of success!" said the private detective with the assurance of Napoléon on the eve of Austerlitz. "I have them where I want them!"

"I sincerely wish you well," said Judex accompanying Cocantin to the door. "However, if you ever find yourself in a precarious position, don't forget I'm here."

"As I am for you," replied Cocantin proudly.

What was this great idea germinating in Prosper Cocantin's brain? After arriving in Paris by train, he went to a clothing store. After purchasing a pair of large silk stockings, he returned to his office in the Rue Milton. Although it was somewhat difficult, Cocantin manipulated the elasticity to cover his face. This stocking originally designed for a woman's leg was transformed into a hood that the detective would use to hide his identity. Meticulously, Cocantin used his nails to scratch eyeholes. With a pair of scissors, he widened the holes. He now could fully see while wearing the mask. Folding up the modified stocking, he placed it in his pocket.

Pulling out his wallet, he removed the leaflet that Belles-Mirettes had thrown into his taxi.

What do you want to know?
Ask the famous seer
LA BELLE FATHMA
139 RUE BERGÈRE
She knows all, sees all, tells all
Consultations between 2 and 7 o'clock on Sundays

"We shall see if she can discern my true identity."

Since it was a Sunday, Cocantin was going to consult the medium. Was this his great idea? Apparently so because he decided to travel the short distance separating the Rue Milton and the Rue Bergère. He rang the door of La Belle Fathma. A woman clothed in the style of a harem slave answered swiftly. Three quarters of her face was covered by the classical veil employed by women of the Near East. After passing through a dark antechamber, she led him to a garish parlor whose bizarre eroticism impressed Cocantin.

"I want to consult La Belle Fathma," he said with a detached air.

On hearing these words, the harem girl knelt and made a series of bows. Rising from the floor, she pointed at Cocantin and then downward to indicate that he should remain here. The harem girl disappeared behind a door.

Somewhat surprised by the course of events, Prosper Cocantin took advantage of the harem girl's absence to don his black silk hood. The harem girl returned and announced that her mistress would receive him. She led him into the den of the seer.

La Belle Fathma resided on a divan in a room lit by an unseen lamp. Her face was even more veiled than that of her servant. Only her dark shining eyes could be glimpsed. She was clothed in a sumptuous dress decorated with sequins.

Upon viewing her hooded visitor, she made a cry akin to a stifled laugh.

"*Bonjour*, Sidi Cocantin."

The detective was pleasantly surprised. *Only a true mystic would have recognized me under this impenetrable mask,* he thought. *She could use her powers to tell me many things. My idea has proven to be truly great. Judex will be amazed.*

Nevertheless, he spoke to the seer with an altered voice. "You're mistaken. I'm not Cocantin."

"Why are you trying to fool me," reproached gently La Belle Fathma. "You are Monsieur Cocantin. To be exact, Prosper Cocantin, director of the Céléritas Agency in the Rue Milton."

"Madame, I assure you."

"Don't insist. Despite all your precautions, I instantly identified you. If you wore a more elaborate disguise, say an iron mask, I would have recognized you out of a hundred, even a thousand men. I know all!"

"Is it possible?"

The voice of La Belle Fathma soothed Cocantin like a beautiful song. It erased any doubts.

"Yes, a gift was given me at birth. It's a gift that allows me to explore the past, analyze the present and foresee the future. I am like an immense eye that contemplates all humanity. For example, you disguised yourself as a manicurist. You also recently eat in the private dining room of a very elegant restaurant."

"That's also true!"

"Your female guest fled abruptly after leaving you an insolent letter."

"Quite right!"

"She has inspired in you a hatred that has become a burning desire for vengeance."

"This is phenomenal!"

"Are you convinced now, Monsieur Cocantin? I'm no carnival trickster. You're faced with a creature endowed with second sight. My gift enables me to discern all secrets and read men's souls."

"Madame, I bow down before the most extraordinary force that I've ever encountered." "Now that you have faith in me. You may ask your questions. I shall answer them."

"What has become of this hateful woman?"

"She left for America."

"For America?"

"Yes."

"Tell me more."

"This lady, Baronne d'Apremont, had been devoured by a profound passion for you."

"I never doubted it."

"She was scared that you wouldn't return her intense desire because of your flighty temperament."'

"Explain that last remark."

"You have the personality of a butterfly."

"What?"

"Like a butterfly, you fly from flower to flower, except your flowers are the women you conquer. Rather than have her heart broken by your inevitable desertion, she put the distance of an ocean between her and you."

"It was only that?"

"It was completely that! Monsieur Cocantin, do you have any other questions?"

"Yes. Can you predict my future?"

"The cards will speak to me."

Seizing a deck of tarot decks, the seer shuffled them and dexterously spread them in front of her. She examined each upturned card before solemnly addressing the hooded sleuth whose eyes denoted wonderment.

"I see something extraordinary!" she announced.

"What?" asked Prosper Cocantin twitching with emotion.

"A great danger threatens someone you know."

"Comte de Trémeuse?"

"No, a man much older. He has white hair. A fog obscures his features. Wait! I see him! It's a former banker believed dead, I see his name. I see letters... F... A... He's named Favraux. "

Underneath his mask, a cold sweat broke out on Cocantin's forehead.

The implacable Fathma continued. "A great danger threatens him. I don't know its exact nature. Yet, I see him. He's retired to the country. It's odd. The name of the place where he's lives is on the tip of my tongue."

The captivated Cocantin naively volunteered the banker's location.

"Is it Sainte-Madeleine-en-Gâtinais?"

Yes, Sainte-Madeleine-en-Gâtinais! That's it!" There was a faint hint of joy in the tarot reader's voice. "I'm not mistaken. This Favraux is threatened with violent death. There's a man with him. An old man. An ex-convict from a penal colony."

"Kerjean?"

"Yes, Kerjean. He wants to kill Favraux." Suddenly the seer issued a loud cry. Falling backward, she remained motionless on the divan.

Slowly the door opened. The harem girl entered and took Cocantin by the hand.

"La Belle Fathma is in a state of ecstasy," she said. "She must rest for at least two hours. The séance is over."

"When can I return?" asked Cocantin.

"Not before three days. It's necessary for Madame to fully recover."

"How much do I owe her?"

"20 francs."

"Here's 25."

Taking off his mask, Cocantin went outside. He gave voice to his thoughts.

"What defeats would Napoléon have avoided with a seer of this magnitude. She would have told him to stop in time. There never would have been a Battle of Waterloo or the subsequent imprisonment in St. Helena."

As soon as the detective left, La Belle Fathma leaped to her feet. Pulling off her veil, Baronne d'Apremont shouted with ferocious glee.

152

"It worked!"

Grabbing a telephone concealed beneath a tapestry, she requested a number that was immediately connected.

"Hello. Is that you, Bébert?"

"Who's calling?"

"The Baronne."

"Any news?"

"Cocantin was here."

"No names!" grumbled *N'a-qu'un-Chasse*.

"The man we expected came. Do you understand?"

"Yes."

"He disclosed the banker's location."

"Where?"

"Sainte-Madeleine-en-Gâtinais."

"Perfect," concluded Bébert. "I had two agents previously searching in that vicinity, but their quest proved fruitless. We must act on this intelligence quickly. You must travel there to confirm Favraux's location. Once you have verified it, telephone me at Domicile #4. Is everything clear?"

"Yes."

"Good work"

"Thanks."

Baronne d'Apremont hung up the receiver. The two criminals didn't need a long conversation to fully understand each other. Before 15 minutes passed, the adventuress left in her car for Sainte-Madeleine-en-Gâtinais.

The Secret Raiders were about to strike.

II. The Living Dead

Cocantin took the train to La Frondaie. He arrived there at 6 o'clock in the evening.

His face radiated pride. He expected to be completely rehabilitated in the eyes of Judex.

Since his earlier interview with Cocantin, Judex had remained in his study to coordinate his campaign against the

Secret Raiders. When the jubilant Cocantin arrived, Judex was surprised.

"I hope you haven't blundered again."

"When I left this morning, my dear Comte, I promised to amaze you."

"I remember it well."

"Well, it's done."

"You didn't waste time."

"I work quickly. I succeeded beyond my wildest dreams."

"Tell me everything!"

"I went to see La Belle Fathma."

"La Belle Fathma? Sounds like the name of a belly dancer."

"Yes, La Belle Fathma. Not a belly dancer, but a seer! The famous seer of the Rue Bergère. She sees all, tells all, knows all!"

"Well?" said Judex who was desperately trying not to burst out in laughter.

"Well? This extraordinary mystic recognized me even though my face was fully covered by a mask. Furthermore, she told me that Baronne d'Apremont had left for America."

"Let's wish her *bon voyage*," skeptically noted Judex.

"But that's not all. She said danger threatens Favraux in his retreat at Sainte-Madeleine-en-Gâtinais."

Judex nearly jumped out of his seat. "What? This woman mentioned my father-n-law?"

"Yes, Monsieur Favraux."

"And she mentioned Sainte-Madeleine-en-Gâtinais to you."

"Are you absolutely sure?"

"Sainte-Madeleine-en-Gâtinais."

" Cocantin, what have you done?"

"You think that I made another blunder?"

"More than a blunder! A terrible lapse of judgment with the gravest consequences!"

"But I felt that I had done an immense service."

"A service! You revealed my family's most closely guarded secret to the Secret Raiders!"

"What?"

"I don't have time to explain. You wouldn't understand anyway." Judex pressed a button to summon a servant. "You've made a real mess this time!"

"How?"' asked Prosper Cocantin, taken aback by hearing for the first time the anger of the man whom he considered his master.

Changing his mind, Judex decided to explain precisely.

"I believe the Secret Riders lured you to this fake seer in order to trick you in revealing Favraux's location."

"I didn't say anything."

"How could this woman have obtained the address?"

"She's gifted with second sight."

"You believe in this absurdity?"

"Yes."

"I don't. Admit it, Cocantin. You were duped."

A servant appeared in the doorway.

"Tell Baptiste to prepare the car," ordered Judex. "I need to leave in five minutes."

The servant turned on his heels.

"Am I going with you?" asked Cocantin.

"No! Do what you want! Dance in the grass under the moonlight! Dress in leotards! Save butterflies in danger! Even visit every fortune-teller in Paris! But I order you to take no action regarding the Secret Raiders! Do you hear me?"

"I promise you," said Cocantin with indescribable remorse. He beat his chest three times in order to emphasize the sincerity of his mea culpa.

Judex had already left. While Cocantin remained standing as an act of contrition, the Comte was inside a small room adjacent to his office. Advancing towards a cage that held two homing pigeons, he opened the door. After hesitating for a while, the birds flew through an open window. Leaving La Frondaie, they flew across the forest of Fontainebleau towards the city of Moret. Bearing to the right, they flew across the

155

locality of Lorrez-le- Bocage. A further course correction to the left took them across several hills and towns. Eventually, they slowed down in order to descend into a garden surrounded by a ring of high trees. Adjacent was a cottage where someone could easily forget the world and be forgotten by it.

Seated on a bench, two old men savored silently the rapture of a summer evening. In their relaxed faces, their sad eyes reflected that both had survived the harsh storms of existence. In their retirement, the pair searched for a tranquility that they had once believed to be permanently abolished.

These two men were the banker Favraux and Pierre Kerjean. One was the financial swindler whom Judex had cast down and then raised to a life of noble redemption. The other was an ex-convict who had been originally corrupted by his current companion and then made a scapegoat. Through the noble influence of Judex, Kerjean was now the custodian of his former persecutor. An implacable hate had once separated these two men, but they had put aside their former feud. No more did Favraux view Kerjean as the living proof of his past crimes. No more did Kerjean see Favraux as the destroyer of his happiness. They lived together in harmony. They trusted one another. Favraux's remorse combined with Kerjean's suffering had resulted in the triumph of compassion over resentment. The two men were resigned to docilely follow Judex's instructions.

Favraux gazed at the blazing crimson sun shining through the trees. "Kerjean, this is a superb sight. Nature is truly beautiful. Visions such as this cause a man to love life."

Kerjean looked up. He made a brief gesture to ask the ex-banker to be silent. Favraux stopped talking. The pigeons landed on the garden table in front of the two men.

"The signal," said Kerjean.

"What should we do?" asked Favraux becoming pale.

"It's time to leave."

"*Mon Dieu!*" sighed Jacqueline's father.

"Fear nothing," advised Kerjean calmly. "The important thing is that we've been warned. The Comte de Trémeuse's instructions were precise. As soon as the pigeons arrive, we must leave the house for the prearranged rendezvous. For several days, I have prepared for this. All the precautions have been taken."

"Then let's leave," said Favraux. He looked sadly at the house which had afforded him sanctuary. He had hoped to finish his life here.

"It would have been better that I had stay buried in the cemetery of Les Sablons. Then I wouldn't suffer the ordeal of a public revelation that I still live."

"There's still time," claimed Kerjean. "I'll defend you until my death! The Comte made me the guardian of your life. In his name, I forbid you to have such suicidal thoughts. He wanted you to live. You shall live! I have suffered more than you. I have no surviving children to love and hence no attachments to this earth. If you want to die, you must kill me first!"

"Kerjean!" said Favraux grasping his companion's hands. "You have brought me back to reality. I have no right to kill myself. I shall follow your orders blindly."

United by an invisible bond, the duo entered the house. While Favraux packed his suitcase in his room, Kerjean entered a study. Opening a desk drawer, he removed several papers and put them inside an envelope upon which he wrote these words: THE FAVRAUX DOSSIER. He sealed the envelope with red wax. He then left the envelope in the drawer. After Favraux finished packing, Kerjean departed the cottage with him without bothering to remove the key from the lock. They went to a remote inn on the outskirts of the town.

Obeying the instructions of Judex, Kerjean briefly conferred with the female innkeeper. After a brief meal, the ex-banker and his companion mounted a horse drawn carriage. Driven by Kerjean, the conveyance proceeded towards an unknown destination.

Night had fallen. It was a serene summer evening. Against the sky full of stars, the fragrance of the forest created an exquisite freshness that replaced the intense heat of a scorching day.

"There must be happy people at this hour," murmured Favraux to Kerjean.

No sooner had those words been spoken than the carriage's horse swerved quickly to the side. It had been dazzled by the headlights of an approaching car. Above these two vehicles flew the two pigeons. Having accomplished their mission, they flew back towards their sweet prison of La Frondaie.

The automobile, a sumptuous limousine, had just visited the village of Sainte-Madeleine. It stopped in front of the *Boule d'Or* (the "Golden Bowl"), the only local inn that provided comfortable lodgings for travelers. An elegantly dressed woman exited the car. The owner of the establishment, Madame Pingaud, immediately rushed outside to meet this wealthy visitor.

III. Ten Minutes of Terror

"I wish to dine," said the haughty Baronne d'Apremont.

"Does Madame want a room?" asked Madame Pingaud.

"No!" the Baronne curtly replied as if it was degrading to be here.

"Is there at least a garage in your establishment?"

"Yes, Madame," replied the somewhat disconcerted hostess. She indicated a large building connected to the inn. "That's it, Madame. You have nothing to fear. My house is a reputable establishment. You can rest assured."

While the chauffeur drove the car into the rather rudimentary structure that served as a garage, Madame Pingaud escorted her guest inside. The Baronne seemed to be in an angry mood.

"Will your driver be dining as well?" apprehensively asked Madame Pingaud.

"It's not my custom to let my servants starve to death. Where is the dining room?"

"Here, Madame." The owner of the *Boule d'Or* opened a door to a room which contained a large table. Seated there were two commercial travelers, a beef merchant and an old lady whose exact profession was unclear.

"Can't I dine alone?" said the Baronne expressing contempt for the ordinary patrons of the *Boule d'Or*.

"If Madame desires. There is a small parlor which will afford you privacy. Please follow me."

Crossing the corridor, the Baronne smelt the stale odor of melted butter escaping from the kitchen. "What a cheap cookhouse," she growled between her teeth.

Madame Pingaud vigorously objected. "Madame is mistaken. The *Boule d'Or* is not a cheap cookhouse. Our house has, on the contrary, an excellent reputation. My husband is the cook. Once you have tasted his dishes, I'm sure Madame will forget her initial false impression."

"We shall see!"said the Baronne. Entering the parlor, she noticed that the room hadn't been dusted for weeks. "It's disgusting!" She sat in an old armchair that creaked like the groan of a man rudely awakened. "I guess I have no choice," she murmured.

Madame Pingaud still hoped to placate her difficult customer. "Tonight, we have vegetable soup, calf's sweetbread, roast beef and baked apples. Does Madame need time to order?"

"It's useless. I'm pressed for time. I'll take the soup."

"Yes, Madame. And wine?"

"Do you have champagne?"

"Yes, Madame."

"Bring me half a bottle. I want it very dry."

"Yes, Madame." The hostess summoned a little waitress working in the other room. "Victoire, set the table. Madame is pressed for time. I shall take care of you, Madame."

"I you wish to ingratiate yourself with me, then you could help me find two old friends who live nearby." The Baronne described Favraux and Kerjean.

"Those two gentlemen dined here a short time ago," divulged Madame Pingaud. "In fact, they gave me their address. Would you like me to write it down?"

"Please do."

After writing the address on a sheet of paper, the hostess departed. The Baronne's chauffeur then entered the room.

"Mimile, investigate this address," commanded the adventuress. "See if it's occupied by the men we seek."

"Can't I eat first?" asked the driver.

"No! Obey my orders! Hurry!"

The chauffeur departed. Less than ten minutes later, the Baronne was presented with bowl of hot soup that gave an appetizing fragrance. Madame Pingaud hadn't been bluffing. Her spouse was a true artist of the cuisine. As the Baronne drank her half bottle of Moét to the last drop, she hardly appreciated the brilliance of the master chef of Sainte-Madeleine-en-Gâtinais.

The Baronne was brooding over the important task entrusted to her by the chief of the Secret Raiders. She had to spy on Favraux's alleged abode, verify Cocantin's information, and then recommend a plan of action. The Baronne ruminated over the details of her mission when Madame Pingaud came to offer her desert.

"Does Madame wish coffee?"

"Yes, if it's good."

"It shall be delicious."

"A small liquor?"

"No, thank you."

The hostess departed. Pulling a pack of cigarettes out of her pocket, the Baronne smoked while complaining.

"Where is my beast of a chauffeur, Mimile? I told him to hurry. I don't want to spend forever in this hellhole."

There was a knock on the door.

"Enter!"

Her chauffeur appeared obsequiously with cap in hand.

"You're here at last!"

"Yes, Baronne. I'm here."

"You found them?"

"Yes, their house is 200 meters from here. It's a nice villa on a large street. It's called the Cottage, and I wouldn't mind retiring there. I talked to the neighbors."

"What did they say?"

"About 7 o'clock, the two old fogeys snuck out of their garden."

"Are you sure?"

"They acted as if they didn't want to be spotted, but more than one neighbor saw them."

"We missed them! But the important thing is to have located their refuge. Leave the rest to me."

"What will I be doing?" asked the chauffeur.

"You shall eat."

"Is the roast beef good at least?"

The Baronne shrugged her shoulders. "I only had the soup. I'll take a taxi to Favraux's house. Maybe I'll find something. Wait here. I'll rejoin you after I'm done."

"Good luck, Baronne."

Exiting the room, the Baronne located Madame Pingaud. "I'm leaving my chauffeur here. Feed him well. I'm going shopping and shall be back shortly."

The Baronne left immediately. She reached the other end of town where she easily located the villa described by her driver. She cautiously inspected the surroundings. They were deserted. Large storm clouds obscured the moon and the stars. There was no gas-burner nearby. The lieutenant of *N'a-qu'un-Chasse* would be able to operate without interference. She entered the property by the main exit. She opened a gate consisting of two thick metal doors. She soon located the small door in the garden wall through which Favraux and Kerjean had left two hours beforehand. To her surprise, the key was still in the lock. Apparently in the haste of their escape, the ex-banker and his companion forgot the key. Without the least hesitation, she opened the door and penetrated the garden. Silently she searched the house. Looking through the window, she saw that the interior was shrouded in darkness. The house was abandoned. Its door was unlocked. The Baronne entered the vllla's antechamber.

"The two madmen left the house without brothering to lock the doors," mumbled the Baronne. "How could they have been warned? Could Cocantin have been fooling me? That's impossible. It was that simple-minded idiot who gave me Favraux's location. Could Judex have interfered? How could he have learned that I located his father-in-law? This isn't the time for questions. It's the time for action!"

Taking a small lamp out of her pocket, she used it to search the room. Noticing a wall switch, she flipped it on. Suspended from the ceiling, a Chinese lantern illuminated the room. Although the town of Sainte-Madeleine-en-Gâtinais possessed few street lamps, it had electricity which would now greatly assist the Baronne. Entering another room, she found another wall switch. Turning it on, she found herself in a study. She immediately spotted the desk where Kerjean had conspicuously left the envelope labeled "THE FAVRAUX DOSSIER."

This may be too good to be true, thought the Baronne. *In their panic to flee, did they leave the secret that we're after? Perhaps this is a trap. That envelope may not contain documents, but a dangerous surprise, such as poison, for anyone who opens it. I must take it to* N'a-qu'un-Chasse. *He'll know how to open it.*

The Baronne cautiously grabbed the envelope. A cry of horror escaped her lips. A metal rod ending in a skeleton's hand had shot out of the desk. The bony fingers clutched her wrist. It was a clever mechanical trap set by Kerjean. As the dead hand squeezed her flesh, she fainted.

When she awoke, she found herself in an automobile traveling at a great speed. Seated nearby, Judex threatened her with a pistol.

"Baronne, if you move or scream, I'll kill you!"

She fainted again.

While this drama unfolded, Mimile, the Baronne's chauffeur, enjoyed his meal at the *Boule d'Or*. Without a thought for the welfare of his employer, he smoked a cigar after his hearty meal.

IV. The Propeller Plans

At a shady tavern in an obscure corner of the Parisian suburbs, *N'a-qu'un-Chasse* read a newspaper in a whispered tone to Belles-Mirettes. He wasn't reading a sensational news story or even an exciting serial. His focus was a personal advertisement.

M. JORIS VANPEPERSTRAET
240 Boulevard Sébastopol
Willing to purchase for cash inventions
relative to the military, naval, aeronautic fields, etc.

Placing the newspaper next to a barely consumed glass of wine on the table, Bébert issued instructions to an extremely attentive Belles-Mirettes.

"You will take the propeller plans to this Monsieur Vanpeperstraet. You will offer to sell him the plans for 100,000 francs, and compromise on 50,000. It doesn't matter that we're selling the originals. The plans have been photographed. I'm relying on you to conclude this transaction."

"Rest easy, I won't fail you."

"Do you remember the name?"

"Joris Vanpeperstraet."

"The address?"

"240 Boulevard Sébastopol."

"All right," said Bébert in English before reverting back to French. "Here are the papers."

He gave Belles-Mirettes an envelope that she quickly placed in her briefcase.

"I won't keep you. Move quickly. This matter must be handled efficiently. Report to me at Domicile #4 where I'm waiting to hear from the Baronne. I'm surprised that she hasn't reported back since yesterday. I fear that we've had a setback.

However, she's quite capable and has performed satisfactorily in the past. At least you should be successful. Since the interference of this cursed Judex, the Secret Raiders haven't played their cards well."

"I shall do my best, chief."

"*Au revoir.*"

"I'll see you tonight."

"In case there are any complications that prevent you from coming tonight. I'll be there for the next two nights as well. Arrive no earlier than 10 o'clock."

Belles-Mirettes went to the nearest underground railway station. As the train transported her towards the center of Paris, her eyes became sad as if she was going to cry. The vision of that lovely child, Jean, appeared before her. Belles-Mirettes wondered why she was thinking of the child since they would never meet again. Her mind became filled with thoughts that revealed her to be less corrupt than her colleagues in the Secret Raiders. There existed inside her soul compassionate feelings that her master had failed to stifle.

He was so gentle, she thought. *I remember him clasping his hands in prayer.*

Would this angelic child from the forest be her personal angel of redemption?

At 3 o'clock in the afternoon, Belles-Mirettes, wearing a black dress and veil suitable for mourning, entered the first floor of a large industrial building on the Boulevard Sébastopol. She entered Joris Vanpeperstraet's offices. At the request of the office boy, she signed a register with the false name of Mademoiselle Marie Roger. She wrote down the purpose of her visit: "Sale of plans of an automatic propeller for the navy." The boy led her to a small waiting room. The register was taken by the boy to his employer.

Joris Vanpeperstraet was pleased by what had been written inside. "Show the lady in."

Some moments later after, Belles-Mirettes; crossed the threshold of the prospective buyer's private sanctum. Her dignified manner impressed Vanpeperstraet. He directed the visitor to be seated opposite him.

Belles-Mirettes examined the man with whom she hoped to negotiate an agreement. He was rather large. His long hair was combed back. A big gray beard adorned his face. Tortoise-shell spectacles hid his eyes. Austerely dressed, Joris Vanpeperstraet was an imposing figure. His emotionless face masked his innermost thoughts. He created the impression of a man accustomed to issuing orders. It certainly wouldn't be easy for Belles-Mirettes to manipulate him.

Looking at the register, Vanpeperstraet spoke with a heavy foreign accent.

"I see, Mademoiselle, that you have plans for sale."

"Yes, Monsieur," she replied in a sad voice. "My recently deceased father had invented a propeller. I read your newspaper ad about purchasing inventions for cash."

"In fact, Mademoiselle," declared the businessman. "I only moved here three days ago. You're the first person to answer my advertisement. I hope that your visit will prove profitable to both of us."

"You're very kind, Monsieur."

"Please show me these plans."

"Here they are." Belles-Mirettes pulled the envelope out of her briefcase.

"May I see them?"

"Certainly, Monsieur."

Joris Vanpeperstraet unsealed the envelope slowly in a meticulous manner. After quickly perusing the documents, he laughed.

"You claimed your father invented this propeller."

"Yes, Monsieur," reiterated Belles-Mirettes calmly.

"Are you sure?"

"Absolutely."

Maintaining his courteous exterior, the potential buyer coldly replied. "You're mistaken, Mademoiselle."

"Monsieur, I spoke the truth."

"Your father had nothing to do with this invention."

"Monsieur!"

"These plans were stolen."

"Stolen?"

"On June 14th, in the Chateau d'Arbois, from James Milton." Removing his glasses, false beard and wig, the businessman shouted "I am James Milton!"

Recognizing the trap into which she had been lured, Belles-Mirettes acted promptly. Inside her briefcase was a container filled with pepper. She could use it to temporarily blind an enemy. Grabbing the container, she tossed its contents into Milton's eyes.

As Milton yelled in pain, Belles-Mirettes grabbed the propeller plans and ran for the door. It opened before she could reach it. Screaming with rage, the bold Raider retreated. Calm but inscrutable, Judex advanced towards her.

"It's the two of us, Mademoiselle!"

The office boy followed Judex into the room. While the lad attended to the stricken Milton, Judex grabbed the minion of *N'a-qu'un-Chasse* by the arm.

"Now you'll tell me how those plans fell into your hands."

Belles-Mirettes defiantly turned her head away.

"So you won't talk? so be it! For the moment, I won't insist. However, you must follow me. I don't doubt that you'll soon become more talkative."

Hearing these words, she looked straight into Judex's eyes. Her own eyes reflected defeat. She didn't know how to outwit this man of mystery.

"Yes," resumed Judex nonchalantly drawing from a pistol from his pocket. "Follow me. You must learn the truth about your employers."

As the Raider docilely obeyed him without a word, a triumphant smile appeared on Judex's face.

"This one will talk! I'm sure!"

45 Centimes.   Tous les Jeudis.

LA
NOUVELLE MISSION
DE
JUDEX

Par ARTHUR BERNÈDE et Louis FEUILLADE

LES CAPTIVES

Part Eight. The Captives

I. Cocantin's Mea Culpa

Les Trois Soldats ("The Three Soldiers") was a stylish inn situated between Mantes and Bonnières. On its terrace, Prosper Cocantin was seated before a green table where rested a full glass of beer. Rather than drink the alcoholic beverage, Cocantin watched the dust, kicked up by speeding cars on the nearby road, fall into his glass. The detective was extremely dejected. The depression about which he had complained to Dr. Howey had returned with a vengeance. He was plunged in that despondency which rejects all the cheerful elements of life. For an instance, he muttered to himself.

"*Mon Dieu*! What an idiot! I'm a brute!"

Pulling out a letter which had been folded with the greatest care, he scanned the letter while his lips moved incoherently. The letter was written in a bold precise handwriting.

My dear Cocantin,

I absolutely need to see you. Meet me tomorrow, Tuesday, at noon in the inn called Les Trois Soldats *on the shore of Rochebois. It is imperative that you understand the consequences for me and my loved ones of the indiscretion that you committed during your visit to La Belle Fathma. I rely absolutely on your presence at the appointed time.*

Good Wishes,

Jacques de Trémeuse

"The devil with Judex!" growled Cocantin. He began to ramble in whispered tones. "His words send chills down my spine. 'It is imperative that you understand the consequences...' What consequences? He makes it sound that I'm responsible for a horrible catastrophe. He then summons me to this country tavern where I dare not even taste my drink because I'm haunted by the possible misfortune that I've caused.

"Fortunately that I received news this morning from Daisy and the Licorice Kid. At least that consoled me... It isn't my fault! I couldn't fight back. The Secret Raiders conspired against me.

"What has happened? Could these criminals have kidnapped Favraux and now be blackmailing the Trémeuse family? Judex's summons indicates that he has suffered a defeat. Ah! That woman! That Baronne! Why the did I meet her on this train? Why did she have such big eyes, such a sweet voice, and such pretty limbs? She caused me to totally lose my reason. Her image haunts my thoughts.

"In this investigation, I sang like a canary. If I live to the age of 98 like my grandfather, I won't be able to use the 60 years of my remaining life to adequately atone for my inexcusable blunder."

Cocantin finally swallowed the mixture of hot beer and gray dust in his glass.

"I would give a year of my life to know what Judex has to tell me."

He didn't have long to wait In less than five minutes, a swift car parked in front of *Les Trois Soldats*. Nimbly alighting from the vehicle, Judex solemnly advanced towards Cocantin.

Things have gone badly, thought the detective. Rising from his seat, he walked slowly towards Jacques de Trémeuse.

"*Bonjour*, Cocantin," said Judex dryly.

"*Bonjour*, my dear Comte. Do you want something to drink?"

"No, thank you. I'm pressed for time." Judex then spoke in a tone that left no room for resistance. "There's no time. Follow me."

Cocantin didn't need to hear those words twice. Leaving a tip on the table, he hurried to follow the awe-inspiring Comte into his car. Judex addressed his faithful chauffeur, Baptiste.

169

"To the Chateau-Rouge."

Those words made Cocantin shudder. Judex never had done him the honor of showing him those ruins.

I now understand, thought the sleuth, *the anguish that Napoléon suffered before embarking on his exile. I'm leaving for my own St. Helena.*

The car moved speedily towards its destination. Although occasionally Judex glanced at his companion, he cryptically never spoke.

Finally Cocantin was compelled to break the silence. "Comte, are you angry with me?"

"You shall learn that in good time."

That's it, thought the detective. *I'm condemned. I can't save myself by jumping from the car. Its speed has to be at least 90. Why didn't I go with Daisy to America?*

Coming to the bottom of a hill, the car stopped. Before it rose the Chateau-Rouge.

"Come," Judex ordered.

The anxious Cocantin obeyed sheepishly. If he had noticed the smiles exchanged between Jacques de Trémeuse and his chauffeur, Cocantin would have been relieved. However, he didn't. Cocantin continued to walked with his head lowered in shame. He was resigned towards whatever fate awaited him. Reaching the summit of the path, Cocantin decided to cast off his trepidation and behave brazenly.

"My dear Comte, you have exercised your rights as my overlord to bring me this far. Despite the deference that I owe you, I have no more patience for this trek through melodramatic ruins."

Delicately Judex placed his hand on Cocantin's shoulder.

"Cocantin, you deserve a lesson. I shall give it to you."

Judex touched a hidden mechanism on the wall. A flagstone was raised in order to reveal the stairwell to the subterranean levels of the Chateau Rouge.

Becoming pale, Cocantin shivered and nearly fainted. "My dear Comte..."

Hoping to relieve Cocantin's terror, Judex softened his voice.

"You imagine that I want to confine you in the prisons of my fortress? Cocantin, your remorse is visibly sincere. I know how devoted you are to me. I have already forgiven your indiscretions. In order to prevent further failures ---"

"I swear that it won't happen again!" shouted Cocantin. "If you knew how much I've suffered! My soul burns from guilt, I can no longer beg forgiveness. Tell me that all is not lost! Tell me that we are still strong enough to defeat the Secret Raiders!"

"Follow me!" replied Judex.

The flagstone closed behind them as Judex and Cocantin descended a narrow stairway. Their journey was illuminated by electrical lights that were the equal of those used in the underground railway.

Cocantin's eyes widened. "This is astounding!"

"As I said earlier, I have no intention of imprisoning you. Your mistakes didn't have the consequences that I feared. I warned Favraux in time that his refuge was discovered. However, you must stay here while I settle accounts with the Secret Raiders. That shouldn't take longer than 48 hours. I'm not using force to keep you here. You're absolutely free to refuse a brief repose beneath the Chateau Rouge, but you would have an excellent room, an ample supply of food, and an abundant library of stimulating books. I believe a voluntary confinement is essential to your security. It will prevent any stratagems against you by the people we pursue."

"I accept," enthusiastically replied Prosper Cocantin. "My only regret is being absent from your side at the moment of the supreme battle. I especially wanted to be present at the punishment of that dreadful Baronne d'Apremont."

"You want to see her punished?" added a smiling Jacques de Trémeuse.

"Do I!"

"And the other one as well?"

"What other one?"

"The little chambermaid with the tousled hair and the hellish eyes!"

"If only they were my prisoners!"

"Come and look." Judex directed Cocantin to a large mirror on one of the walls of his laboratory. The Comte turned the mirror on a stem by moving a gear. The mirror could be orientated in any direction.

"It's her!" cried Cocantin.

Due to an electrical system invented by Judex, the detective could behold the image of the Baronne prostrate on a bench in a prison cell.

"The swine!" sneered Cocantin. "If I could only make her pay. At last, you have captured her! It's vital!" He shook his fist at the image of the Baronne. "I hate you!"

Suddenly the Baronne disappeared as Judex maneuvered the mirror. The image of Belles-Mirettes appeared. She was in a similar cell. Seated on a stool, her hands was raised to her face as if she was lost in deep mediation.

"You've beaten them!" shouted Cocantin in wonder. "It's fabulous. I hope, my dear master, that you won't hesitate a moment to deliver these two women to the police."

"You forget, Cocantin, that in order to render my own justice, I have placed myself outside the law. It's impossible for me to invoke the law in my own defense."

"It's true," acknowledged the detective.

"Furthermore, my enemies know the secret of Favraux's survival. I can't expose them without exposing my family to the irreparable shame of a scandal."

"This all my fault!" said Cocantin beating his chest.

"Therefore, I'm obliged to use the only option available to me. I must rely on my own devices. I believe that the battle will be brief, and your tenure, my dear friend, as host of the Chateau Rouge won't be long. Through these two women, as well as a male accomplice apprehended earlier, I shall unmask the sinister chief of the Secret Raiders. I intend to question my two new captives. Through this mirror, you will be able to observe the results of my interrogation. Hopefully, one or the other will disclose the desired information. My dear Cocantin, you have no more penance to perform. In fact, your unfortunate encounter with the seer caused me to fly to Favraux's relief and trap the Baronne d'Apremont."

Cocantin was exuberant.

"My dear Count, may I say something before you depart."

"Speak."

"You have surpassed Napoléon."

Jacques de Trémeuse laughed. "Let me demonstrate how to operate the mirror."

Once Cocantin had mastered the mirror, Judex left his laboratory. The private detective's eyes were fixated on Baronne d'Apremont savagely snarling in anger as Judex entered her cell.

II. Belles-Mirettes

"Are you ready to talk?" forcibly asked Jacques de Trémeuse.

The Baronne merely shrugged her shoulders.

"I see that you haven't accepted your situation even though you had ample time for reflection. You must be intelligent enough to conclude that silence merely extends your captivity indefinitely. A single word could cause you to leave this cell."

The eyes of the Baronne reflected burning hatred.

"Monsieur, I don't know what you want me to say."

"I shall be brief. Give me information that will result in the capture of the chief of the Secret Raiders, and I shall grant you your liberty."

"Never!"

"Perhaps you're afraid that I won't keep my word. You must have investigated me. Your research would have revealed that I always abide by my agreements, even when I'm forced to deal with people of your ilk."

"My ilk will prove more than a match for you!"

"Permit me, Madame, to dispute your opinion. However, that's not the issue. I deal with you in good faith. I repeat my offer."

"You're wasting your time!"

"Then you shall remain here."

"For how long?"

"As long as it pleases me."

Roaring like an injured tigress, the Baronne leaped to her feet. She shook her fists at Judex. He calmly contemplated her with his arms crossed. His splendid self-control contrasted with the wild exasperation of the prisoner.

"What do you intend to do with me?" she screamed.

"You shall remain confined for your infamy. You have allied yourself with a monstrous criminal. You're worse than a slave to him. You're little better than a toy or a plaything. Yet you refuse to negotiate your liberty out of loyalty to him."

"I shall be true to myself," asserted the insolent Baronne. "I'm a woman who after savoring all the pleasure of life found herself unfairly betrayed by a jealous husband. Following his death, his will disinherited me. I was reduced to the most abhorrent poverty. I was too proud to take a lover. The idea of selling my flesh disgusted me to a point that I preferred death. I would rather sell my soul to a man who values my intelligence and talents, the leader of the Secret Raiders. This all may sound bizarre, but it's the truth. I'm not a woman who can lead an ordinary life. If I told you my history in detail, you probably wouldn't believe me. My life reads like a book of incredible adventures. Yet, I am still not yet 30 years old. I won't reveal how I became the associate of the man you're hunting, but I'm tied to him by an unbreakable bond. I'll never betray him."

"Do you love him?"

"Love? No, it's been a long time since that feeling has been aroused inside me. Instead, I have a boundless admiration for him. And do you know why? Because he introduced me to a life of continual excitement. Although he demanded much, he gave me more than I ever hoped for. I'm not talking about money, but about the thrill of danger and the intoxication of revenge. Even in this prison, my courage hasn't left me. You know why? Because I know what endeavors your quarry is capable of. I'm confident of his ultimate victory. I won't remain defeated for long unless you kill me --- and you wouldn't dare! The leader of the Secret Raiders won't delay in removing me from your hands. Then we shall strike at you and enact a terrible vengeance. "

"We shall see!" replied Judex simply.

Exhausted by the vehemence that she had unleashed in her challenge to her nemesis, the Baronne sat down. She was tired but still defiant. With nothing more to say, Jacques de Trémeuse left the cell of Baronne for that of Belles-Mirettes.

Back in the laboratory, Cocantin had followed Judex's entire interview with the Baronne on the electric mirror.

"What a virago! If it had been me instead of Judex, I would have mercilessly strangled her."

When Judex entered her cell, Belles-Mirettes slowly raised her head. This time Judex didn't see fury in the eyes of a prisoner. He saw despair. It was despair begging to be relieved.

Her anguish revealed the possibility of remorse. A desire to do penance had begun to penetrate the captive's mind as she weighed the inevitable consequences of her incarceration.

Judex understood instantly that this was a different woman than the sadistic monster he just left. He hoped that she wasn't as corrupt as the Baronne. If he called upon the remaining goodness inside her, would he be able to reawaken her conscience. Of all the battles that the champion of justice had fought, this could be the most stirring.

With his harmonious voice, the master of the Chateau Rouge went on the offensive immediately. He would treat the prisoner not with harshness but with compassion.

"You seem to be in an unfortunate state."

"Yes," replied Belles-Mirettes. "I'm very unfortunate."

"Do you suffer?"

"Yes, I suffer." All of a sudden, the strange being that was Belles-Mirettes regained her bitterness. "Why did you ask me that?"

"Because you intrigue me!"

"Me!"

"You aren't a vulgar woman. Not only are you endowed with a rare intelligence, but I'm convinced that you're destined to pursue a different path than the one you're currently pursuing."

"You may be right!" Belles-Mirettes was strongly affected by the kind words of her enemy.

"Look at me," requested Judex. Belles-Mirettes turned her head away. "Look at me," insisted her jailer. "I need to understand you completely. Your eyes are a deep enigma. If I could read your wounded soul through them, I'll be able to judge it better. Perhaps I may even be able to heal it."

As Jacques de Trémeuse spoke, Belle-Mirettes raised her head gradually. The previous hostility in her eyes abated.

"Poor child," said Judex. "I can finally gauge you totally. You only became a criminal because you've never been happy."

"It's true!" murmured the accomplice of *N'a-qu'un-Chasse*. Tears began rolling slowly down her cheeks. The man who had seemed so terrible to her now seemed an angel of mercy.

"My poor life has always been chaotic. I never knew my parents. I never had anything that resembled a family. My first memories are painful. A stranger raised me without a gesture of kindness or affection. She claimed to have found me in the streets. Perhaps it's true. She taught me nothing but evil. I was scarcely five years old when she taught me to steal! What a wonderful apprenticeship. The miserable woman was skillful. She knew how to make the lessons interesting. I had to obey her. She beat me when I didn't. I was terrorized. That lasted years until Bébert, alias *N'a-qu'un-Chasse*, found me and asked me to work for him.

"I accepted. I had enough of that shrew. I followed this man. He's an incredible master! No one can resist him! He ensnares you in a web of fascination. One obeys him like a slave. Once you become his prey, there is no deliverance. He never threatens. He never yells. This individual is terrifying because his voice invokes infinite kindness. He's a master of cynical pleasantries. No one else could give an enticing appearance to such horrifying orders.

"In reality, there are two men in him under the same mask. One is Bébert, alias *N'a-qu'un-Chasse*, the Apache of the dark underworld, who speaks in the slang of the men who prowl the outskirts of Paris. The other is an aristocratic gentleman whose impeccable manners and extremely polished language reveals an extensive education.

"Which one is his true self? Where did he come from? I don't know. I've never fully seen his face. I know only his name and his voice. I would recognize his seductive voice in a group of a thousand men.

"None of his servants, not even Baronne d'Apremont, has been able to pierce the mystery surrounding him. Those that try don't even have time to regret their curiosity. They all perished as if they were struck down by invisible lighting.

"Monsieur, this man has unbelievable power. You may be brave and resolute, but I fear you aren't the stronger. *N'a-qu'un-Chasse* will break you as he's broken a hundred others. He isn't a man. He's a demon!"

Having attentively listened to the long narrative, Judex decided to issue his judgment.

"As with others, this man is also your evil spirit. I shall crush him!"

Belles-Mirettes shook her head. Recognizing that he hadn't yet exorcised the mastery of the chieftain of the Secret Raiders over her, Judex resumed his campaign to shift her loyalties.

"From what you told me, it's clear that you're more unfortunate than guilty. Your harsh upbringing and the perverse influence of the Secret Raiders hasn't completely destroyed your natural good instincts. An honest man could have cultivated your goodness just as *N'a-qu'un-Chasse* has nurtured your evil. Do you want me to be that man? You could have a normal life that obliterates all the filth into which you've been dragged. You could know all the bliss of a purified existence. At last, you could live in an atmosphere purged of harmful poisons. I can introduce you into a happiness whose existence you certainly suspected and perhaps consciously desired."

The young miscreant was conquered by the benevolence of Judex.

"Yes!" she shouted. "I want it. You have opened my eyes to the light. I've had enough of this shameful life. Save me, Monsieur. Save me!"

"I shall," promised Jacques de Trémeuse. "Although I have no doubts about your remorse, you must give me proof."

"Speak!" declared Belles-Mirettes, completely transformed. "I shall obey you in the cause of righteousness just as I obeyed *N'a-qu'un-Chasse* in the cause of evil."

"Tell me where to find *N'a-qu'un-Chasse*.

"Tonight he's in Auteuil, 21 Rue du Docteur-Pelet. He's waiting for me and the Baronne to arrive at 10 o'clock."

"Will you accompany me there?"

"I'll go with you."

"From this moment onwards, you can consider yourself reborn and forgiven."

Seizing the hand of the righteous judge, Belles-Mirettes kissed it.

"Remain here for a short while," stated the Comte, "and have full confidence in me. Soon you shall be free!"

"Soon!" shouted the young woman. Tears of sublime hope bathed her face.

Returning to his laboratory, Judex found a tearful Cocantin.

"I couldn't hear anything," said the detective, "but I saw everything in the mirror. You moved me. It didn't take you long to convince her."

"At least that one has a soul," said Judex.

"While the other is a ferocious beast! I won't lie to you, my master. I would rather face a tigress that escaped from the zoo than face Baronne d'Apremont."

"Even in a private dining room," said Judex mischievously.

"Especially in a private dining room," stressed Cocantin with a noticeable grimace.

Judex picked up the telephone. He asked the operator to connect him to the Chateau de Joyeuse. Once the connection was made, a servant answered. Judex asked to talk to his brother.

"Hello, Roger! Everything's going well... admirably well... Tonight, at 10 o'clock precise, meet me in Auteuil at the intersection of Rue du Docteur-Pelet and Avenue de Billancourt... I have the one-eyed man's address... Understood... I look forward to tonight!"

"Now," said Jacques de Trémeuse to Cocantin, "our goal is within reach. Soon the Secret Raiders will pay for their crimes."

"I'm in total agreement," added the director of the Céléritas Agency.

"While we wait," declared Judex, "I shall finish the conversion of Belles-Mirettes!"

III. The Dance in the Mirror

Around 6 o'clock in the evening, Judex left the Chateau Rouge. He was accompanied by Belles-Mirettes. When Judex had captured Belles-Mirettes, he had found the key to her apartment. While searching her flat, he had retrieved some of her clothes. She was now dressed in a masculine suit.

Prosper Cocantin was left in charge of the two other prisoners, Baronne d'Apremont and Louchard. Judex was quite confident. He knew he could rely on Cocantin for two reasons. First, Cocantin desired to make amends for his earlier blunder. He would rather be cut in half than fail Judex. Second, the Baronne inspired in him such a fear that he would

179

scrupulously avoid entering her cell. Cocantin had no wish to tame this tigress.

Left a basket of provisions by Judex, Cocantin quietly sat at the table in the center of the laboratory. Following a brief meal, he became absorbed in reading a novel from the Chateau Rouge's library. While reading was one of his favorite past times, he wasn't able to focus his attention on the book. After a quarter of an hour during which he had repressed several yawns, Cocantin closed the book. Getting up, he checked all the scientific devices in the room. He marveled at how these mechanisms reflected Judex's vast knowledge of chemistry and physics.

He went to the mirror to observe the prisoners. In her cell lit by an electric lamp, Baronne d'Apremont reclined on her couch. She was displaying her natural savagery by rolling her eyes and constantly moving her lips. Although Cocantin couldn't hear her words, it was obvious that she was indulging in outbursts of anger and hate.

"She remains defiant," noted Cocantin. "Maybe she would be less rebellious if she knew of my presence or that the chief of the Secret Raiders was about to fall into Judex's hands. How to tell her? Judex ordered me not to enter into the prisoner's cell. It was an unnecessary command because I have no desire to confront this enraged tigress. However, I must communicate with my enemy in order to savor my well-deserved vengeance."

A very pale Cocantin reached the large crypt where a series of locked doors had to be opened in order to reach the cells where Judex kept his prisoners. Silently Cocantin reached the door of the female Raider's cell. He opened a panel that revealed a barred window in the top of the door.

"Good evening, Baronne." After uttering those words, Cocantin instinctively backed away three steps.

Some moments later, the face of the Baronne stood out behind the barred window.

"So it's you!" She recognized Cocantin whose figure was illuminated by the glimmer of a strong electric light suspended from an arch.

"Yes, it is I!" retorted the detective. "I, Prosper Cocantin, am now your jailer."

"My jailer?"

"Yes, Baronne, and a jailer what won't let you escape!"

The sight of the private detective had caused a vague hope to arise inside the Baronne. She decided to adopt a meek demeanor.

"Did Monsieur Judex deputize you to watch me?"

"Exactly, Baronne. It was Monsieur Judex."

"Is he doing well?"

"Very well! Soon things will be a lot better for him." Cocantin was drunk with vengeance. "Tonight, something amusing will happen in Auteuil."

"What are you saying?" The Baronne was stunned by the comment.

"I'm talking about the Rue du Docteur-Pelet."

"The Rue du Docteur-Pelet," anxiously repeated the Baronne.

"Your patron, Bébert alias *N'a-qu'un-Chasse*, will be there."

"Belles-Mirettes has betrayed me!"

"Excuse me, Baronne. Belles-Mirettes didn't betray you. She avenged me and Judex. It's not exactly what you said, but the net effect is the same. Belles-Mirettes will introduce Judex to *N'a-qu'un-Chasse*. In a couple of hours, we should know the consequences of this meeting."

"You swine!" roared the Baronne furiously shaking the bars.

"All this racket is futile. It won't alter the course of events. You can't deceive me. I'm able to monitor all your movements through a metallic mirror. My eyes will continually be fixed on you. I advise you to behave. Otherwise, there will be consequences."

Closing abruptly the window in the cell door, an ecstatic Cocantin returned to Judex's laboratory. Hearing him depart, the Baronne smiled cryptically.

"The fool! He doesn't know what I, Baronne d'Apremont, can do even in the depths of a prison."

Grinning hellishly, she returned to her cot and seemed to fall into a deep sleep. The scheming woman was about to submit the director of the Céléritas Agency to one of the most fearsome tests than he had ever endured.

Continuing to use the mirror, Cocantin noticed the motionless Baronne.

"All's well! I crushed her! I conquered her! She'll be quiet!"

Swelling with pride, he walked up and down the laboratory with his hands in his vest. After a few minutes, he resumed his observation of the Baronne. A cry combining fear and anger burst from his lips.

Resting on her pearl white shoulders, her magnificent black hair had been undone. Her hands stretched forward in a gesture of subservience. Her chest vibrated with intense emotion. Her eyes smothered as her lips trembled. Baronne d'Apremont, one of the most alluring women on earth, was calling Cocantin to her like a legendary siren.

Cocantin was heroic. He didn't falter. Yet the devilish Baronne had never seemed more beautiful. She moved like a cat. Her half-opened mouth invoked images of ecstasy. Like Salome dancing before Herod, she used all her feminine wiles to entice her stern custodian.

Still Cocantin didn't falter. Recognizing the powerful desires inside himself, he refused to yield to them. Cocantin turned off the mirror. This time, he had triumphed over temptation. The Baronne had failed to ensnare him.

Seated at the table, he picked up his novel. The director of the Céléritas Agency congratulated himself on his victory.

"Prosper, I'm happy with you!"

He wanted to return to his reading, but the real events transpiring at the Chateau Rouge made the fictional musing of the author seem bland by comparison. Quickly he reactivated the mirror hoping to view his enemy's desolation. He wasn't disappointed.

The Baronne was spread on her cot. Turned against the wall, her face showed signs of a horrible despair. If Cocantin couldn't see her face quickly, he was able to observe the spasmodic twitching of her body.

She's having a nervous fit! thought the detective. *It's the fate she deserves. She can't escape it! The swine! What if she dies from this attack of nerves? Judex wanted me to watch her! How do I prevent her from dying! Should I enter her cell to calm her? No! She'll jump on me and rip open my face with her nails. Or she'll try to charm me into making another blunder. In either case, it won't happen. Someone can trick me once. Maybe even twice. But never three times! Baronne, your mischief is at an end. I must be a man of iron. Tonight, the director of the Céléritas Agency is not disposed to leave his post. Bonsoir, Madame. Rest well. I shall try to do the same.*

Cocantin was about to turn the mirror off when the Baronne made a sudden movement. She rose showing a face filled with hate.

What she's up to? wondered Cocantin. *What an awful face! She really has the look of a killer! I must stay here rather than go to her cell. She sends chills down my spine. She wants to murder someone. I pity anyone falling into her hands. Even a gun or knife would be inadequate protection from her. She's moving around. What's she planning? She can't demolish the cell door. What a ruthless beauty! I doubt that she shall ever die! Wait! She calmed down.*

In fact, the Baronne had stopped pacing around her cell. With an extraordinary mobility, her facial expression had completely changed. Her angry disdain had been replaced by total tranquility. She stood frozen for an instant, and then looked at the electric lamp that hung from the ceiling. Words escaped from her mouth, but Cocantin couldn't hear them. She smiled as she crossed her arms against her chest. For a brief moment, the Baronne seemed lost in a dream. She then grabbed a stool that was nest to her cot. Moving it to the middle of the room, she climbed up on the stool. She detached the circular glass covering that was around the glass. Stepping down, she advanced toward a small table containing a jar and a bowl. She smashed the glass covering against the table.

"Damnation!" yelled Cocantin. "Does she want to kill herself?"

The Baronne closed her eyes as if she was about faint.

Cocantin's brain became filled with panic.

She may be planning to cut her throat. Do I let her commit suicide? To prevent it, I'll need to go into her cell. I promised Judex that I wouldn't, but I also promised to monitor the prisoners. Diable! *Do I go or not? What responsibility!* Mon Dieu! *If I keep one promise, I break the other!*

The Baronne reopened her eyes. She looked at the piece of glass as thin as a razor blade in her right hand. Her left hand touched her neck searching for the carotid artery.

"That's it!" screamed Cocantin. "She's cutting her throat!"

Slowly the Baronne's right arm moved the glass towards the veins on her neck.

"I must stop her!" yelled Cocantin. Running to her cell, he unlocked the door. The Secret Raider rested on the bed with her head in the covers. Afraid that he might slip in a pool of blood on the ground, Cocantin walked slowly without looking at the ground. He would have given 10 years of his life to be 100 leagues from here.

I must gain control of my emotions. he thought. *It's hard to imagine that this vibrant woman is now a corpse! Maybe there's still hope. Could her hand have faltered at the last minute? Could her suicide have been a failure?*

He touched the prisoner's shoulder.

"Baronne! Baronne!"

He didn't get a chance to say anymore. Leaping like a panther, the Baronne grabbed him by the collar

"I tricked you!" she screamed. "I'll beat you, your precious Judex, and all your friends!"

Cocantin tried to defend himself, but it was futile. Using the element of surprise, she pushed him on the cot. Consumed with anger, she unleashed a sting of blows worthy of a professional boxer. In a matter of seconds, Cocantin's cheeks were bruised, his eyes blackened, his forehead battened and his nose smashed. She then fled. Blinded by his own blood, Cocantin courageously garnered al his strength to raise himself from the bed. Seeking to follow her, the temporarily blind Cocantin bumped his head on the cell door that the Baronne had closed and bolted behind her. The battered detective fell unconscious on the cell's flagstones.

Noting that Belles-Mirettes was no longer in her cell, the Baronne released Louchard. The two Raiders found the laboratory. There the Baronne grabbed the phone. She hoped that there was still time to contact Paris. After some anxious moments, she reached the operator.

"Passy 01-28," she feverishly stated into the instrument. In a few seconds, a voice answered.

"Who's calling me?"

"Hello! Bébert, it's the Baronne. Belles-Mirettes betrayed you. She told Judex everything. She's coming with him tonight to the Rue du Docteur-Pelet."

"Are you sure?" asked the voice of *N'a-qu'un-Chasse*.

"Absolutely."

"Thank you for that information," Bébert said unemotionally before erupting in a laugh. "Don't fret! I shall prepare a reception for them! It shall be a big surprise!"

IV. The Wounded

At 10 o'clock, Judex's car stopped at the intersection of the Rue du Docteur-Pelet and the Avenue de Billancourt. Prepared for any eventuality, Baptiste remained in the vehicle as Judex and Belles-Mirettes alighted. Hidden behind a tree, a young man observed them. Leaving his hiding place, he advanced towards them. It was Roger following his brother's orders. Jacques de Trémeuse related the events that had unfolded at the Chateau Rouge.

"Now we can proceed," decided Judex.

Having shifted her loyalty to Judex, Belles-Mirettes was visibly anxious to play her designated role. Her new master explained the plan.

"Mademoiselle will ring the doorbell. Once the door is opened, we shall rush in with guns and capture the ringleader. Once he's incapacitated, we'll take him to the car and depart for the Chateau Rouge. There we shall settle accounts with him."

"Understood," said Roger. "What if this criminal resists?"

"I can render him unconscious without doing any harm," claimed Judex.

"Let's do it!" declared Roger.

"Come, sirs," urged Belles-Mirettes, "I'm even more anxious than you to finish this!"

She directed the two brothers to the corner of the Avenue de Billancourt opposite 21 Rue du Docteur-Pelet. The house had a decrepit appearance. A weather-beaten sign with faded letters indicated that a wine merchant had once lived there. The ground floor of the residence had decaying shutters covering the windows. There was no light visible in the upper floor, but the skylights of the attic glimmered faintly.

"He's here," explained Belles-Mirettes. "He has several residences spread throughout the four corners of Paris. He's always in the garret when he's here. He has a small chamber there consisting of a table, a chair and a closet. There's no bed. He's installed a mechanism that allows him to open the front door from up there. Once he lets you in, you have to wait for a special signal.

"Both of you must remain hidden behind this kiosk. If he sees you with me, he won't open the door and will probably escape. He's rumored to have the power to pass through walls. I must ring the doorbell alone. Then you can follow me into the house. The rest I'll leave to you."

"Very well!" approved Judex. He was convinced that the key to the mystery was within his grasp. He would pay any price to obtain it.

Placing her hands in her pockets, Belles-Mirettes resumed the attitude of an elegant Apache. Walking towards the den of *N'a-qu'un-Chasse*, she was confident. The mastermind would open the door even though he could see from his observatory that the Baronne wasn't with her. For their part, the concealed Judex and Roger closely observed 21 Rue du Docteur-Pelet as they tightly grasped their guns. They were ready to strike once the door opened.

The moment of decision was at hand. If the operation succeeded, the Secret Raiders would become little better than a headless corpse once their leader was apprehended.

Belles-Mirettes was less than two meters away from the weathered-beaten door whose upper portion consisted of a broken window. She raised her head to make sure that *N'a-qu'un-Chasse* could see her and then rang the doorbell. Suddenly the light in the attic was extinguished. The young woman opened the door. Two detonations resounded followed by thick smoke gushing through the entrance. Belles-Mirettes screamed.

Waving her hands in the air, she fell backward into the arms of Roger who had rushed forward with Judex. The unfortunate woman had been shot in both the shoulder and the chest. Jumping through the door, he spotted a booby trap consisting of a smoking double-barreled rifle. Located in the front corridor, it had been positioned on an easel. The mechanism must have been rigged to fire once Belles-Mirettes opened the door.

Roger carried the bleeding Belles-Mirettes back to the car. Judex quickly rejoined him there.

"*N'a-qu'un-Chasse* was prepared," said Judex. "It's useless to search the house. He's either already fled or has some inaccessible hiding place inside. Further pursuit will just allow him to taunt us and possibly even kill us. The neighborhood will also become aroused. We must flee. You told me that Dr. Howey had returned to Paris yesterday morning?"

"Yes, brother," confirmed Roger.

"He's two blocks from here. Let's take our wounded friend to him. It's better that we confide in a doctor known to us."

People from the neighboring house opened their doors. They were attracted by the two gunshots.

Judex issued orders to Baptiste: "Rue du Lamp." The car started up immediately.

Two minutes later the vehicle parked in front of a small house from the Louis XVI period. It was constructed in the middle of a garden surrounded by a wall. Its overall structure was vaguely similar to the house at 21 Rue du Docteur-Pelet.

"An odd coincidence," commented Judex who never overlooked a detail. He rang the bell next to the wide gate in the wall. No one answered even though lights shined on the first floor. Judex tried again. No one came. At the third try, a side door on the ground floor opened.

"Who's there?"

"Count de Trémeuse."

"My dear friend!" replied an astonished Dr. Howey. "I'll be there in a moment." A few seconds later, he opened the gate. "Forgive me. I was outside enjoying the night air in the back of my garden. I'm alone. The servants have the night off. My dear Comte, how can I be of service?"

"I have an injured patient."

"Injured!"

"Yes, the patient in my car. We were passing the Rue du Docteur-Pelet and saw the poor unfortunate lying on the ground. We immediately decided to help."

"You did well, my friends," concluded Howey. "Come inside."

Holding Belles-Mirettes in his arms, Roger followed Howey into his office. There Roger gently deposited her on a couch. Following them, Judex scanned the room with a critical eye.

Howey examined Belles-Mirettes in her masculine attire.

"This patient is a woman!" said Howey.

"A woman!" repeated Jacques de Trémeuse feigning surprise.

" Yes," resumed the doctor while continuing his examination. "Two bullet wounds. One skimmed the shoulder. A minor injury. The other penetrated the middle of the chest. Not much hemorrhaging. I shall probe the wound to determine the exact path taken by the bullet."

Calmly Howey opened a closet filled with shelves cluttered with surgical instruments. At that moment Belles-Mirettes opened her eyes. She gazed around the room. Recognizing Judex and Roger, she smiled.

"You're here. I'm not afraid."

"Comte, place her on the operating table," said Howey holding instruments he had removed from the cabinet.

"Don't let him touch me!" yelled Belles-Mirettes. White as a ghost, she rose from the couch. Raising her arm, she pointed an accusing finger at Howey who had become deathly pale.

"I know his voice! He's *N'a-qu'un-Chasse!*"

Exhausted by her exertion, Belle-Mirettes fell unconscious into Roger's arms.

Judex leaped at the doctor. However, Howey dodged the Count and jumped into the closet. A hidden spring caused the wall of shelves to pivot forward revealing a stairway that led below. Howey ran down it. Following him through the subterranean passage, Judex found his progress blocked by a metal barrier that had lowered from the ceiling once Howey had passed by.

Returning upstairs to the doctor's office, Judex addressed his brother.

"Howey is the evil spirit. We no longer fight in the shadows, but in the light. You will take this unfortunate woman to Dr. Rambert's. Then go to the Chateau Rouge and see how Cocantin managing."

"What about you?" asked Roger.

Judex pulled out his pistol to verify that it was fully loaded.

"I'm staying here."

Part Nine: The Papers of Dr. Howey

I. The Bianchini Dossier

Judex had remained at Dr. Howey's house to search for clues that could help in the campaign against the Secret Raiders. Jacques de Trémeuse wasn't acting instinctively. By remaining in the house, he coldly reasoned that there wasn't any risk of a renewed attack from his enemy. The sudden flight of the mastermind indicated that he had been totally unprepared to battle Judex in this house. Frightened by the consequence of the revelation of his identity, the criminal had only sought to secure his personal safety. Doubtlessly, *N'a-qu'un-Chasse* was already planning a fearsome revenge. However, Judex predicted that his nemesis would reinitiate hostilities only after he had marshaled his forces. Therefore, there was time to search the residence. Remaining on his guard against a possible trap like the one encountered in the Rue Musset, Judex began a meticulous search of Howey's office.

Beside the secret passage through which Howey had escaped, the only other exits were a door leading to the antechamber and a wide window opening out on the garden. Inspecting the passageway in the closet, Judex concluded that it was impossible to raise the barrier.

His attention focused on a desk with a rather large locked drawer. Using a small hook from his ring of skeleton keys, Judex opened the drawer in the wink of an eye. It contained an appointment book for the last year and an album of photographs. The Comte's keen eye immediately noticed that the dimensions of the drawer's interior seemed smaller than those of its exterior. Immediately he concluded that the drawer had a false bottom. Without wasting time to find a mechanism to open the false bottom, he pulled out the drill that he had used effectively to escape the trap at Baronne's house. Cutting through the false bottom, he made a hole large enough for his hand to pass through. Reaching inside he didn't find the papers that he expected.

Instead he removed a small key for an ordinary clock. Attached to the key was a label that bore this inscription:

B 45 X .9.1.22

The Comte wondered what these esoteric characters meant. Clearly the key was important enough for Dr. Howey to hide it. Spotting a large wooden clock in a corner of the room, he decided to see if the key opened its face. Standing on a chair, Judex discovered that the key was too small for the lock. Disappointed, he was about to search the other rooms starting with the antechamber. Suddenly a series of chimes erupted announcing it was 11 o'clock. The noise led the Comte to a Louis XVI wall-clock barely visible in a shadowy corner. Its silent pendulum rhythmically swung back and forth.

The hands on the clock indicated 3 minutes after 11. Beside the two normal holes in a clock's face, Judex discovered a third hole obscured by the Roman numeral eight. Without hesitation, he placed a key in the third hole. On the first turn, a clap sounded. A part of the wooden base beneath the pendulum opened revealing a secret compartment with a height of 50 centimeters and a length of 18 centimeters. Inside was a pile of carefully stocked files. Convinced that he had discovered valuable documents, Judex grabbed a file.

In case of the return of the leader of the Secret Raiders, Judex positioned himself in a corner of the room that allowed him to view the door, the window and the secret passage in the closet. Holding his pistol, he flipped through Dr. Howey's papers. They constituted the operational plans of the Secret Raiders in France for the next few months.

Every matter was detailed with extreme care. The goal of each operation, the nature of the secret to be stolen, was described. There was an estimation of the profits to be made. The victims to be robbed were described in detail. Their relatives, their habits and even their personalities were fully documented. There were geographical layouts of the locations in which the crimes were to be committed. The personnel assigned to each illegal operation was named. Each operative was listed alongside detailed instructions of their assigned tasks.

How tragic that all the planning in these documents wasn't put to a good cause, thought Jacques de Trémeuse. *This work of criminal mobilization was a true masterpiece of organization and methodology! This Howey was capable of great things. I never fully appreciated his genius. Why did such a gifted man chose such an abominable path! Was it money! He could have accumulated it through honorable means. In any case, the tremendous toil to which he was committed, along with the different identities that he undertook, couldn't have left him the time to spend the loot he has stockpiled. The man has been leading a double, a triple, even a quadruple life! Is he motivated by an addiction to crime? Is he enraptured by an infamous delight in evil and sadism? Primrose was right to call him an evil spirit!*

Thanks to these files, I shall be able to frustrate the Secret Raiders' plans. I can warn the victims that this gang threatens from the shadows. I shall book no delay in bringing Howey to justice. Since I have nothing more to do here, I must make sure that the tragically wounded girl recovers and continues along the road to redemption.

Assembling the papers of the absconding doctor on the table, the Count was ready to tie them together in a package when he received a shock. On the cover of a file were two words: BIANCHINI DOSSIER.

"Bianchini!" shouted Judex. Could this be the brave man who had earlier prevented his family's impoverishment, but arrived too late to forestall his father's suicide? While leafing through the papers in the file, he recalled the early drama that led him to assume the role of a self-appointed judge.

One evening, Madame de Trémeuse mother took her two sons in front of a bed containing the corpse of their father. She made them both swear an oath of vengeance. The grieving wife explained how her husband had been financially ruined by the schemes of a banker named Favraux. The next day an honest big man named Bianchini visited. This big engineer had been sent by Monsieur de Trémeuse to locate an African mine with a valuable lode. Arriving in Paris after dodging assassins that Favraux had put on his trail, Bianchini brought to the widow and the two boys a new and inexhaustible fortune.

For several years, Bianchini had lived in South America managing another mine that he had discovered earlier for Judex's father. As a reward for that discovery, he been made joint owner of the mine by Judex's father. A campaign of sabotage by Favraux had temporarily compromised that mine's operations and prevented it from relieving the financial misfortunes of the Trémeuse family. After the discovery of the African mine, Bianchini had been able to make the South American mine fully operational again. Although Judex's mother had made him joint owner of the more profitable African mine, Bianchini preferred to stay in South America since he had purchased a home there for his family.

As joint owner of the South American and African mines, Bianchini's relations had been most cordial. Misfortune had befallen him with the speed of lighting. Almost simultaneously, he had lost both his wife and his two young daughters. Beset by grief, he had sold his mining interests to the Trémeuse family. From that moment, there had been no further word of him.

Now the name of the man to whom Jacques de Trémeuse was eternally grateful had surfaced in Dr. Howey's papers. Was this a coincidence? In order to determine the truth, Judex examined the file. Judex discovered a newspaper advertisement in the file.

French engineer residing in the Americas for 30 years, seeks to find two young girls, age 17 and 20, in France. Relay any information to this address: M. Bianchini, Hotel Crillon, Paris.

The dossier contained a second advertisement in the same vein.

M. Bianchini, Hotel Crillon, Paris, offers 50,000 francs to whomever can locate his two daughters, Maria and Clara Bianchini, respectively 17 and 20 years old today. Both vanished 16 years ago.

There wasn't any shadow of a doubt. This Bianchini seeking his two children was the same man that had earlier saved the fortune of the Trémeuse family. Judex remembered certain details that his mother had told him. Bianchini was in France when he had abruptly been called back to America. He had been forced to leave his sick wife and his two young daughters in Paris. Within a few weeks, Madame Bianchini had succumbed fatally to a lingering disease. Some days later, Bianchini's governess and secretary had left with the children under the pretext that they were returning them to their father. They completely disappeared. A long and laborious search by police departments around the world had failed to yield any results.

Then Bianchini had dropped out of sight. With a sublime persistence, he devoted his time and money to find the children. He couldn't resign himself to the possibility that they were dead. He stubbornly clung to the belief that they would be found some day.

Deeply moved, Judex looked at the two newspaper ads that he had found in the files of the Secret Raiders. Better than any narrative, they showed the horrible ordeal that this worthy man had suffered. Therefore, Judex was no longer fighting to save a nameless mass of victims from the depredations for the Secret Raiders. He was now seeking to avenge a great wrong done to a loyal friend of his father. This was the repayment of a sacred debt.

Placing the two clippings to the side, Jacques de Trémeuse continued to study the dossier. It contained several handwritten pages in code. Possibly the sheet of strange symbols found in the secret drawer was the key to this code. A deep secret must hidden in these words composed of numbers and weirdly assembled letters. Perhaps the chief of the Secret Raiders, more fortunate than the wretched father, had found the two girls and intended to claimed the reward. Worse yet, perhaps he intended to use the two girls to extort a large ransom from Bianchini. Judex would have to rush to the Hotel Crillon and warn his father's friend.

The Comte wished he could decipher the pages written in code. Feverishly putting all the items back into the folder, he noticed a card pinned to the inside cover. His exertions caused the card to become detached and fall to the ground. Retrieving it, the Comte put the card under the lamp. He was stunned by what he read. His face became extremely pale. The mystery had become unexpectedly clear.

Clara Bianchini - Belles-Mirettes
Maria Bianchini - Primrose Milton, Chateau d'Arbois

Jacques de Trémeuse had material proof in his hands that Primrose and Belles-Mirettes were the daughters of Bianchini the engineer!

Although his life had been far from ordinary, Judex hesitated for a moment. This new development distressed him because of its connection to its past. This seemed the most extraordinary event in his entire adventures.

This is impossible, he thought. *It's crazy. Am I dreaming or hallucinating? Nevertheless, the document exists. The handwriting must be Howey's. It's neat and precise like his usual penmanship. This must be the truth! Howey would never have placed this note in the dossier unless it was absolutely true. These hieroglyphics that I can't decipher must describe the facts that preceded, accompanied and followed the theft of the two children. We must have them translated. My immediate priority is to inform Bianchini. As early as tomorrow, I shall check Belles-Mirettes in Rambert's nursing home. Next I shall go myself to the Hotel Crillon and put this dossier in the hands of our family's friend.*

Judex's eyes became clouded.

Primrose and Belles-Mirettes are both children of the same father. He's probably the most honest man that I ever met. One daughter is the embodiment of charm and purity. But the other! The tragic girl! Both are victims of the evil spirit! Why did Howey choose to manipulate them several years apart! One became the experienced accomplice progressively corrupted by hid shameful infamies, while the other is the unconscious instrument of his criminal stratagems. How was he able to discover the secret of the birth of these poor children? Could a third party have sold that information to the Secret Raiders? Or was Howey involved even earlier in this inexplicable conspiracy directed against the Bianchini family? Could he have been the instigator of the original kidnapping? Then why abandon one daughter and keep the other?

I must logically solve this mystery. How? By forcing Howey to speak. Where do I find him? How do I capture him?

These questions plagued Judex. Suddenly he heard the grating sound of the front gate opening. Had Howey returned? He placed Howey's files in the desk drawer. Turning off the lights, Judex pulled out his pistol and looked outside the window. He saw a feminine silhouette moving in the garden. She boldly approached the house without any effort at concealment. Judex had an uneasy feeling. He hid behind the thick drapes surrounding the window.

The woman entered the antechamber and walked into the doctor's office. She turned on the lights. The figure of Baronne d'Apremont was fully illuminated. Judex wondered how she had escaped the Chateau Rouge.

The Baronne was perplexed. The female Raider had thought that she had seen a light in the house. Where was Bébert? Has he fallen victim to Belles-Mirettes's betrayal?

Suddenly a ringing sound erupted in to the room. There was a large telephone on a table near the drapes. The communication device had two round receivers in order to allow more than one person to listen to the conversation. Both receivers was attached to the telephone by lengthy cords. The Baronne picked up one receiver. Without suspecting the hidden presence of the sworn enemy of the Secret Raiders, she answered it with a joyful smile.

"Hello! Bébert?"

There was a silence. The Baronne had turned her back on Judex still secreted behind the drapes. Taking advantage of the situation, Judex's hand stealthily moved to grab the other receiver and bring it to his ear.

"Is that you, Baronne?" asked Howey. "What are you doing there?"

"I was able to escape the Chateau Rouge?"

"Congratulations!"

"I'll tell you about it later. What happened here? I found your door open and the house empty."

"Don't worry about that. Return to the Rue Bergère. Tomorrow at 3 o'clock, come to the Pavillon de la Puerta in Les Buttes-Chaumont. I have an appointment there with my old friend, Bianchini. I'm counting on you to be there."

"Understood."

"Don't linger in my apartment. It may be unhealthy."

Judex replaced the receiver while the Baronne still had her back to him. She then hung up.

Judex had regained the trail of Bébert alias *N'a-qu'un-Chasse* and Dr. Howey. For the moment, that was sufficient. Motionless behind the drapes, he observed the Baronne.

How did she outwit Cocantin, Judex wondered, *and escape her prison cell? Clearly the brave Prosper has accumulated another blunder. Knowing him as well as I do, I shouldn't have left him alone at the Chateau Rouge. But I had no other choice. Someone had to remain there in my absence, and he was the only person available. He was so resolved to scrupulously follow orders that I couldn't imagine him risking a confrontation with the lady of the Rue Musset. What infernal trick did she use to overcome Cocantin and arrive here an hour after me? If Cocantin is unhurt, this may turn out to be a fortunate development. For if the Baronne hadn't come here, I wouldn't have discovered the Secret Raiders' current plan to move against Bianchini.*

As Judex had contemplated his course of action, the Baronne had followed her superior's advice by leaving the house. He had considered using his gun to inflict the supreme punishment on this criminal who so richly deserved it. However, Judex was too chivalrous to strike at a woman from the shadows.

Removing Howey's secret files from the drawer, Judex went outside

"Tomorrow at 3 o'clock, I shall be there!"

II. Cocantin's Suicide

Following his brother's instructions. Roger had transported Bells-Mirettes to Dr. Rambert's nursing home. The intern on duty had immediately attended to the injured woman. After a detailed examination, he had completely reassured Judex's brother. The injury of the shoulder was insignificant. As for the bullet that was lodged in the middle of her chest, it had been deflected by a button on her vest into a gap between two ribs without hitting any vital organs. The quick extraction of the bullet was relatively easy. As soon as she regained consciousness, Bells-Mirettes gave Roger a look of sincere gratitude. Invoking the name of Comte de Trémeuse, Roger asked the interne to keep a discreet silence regarding the woman's admission.

Returning to the car, Roger ordered Baptiste to take him to the Chateau-Rouge. Precisely at that same moment in the underground depths of the feudal castle, Prosper Cocantin regained consciousness.

"What a beating," was his first words. He felt as if he had received 100 lashes. "She was strong! That swine! I never had time to defend myself. I see stars. What determination! What fire! What muscles! She must have learned Swedish gymnastics and English boxing! Here's someone who doesn't need to perform Howey's exercises. She's not a woman. She's a Hercules!"

While each of his movements was full of aches and pains, he moved towards the door. It was locked.

Who can I call? he thought. *Judex isn't here and won't return for hours. Oh my face! It must look like marmalade. My eyes! I can scarcely open them. They must look like poached eggs.*

Cocantin went to the water jar and soaked his face.

This is the last straw. What will Judex say when he finds me here in place of the prisoner? He will believe that I succumbed to temptation and went from being Joseph rejecting Madame Potiphar to Samson accepting Delilah. His punishment will be to imprison me where Marguerite de Bourgogne expiated her sins.

It's an abomination! I'm innocent. I followed the voice of my conscience. I thought that I was preventing the suicide of that swine! She tricked me! She nearly bashed in my skull! My ears are humming! My nose! My poor nose! It's tragic!

Exhausted physically and morally, Cocantin was on the verge of a nervous breakdown.

He collapsed on the cot. For an hour, he remained motionless. Ironically the cot was impregnated with the Baronne's perfume that had once entranced the detective. Cocantin then experienced a fever accompanied by delirium.

He believed himself transported to the time of the Middle Ages. He was accused of being one of the lovers of Marguerite de Bourgogne. Furthermore, he was charged with having participated in the assassination of Philippe d'Aulnay during a dark orgy in the Tower of Nesle. His main accuser was Buridan, who now physically resembled the Comte de Trémeuse. In his nightmare, Cocantin learned the hard way that justice was swift in previous eras. Claiming his innocence, Cocantin pointed an accusing finger at Marguerite de Bourgogne, who greatly resembled Baronne d'Apremont. Also present were two officials dressed in modern clothes as a reflection of the incoherence of nightmares. Scarcely had he accused the true malefactor than two officials seized him and threw him into a pit.

"Liar, burn in Hell!" screamed the men in modern clothes.

Cocantin then suffered a gruesome hallucination that lizards were swarming all over him. An even worse delirium followed. He imagined his body swelling and growing until it burst the wall of the prison cell. He became a tremendous giant like the one appearing in illustrations from *Gulliver's Travels*. Then Cocantin heard the ferocious grating of teeth. Giant crocodiles were advancing towards him!

Surrounding him, the saurian predators performed a spectacular dance in the style of the *Théâtre du Châtelet*. Cocantin's nightmare then became a reptilian circus. The crocodiles retreated in order to yield center stage to a group of giant chameleons who entertained Cocantin by constantly shifting color. Further waves of reptilian monstrosities followed. There was a detachment of dragons and chimeras, succeeded by a procession of salamanders. Suddenly Cocantin was attacked by batrachians of all kinds. An army of frogs and toads leaped on him. Their cold paws stuck to his face and hands.

In a wink of an eye, the scene changed. The reptiles and batrachians vanished. From a hole in the ground rose the head of a boa constrictor. The detective found himself alone in the presence of the snake. With blazing eyes, the snake's head descended towards Cocantin. Stopping a meter in front of the terrified sleuth, the snake opened its jaws to vomit fire and smoke. At the same time, an awesome voice spoke.

"Cocantin, you're a traitor!"

The detective finally awoke. He believed that the voice belonged to Judex. Cocantin's greatest fear was that his patron and friend would never forgive him for letting the Baronne escaped. The sleuth viewed the atrocious dream as a warning that there was no clemency awaiting him. Due to his feverish delirium, as well as the tortures of hunger and thirst, Cocantin suffered from the delusion that he had been confined in the

Chateau Rouge for several days. He imagined that Judex had decreed a slow and lingering death as punishment for his blunders.

"Daisy!" he cried. "Why didn't I go with you to America! I can't endure this torment any longer! Napoléon survived for over five years in St. Helena because he had the hope of being rescued. I know too well that my days shall end miserably in this cell. Five minutes more here is too heavy a burden to bear. I shall take my own life.

"It is tragic. At my age, I had so many happy days ahead of me. When Daisy returned with her uncle's inheritance, fortune as well as love would have smiled on me.

"I must be resolute. I don't want this Judex to view my mortal remains and think that I shook in front of death. He must know how proudly I walked towards the great beyond. Yes, I must die. But how?"

The fever had given the director the Céléritas Agency a martyr's passion, but had weakened his imaginative faculties.

"Strangle myself. I don't have the strength. Bust my skull against the wall? My head already hurts too much. If only I had a knife or a gun."

He recalled a night that he recently passed at the opera.

"Yes, a gun as in Massenet's *Werther*. The curtain rises..."

Cocantin went no further in his theatrical reminiscences. He noticed on the table a piece of broken glass that Baronne d'Apremont used in her feigned suicide attempt.

"I know what to do! I'll cut my throat!" He grabbed one of the shards. His hand trembled.

"Courage, Prosper," he said as he rose the piece of glass to his throat. "Farewell, Daisy. Farewell, Licorice Kid. Judex, I forgive you. Baronne d'Apremont, I cursed you for all eternity!"

He felt his improvised weapon press against his flesh. Drops of blood fell to the floor.

"Already!" exclaimed Cocantin. He found it difficult to breathe. His legs buckled under him. Collapsing on the flagstones, he made a sublime statement.

"I never knew how easy it was to die!"

With great speed, Baptiste drove along the Mantes road to the Chateau Rouge. Illuminated by moonlight, the ancient fortress appeared before him. Stopping the car abruptly, Baptiste turned to Roger who was seated next to him.

"Those men on the road are signaling to us, sir."

Two agitated policemen walked up to the car. "You come from Paris?" abrasively asked one of them.

"Yes," replied Roger.

"Do you intent to give us a traffic ticket?" questioned Baptiste. Considering the enforcers of the law to be the bane of motorists, the chauffeur had no desire for a prolonged argument.

"It's not that!" replied the policeman.

"We want to know if you passed a gray car carrying a man and a woman. The vehicle was headed towards the capital."

"It's possible," acknowledged Baptiste. "We passed several cars, but I couldn't discern their color or their passengers."

"Do you want to question the people in the gray car?" asked Roger.

"Not exactly," said the first policeman.

His colleague, who hadn't spoken a word until now, gave a gruff and precise explanation of the situation.

A young man from this neighborhood was returning from Le Havre. His car was stopped by a man and a woman near the Chateau Rouge. At gunpoint, he was forced to leave the vehicle. The two bandits then entered the car and drove in the direction of Paris."

"Very strange," noted Roger fearing that something had happened at the Chateau Rouge. "Unfortunately, as my chauffeur explained, we can't help you."

"Thanks, anyway," said the second policeman. "You can leave," said the other.

"The prisoners must have escaped," said Baptiste as he drove towards the Chateau Rouge.

Roger didn't reply, although he shared the chauffeur's suspicion that the Baronne and Louchard were now free. After traveling hundreds of meters, Baptiste parked the car near the short zigzagging path that led to the ruins of the Chateau Rouge.

"Conceal the car on the road that bypasses the hill," ordered Roger as he left the car. "I'll join you there later. I may be a while."

As Baptiste disappeared into the night, Roger vigorously ascended the hill. Opening the flagstone, he descended the stairway into the subterranean depths. The pathways were still illuminated by electricity. In their haste, the Baronne and Louchard hadn't extinguished the lights. Primrose's fiancé went directly to the laboratory. Its door was open. He immediately noticed that a drawer containing several pistols was empty. There was no doubt that the Baronne and Louchard were the car thieves mentioned by the policeman.

Roger utilized the mirror to check the cells. Louchard's was empty. There was a lifeless body lying in the Baronne's cell. Roger recognized Cocantin.

"They murdered him'" exclaimed Judex's brother. He ran to the cell and unbolted the door. He heard Cocantin breathing through that large nose that could absorb air like a vacuum cleaner.

"He's alive!" shouted Roger kneeling next to the detective. Grabbing the half-filled pitcher or water from the table, he poured its entire contents into Cocantin's face. This brutal means of revival yielded immediate results. After his chest raised in a sigh of deep relaxation, his nostrils exhaled like the bellowing of an angry elephant. Like a character in a dramatic scene from one of Shakespeare's plays, the bruised Cocantin furiously shouted.

"Blood! Blood! Blood!"

"Where the blazes do you see blood?" said Roger scanning the cell.

"It's everywhere!"

"What?"

"My body's covered with it!"

"That's water!"

"Water!"

"I used it to revive you."

"I tell you it's blood!" screamed Cocantin. "I cut my throat!"

Roger couldn't see any sign of injury on Cocantin's neck.

"You're crazy!"

"I cut my throat with a piece of glass!"

"You only cut your finger!" Roger pointed to a wound on Cocantin's finger.

"Is it possible?" asked Cocantin as his hand sought his carotid artery. His throat's skin was undamaged. There wasn't even a scrape.

"It's good to be alive," admitted Cocantin. "Even when I have a crime on my conscience."

"A crime?"

"A crime..." repeated Roger.

"Yes, my friend. I committed a crime. I permitted the Baronne to escape. That female snake beat me to a pulp! Judex would never forgive me. I wanted to die. I tried to kill myself. "

"Calm down." consoled Roger. "I can't leave you here in this state. You're returning to Paris with me. On the drive back, you can tell me in detail how the Baronne escaped."

"I don't want to talk about it." Leaning on Roger, Cocantin rose from the ground. The detective was on the verge of tears. "I can't face Judex. He'll curse me. I should never have been born!"

Roger smiled. "I think my brother will simply tell you to forget your ordeal by taking a ride in the country."

III. *At Les Buttes-Chaumont*

The Pavilion de la Puebla in Les Buttes-Chaumont was a restaurant which preserved the best traditions of the French cuisine. Seated at a table was a middle-aged man with a beard and graying hair. He was located next to a window that gave him an excellent view of the outside. Ignoring the glass filled with an excellent wine of 1874 vintage, his two eyes gazed through the window. Was he waiting impatiently for someone? O r was he just daydreaming? No clues could be gleamed from his expressionless face. It revealed nothing of his soul.

Suddenly he quivered. A hand had grasped his shoulder firmly. Dressed in a black hat and cloak like a Spaniard, a tall man with an elegant profile stood before the bearded man. The eyes of the newcomer gazed into those of the bearded man. The cloaked man spoke incisively with an implied threat.

"I have something to say to you."

The disguised chief of the Secret Raiders wanted to flee from the speaker. However, the hand of the intruder weighed on the master criminal's shoulder. Almost rendered speechless by the dominating eyes, *N'a-qu'un-Chasse* finally stammered a reply.

"Speak, Monsieur de Trémeuse."

Releasing his enemy's shoulder, Judex took a seat next to him. "This is no longer a matter of Comte de Trémeuse and or Dr. Howey. This is a duel between Judex and *N'a-qu'un-Chasse.*"

"True!" said *N'a-qu'un-Chasse* recovering his composure.

"You weren't expecting me."

"No. How did you arrive without attracting my attention?"

"I came through the store used to deliver supplies to the restaurant. I avoided making a sound as you looked outside for signs of your accomplice, Baronne d'Apremont, and your once and future victim, Monsieur Bianchini."

N'a-qu'un-Chasse became pale under his false beard. Marshalling his nerves. he replied arrogantly.

"Monsieur Judex, you are admirably informed. I do indeed have an appointment with both the Baronne and Bianchini. How does that concern you?"

"Listen well. You are the man who through an abominable subterfuge entered my home to spread despair. I intend to expose you as chief of the Secret Raiders."

"Really?"

"You shall learn that there is a price to pay for declaring war on me."

N'a-qu'un-Chasse drank from his glass before replying. "My dear Judex, you're wrong to continue this fight against me. Return to your private matters, and leave me to mine. Accept this condition, and we can declare a truce. Promise not to attack me and my agents, and I will leave you and your family alone. Do you agree?"

"No."

"Why?"

"It would be an act of cowardice to allow your crimes to continue."

"In that case, I must oppose you. There are two policemen patrolling outside. There will pass this restaurant. Denounce me to them and our struggle will end."

Judex didn't reply.

"You won't denounce me," continued *N'a-qu'un-Chasse*. Laughter escaped his lips. "You don't want the law interfering in your affairs, Judex. Better to leave Favraux resting soundly in the small cemetery of Les Sablons than have him resurrected."

The erstwhile Professor of Physical Culture drained the remainder of his glass. Jacques de

Trémeuse looked at him with an expression of pure contempt.

"I'm unaware of the circumstances that transformed you into a criminal, but I don't need that knowledge to settle accounts. Nothing you can do will persuade me to back down.

You can never be swayed from the evil existence you've chosen. You may not fear me, but I don't fear you. I have the strength to defeat you!"

"We shall see!"

"Do you accept the challenge?"

"I accept it!"

"From this moment onward," declared Judex, "you and I will be engaged in a merciless war in the shadows."

"So be it!"

"Whenever you commit a crime. I'll be there to prevent it."

"You will need a lot of preparation."

"Actually not much. I warn you, Bébert alias N'a-qu'un-Chasse, on the first opportunity, I will ruthlessly cut you down like a mad dog."

"Why not do that now?"

"I'm no assassin."

"It's true. You naively believe yourself to be a judge."

Judex rose from the table.

"There is no more to be said, " added *N'a-qu'un-Chasse*, "unless you desire to attend my meeting with the Baronne and Bianchini."

'"It's unnecessary. I know exactly what you're going to tell them."

"*Au revoir*, Monsieur Judex."

"We'll be seeing each other very soon, Monsieur *N'a-qu'un-Chasse*."

"One final word. Guard your father-law, your wife and your precious little Jean. I haven't finished with them."

"Monster!"

"This is war."

"It is war!" confirmed Jacques de Trémeuse. He gazed down on the leader of the Secret Raiders with a combination of defiance and contempt. Turning away, he exited the restaurant.

N'a-qu'un-Chasse summoned the manager of the restaurant. "Monsieur Chevy, another drink please. I'm a little depressed and need to raise my spirits. "

After crossing towards the parking lot near the restaurant, Judex stopped near the entrance facing the Rue de Rébeval. Concealed behind a group of trees, he scrutinized the cars entering the lot. A chauffeur-driven car arrived. In the back seat of the roofless vehicle was a fifty-year old man whose hair was tinged with gray. His clean-shaven face indicated a deep sadness and a big heart. The vehicle stopped. Judex hesitated for an instance. Removing his hat, he stepped up to the car.

"Excuse me, are you Monsieur Bianchini?"

"Yes."

"Do you recognize me?"

"No."

"I am Comte Jacques de Trémeuse. You saved my family from bankruptcy."

"*Mon Dieu*! Of course, I remember you!"

"My friend, it's necessary that we talk."

"Please come into the car."

Judex did so.

"I'm so happy to see you, Monsieur Jacques," said Bianchini.

"Tell your driver to take us to the Hotel Crillon," insisted Judex.

"I can't. I have an important appointment."

"With an individual that claims to be able to restore your two daughters."

"How do you know that?"

"It's a long story, but there's no need to meet with this man."

"Why?"

"Because someone else knows where to find your lost children."

"Who?"

"Me."

"Are you telling me the truth?"

"You have my word. I'm repaying the debt that my mother, my brother and I owe you!"

"Will I be able to see my daughters?"

"Yes."

"When?"

"In a few hours."

"Driver, take us to the Hotel Crillon."

During the trip, Judex briefed Bianchini on the situation. The Comte removed from his pockets certain items taken from Howey's dossier.

When the former explorer read the card containing the true names and the current identities of his two daughters, he reacted strongly.

"This is the handwriting of Friedrichs, the kidnapper who stole my children!"

Judex gazed up at the sky from the car. He looked like a man thanking God with ardent fervor.

"The truth is becoming clear. Today we have taken a giant step forward!"

45 Centimes. Tous les Jeudis.

LA
NOUVELLE MISSION
DE
JUDEX

Par ARTHUR BERNÉDE et Louis FEUILLADE

LES DEUX DESTINÉES

Part Ten: The Two Destinies

I. An Important Development

"Are you happy, Jacques?"

"Yes, my darling, I'm very happy," asserted Judex just before returning the kisses of Comtesse de Trémeuse. Clasping the hands of his beloved wife, he continued to speak with great emotion.

"I feel stronger now that I know Providence is with us. God has allowed me to unmask the traitor Howey who had succeeded in infiltrating our home. Our Good Lord has also allowed me to return to Bianchini, my family's generous benefactor, his two children."

"The last event was marvelous," emphasized Jacqueline.

"I wished you could have witnessed it," added Judex. "Bianchini became filled with indescribable joy upon learning that Belles-Mirettes and Primrose were his daughters. When we reached the Hotel Crillon, I had finished my account of the subsequent lives of his two daughters. He seized my hands. 'Let's go first to the one who's wounded,' he said. 'She's more in need of my love.' I took him to the nursing home where Belles-Mirettes was. We must stop referring to her by that alias, but use her real name, Clara. Her injuries had been more moral than physical. Upon seeing me, she was so full of gratitude that I knew her reformation was complete. Gradually I revealed that her father was still alive. I also told how good and generous he is. At that moment the door open. Bianchini ran to his daughter. I don't know what was said during their long interview because I left them alone. However, I saw tears streaming down their faces. I firmly believe that the angel of redemption has completed the transformation of the former Secret Raider."

"You are truly the Knight of Justice!" exclaimed Jacqueline. "As always, you acted nobly. Heaven has rewarded your efforts."

"Clara was discharged from the clinic this morning. She had been galvanized by the unforeseen happiness resulting from the reunion with her father. She's currently with him in the caretaker's cottage outside the Chateau de Joyeuse. They're waiting to meet Primrose and Monsieur Milton. This is a delicate situation, and it would require a tactful woman like you to arrange this meeting. You must be the bearer of good tidings."

"I shall do my best to be worthy of such responsibility," replied Jacqueline.

"I shall send you Milton and his foster daughter. Once you've explained the situation to them, signal from the window. I will then send Bianchini into the Chateau to be reunited with his younger daughter."

"Understood."

Jacques de Trémeuse was going to leave, but he then noticed a look of concern on the Comtesse's face.

"Do you want to say something, darling?" asked Jacques.

"You read me well," Jacqueline replied. "A question troubles me. You may think that I'm being nervous and apprehensive..."

"Please speak freely."

"Having been frustrated by you, won't an enraged Dr. Howey seek vengeance?"

"It's quite likely," admitted Judex with complete honesty, "but I'm certain that he'll be decimated by me. I say this without foolish pride. I overcame this evil spirit when he hid in the darkness. I shall combat him much better now that I know his face and name. Despite my confidence, we still must take precautions. When confronting such unscrupulous opponents, we can't afford a single mistake. More than ever, I remain vigilant. Since I swore to finish this criminal once and for all, I won't miss a single opportunity to remove him from this earth. If he shows himself here, I won't hesitate to slay him! Howey will pay for his crimes!"

"Then I'm completely assured," said a smiling Jacqueline while Judex moved away.

For a moment, Jacqueline felt free of anxiety for the first time since she arrived at the Chateau de Joyeuse. However, a deafening fear gradually invaded her. She immediately fought it. This despair quickly dissipated. However, she realized that her tranquility would only return when Judex "crushed the head of the snake." In her role as a loving spouse and a mother, she prayed for the triumph of her champion of justice over this evil spirit.

"I know he shall triumph. God is with him. God is with us."

After Milton and Primrose entered the large parlor, they noticed that the Comtesse's face had become radiant due to the sublime confidence generated by her love for her husband.

Upon seeing the American and his foster daughter, her eyes reflected sadness and the smile disappeared from her lips. Comtesse de Trémeuse understood the difficulty of her task. These two individuals loved each other as father and daughter. Their bond was as strong as that of a parent and child linked by blood. Now a stranger would assert his paternal rights to break that exquisite bond.

"My friends," said Jacqueline, "I'm obliged to inform you of an important development."

Seated close to the Comtesse on a couch, Primrose was visibly upset.

My dear child," emphasized Jacqueline, "you have nothing to fear. I have happy news to relate. Dear Primrose, you have often expressed pity towards parentless children. You have wondered what would have been your fate if you had fallen into the hands of people far less scrupulous than Monsieur Milton."

"Quite true," acknowledged Primrose. "I thank Heaven that Monsieur Milton found me."

"My little girl," murmured Milton. Due to the Comtesse's tone, he was convinced that the conversation would inevitably take a very serious turn.

"My sweet Primrose," continued Jacqueline, "although you were spared this misfortune. Other abandoned children have not. Instead of experiencing the light and joy of your life, they only know shame and misery. It's monstrous!"

"Yes, monstrous!" repeated Primrose with tearful eyes.

"I can't hide from you an event that will change your life forever," revealed Jacqueline.

"God has revealed to my husband the secret of your birth."

Upon hearing these words, Milton and Primrose linked their hand together, they feared that the Comtesse's revelations would lead to their separation.

"You have nothing to fear, my friends," assured Jacqueline. "The Good Lord that shapes our destinies wouldn't want to break two hearts such as yours. This news that I impart must not disrupt your mutual devotion. Providence wanted, my dear Primrose, that we rediscovered simultaneously your father and one of my family's oldest friends. The man who will embrace you as his daughter is Monsieur Robert Bianchini, who courageously saved the compromised finances of my family in the remote corners of the world. He is a man of incomparable integrity and tenacity. You can be proud of him and trust him thoroughly. You are worthy of each other."

Jacqueline then turned to an attentive James Milton. "Rest at ease, my friend, Monsieur is anxious to thank you for raising his daughter. He would never challenge your affection for his child. He merely asks to be allowed to love her as you love her. The debt he owes you forbids him from acting selfishly. He's already your friend. Before long, you shall be his. Of that I'm sure. "

"That is my firmest desire," replied the American.

Primrose was effusive in her response to the Countess. "Madame, thank you. You have assured me that no ulterior motives exist in this reunion. My present happiness remains intact, and this development will only augment it. I shall now have two fathers."

Primrose became deathly pale before continuing. "Madame, may I ask a question?"

"Of course, my dear."

"Why didn't you mention my mother?"

"My poor dear!" said the Comtesse. "I must diminish your joy. Many years ago, your mother died. You were only a year old when the Good Lord called her to him. I had intended for your father to console you with the knowledge that she loved you very much."

As two tears rolled down Primrose's face, Jacqueline continued. "Your sorrow at your maternal loss shall be compensated by the existence of your sister."

"A sister!" exclaimed Primrose.

"Yes," confirmed Jacqueline, "but she suffered. She wasn't raised by a man as noble as James Milton. She didn't have the advantages of a moral upbringing. I won't say anything more for now. Know only that the child was deeply unfortunate. If her wounded soul heals due to the loving care currently surrounding her, it's important that she forget the abyss that nearly swallowed her. This will be your task, dear Primrose, more than the ours. When you meet her, you will notice that you physically resemble her."

"A sister," murmured Primrose in ecstasy. "I will love her!"

Jacqueline smiled. "Now that I've told you the important news, I can call your relatives. They've been patiently waiting nearby."

"They are here!" exclaimed Roger's fiancée. "Both of them!"

The Comtesse approached the bay window. She made the signal.

Discreetly James Milton started to leave, but Primrose gracefully held his arm.

"You must remain, Father. I want you here. You shall always be close to my heart."

"My child! My daughter!" Milton kissed her.

Outside the window, they could see Robert Bianchini approaching. His handsome face reflected his noble character. Seeing him, both Milton and Primrose realized that Jacqueline had accurately described the engineer.

After a charming embrace between Bianchini and his daughter, Primrose took her father by the hand and brought him towards Milton, who had observed the touching scene without any anxiety.

"This is my other father," said Primrose in her angelically musical voice.

Looking into each other's eyes, the two men shook hands. An unalterable friendship had been sealed.

"Her heart is big enough to love us both." said Milton.

A young lady who seemed to be dressed in morning clothes then appeared. Pale and trembling, Belles-Mirettes was leaning on Judex's arm with Roger behind her.

"Your elder sister," Bianchini simply said.

Belles-Mirettes clumsily advanced forward as if she was ready to faint. Although both Judex and her father had promised not to disclose the details of her criminal life to Primrose, Belles-Mirettes still feared that her sister would reject her. Belles-Mirettes even imagined that her involvement with the Secret Raiders would cause Primrose to feel undying hatred. An awkward scene then followed.

Although her first inclination was to embrace her sister, Primrose suddenly stopped. She stared at Belles-Mirettes.

"Maybe I'm mistaken," said Primrose, "but it's seem to me..." A brief silence followed after which she advanced closer towards Belles-Mirettes. "I've seen you before."

Judex intervened. "No, Primrose. You couldn't have met Clara because she lived abroad."

Once this pious lie dissipated her confusion, Primrose reacted quickly. Opening her arms wide, she hugged and kissed her sister. Emotionally exhausted, a crying Belles-Mirettes nearly fell to the ground.

"And now, my dear friends," announced Bianchini, "it's time for you to hear the story of my life. Remain also, my friends. You too should hear this."

As everyone gathered around Bianchini, Judex took Roger aside. This was their first conversation since Roger had returned from the Chateau Rouge.

"What happened to Cocantin?" asked Judex.

"I found him in Baronne d'Apremont's cell," explained Roger. "He was knocked half-senseless. Pretending to commit suicide, the Baronne had tricked him into entering her cell where she overpowered him."

"And Louchard?"

"He escaped."

"Naturally, That outlaw doesn't worry me much. I'm concerned about this cursed Baronne. We aren't yet at the end of our task."

"I feared as much."

"What about Cocantin?"

"I took him home. He's recovering under the care of his housekeeper, Madame Robbes. She shall nurse his bruises."

"Did you tell him our address?"

"I was as close-mouthed as a clam."

"We must continue to be on our guard. The Secret Raiders will only surrender once we hold a knife to their throats. Let's listen to Bianchini."

II. The Prospector's Story

Seated between his two daughters, the old friend of the Trémeuse family prepared to relate the story of his life. After a brief silence during which he regained his composure, he looked at Primrose and Clara successively before beginning.

"The mine of Santa Juana, which the Trémeuse family had entrusted me with the management as well as a substantial share of the profits, assured me a considerable fortune to support my wife and my two lovely children, Clara and Maria. For five lovely years, I had the pure happiness of marriage. I assumed that those dream-like years would never end, Alas! I was to be confronted with a terrible wakening, I paid a price to experience Heaven on earth. Forgive me, my dear children, but my pain becomes unbearable when I remember the loss of your incomparable mother.

"Every year that I returned alone to France to confer with the Trémeuse family, my dear Rosita pleaded with me to take her and our two babies there with me. Eventually I relented. How many times have I regretted that decision? Yet I must not linger on past mistakes. I'm sure your mother has forgiven me in Heaven just as you, my daughters, must forgive me on earth."

"Yes, Father," said the two young women as they kissed their father.

"After a pleasant voyage, we arrived in Paris without incident. As was my habit, I registered at the Great Palace Hotel. My young secretary, Carl Friedrichs, accompanied us.

He supposedly was of Polish origin, but I now believe that he was German. He skillfully concealed his identity to enter my service. His papers indicated that he was a recently naturalized American. He had extremely correct manners, and his conversation indicated that he had been superbly educated. Besides being fluent in several languages, he was extremely well versed in medicine. After serving me superbly for nearly a year, he had completely gained my trust.

"The governess of my children, Mademoiselle Elsa Rhener, claimed to be Swiss. Appearing to be as devoted as Friedrichs, she also traveled with us to Paris. I was living in an atmosphere of false security. I never suspected that Friedrichs and Elsa were engaged in a secret intrigue prompted more by mutual greed than love. They were preparing to betray me in a horrible manner."

Monsieur Bianchini paused. In the vast parlor of the Chateau de Joyeuse, one could hear a pin drop. Captivated by these revelations, Primrose and Clara moved closer to their father. His voice became harsh and painful.

"Within a few days, my wife, who had always been in good health, fell ill. Thanks to the intervention of an excellent physician, Dr. Martens, the process of the malady was quickly halted. My precious Rosita began her convalescence. I then received a cablegram from South America. Agents of my competitors had taken advantage of my absence and bribed several of my workers in Santa Juana. A campaign of sabotage had begun. Its purpose was to gain control of the concession owned jointly by me and the Trémeuse family. I consulted Dr. Martens. He declared that Rosita wasn't healthy enough to travel. Since the patient was recovering nicely, nothing prevented me from taking the trip alone. The doctor additionally assured me that he would watch over Rosita. I accept all responsibility for what subsequently happened. I decided to leave for San Juana alone."

The former prospector than spoke directly to his daughters.

"When I announced my decision to your mother, her eyes filled with tears. Despite her sorrow, she refused to act selfishly. I'll never forget her words: 'My beloved, you don't have the right to remain here not only because our fortunes and those of our children are at stake, but also because we are sworn to protect the interests of the Trémeuse family.' This noble declaration was in accord with the principles that had been the rule of all my life. It removed any doubts about my decision.

"After giving precise instructions, I entrusted my funds in Paris to Friedrichs, my secretary; and I left my two daughters under the care of their governess, Elsa. Both of them swore to me that I could count on them. I then kissed Rosita for the last time. After that final embrace, I had the fervent hope that I would return to Paris after a few weeks in Santa Juana.

"Alas, my darlings, I never saw your mother again. I didn't find you again until after 16 years of a terrible ordeal. I owe that reunion to Comte de Trémeuse, an admirable man whom you must love and revere.

221

Tears streaming down his cheeks, Bianchini stood up. Judex went up to him.

"You can sit down and continue your story, my friend."

"Not before I thank you in front of everyone! Not before I hug my old friend's son, the hero who has rescued me from despair."

The embrace of these two men was a scene of unforgettable emotion. Returning to his seat between his two daughters, Bianchini resumed his narrative.

"Now, my friends, the frightful facts that I shall relate were unearthed by me after my return to France. Almost immediately after my departure, my wife's health inexplicably worsened. Dr. Martens ordered Friedrichs and Elsa to wire me the terrible news. However, this is an example of the cablegrams that I received up to day my poor Rosita die."

Pulling a document of his pocket, Bianchini showed it to his companions.

Madame Bianchini in satisfactory health. Children well. Yours truly,

Friedrichs

"What actually happened?" shouted Robert Bianchini. "I shall tell you, and you will judge fully their crime. Friedrichs and Elsa betrayed me. Attracted by the large sum that I left at their disposal in my checking account, they had resolved to embezzle all my funds in Paris. Their plan had begun with the poisoning of my wife! The murder was performed slowly and skillfully in order not to awaken the suspicions of the doctor or the police. They pretended to lavish affection on my wife by standing constant vigil at her bedside. They played their infamous roles so well that my cherished Rosita in her deathbed begged these butchers to watch over our children.

"Once my poor wife was buried in the cemetery, Friedrichs and Elsa vacated the Great Palace Hotel. Pretending that they had received from me instructions to take the two children to South America, they were viewed sympathetically by the hotel staff. Probably in order to make themselves less easy to trace, they jettisoned my precious Maria, my younger daughter, the next day. Luckily you were found by an honorable man whose name I shall bless until my dying day. Becoming your foster father, he christened you with the pretty name of Primrose. You must maintain that name.

"Based on your account of your early life, Clara, you were entrusted to Elsa. She decided to disappear with you. Perhaps she was fleeing Friedrichs. He may have wanted to kill his female accomplice in order to avoid having to divide my fortune with her. He was already a formidable criminal. Information from the Comte de Trémeuse concerning his activities as Dr. Howey show that he has grown more dangerous with time. With Machiavellian skillfulness and infernal audacity, this monster, implemented a long-range plan. He disappeared for several years. We don't know what he did during this period or what aliases he hid himself under. Doubtlessly, he worked in the shadows to erect the frightening organization known as the Secret Raiders. Eventually he used his agents to locate Clara.

As for me, I was in the South American desert where the Santa Juana mine was located. Waiting impatiently for Rosita's first letter, I received this communication from Paris. Bianchini showed everyone a letter.

Monsieur Bianchini,

I must regretfully inform you of Madame Bianchini's death. Regarding myself, I have removed all your funds from the banks, and have no desire to return them to you. In order to protect myself, I'm keeping your two daughters as hostages. When I'm no longer in any danger of prosecution, I'll allow you to purchase their freedom. Hopefully you'll be willing to pay the ransom. Please accept my gratitude for all the trust that you placed in me. I mean that sincerely.

Your former secretary,

FRIEDRICHS

P. S. It's useless to try to find me. You'll just be wasting your time and money.

"At first, I thought the letter was an abominable trick, a hellish ruse by the saboteurs to lure me back to France. Having wired to Paris, I received the confirmation of my poor Rosita's death and the departure of my children in the custody of my secretary and their governess. I now knew the letter was the truth.

"I won't relate my grief. You already understand it. Especially you, my dear James. The Comte de Trémeuse has told me about the tragic accident that claimed your wife and daughter.

"For 24 hours, I nearly went mad. I wandered crying in despair. I considered suicide. Only the thought that my children still needed me swayed my hand. I couldn't abandon you to a horrible fate. I swore to devote the rest of my life searching for you.

"I was able to find an intelligent young man to take over my responsibilities at the mine. Loyal to the Trémeuse family, my successor never betrayed the trust that I placed in him.

"I left for France to begin my investigation. I was able to ascertain the truth about my wife's death, but, despite my best efforts, it was impossible to locate my children. The passage of trail had erased the criminals' trail. Friedrichs had taken amble precautions to assure his safety. For 16 years, I continued my search. Hopeful leads would wither in the face of harsh reality. Finally the infamous Friedrichs under another name answered my newspaper advertisements. What would have happened if I hadn't been warned by Jacques of Trémeuse? Probably the master criminal would have used Clara as a hostage in a campaign of extortion.

"My narrative has reached the present. We must forget our hardships and live happily under the same roof. We must use our new found unity to heal our souls."

"And to punish the guilty!" energetically added Judex.

Everyone crowded around Bianchini.

"Dear friend," declared Jacqueline, "you and your two daughters are our guests. I don't know what your plans are, but our house shall always be yours."

"My plans are very simple," replied a smiling Bianchini. "Live happily and not disrupt anyone's else happiness. My intention is to buy a residence next to yours. Not only will I be close to my dear friends, the Trémeuse family, but Primrose would be able to divide her attention between both her fathers."

"Monsieur Bianchini. there's another person that you must take into account," said James Milton pointing to Roger. "This handsome young man must be part of any arrangement."

"I know!" said the former prospector placing Primrose's hand insides Roger's. "These two hearts ask only to be one."

Hearing those words, Clara Bianchini felt lonely. Jacqueline approached her.

"Mademoiselle, would you like to see the room that we've prepared for you."

"Yes. .. Madame," gratefully stammered Bianchini's daughter.

Divinely compassionate, Comtesse de Trémeuse detected that the young girl was in the throes of repentance.

"Let me help you, my child, to forget your former life. If you feel moments of anxiety or uncertainty, I'm here to advise you. Please accept me as your confidante and friend."

"Thank you, Madame," said a deeply moved Clara.

"Come also, Primrose," said Jacqueline.

The trio of ladies departed with an aura of joy capable of dissipating any gloom.

"Look at them!" said Judex to Bianchini and Milton. "They look so happy! The first part of my mission is finished! Now I shall attack the other!"

Scarcely had he finished this sentence than a footman appeared in the doorway.

"Monsieur Prosper Cocantin requests the Comte to do him the honor of being received."

Judex moved towards his brother. "Cocantin here! How could he have discovered our new address?"

"I have no idea?" replied Roger.

Jacques de Trémeuse then gave his orders to the servant. "Take Monsieur Cocantin to my study."

"Pleases excuse me, my friends," said Judex. "It's absolutely necessary that I see this man.

As he was leaving, the Comte muttered under his breath.

"I hope that jackass hasn't made another blunder!"

III. At the Chateau de Joyeuse

"Ah! There you are!" said Judex as he entered his office to greet the director of the Céléritas Agency. The conversation quickly grew bitter. "Look what you've done. You let my prisoners escape! An agent of the Secret Raiders couldn't have done any better! Obviously..."

He didn't get a chance to finish his sentence. Prosper Cocantin fell on his knees.

"No, Judex don't say that!"

With his two black eyes, bruised forehead, battered cheeks and his swollen nose, the private detective was a pitiful figure.

"Call me a fool, an idiot, a moron, a simpleton, a king of fools! Reproach me bitterly! Sentence me to many years of imprisonment in the Chateau Rouge! I shall willingly accept any punishment that you decree for my inconceivable stupidity, but don't accuse me of betraying you! If you believe me capable of such a felony, I would end my own life! I already tried!"

"Stand up!" commanded Jacques de Trémeuse. He had been surprised by the passion with which Cocantin had regretted his blunders.

Painfully Prosper rose on his stiffened legs.

"Yes, Judex, I wanted to die."

"Really?"

"I swear it's true. In the Chateau Rouge, this swine of a Baronne attacked me by surprise in her cell. You see the brutal results of her assault. Realizing that I had been once again duped by this she-devil and deserved your disdain, I was convinced that you wouldn't forgive me for putting you and your loved one in jeopardy once more. Terrified by the consequences of my action, I bade farewell to Daisy and the Licorice Kid, and then tried to cut my throat with a piece of broken glass!"

Cocantin had pronounced this last sentence with comical intensity that Judex forgave him completely.

"Undoubtedly, the glass must have been of poor quality," said a smiling Judex.

"Not at all," protested Cocantin. "It was excellent quality. I lost consciousness a little too quickly. I started to implement my plan, but I didn't finish it."

"You always do that!" concluded the Comte de Trémeuse. "Cocantin, you're not suited to be a detective!"

"You're quite right, my seigneur!"

"I recommend that you give up running your uncle Ribaudet's firm."

"When Daisy returns from America with her uncle's inheritance, I shall close down the Céléritas Agency. However, I don't want to be a husband that lives off his wife. What could I do? I know. I'll become a movie director!"

"It's settled!" approved Judex. "Only I advise that you find a movie producer to finance your films. You don't want to risk your own money."

"Thank you for the sound advice!" said Cocantin. "I shall certainly follow it, my master!"

"How did you discover my whereabouts?" asked the Comte de Trémeuse.

"It was easy. After your brother dropped me off, I didn't go to my third floor apartment. I hid behind the door and overhead Roger tell your chauffeur to take him to the Chateau de Joyeuse. Once my housekeeper saw to my injuries, I wanted to vindicate myself in your eyes. I had never heard of the Chateau de Joyeuse, but it didn't take me long to locate it.

"My heart beat heavily when I entered this abode. I was afraid that you wouldn't receive me. However, my fear proved baseless. You agreed to see me. I read your merciful verdict in your eyes. You are a man of infinite nobility who shall always have my affection, my respect and my devotion."

"Cocantin," declared Judex, "you indicated your intent to be a movie director."

"Yes."

"I have a better idea. Become a lawyer instead. Your eloquence makes you more qualified than anyone else to argue that the guilty should be punished and the innocent acquitted."

"I'll consider your suggestion," said the private detective with grave seriousness.

Judex resumed his authoritative tone. "You shall remain here for the foreseeable future.""I promise to follow your order."

"You shall be installed in an isolated cottage at the end of the courtyard. Meals will be brought to you regularly. The house has a library that should provide you with ample diversions. You shall not leave until I command."

"Understood, my master."

"I have a simple question. Are you sure that no one followed you here?"

"Have faith in Cocantin! You can sleep soundly on this matter."

"We shall see," said Judex skeptically.

In a corner of the large parlor of the Chateau de Joyeuse, Primrose and Roger were alone. The lovers had much to say to one another. They spoke of the radiant future before them. They were confident that Judex would have the power to deflect the influence of the evil spirit. Certain that no storm would darken their blue sky, they no longer doubted their dream of happiness.

228

Judex, Jacqueline, Milton, Bianchini and Clara all took advantage of the serene splendor of the night from the magnificent terrace which permitted a moonlight view of the winding Seine River. They all had an intimate and charming conversation against this enchanting setting. Bianchini noticed that his older daughter had left her seat next to him. Having observed Clara fighting her melancholy during the evening, he wasn't too worried. Assuming she had gone to her room, he entered the main house to look for her. Inside the parlor, he saw Clara hidden behind a screen tearfully spying on Roger and Primrose. Absorbed in viewing this sweet romance, she didn't notice her father approach her. Taking a deep breath, she extended her hands in a gesture of despair. Robert Bianchini realized that Clara was distressed by her sister's romance.

"Clara," whispered Bianchini. Without saying a word, the sobbing woman rested her head against her father's shoulder. "Why are you crying, my daughter?"

"Because I will never be as happy as them."

"Why do you say that?"

"I remember what I was?"

"Think about what your future rather than your past. When Comte de Trémeuse tactfully revealed the circumstances in which he found you, I was greatly distressed. The Comte explained how the reawakening of your better instincts had been spontaneously sincere. To be completely reassured, I needed to meet you. I saw an unfortunate who had left a life of darkness to live openly in the light. Just as a miracle can heal a bodily injury, so can it heal an injury to the soul. You became morally cleansed once you chose the side of truth and justice. It isn't your fault that your life was the opposite. You were a victim of chance. You and your sister followed two different destinies. Yet all divergent paths, no matter how remote, can still meet. You were returned to me at the same time. If Primrose is destiny's favorite, you're already enshrined in my heart."

"Father, I never expected to hear those words. You have dispersed my doubts. Leaning on you, I feel strong. Looking at you, I understand myself better. Loving you, I have found happiness. You have opened for me new horizons. Until this day, I lived among the selfishly corrupt. It was impossible to distinguish between good and evil because I didn't understand the former. You have shown me the true nature of goodness through your love. Close to you, I breathe a new atmosphere. I am surrounded by your benevolence. I hear only just words. I see only honest faces. I never suspected this happiness existed. I was unworthy of this happiness, but your paternal love has given it to me."

"You were dead, my child, but now you are resurrected!"

N'a-qu'un-Chasse had accepted the challenge that Judex had delivered in the restaurant. Just as the Knight of Justice had decided to decimate the leader of the Secret Raiders, the evil genius had sworn to thoroughly crush his opponent. He had learned the location of Judex's sanctuary by having Cocantin followed. The master criminal was convinced that Jacques de Trémeuse could not expose the Raiders to the police without revealing the illegalities of his own mysterious exploits. Still the master criminal didn't delude himself. Vanquishing Judex wouldn't be easy. All the traps woven against him had backfired on his enemies. It was as if he was invulnerable.

I shall succeed in defeating Judex, thought *N'a-qu'un-Chasse*, *I can unearth any secret. I've eluded all the human bloodhounds who picked up my trail. I've mocked all the police forces of the world.*

Nevertheless this situation is intolerable. If it does not change, it may be my downfall. Compared to Judex, I am the superior man who stops at nothing to attain his goal. I shall destroy everyone he loves!

Alone in a secret den, the mastermind grinned ferociously as he rubbed his hands together. At the end of an hour of uninterrupted meditation with his face frozen with that expression, he rose from his chair. His grimace had been replaced by a slight smile. His eyes widened as if they were seeing a desirable vision of the future. Opening a closet containing a simple wardrobe, he chose a suit that could belong to a modest tradesman. Donning a wig and a beard of dark hair laced with gray, he went out on the street to hail a cab. It took him to the residence of Baronne d'Apremont on the Rue Bergère.

Received by the bogus harem girl who had attended Cocantin, *N'a-qu'un-Chasse* made himself known to here through a secret gesture known only to members of the Secret Raiders. He assumed a harsh domineering demeanor.

"Is the Baronne here?"

"Yes, Monsieur."

Without waiting for any further explanation, Howey entered a room in which the Baronne was packing suitcases with clothes.

"My dear, are you going on a trip?"

The Baronne was visibly uneasy. Despite his disguise, she recognized her superior.

"I ask you again," repeated an angry *N'a-qu'un-Chasse*, "are you going on a trip?"

"Why not?" bravely replied the Baronne.

"Without my permission?" emphasized *N'a-qu'un-Chasse*.

"It seems, my dear, that you're becoming a little too concerned with your own comfort. "

"I've had enough!" shouted the temptress.

"I don't understand you!" taunted the criminal doctor.

"You want me to spell it out? I'm certain that the Secret Raiders are doomed."

" Really?"

"Since this Judex has entered this fight against us, success has eluded us. It's only by a miracle that I was able to escape from his hands. I don't want to test my luck against him again. We don't have the power to defend ourselves against this man. I'm retreating from the battlefield."

"Weak woman that you are," laughed *N'a-qu'un-Chasse*. "Alfred de Musset was right!"

"What are you trying to say?"

"Nothing that need concern you. I don't have time for literary discussions. Baronne, you will do me the pleasure to leave here your luggage. You shall come with me, I have further need of your services."

"And if I refuse?"

"You won't"

"How can you be sure?"

"Because you wouldn't dare."

The Baronne could repress her terror.

N'a-qu'un-Chasse became threatening.

"Did you really imagine that I would allow you to leave? Even if you had succeeded in fleeing here, you wouldn't have gone far. You aren't aware of all those I've punished in the past for betrayal or cowardice. No matter what you think about the dangers threatening us, the Secret Raiders remain all powerful! I, *N'a-qu'un-Chasse*, its leader, have an arm long enough to find you no matter where you hide! Others before you have learned that lesson to their detriment! Don't even think about violating your oath of loyalty to me!"

Doubtless the words of the criminal doctor took their toll. The Baronne's arrogance was replaced by meek submission. Dominated completely by the evil genius, she realized that her eternal destiny was to be his slave.

"You're right." she admitted. "I was mad. I'll obey you."

"Good!" exclaimed *N'a-qu'un-Chasse*. "Judex has provoked me into a merciless duel to the death. I pick up the gauntlet and enter the fray without delay. One of us shall fall. It shall be him. In order to dispose of Judex, Baronne, I have conceived a method far deadlier than knives or bullets. To implement it, I need your talents. En route, I shall tell you what must be done. You won't be unhappy with the role that I've assigned you in the climax of this drama. Once we succeed, you'll have no regrets about remaining in the Secret Raiders."

The two fiendish conspirators left the house in the Rue Bergère. What scheme had germinated in the mind of the sinister being known as Dr. Howey?

Around 11 o'clock in the evening. everyone slept in the Chateau de Joyeuse. As the moon hid behind the clouds, a mysterious shadow entered the courtyard. It was a woman dressed in a skintight black leotard that covered her entire body. Her head was covered by a hood with an oval opening for her face. Baronne d'Apremont was executing the orders of her master.

Part Eleven: The Involuntary Crime

I. The Sick Child

"Mama?"

"Yes, Jean?"

"I want to take a walk,"

"Come with me to the medical center. The fresh air will do you good."

"Yes, Mama?

Taking the small child by the hand, the Comtesse left the Chateau de Joyeuse. They walked 500 meters from the magnificent property where Judex had taken his family. Jean left his mother's side to run after a butterfly flying among the flowers. Soon the child shifted his attention to a bird that flew out of its nest in the tree. The boy took a deep breath to enjoy the reinvigorating air. He relished the sunlight and the lush foliage.

Jacqueline contemplated her son with pride. Her son has thoroughly charmed her. Yet Jacqueline was too intelligent to exclusively idolize her son. Like all children, he had his flaws. As Jacqueline stove to cultivate his talents, she sought to correct his shortcomings. This task became easier with each passing day.

Her son filled her with wonder. She knew that he would inevitably become more independent. However, Jacqueline was convinced that he would never ignore her. She would always be his confidante.

While Jacqueline mused about him, Jean looked around to make sure that no one could overhear them. He then whispered a question.

"Mama, will I be able to see Grandpa soon?"

"Yes, darling." Jacqueline trembled nervously as she answered. Her father was the biggest burden in her life.

Jean was silent for a moment. The boy behaved as if he wanted to say something, but wouldn't dare.

"What's wrong, darling?" asked Jacqueline.

"Nothing, Mama."

"Only a moment ago, you were running and playing. Now you're sad."

"Nothing's wrong, Mama."

Jacqueline pressed her hand against Jean's forehead. It was burning.

"This is strange," noted the banker's daughter. "You're not in pain?"

"No, Mama, I feel good... very good."

"My little one!"

"Why isn't Grandpa Favraux with us?"

"I already told you."

"Because bad men want to kill him."

'"That's the reason."

Jean objected with the implacable logic of a child. "Why can't these bad men be thrown in jail?"

"A young boy of your age doesn't ask such questions." Jacqueline was becoming increasing unnerved by this conversation.

"Why?" insisted the child.

"Because you'll only understand such things when you're big."

"When will I be big?"

"In a few years."

"Then when these bad men try to kill Grandpa, I'll beat them up." His eyes sparkled as new ideas entered his brain. "Is Grandpa scared all the time when he's hiding?"

"Jean, don't talk about such things. Don't even think them. These matters are very troubling, and talking about them makes me worry."

"Oh! I won't say anything more. I don't want you to worry, Mama."

Stepping on his toes, Jean stretched his arms towards his mother. Hugging him, she showered his forehead with kisses.

"Are you happy now?" asked Jacqueline lowering her son the ground.

"Yes, Mama," replied Jean. He ran after a dragonfly that flew around his head.

Some minutes later, Jacqueline and her son arrived at the Sainte-Marguerite Clinic. It was a large well-ventilated building. Recently built, it was located near the town's entrance. Wishing to honor the memory of her late husband, the Dowager Comtesse de Trémeuse had generously funded social works in the communities where she maintained residences. Under the direction of the talented Dr. Verchin, this clinic provided essential health services to the surrounding population. Examinations and medicines was given with no charge.

During her stay at the Chateau de Joyeuse, Jacqueline visited the health facility frequently. Believing that donating money to the poor wasn't enough, she believed in working at the clinic as a volunteer. Thanks to her kind and generous nature, she became quickly popular among the local inhabitants. Upon her entrance into the waiting room, there was a spontaneous outburst of applause. They were about to give Jacqueline a standing ovation, but she restrained them.

"Remain seated, my friends, I thank you for your warm welcome."

Walking among the patients, she charmed them with her kindness. Dr. Verchin joined her to provide advice when necessary. Jean tried to become friends with the pale and thin children who had been brought here by their mothers.

"Who is this man?" asked Jacqueline of Dr. Verchin.

She was referring to an old man seated on a bench. This bent figure gazed at the ground with eyes that mirrored an approaching death.

"He's a vagrant who arrived in town yesterday," explained Verchin. "Since he appeared to be in poor health, I let him spend the night here. I questioned him this morning, but he replied incoherently. I suspect that he's mentally deficient. Now that he's installed here, I dare not discharge him."

237

"Let him stay here," recommended the Comtesse. "Are you in pain, my friend?"

Raising his head, the elderly man raised his head to reveal an unshaven face ravaged by suffering. His wild appearance frightened Jean, who instinctively tugged on his mother's dress.

The derelict's dead eyes lit up with a mysterious flame. He seized Jacqueline's arm.

"Thank you, my good lady," he hoarsely muttered. The vagrant then extended his callous hand towards Jean. "Bless you, my child!"

"Doctor, please do all you can for him," said Jacqueline.

Scarcely had she pronounced those words, then Jean became pale and fell to the ground. The terrified Comtesse grabbed the child and brought him into the doctor's office. She spread out his small body on a couch. The doctor was about to attempt to revive the child, when Jean's eyes opened. He raised his hands to his head. "Mama, I'm sick. Very sick." He then closed his eyes as if the light was hurting them.

"Doctor," asked an anguished Jacqueline, "this isn't serious? Is it?"

"I hope not," responded Verchin. "He was unquestionably already weak, and the vagrant may just have frightened him into fainting. While he rests here, call the Chateau and summon your chauffeur. Once he drives you home, confine your son to his bed. I'll give you some medicine. Every hour, give Jean a spoonful. Around 5 o'clock tonight, I'll drop by to see him."

"Mon Dieu!" sighed the Comtesse.

"Madame, I assure you that there is no cause for alarm. I don't foresee any dangerous complications. Look how calmly he rests. He has no fever. Don't torment yourself. I expect that by tomorrow at the latest, he'll be fully recovered."

"Thank you, Doctor."

Despite the doctor's optimism, Jacqueline was far from assured. Despite her misgivings, she acted as Verchin prescribed. Upon returning, she informed her husband. Once Jean

238

had been placed in bed, he soon reopened his eyes and kissed his parents. After taking a dose of the medicine, the young boy asked for his toys. He was granted his desire. After playing with his Punch and Judy dolls, he quickly wearied. As his head rested on the pillow, he raised his hands to his head.

"Mama, it still hurts."

Some moments later, a burning fever appeared. The Comtesse feared that it was meningitis. Immediately she summoned Verchin. After an extremely thorough examination, he told Jean's mother that her suspicions were baseless. Nevertheless, he was perplexed.

"If the fever doesn't subside by morning, don't hesitate to call me. However, I still see no immediate danger. Children often run high temperatures without any fearful complications. Give him the medicine regularly. I remain convinced that he'll be much better in the morning."

The Comtesse de Trémeuse remained faithfully at her son's bedside. Despite being consumed with worry, no tears flowed from her eyes. Her hand calmly held the hand of the sleeping child. She remained motionless with her mouth half-opened in a mute invocation.

How strange Jacqueline looks, thought Judex. *I have only seen her like that once before. It was when she handed her father's letter to Primrose at La Frondaie when both of them were hypnotized by Howey. These are the same symptoms. Could that evil hypnotist have discovered our refuge? If he had done so, he would have manipulated Primrose into committing a new crime.*

The child's sickness defies explanation. Dr. Verchin can't make a firm diagnosis. This mystery disturbs me.

Are you, Howey, the demon that I'm fighting? Are you the Satan that I must defeat? Calling upon all his powers of self-control, Judex approached his beloved wife.

"Jacqueline, my love," he gently said.

The young woman's hands trembled. Her eyes opened wide in terror.

"I'm afraid."

"Why?" asked her husband.

"I fear for my child, for you and all that we love."

"That needed to be said. When did Jean show signs of being ill?"

"This morning when we visited the clinic."

"Did he sleep well last night?"

"Superbly."

"Did any stranger come here since yesterday?"

"None."

"What about Primrose?"

"She hasn't seen him for days."

"Did you meet any strangers on your way to the clinic?"

"No, but Jean wasn't as cheerful as usual. He kept asking me about his grandfather."

"Who did you talk to at the clinic?"

"Dr. Verchin and his patients."

"Were any of the patients new?"

"There was an old vagrant who had recently come here. Verchin kindly let him stay at the clinic."

"Did this vagrant talk to you?"

"He thank me effusively. It was a very touching scene."

"Did he speak to Jean?"

"Yes. He raised his hand over Jean to bless him." Jacqueline began to glimpse the truth. "That's when Jean fainted!"

Judex didn't ask any more questions. He had the information necessary for his investigation.

"Jacqueline," said Jacques de Trémeuse, "you must stay by your son's bedside. Once you feel the need to sleep, you shall call our devoted servant, Martine, who has already proven her loyalty and intelligence. She will take your place next to our child. Only ask her for help and no one else."

"It's the evil spirit again!" said a terrified Comtesse.

"Yes," bluntly stated Jacques de Trémeuse, "but don't panic. We have enough time to forestall this threat. I give you my word that no harm shall befall Jean."

"I know that you'll protect him!"

"Focus on caring for Jean, and leave the rest to me. *Au revoir*, my darling!"

"You're leaving?"

"Don't worry. I have an important task to perform. I won't be far away. More than ever, I shall be vigilant, I shall not fail to protect you."

After kissing Jean's forehead, Judex embraced his admirable spouse.

"Courage, Jacqueline. We're near the end of our ordeal. The last act of the drama is about to be performed."

"Will the guilty be punished and the good rewarded?"

"So it shall be!" The Comte de Trémeuse once more embraced his destiny as the Knight of Justice!

II. In the Shadow of the Night

Upon leaving the Chateau de Joyeuse, Judex drove immediately to the Sainte-Marguerite clinic. He asked Dr. Verchin about the vagrant. The doctor revealed that the derelict had disappeared shortly after the Comtesse's visit. Judex had no doubt about what had transpired. The vagrant was another of Howey's identities. The master criminal had used this disguise to exercise his malign powers.

Having confirmed his suspicions, Judex returned to the Chateau. As always, he took time to reflect before acting. Once he had decided on a plan, he summoned his brother.

"Roger, Dr. Howey has resumed hostilities. Thanks to Cocantin's carelessness, that wretch has discovered our sanctuary and attacked Jean. Either through poison or some other means beyond my comprehension, Howey has unleashed a mysterious malady that defies Dr. Verchin's science. I don't believe that this criminal is solely committing a vindictive crime of vengeance. He must intend to take advantage of Jacqueline's anguish in order to mercilessly blackmail all of us. Consequently, the monster will make his presence known. We must stand our ground and fight him. He won't delay in launching his assault. It might even happen tonight. Our course of action is clear. We must prepare. Howey doesn't know that we're ready to launch a counterattack. There's no need to inform Milton, Bianchini or his two daughters. Not that I'm afraid that they would accidently leak our plans. We may be surrounded by an invisible cloud of spies watching our movements. It's essential that Howey be ignorant of our preparations. Therefore, there is no need to take others into our confidence.

"Howey's goal must be to learn the new location of Jacqueline's father. Once Favraux is in his power, the Secret Raiders can launch their extortion campaign."

"How could Howey know that Favraux didn't die last year?" asked Roger.

"Remember Captain Martelli?"

"He's the smuggler whom you bribed to betray Diana Monti."

"He knows not only that Favraux lives, but also that I'm Judex. He even knew about my links to Kerjean and Cocantin."

"You think he told Howey all this?"

"Either him or one of his crew. Anyone of those cut-throats could have betrayed my secrets for the right price."

"What about that mysterious letter you found over a week ago? The one that extorted you to become Judex again. Could Howey have been behind it?"

"Originally I thought that the author was our mother, but now I'm not so sure. Perhaps Howey sought to trick me into revealing the location of Jacqueline's father by vainly searching for the letter's author. I briefly suspected Favraux of being the author, but I dismissed that possibility. Howey may have hoped that I would have taken my suspicions more seriously and visited my father-in-law. That would have led Howey straight to Favraux."

"Since you didn't act on the letter, Howey then hypnotized our loved ones in an effort to expose Favraux's whereabouts. One thing confuses me."

"What's that?"

"Howey was able to mesmerize Primrose into revealing your visit to the Basket-Maker's Cabin. He has the same power over Jacqueline. Why doesn't he just simply compel her to reveal Favraux's location?"

"Howey has known Primrose for a much longer period than Jacqueline. He must have a firmer control over your fiancée. With my wife, his power is more limited. He can only force Jacqueline to perform involuntary actions. Unlike Primrose, he can't compel my beloved to reveal important information."

"Could Howey have any influence over Jean?"

"That monster has had ample opportunity to corrupt Jean. However, the failed kidnapping demonstrates that Howey couldn't force Jean to leave La Frondaie. Our foe's only option was to use Primrose to abduct Jean."

"Still Howey may have established some mental rapport. I've heard of hypnotists who can compel a man to become ill or even die. Howey's mesmerism could be the source of Jean's illness."

"Therefore, we must prevent Howey from ever coming into contact with Jean again. There can be no margin for error."

"What do we do about Cocantin?" asked Roger.

"Cocantin," said Jacques de Trémeuse with an enigmatic smile, "shall be kept in reserve to play a very important role."

"What! After all his blunders!"

"Yet all his blunders have inadvertently benefited us."

"*Mon Dieu*! You're absolutely right!"

"Was it fate? Or because I responded appropriately to those blunders? For the moment, let's defer that discussion. Despite his faults, Prosper Cocantin has been useful to us. It would be a mistake to deprive us of his services. Perhaps he will make the ultimate blunder that secures our victory. This may appear paradoxical, my dear Roger, but my reasoning is based on a logical examination of recent events."

"I want to believe you, but I still have doubts."

"Cocantin is destined to play a very big role in the coming battle."

"I trust your judgment, Jacques."

"Now let's talk about what we have to do. As I mentioned earlier, it's essential that Howey never suspect that we've figured out his new scheme. To ensure this goal, there must be no alteration in the daily operations of the Chateau de Joyeuse. Furthermore, Howey must be convinced that we have relaxed our safeguards.

"Here's how we'll proceed, After the dinner, while I check with Jacqueline on Jean's condition, you'll take our guests for a walk in the park. Upon your return to the house, you will organize a game of bridge that lasts until 11 o'clock. When everyone goes to bed, you will return to the ground floor billiards room. Extinguish the lights and leave a window partially opened. Listen for sounds from outside. If you hear a whistle blown three times, then the battle would be engaged. Don't hesitate to intervene. I'll need reinforcements.

"As for me, I shall pretend to leave with Baptiste in our car. However, I will secretly return. If the evil spirit tries once more to invade our abode, this shall be the last time he attacks us. I shall destroy him."

Assisted by Martine, Jacqueline had remained at Jean's bedside. The medicine prescribed by Dr. Verchin seemed to have improved the young patient's condition. Anxious to give his guests an update on his stepson's status, Jacques de Trémeuse presided over a cordial dinner. Near the end of the meal, a footman arrived to notify the Comte de Trémeuse of a telephone call. Making his excuses, Judex took the call. Upon his return, he informed everyone nonchalantly that he most leave for Paris immediately on an urgent matter. Asking Roger to entertain the guests, the Comte changed into a modest suit. Around 9 o'clock, he left that evening in a limousine piloted by Baptiste. Passing through Sainte-Germaine, the car took the Paris road to the coast of Monte Cristo. The car then turned around and took a steep road that passed by the former property of Alexandre Dumas, the immortal creator of the Three

Musketeers. Upon reaching Marly, the car passed through the forest and then maneuvered through a maze of roads. Eventually the car extinguished its lights as it parked at a side road close to the Chateau de Joyeuse.

Ready to confront the enemy, Judex left the car. He had changed from an ordinary suit into the black outfit that included his hat and cloak. Under the camouflage of the opaque shadows of the stormy night, he walked towards the Chateau de Joyeuse. Instead of entering through the principal entrance, he went to the high wall that bordered the courtyard. He scrutinized it thoroughly. His discerning eye noticed recent footprints near a section of the wall.

I wasn't mistaken, he thought. *My enemy has been inside the grounds of my house for at least 15 minutes.*

Judex located a section of the wall that was easy to climb. He nimbly scaled up the barrier. Once over the side, his feet landed in the courtyard. He listened momentarily. No noise reached his ears. Reaching a clump of trees, he looked at the windows of the Chateau de Joyeuse. Intense lights shined in some of the windows. He circled around the house like a hunter seeking to surprise his prey in the darkness. Taking a deep breath, he concealed himself behind a tree. He heard footsteps. Waiting patiently, his vigilance bore fruit. The sound of the footsteps was moving closer to him. Removing his pistol from his jacket pocket, he noticed a shadow advancing in his direction.

Jacques de Trémeuse was surprised. The figure moving forward wasn't Howey. The doctor was much thinner. The individual walked slowly. A hat covered his head, and his features were obscured by the raised collar of his coat. Judex followed the intruder as he moved closer to the Chateau.

Upon reaching the front steps, Judex leaped at his quarry. Judex grasped the other man by the shoulder.

"Who are you? What are you doing here?"

The intruder's hat fell to the ground. A face full of fright was exposed.

"Favraux!" exclaimed Judex harshly. "Why did you disobey my orders? You were to remain in hiding and avoid all contact with us!"

"Jacques, I couldn't fight any longer the desire to see my daughter and grandson. This morning, I was in the neighboring property where you had moved me and Kerjean. I saw my daughter passed by. She was carrying Jean. He was pale and unconscious. I couldn't communicate with you. The special telephone that links directly to the Chateau wasn't working. Without being seen, I watched your house. I saw the doctor arrive. Imagine my despair! I love my grandson deeply. He's the reason I reformed. He revived the goodness that had been buried inside my soul. A terrible idea consumed me. I feared that he was dying. I wanted to kiss him one more time before he perished. Kerjean prevented me from coming to the Chateau. Once he went to bed this evening, I left our residence."

Favraux's voice became extremely agitated.

"How is my grandson?"

"When I left tonight, his condition had greatly improved."

"Will you kiss him for me?"

Judex was filled with a deep pity for the man whose remorse had surpassed his crime.

"I'll do more than that! Come with me. I'll take you to Jean."

A terrible cry rose from the back of the courtyard. Judex rushed inside the house. Running up the stairs, he ran into Jacqueline's room. The loyal Martine stood guard at Jean's bedside. The child rested calmly. The fever had subsided.

"Where is my wife?" demanded Jacques de Trémeuse.

"She went outside 10 minutes ago," replied Martine.

"How could you let her do that?"

"Madame had fallen asleep on the armchair. She suddenly awoke. She had a horrible dream that Jean was going to die. In response to this horrible nightmare, Madame said that she was going to the chapel in the courtyard where the two of you had been married. She wanted to beg God to spare her son's life. I did all I could to dissuade her, but-"

Judex didn't listen any more. The cry that he heard outside came from the direction of the courtyard. Rushing outside, Judex blew on his whistle three times. Roger quickly ran from the house towards him.

"Brother! Jacqueline has been abducted by Howey! We need to save her!"

Running with his brother towards the chapel, Judex swore to crush this evil genius once and for all.

As for Favraux, he had vanished.

III. On the Chapel's Steps

Walking in the middle of the night towards the small chapel where a year earlier she had exchanged marriage vows with her spouse, Jacqueline de Trémeuse was responding to a gradual suggestion in her mind rather than an act of religious faith. Guided by an implacable will whose existence she hadn't even suspected, she had left the safety of the Chateau. The chapel was a small structure created in the Gothic style. Its graceful proportions gracefully harmonized with the surrounding landscape. Climbing the chapel's front steps, Jacqueline found the doors locked. Kneeling on one of the front steps, she began to pray aloud.

"My Lord, perhaps in your unfathomable will, you are testing our faith. Please don't strike at the innocent. Spare my child! You gave us an angel, don't take him away.

"Virgin Mary, you have known all the sufferings that a mother can endure. You of the Sacred Heart, intervene for me with your divine son. Save mine! More than ever, you shall be the most blessed of all women!

"Mercy! My Lord! Mercy!"

A sinister laughter erupted next to her.

"It isn't God whom you must beg for mercy! It is I!"

The voice was laced with mocking hatred. Upon hearing it, Jacqueline rose to her feet as if a supernatural force had plucked her from a dream into reality. A groan of horror erupted from her. Howey was there. His eyes blazed enigmatically at her.

"You!" shouted Jacqueline.

"Yes, Comtesse, I won't keep you here long. I have a simple message for you. I hold the life of your child in my hands. I can spare him or kill him. You've seen enough proof of my power to know I'm not bluffing."

"How can you be so cruel?"

"Madame, I only use the weapons available. Monsieur de Trémeuse wasn't willing to avoid crossing my path. In fact, he even declared a merciless war on me. I merely defend myself by launching a counterattack."

"Your vendetta doesn't have to include my son."

"Believe me, Madame, I'm quite willing to spare him. After all, he's quite a sweet boy. In exchange for his life, I expect a small concession. Tell me where I can find Favraux the banker."

"You know my father is dead!"

"I know that your father is alive."

"Monsieur!"

"We both know he still lives. He possesses a secret that's a key to a fortune. You must choose. Your father or your child!"

"Monster!"

"That's not an answer."

"Help!"

"Shut up!"

Falling down on the steps of the chapel, the Comtesse screamed. This was the cry heard by Judex and Favraux.

"If that's your answer, then your son shall be dead by tomorrow morning."

"Not that! Not that!"

"Then speak!"

Footsteps could be heard in the distance. Howey grinned.

248

"Someone's coming. I must depart." Disappearing behind a tree, the doctor made one last threat. "Be damned! You've chosen unwisely!"

Crawling towards the direction in which her tormentor fled, Jacqueline still pleaded for Jean's life.

"Mercy! Mercy!"

Losing her balance, she was about to roll down the stairs when a man caught her.

"Father!" yelled the Comtesse upon recognizing Favraux.

"What happened? Jacqueline, my child, speak to me."

However, the young woman had fainted. Favraux was vainly trying to awaken her when Judex and Roger arrived.

"She's alive!" said Favraux to the new arrivals.

The three men took her to the Chateau. They placed her on her bed. After being rubbed gently by her husband, Jacqueline regained consciousness.

"It's horrible! Horrible!"

These were the first words from her bleached lips. She grabbed her husband's hands.

"Jacques, Howey was at the chapel. He told me that if I didn't surrender my father, he would kill my child! He can do it. I'm sure he can do it!"

Before Judex could stop her, Jacqueline rose up and ran towards Jean's room.

"I'll protect him! I'll defend him! Come, Jacques! We shall save him!"

Inside his room, Jean slept under the vigilance of the loyal Martine.

"Take a rest, my girl," said the Comte to Martine. "My wife and I shall stand watch over Jean."

Turning to his wife, Judex explained how her son's condition had improved.

"See how calm he is. His fever had gone. He's almost fully healed."

Making a deep sigh, Jacqueline collapsed into an armchair. Immediately her head dropped forward as if she was sleeping. Judex examined her. She wasn't asleep, but in a deep trance. Judex's eyes gleamed strangely. Glancing at Jacqueline and then Jean, two tears appeared in the eyes of this man of iron nerves.

"The monster! What will he do now!"

Silently a shadow passed into the neighboring room.

Throughout the Chateau de Joyeuse, everyone seemed to fall asleep within the next 15 minutes. Jacqueline seemed to awaken from her trance. She left the armchair. Walking clumsily with an unemotional expression, she moved towards the sleeping Jean, who began to show signs of agitation in his bed.

Walking robotically, she removed a pharmaceutical flask from a cabinet. It resembled the medicine prescribed by Dr. Verchin. Opening the flask, she poured a spoonful in a glass of water on the night table. She was about to awaken her son to drink the glass when a hand grabbed it from her. Hidden behind a screen, Judex had intervened.

His wife remained in a hypnotic state as Judex raised the glass to his nose. He recognized the odor.

I wasn't wrong, he thought. *Howey planned to have the child poisoned by his mother. This surpasses anything that a criminal imagination could conceive. Now I shall no longer be restrained. I shall enjoy killing him.*

He seized the flask containing the poison.

This bottle contains a poison that I was using for my own chemical experiments. It was locked in my safe. How did it end up in this cabinet?

Remembering that Jacqueline also knew the combination of the safe, Judex reconstructed the diabolical events that almost led to his wife committing an involuntary crime. Howey had ordered one of his agents to secretly go inside the Chateau de Joyeuse. This spy gave him information on the internal layout of the house and the habits of its inhabitants. The operative also burglarized Judex's safe and discovered the poison. Acting on this intelligence, Howey had hypnotically suggested to Jacqueline to remove the flask of poison and to pour its contents into Jean's glass.

As usual, Judex's reasoning was sound. Earlier events had proceeded along those lines. The burglar had been Howey's usual collaborator, Baronne d'Apremont. The Knight of Justice had successfully foiled the attempt of the evil genius to commit the most hateful crime imaginable, the murder of a child by its mother.

Jacques looked sadly at his wife. Escaping the occult influence of Dr. Howey, she began to awaken from her hypnotic trance.

"How strange! I seem to have fallen asleep." Suddenly she remembered the events at the chapel. "*Mon Dieu*! That man, that monster, told me---"

"Have no fears for your son's safety, Jacqueline." He pointed to Jean who was opening his eyes. "He shall be safe. No corrupting influence, no dark power, will triumph over the guards that shall be placed around him. Jacqueline, you're exhausted. You must rest. I shall finish the nightly vigil over our son."

The young boy opened his eyes.

"I feel better, Papa. Please stay. Mama, get some rest! I promise you that everything will be fine!"

IV. The Success of Prosper Cocantin

The next day, around 9 o'clock in the morning, the Comte de Trémeuse wearing a sports suit left the Chateau de Joyeuse and walked into the courtyard. Pretending to be merely taking an evening walk, he soon disappeared under the shadows of a clump of big trees. He moved towards a large cottage located on the opposite end of the courtyard from the chapel. Formerly a caretaker's residence, the house seemed completely abandoned. Instead of knocking on the door or the hermetically sealed shutters, he knocked three times on a cellar door that was nearly hidden by grass.

A voice came from the interior. "Is that you, my master."

"Yes." replied Judex.

The door slowly opened on its rusty hinges. A large nose appeared in the gap as if it was heralding the appearance of an important personage. Entering the basement, Judex quickly closed the door behind him. He followed a sheepish Prosper Cocantin into a dark chamber dimly lit by an oil lamp. The room had been recently furnished as modest living quarters.

"Well, Cocantin, how do you feel?"

"Better! Yet I still haven't fully regained my good looks." His face still bore the bruises inflicted by the Baronne's blows. "If I applied face powder, my bruises might be rendered invisible."

"I agree. I'm here to tell you some good news. You're free to leave."

"Thank you, but I intend to stay here."

"How could you refuse to leave?"

"I refuse, my dear master, because I've had a string of failures. I don't want to repeat my blunders. "

Cocantin's decision was interfering with Judex's plans.

"What if I ordered you to leave?" asked Judex.

"I would obey!"

"Well! I order you."

"Do you want me to be slaughtered by the Secret Raiders?"

"I'm giving you an opportunity to have your revenge."

"I must tell you, my master, that I don't feel up to the task."

"That is unimportant for the role that you're slated to play."

"What is this role?"

"I want you to leave the Chateau's grounds and stroll around the town and the edges of the Seine. In other words, you need to go wherever you can be seen."

"Judex, you want me dead!"

`"I want you to help me achieve a victory beneficial to us both."

"That's all that I have to do?"

252

"That's all."

"It's not much."

"A lot more than you can imagine. I don't need to tell you that you must report any sightings of suspicious characters immediately to me. I'll be at the Chateau de Joyeuse all day long."

"Understood," said an unenthusiastic Cocantin. "Beside what you just told me, do you want me to do anything else?"

"Nothing, but you have total freedom to carry out this assignment anyway you want. You can even flirt with any pretty girls whom you encounter."

"That's perfect," said the detective despite the fact that he had a wife.

After washing all the bruises remaining on his face, he meticulously shaved and applied facial powder. Wearing a hat and carrying a cane, he went into town. Not finding anything there, he strolled along the banks of the Seine.

I know my Judex, thought Cocantin. *No matter what mistakes I've made in the past, he would never let me walk into a trap. He wants me to stay alive.*

Barely had the detective pondered these consoling thoughts when he spied a pretty girl.

Before him stood one of those plentiful young ladies who decorate the French countryside. Young, sturdy and buxom, she had a charming mouth full of perfect gleaming teeth. She exhumed cheerfulness and strength.

She was sufficient to render Cocantin smitten. Without losing a second, he delivered the classical line used by a man to introduce himself to a female.

"It's a beautiful day for a walk, young lady?"

"Yes, Monsieur."

"What lovely weather! Can I walk you home?"

"Monsieur, you can't. I'm married!"

"That's not a problem!"

"Maybe not for you, but for me it is."

"You're an honest woman."

"Yes, Monsieur. A very honest woman. There are many such women. More than you can imagine."

"What a pity!"

"Bite your tongue!" said the woman, half-amused and half-angry. She was visibly entertained by Cocantin's remarks. "You're wasting your time with me. However, there are several young ladies who would enjoy making your acquaintance."

"Where can I find them?"

"They might not want to be found."

"You're being overly virtuous again, Madame."

"For you, but not for others!" The young lady's eyes flashed mischievously. Seeking to rid herself of Cocantin, she decided to play a joke on him. "After all, you're free to do what you want. If you want to do something stupid, it isn't my role to stop you."

"True."

"If you're looking for a romantic diversion, you'll probably find one in that small inn near the water."

"Why are you so sure?"

"A lady from Paris has been staying there for some days. She seems the type of woman who would interest you."

"What does she look like?"

"Tall and attractive. Dark hair. Black eyes. She has a mouth that seems to want to devour all males."

"That's an intriguing description."

"If I were you. Monsieur, I would visit this woman. Undoubtedly a handsome man like you need only wink to get her attention."

"You've given me excellent advice," declared Prosper Cocantin well aware of the sarcastic irony in the last remark. "I intend to profit from it. Farewell, Madame, and a thousand thanks."

Walking 300 meters, Cocantin reached the inn. The establishment was picturesque and engaging. The spacious dining area was decorated with sketches made by artists who had appreciated the innkeeper's hospitality and cuisine. Behaving like a cynical man of wealth, Cocantin sat down at a table. A smiling blonde, full of youth and beauty, approached the private detective.

"What does Monsieur desire to order?" she asked.

"White wine and soda water."

She's quite attractive, thought Cocantin. *However, she's not the Parisian lady described by my female friend. Like an artist, I have "periods." I'm currently in a brunette period. If I ever shift to a blonde period, then I shall cultivate the company of this young waitress. She's extremely enticing.*

The waitress returned with Cocantin's glass.

"What is your name?" asked the director of the Céléritas Agency.

"Catherine, Monsieur."

"You must have a lot of suitors."

"Why do you sat that?"

"Because you're very pretty. You must have difficulty in choosing a husband from so many men."

"What if I don't want to get married?"

"Why wouldn't you?"

"Maybe I want to be free."

"It's your right!"

"All you men think alike."

"Mademoiselle, you misunderstand me."

"You're as bad as the other men, maybe even worse."

"I have an irresistible fondness for the opposite sex."

"So you admit it!"

Shrugging her shoulders, the waitress prepared to move away when Cocantin made a further comment.

"Rest assured, my child, I'm only being protective in a paternal manner." He slipped a gratuity into her hand. "I simply want information."

"I'm happy to oblige."

"You you have a wealthy guest staying here?"

"A wealthy guest?"

"A lady from Paris. Dark hair and black eyes."

"In fact, a lady answering that description is staying here."

"Is she nice?"

"She is very sarcastic and not easy to serve."

"*Diable!* Is she alone?"

"Only during the day. In the evenings, she is often visited by an elderly gentleman. She never spends time at the dining table. She only comes down briefly to talk to the person on duty at the front desk."

Cocantin thought it odd that this guest was spending her entire day in her room.

"What is this lady's name?"

"You're very nosey, but I'll tell you anyway. Her name is Mademoiselle Durand."

"Tell me, my child," whispered Cocantin, "would you inform Mademoiselle Durand that a man is seeking to make her acquaintance."

"What do you take me for? I don't arrange assignations!"

"You're virtue personified!"

"Besides you can simply tell her yourself. She's over there." The waitress departed.

The director of the Céléritas was stunned. On the threshold of the dining room stood Baronne d'Apremont. Seizing a newspaper from the table, the private detective opened it to hide his face. Walking by without noticing him, the adventuress exited the inn. Finishing his drink, the detective got up and left. He ran to the Chateau de Joyeuse.

Upon seeing Cocantin's joyous face, Judex knew that the detective brought good news.

"What's happened?" asked Judex.

"I spotted the Baronne," triumphantly declared Cocantin.

"Are you sure?"

"I saw her with my own eyes, my master."

"Where?"

"At the inn on the edge of the river."

"Did she see you?"

"No."

"You're positive?"

"Absolutely"

"And Howey?"

"I didn't see him."

"Did you observe anything that indicates he's also at the inn? Think."

"As God is my witness, I... A waitress named Catherine said an old man visits the Baronne in the evenings."

"That has to be Howey. Now I have them!"

"Did I do well?"

"Very well."

"What must I do?"

"All in good time," answered Judex cryptically. He summoned a servant. "Tell Monsieur Roger that I need to talk to him."

As the servant left, Judex turned to Cocantin.

"The hour of vengeance has come. "

45 Centimes.   Tous les Jeudis.

LA
NOUVELLE MISSION
DE
JUDEX

Par ARTHUR BERNÈDE et Louis FEUILLADE

CHÂTIMENT

Part Twelve: Punishment

I. The Supreme Scheme

Towards the afternoon, an old vagrant, who seemed weakened by illness and starvation, was walking along the large road from Triel to Mantes. To an outside observer, he seemed to be strolling along a shady path near the Seine in order to escape the heat. After walking 200 meters, he stopped at an oak tree. Three times he made a hoarse wheezing noise that sounded more like a wild animal than a human being. Patiently he waited. Responding to an approaching figure, the vagrant revealed that he was more agile than his earlier actions indicated.

An elegantly dressed woman with a veil came from the opposite direction. She was the Baronne d'Apremont. Her presence galvanized the vagrant who quickly ran to her.

"Any news?" asked the adventuress.

"All goes poorly," replied Dr. Howey alias *N'a-qu'un-Chasse*.

"I feared as much."

"I nearly succeeded."

"What went wrong?"

"Using hypnotism, I wanted to make the Comtesse betray her father."

"A brilliant stratagem."

"My plan blew up in my face. For the first time, my mesmerized subject rebelled. Despite all my efforts, I couldn't break her resolve."

"Very strange."

"I successfully commanded the Comtesse to come to the chapel. There I presented her with a dilemma. She had the choice of surrendering her father or letting her child die. As I foresaw, she initially implored my mercy. Exhausted and broken, she was close to revealing her father's secret whereabouts when approaching footsteps forced my flight. Since I still maintained my hypnotic influence over Jacqueline de Trémeuse, I ordered her to poison her son in order to punish that cursed Judex for his interference. Earlier she had docilely poured a little poison to augment the boy's illness already caused by my mesmerism. I was resolved that she would now finish him off with a large dose. She must have defied my command because I received proof this morning that Jean is alive and well.

"Instead of continuing a line of attack that was failing, I've decided to strike directly at Judex himself. Since this morning, I have been far from idle. I heard about the nearby construction of a new railway. Encountering two workers on that project, I discovered them to be men whose morality was even lower than their intelligence. They were easily corrupted."

"It was child's play for you to bribe them."

"Yes, it wasn't difficult to gain their cooperation. Briefly, they removed a case of explosives from their construction site. I rented a small boat from an agency that provides transportation along the Seine. My two new underlings placed the explosives on the boat which is now hidden about 500 meters from here. I covered the case of explosives with a tarp. If anyone on the shore notices it, they would never suspect that this flimsy craft contains enough explosive to destroy the Chateau de Joyeuse and all its inhabitants."

"Then your intention is..."

"To blow our enemy to kingdom come. It will be a perfect crime. As always, I count on you, my sweet, to aid me. The execution of this plan presents some difficulties. Let's evaluate the scenario. First, we must convert the explosives into a bomb by attaching to them a timing device that I have ordered Louchard to bring from Paris. Second, we must simply introduce the bomb into the Chateau."

"I commend your ingenuity."

"This first part of the plan involves me. The second part of the plan must be implemented by you. After I attach the timer, your responsibility will be to plant our bomb inside the Chateau. Don't wrinkle your brow, my Juno. This isn't a difficult task for a Raider of your caliber. Clothed in black tights that blend into the shadows, you have invaded many supposedly impenetrable houses in the past. You shall slip into the Trémeuse abode just as you did earlier. We have nothing to fear. Since we poisoned Judex's dogs, he hasn't replaced them.

"I shall be waiting outside attired similarly as a burglar. Once you have finished your task of placing the explosives, you shall set the timer and then rejoin me. The rest will be up to our bomb. You clearly see that this operation isn't dangerous."

"Really!" exclaimed the Baronne. "After what happened yesterday, won't Judex be expecting you to launch another attack?"

"So?"

"Besides being increasingly vigilant, he must be trying to find us."

"That's certain."

"Aren't you afraid?"

"The ongoing duel between us is a merciless battle. The best course is to strike bravely without hesitation. The stake is our survival. We must be ruthless, my beauty. *We have no other choice. We must destroy our enemies in a single blow!* There may never be another opportunity."

These stern words dispelled any fears on the part of the Baronne.

"You're right as always, chief. I shall obey you."

"You won't regret this," predicted Howey. "We must separate. Return to the inn. I shall see you later there. Don't get nervous."

"I shall try to be as confidant as you."

"You will be!" said the master criminal hoping to impart his own personality into his accomplice's soul.

261

The pair went their separate ways. The man feared as *N'a-qu'un-Chasse* continued to journey along the shady coastline where he had just woven his supreme scheme. Resuming the shambling gait of a tramp, he reached the open countryside. Halting in a deserted field, he took a rest near a big poplar. He spread his face on an old handkerchief and became suddenly still as if he was in a deep sleep.

Was he thinking about the implementation of his devilish plan? Or was he just merely resting to gather his strength for his upcoming task. Whatever his reasons for this respite, he stayed there with his eyes shut for nearly an hour before slowly raising himself from the ground. In case anyone was watching, he simulated a slow gait. Following the main road, he came to a tavern in a bushy area.

Dr. Howey would have been less than confident of success if he knew that two men were observing him from behind a shrub. These men were Jacques de Trémeuse and Robert Bianchini.

"It's him," whispered Judex to his friend.

"This hobo matches the description given us by Dr. Verchin," noted Bianchini.

"This bar is a disreputable house in every sense of the word. This criminal will have little difficulty in recruiting accomplices there."

"Should we go inside?" asked Bianchini.

"That would be futile," replied Judex. "We would risk falling in to a trap. Our quarry also could easily slip through our hands. Let's just spy on this dive. We'll continue to secretly pursue his trail. Based on Cocantin's information, Baronne d'Apremont is installed in the inn near the river's edge. Howey shall eventually join her there. Once they're together, we can capture both of them at once. For reasons that you know, I can't publicly accuse these criminals. You, Robert Bianchini, are free from this restriction. You can publicly unmask this fake American doctor as both the kidnapper, Carl Friedrichs, and the leader of the Secret Raiders."

"Provided I don't throttle him with my bare hands," declared Bianchini full of unspeakable hatred.

II. Comparison

While entering into the establishment, Howey didn't go into the tavern's main room where disreputable patrons drank cheap wine and smoked stale tobacco. Instead, he walked up dusty stairs to the upper room of the decrepit establishment. Opening a door barely hanging on its hinges, he went into a garret which contained a suitcase resting on a grease-stained table. In accordance with Howey's orders, the suitcase had been delivered by Louchard. Removing the suitcase from the garret, Howey placed it on a small couch in the hallway. The couch's four legs almost broke under the weight of the suitcase. Taking a key from his pocket, the master criminal opened the bag. He withdrew a small metallic machine with a winding mechanism similar to a clock's. A long cord of some centimeters hung from the device.

Turning the winding mechanism, the chief of the Secret Raiders took out a stopwatch hidden in a pocket of his ragged jacket. Starting the stopwatch, he watched the device closely. After two minutes, an electric spark gushed strongly out of the end of the cord.

The doctor was pleased with the results. Unless there was an unforeseen complication, tonight, Judex and his family would cease to be among the living. The Comte de Trémeuse would learn the folly of declaring war on *N'a-qu'un-Chasse*.

The suitcase brought by Louchard also contained everything necessary for the mastermind to alter his appearance. Inside was a makeup kit, a set of regular clothes, a burglar's black tights, and a pouch with a shoulder strap. After removing the vagrant's wig and beard, he placed a fake mustache on his face. The vagrant's rags were replaced by an expensive suit and a felt hat. A pair of tinted spectacles covered his eyes.

Howey wrapped the black silk tights around the timing device, and then covered everything with an old newspaper.

He then tied the bundle with a string to create a package. He placed it in the pouch which he then slung over his shoulder. Abandoning the suitcase, he went downstairs. Without disturbing the occupants of the inn, he went outside. He reached the main road without incident. As Howey walked, he occasionally glanced at a small mirror in the palm of his hand. He was positive that no one followed him. Howey finally reached the inn on the river's edge.

Baronne d'Apremont had scrupulously followed her master's instructions. She was in her room when Howey arrived.

"How are things?" he asked.

"Everything is going very well." she replied.

"Nothing new?"

"Nothing."

"Then all is well. Our patience has been rewarded. The quicker we leave here, the quicker we can act."

Removing his hat and false mustache, he sat on an armchair next to a window. He made a sigh.

"I would give 50,000 francs for this affair to be over. I bear a heavy burden on my shoulders."

"Do you fear some unexpected development?" questioned the Baronne.

"No!" stated clearly the leader of the Secret Raiders. "Everything is proceeding admirably. It's time for this duel to end. This is no longer a business matter. It's impossible to undertake any serious operation without imaging the dark shadow of that modern paladin blocking my path."

Taking out an expensive cigarette case, Howey smoked as he eulogized the enemy whose assassination had been planned.

"This Judex is obviously a tough opponent. He has been a constant thorn in my side. Once he's dead, he'll no longer occupy my thoughts."

Abruptly he abandoned his morose brooding.

"Tell me, Baronne, can one get a good meal here?"

"The food isn't bad."

"Order us a modest dinner."

"I'll go downstairs now."

As the Baronne moved away, her superior made further comments.

"I'm very happy with you, Baronne. Very happy. If we had decided to marry, imagine the children that we would have had!" The mysterious doctor soon regained his stoic composure.

"Leave. I'm talking nonsense. Order dinner."

Left alone by the Baronne's departure, Howey gazed at the ceiling as he consumed his cigarette. He became lost in a daydream. What thoughts filled the mind of the leader of the Secret Raiders? Was he thinking about this evening's expedition? Did he think of the perils which he confidently believed his infernal genius could overcome? Did he relive the spectacular thefts that he had engineered? Did he meticulously recall all the unspeakable atrocities of his criminal career?

No! For the first time, he compared his current existence to what his life might have been. In fact, even though he was intoxicated by the wealth stolen to satisfy his vices, he wondered what it would have been like to be a man who only trafficked in scientific research. Since encountering Judex, an intellectual giant of total honor, the master criminal had begun to doubt himself. Howey had always considered honest people to be inferior beings suitable only as prey. Although he had never showed the least remorse in the exercise of his horrible profession, he now wondered what would have happened if he had chosen another path.

Faced with the compelling character of his nemesis, Dr. Howey engaged in a soliloquy.

"I was wrong. Evil isn't the only dominant force on Earth. Good is also powerful. It can combat Evil. I have outwitted all the police forces of the world, but I am now blocked by a mere gentleman who draws his strength not only from intellect and determination but also from loyalty and of courage. This man is happy. He loves and is loved. He tastes all the sovereign pleasures of being an important lord of immense

265

power. He has no concern for the next day. He isn't forced to hide like me. He lives for the moment!

"Although I know tonight will see all his happiness buried under the ruins of the Chateau de Joyeuse, I can no longer ignore an inescapable fact. I can no longer conceal the truth from myself. All my attacks on this man have backfired. If he hasn't stopped me, it's because he declines to do so. If he hasn't killed me, it's because he doesn't want to. After what happened last night, there will be no more restraints on my opponent's actions. He knows that I have condemned him to death. In retaliation, he shall condemn me to death."

Realizing for the first time the absurdity of his own criminal existence as well the peril threatening to overwhelm him, Howey slapped his hand against his forehead.

"What I might have been! An admired and honest man!" He laughed. "Honest man? Who knows if that would have been a better life? It's useless to have any regrets about the past. It's too late to change. Let's concentrate on the present. I must preserve the Secret Raiders."

The door opened as the Baronne d'Apremont returned.

"We've lost," she claimed. "They're downstairs."

"Who are you talking about?" asked Howey.

"Judex and Bianchini."

"Did you see them?"

"Yes, they were hiding in a small parlor that communicates directly with an exit and the inn's lobby."

"Did they see you?"

"I hope not."

The man known as *N'a-qu'un-Chasse* remained master of his emotions as the Baronne was clearly in a state of panic.

"You have concluded that everything is going wrong, Baronne."

"I have. I'm afraid."

"Why?"

"I have a premonition of death for both of us."

"In that case, you have only yourself to blame."

"Me?"

266

"Yes. I have not committed any blunders."

"I assure you this isn't my fault."

"Despite my orders, you must have left the inn and been seen by Judex or one of his allies."

"I swear that I didn't."

"This isn't the time to engage in recriminations. We must defend ourselves against Judex's inevitable attack. Fortunately, I have enough self-control for the two of us. I have foresight. Calm yourself, Baronne. You must avoid any crisis of nerves that would compromise us. *Diable!* We must act."

Approaching the locked door, the chief of the Secret Raiders moved a heavy chest of drawers against it as a further precaution. He looked outside the window. He saw a shadow near a tree.

"Exactly what I suspected," observed Howey. "We're like rats in a trap. You're very cunning, Lord Judex. Let me show you how negligence can cause a clever ambush to fall apart."

The criminal began to meticulously plot his escape. He moved towards a locked door that communicated with a neighboring room. Pulling a pair of pliers from his pocket, he picked the lock. He entered an unoccupied room where the window opened on a clump of large trees on the opposite side of the inn.

"Wait for me here," commanded the doctor. "Your safety depends on your obedience."

Exiting through the window, he climbed down the trellis attached to the wall. He nimbly reached the ground without a hitch. He quickly glanced around.

"Perfect," he muttered. Judex had not placed a sentinel on this side of the inn. Yesterday, he had inspected a shed near the main building. There was a ladder inside. Retrieving the ladder, the doctor placed it against the wall. Ascending to the window, he entered the room."Baronne, we're safe."

"The Comte de Trémeuse is guilty of a major oversight," noted the female Raider.

"Have no fear," assured the doctor. "Our avenue of escape is secure."

Despite all the influence that her formidable superior exercised on her, Baronne d'Apremont remained terrified. She feared the fate that would befall them.

The doctor picked up a telephone in the room. It communicated with the lobby. Talking to a woman at the front desk, Howey requested that Monsieur de Trémeuse be paged.

"Monsieur de Trémeuse!" replied the hostess.

"Yes," replied the doctor.

"Monsieur de Trémeuse isn't here."

"I beg your pardon, Madame. He's in the small parlor next to the lobby. Please inform him that Dr. Howey would be honored if he came up to Mademoiselle Durand's room."

"Well, Monsieur, I shall inform him," said the hostess somewhat dazed.

Howey hung up. "Let's flee," he said to the Baronne.

He locked the side door to the room where his female accomplice was registered. From the adjacent room, the two conspirators descended the ladder to the ground outside. The doctor returned the ladder to the shed.

"We must go to my boat," he told the Baronne. "While Judex goes to your room, we shall put the Seine between ourselves and our enemy. That will be quick and easy."

Bypassing the front entrance of the inn, the two criminals slipped away towards the banks of the Seine. Concurrent with their flight, the hostess performed the task requested by Dr. Howey. She deferentially addressed Jacques de Trémeuse.

"Comte, a gentleman desires to speak to you."

"A gentleman?" repeated a stunned Judex.

"Yes."

"Did he give his name?"

"Yes, but I've forgotten it. Wait here. I may have written it down." She fruitlessly searched among her papers at the front desk. "I can't find it. I only recall that he was a doctor."

"Was his name Dr. Howey?"

"That's it. Dr. Howey."

"How could he dare?" exclaimed Judex. Recovering his composure, he winked at Robert Bianchini. "Where is the doctor?" Judex asked the hostess.

"In Mademoiselle Durand's room," she answered.

"Madamoiselle Durand?" Judex had already heard the name from Cocantin, but he thought it prudent to pretend ignorance.

"Yes," confirmed the hostess. "She's a dark-haired lady who's been here for several days. She just ordered dinner for two."

"Very well," said Judex acting nonchalantly. He turned to Bianchini. "We shall accept the dear doctor's invitation."

The hostess summoned a bellhop. "Théodore, take these two gentlemen to Madamoiselle Durand's room."

"I'll see to it straight away, Noémie," replied the bellhop.

Upon reaching the Baronne's room, Théodore knocked on the door. When no one replied, he knocked three more times with greater intensity.

"This is odd," said Théodore. "I'm sure Noémie gave me the correct information."

Judex press his ear against the door.

"There's no one inside," deduced Judex.

Théodore rolled his eyes in surprise. "I was working in the kitchen. The kitchen door was open, and I would have see anyone using the back exit."

"What is your full name, young man," asked Judex.

"Théodore Baron."

"Monsieur Baron, are you an honest man?"

"I try to be one, Monsieur le Comte."

"Would you help to bring two criminals to justice?"

"It would be my duty. I would help without hesitation."

"Well, Monsieur Baron, Please open the door of this room. It was a refuge for two of the greatest criminals of our time."

"Are you joking, Monsieur le Comte?" asked Théodore becoming pale .

"Not at all."

"What if I get into trouble?"

"I shall take full responsibility!" exclaimed Judex.

Taking out his master key, the bellhop unlocked the door. However, the chest of drawers pressing against the door prevented entry.

"Take care!" warned Bianchini. "It may be a trap!"

"No!" declared Judex. "The doctor has diverted us in order to flee. Let's go downstairs." Followed by Judex and Bianchini, Monsieur Baron rushed down the stairway. Upon reaching the lobby, Judex questioned the bellhop.

"Where does the window of Mademoiselle Durand's room face?"

"The front of the hotel."

The three men went outside. The window of the Baronne's room was ajar.

"Fetch a ladder," ordered Judex.

As Théodore departed, Judex whistled. He was joined by Baptiste, who had been watching the front of the inn from the woods. Baptiste informed his master that he hadn't seen either Howey or the Baronne.

After a few minutes, the bellhop returned with the ladder from the shed. Supporting it against the wall, Judex ascended up to the window. He peeked into an empty room. Judex entered the room. He hadn't been mistaken. The birds of prey had flown.

"No one's here," said Judex to Bianchini, who had followed his friend up the ladder into the room.

Hearing this statement, the cautious Théodore ascended the ladder to join the two men. Judex noticed the door to the adjoining room as well as a nearby coat that the Baronne had dropped in her flight.

"If I'm right, this was a carefully crafted ruse for a clever departure. Howey has no desire to fight me face to face. He's afraid. It's a good sign."

The bellhop was totally confused by the Comte's statements. He had no idea what was going on.

"My dear Bianchini," said Judex, "we must somehow regain the trail of our quarry."

Removing the barricade from the doorway, Judex and Bianchini went downstairs. A breathless Théodore went straight to the kitchen where he drowned his confusion in a glass of wine.

Judex was determined to locate the fugitives. He went to the back of the inn. He saw that the window of the room adjoining the Baronne's was open. The two Raiders must have used it to escape. Did they flee into the woods or towards the river? The answer was ascertained using sound logic.

"The woods are too difficult to navigate," argued Judex. "They would have maneuvered themselves under the cover of the trees towards the river bank. Come, my dear Bianchini. Baptiste, stay here in case our enemies return."

Bent on ending the careers of the criminals, Judex and Bianchini ran towards the shore. Once they reached their destination, a cry of anger erupted from both their lips. In the middle of the river, they beheld a small boat carrying the doctor and the Baronne. Unknown to Judex and Bianchini, the boat also carried the explosives intended to destroy the Chateau de Joyeuse. Howey vigorously rowed to reach the opposite shore

"They escaped us again!" shouted Bianchini hopelessly.

"Not for long!" predicted Judex whose eyes burnt with vengeance.

III. Deus Ex Machina

While Judex prepared for the final battle with the leader of the Secret Raiders, Prosper Cocantin had not remained idle. Never had the director of the Céléritas Agency been in better spirits. That morning, he had experienced one of the greatest joys of his life. Judex had praised him highly.

"My dear friend, I'm extremely happy with you. By alerting me to the presence of the Baronne d'Apremont at the

271

inn near the river's edge, you have done me a great service. I shall now give you a new assignment."

"Wonderful!"

"It's an easy mission that presents no danger."

"Regrettable!"

"You shall walk along the shore near the inn."

"Perfect!"

"It would be futile to wear a disguise."

"Yes, I know, my dear master," acknowledged Cocantin pointing to his nose.

"You will be looking for suspicious activity. If you notice anything, contact me at the inn. I will then act accordingly."

"Understood!"

Cocantin's natural innocence had its limits. He smiled.

"Do you really want to use me as bait?"

"You would be that."

"Then I'll do it. Hopefully, my master, you would be satisfied with my performance."

"If I didn't believe that I would be satisfied," said Judex with a touch of irony, "I wouldn't have trusted you with such a delicate task."

Upon saying those words, Jacques de Trémeuse left the director of the Céléritas Agency. Cocantin was in a state of bliss beyond description. He was totally free from the state of depression that overwhelmed him in the underground passages of the Chateau Rouge.

"One of Napoléon's truth holds true for me," the detective joyfully declared. "To truly appreciate victory, you must experience some failures before your great successes."

Cocantin's enthusiasm didn't take long to decline. The detective had a pure loyal heart. He was incapable of cheating a stranger or betraying a friend. Once he gave his word, he kept it no matter what the consequences. He had taken Napoléon for a role model. Although he had literally stuffed his skull with all the military campaigns of the First Empire, he had never been able to obtain the calm bravery to confront peril without flinching. It must be admitted that Cocantin suffered from cowardice. Despite his willingness to punctually execute Judex's orders, he was filled with anxiety.

My only role is that of decoy, he thought. *Judex claims that I have nothing to fear. Damnation! He's underestimating the birds that he wants to cage. Suppose they see me first. They won't hesitate to rid themselves of a troublemaker like me. They'll stab me in the back or throw me in the Seine. Not only must I be on my guard, but I must be armed to the teeth. I must be prepared for any attack.*

This decision caused Cocantin to regain his courage. Pulling out his pistol, he checked the cartridges before slipping it into his pants' pocket.

That's insufficient, he thought. *I need to find more weapons to augment both my offensive and defensive capabilities.*

In a small room, he found an expertly crafted Hammerless rifle with a shoulder strap, as well as an ammo belt of 25 bullets. Slipping into the kitchen, he found an immense knife, freshly sharpened. He tucked the blade inside the ammo belt that now encircled his waist. Placing a coat over the ammo belt, he strapped the rifle over his shoulder. He then walked to the Seine.

It was a superb scene. The birds sang. The butterflies flew. The flowers bloomed. Nature appeared more willing to be a celebration of love rather than be the setting for some dark melodrama.

Feeling confident since he had transformed himself into an arsenal, Cocantin paced back and forth. Almost forgetting the mission assigned him by Judex, he savored the delights of a serene stroll along the Seine.

An unforeseen event would bring him back to reality. Scarcely had he paced along the river for two minutes when twenty meters ahead of him appeared a superb wild duck motionless in the river. Cocantin remembered he carried a rifle. The detective had a great love of hunting. Every year, he and some friends hunted rabbits and partridges along the vast plains between Antwerp and Valmondois. However, the quantity of game found was insufficient to be shot by every hunter. Cocantin returned every year empty-headed. Unfortunately, Cocantin had boasted to his housekeeper, Madame Robbes, that he would return with an ample supply of game. In order to avoid her biting sarcasm, he had to purchase dead rabbits and partridges from another hunter, who profited handsomely from the yearly transactions. Despite these repeated failures, Cocantin always harbored aspirations of finally "bagging something." Now Cocantin was offered the opportunity to slay a magnificent duck.

The fowl didn't fly away at Cocantin's approach. The bird was oblivious to the approach of the private detective.

It's like he's daydreaming, thought Cocantin. *Maybe he's thinking of his girlfriend.*

Cocantin's instinct of a hunter began to conflict with his beliefs as a member of Society for the Protection of Animals. However, he finally decided to shoot the duck with his rifle.

Cocantin fired. Struck in the middle of the body, the duck dived downward into the water.

"Touché!" shouted the detective triumphantly. Barely had he made this exclamation than the duck reappeared on the water and oscillated slowly on the water. "It's only injured!" exclaimed Cocantin. Excited by the thrill of the hunt, he fired a second shot. Again the duck dived and then reappeared to defy its would-be assassin.

"This is extraordinary! This bird won't die! We shall see if it can outlast me."

Loading two bullets into his rifle, Cocantin fired twice. The result was the same. For the third time, the duck dived and returned undamaged to the surface.

"Am I hallucinating?" wondered Cocantin. "Is this duck bewitched? I'm sure that I hit him every time. I saw feathers fly."

Cocantin was going to take further shots when an incensed voice interrupted him.

"Are you trying to destroy my decoy?"

Cocantin was faced by big man in a flannel shirt. His rolled up sleeves revealed muscular arms. He angrily raised a threatening fist in the air.

"Your decoy?" repeated the director of the Céléritas Agency.

"You're telling me that you don't know what it is?"

"I swear that I didn't."

Cocantin's tone of honesty placated the other man.

"Oh well. I see that you didn't. It's a dead duck stuffed with straw. I let it float on the Seine to attract the 'real' ducks. I use a thin, almost invisible, string to keep the decoy from floating away."

The owner of the decoy reeled it in. Inspecting the damage done by Cocantin. The other man became incensed.

"Look at its condition! It's now worthless! You have to pay me damages! 10 francs!"

"10 francs!" repeated Cocantin.

"Not a penny less!"

"Can you prove that this phony duck is your property? After all, I don't know you."

"You don't know me! Everyone will tell you that Père Leupré is incapable of lying."

"Let's stop right there, Monsieur!"

"You want to fight me?"

"Not at all!" protested Cocantin, "but I don't want to be a dupe. Here's my card. If you have rights, they shall be respected! Let the courts settle our disputes. The justice of the peace will render judgment."

An outraged Père Leupré seized the business card of the director of the Céléritas Agency As he read it, Cocantin started to move away. Suddenly he was plagued by doubts. He realized that a private settlement was preferable to a convoluted court case. Changing his mind, he took 10 francs out of his pocket

"Wait! You seem an honest man. With this, you will be able to buy a new decoy. If you have any money left over, buy a glass of wine and toast my health."

Leaving the decoy's owner very satisfied, Cocantin continued his patrol by the Seine. Determined to refrain from further duck hunting, he flung his rifle over his shoulder.

"When I finally shoot some game, I don't have any luck!" he muttered.

Momentarily cured of his hunting mania, Cocantin took a moment to sit under the shade of a large tree whose roots extended to the river. While contemplating the beauty of the Seine, he thought of his beloved Daisy. Once she returned to France, he would take her on a second honeymoon.

The detective's romantic thoughts were interrupted by a small boat advancing near. Believing this to be an insignificant event, Cocantin was about to resume his daydreaming. However, he noticed something unusual on the boat. While a man strove to reach the Seine's left bank by rolling against the current, a woman sat in the back. She was clearly in a state of panic as if threatened by some unknown peril.

Prosper Cocantin wondered why she was so terrified. The boat was drifting due to the current, but that posed no danger. From his position of perfect security, Cocantin smugly concluded that the woman was a coward. Suddenly his eyes widened.

"It's them!" he yelled.

Judex's ally had recognized Dr. Howey and Baronne d'Apremont.

"Those crooks won't escape under my nose! I shall stop them!"

Concealing himself behind the tree, Cocantin grabbed his rifle and aimed it at the boat that was coming nearer.

"I'll wound Howey in the arm! He and that monstrous Baronne must be taken alive! Judex will know what to do next!"

The boat was only a few meters from the opposite shore. It passed in front of Cocantin. He fired.

A tremendous explosion erupted. The small boat shattered in a whirlwind of smoke and flame. Fragments of wood and human flesh were thrown upward before falling in the river.

Cocantin had failed in his intended goal. His bullet didn't wound Howey. Instead, it hit the hidden explosives being transported by the dinghy. Tossed into the air, the dismembered corpses of Dr. Howey and the Baronne landed in the river.

From another point near the river bank, Judex and Bianchini witnessed this tragic and unexpected event. Quickly they ran towards Cocantin. Pale and shaking, the detective watched the fragments of the two cadavers as they floated nearby.

Holding his smoking weapon, the director of the Céléritas agency stammered incoherently.

"*Mon Dieu! Mon Dieu! Mon Dieu!*"

"How did that happen?" asked Jacques de Trémeuse. "Did you do that?"

"Yes, it was me. I didn't do it deliberately." Briefly, he confused Père Leupré's decoy with the two Raiders. "I only wanted to hit him in the wing. The next thing I knew... Boom! I didn't know my bullets were so powerful!"

"You aren't to be condemned," advised Judex. "Savor the joy of your triumph. Thanks to you, the Secret Raiders have been decapitated with the loss of their two principal bosses. You have become the *Deus Ex Machina* that in classical plays brings a happy resolution to tragic events. I hail you, Prosper Cocantin, as the instrument of Providence!"

"It's true!" realized Cocantin. "Yes, master! It's true!"

"And now," announced Judex, "let's collect Baptiste at the inn. We'll then return to the Chateau de Joyeuse and tell everyone the good news."

As the radiant sun shined on the hills that encircled the Seine valley, Cocantin tucked his hand inside his waistcoat.

"Now I've achieved my Austerlitz."

Some moments later, Judex, Bianchini, Baptiste, and the hero of the day arrived at the Chateau de Joyeuse. Judex related to all the truly tremendous exploit of which the private detective was rightfully proud. There were many cheers, hand-shakes, hugs and kisses.

In the course of these celebrations, Prosper Cocantin demonstrated that he was a simple soul not intoxicated by success.

"Considering, my friends, that I have committed so many blunders, it was only natural that I made up for them."

"The nightmare now is over," concluded Judex. "Deprived of their leaders, the Secret Raiders will fall apart and disappear into the shadows. Now, Roger and Primrose can marry. The evil spirit is exorcised. It's their turn to be happy!"

Epilogue

Some weeks later, Roger de Trémeuse married James Milton's adopted daughter in a private marriage ceremony. The loving couple immediately departed on their honeymoon trip.

Cocantin returned to Paris to await the return of his precocious Daisy. While his day proceeded normally, his nights were less sweet. His sleep was frequently disrupted by terrible nightmares. He would remember being on the edge of the Seine. He would aim the rifle at Howey and shoot causing the horrible deaths of the doctor and his accomplice. Then he imagined that the scattered fragments of his two victims reassembled themselves. His resurrected victims then proceed to mercilessly dismember him with knives. Upon awakening, Cocantin gave voice to his anguish.

"To kill a criminal is justifiable even though I have no aptitude to be an executioner. But to tear a woman apart! For that is what I actually did. Uh! It's disgusting."

His remorse would dissipate once the bad dream was over, and he would then rationalize his actions.

"When all is said and done, Napoléon was right to shoot the Duc d'Enghien in the ditches of Vincennes. That may not be the most noble page in the Emperor's history, but it proves that there are circumstances where any means necessary must be employed to remove enemies especially when they threaten all mankind."

This philosophical reasoning steeped in historical precedent calmed Cocantin's troubled spirit.

One morning, Cocantin's housekeeper, Madame Robbes, awoke him and announced that a policeman wanted to see him. Upon hearing these words, Cocantin's body contorted and his nose began to assume a purplish complexion.

"A policeman?"

"Yes, Monsieur."

"What did you tell him?"

"I said that you were in."

"What? You should have said that I took a trip to India, Japan or Madagascar,"

"Why should I lie?" Unaware of her employer's last exploit, the housekeeper feared that he had lost his reason.

Jumping out of bed, he ran around in his pajamas.

"What have I done to deserve this? They have come to arrest me!"

"Arrest you?"

"I'm a murderer. I killed two people, a man and a woman."

Madame Robbes was shocked. "How horrible!"

Cocantin was resigned to his fate. "Tell the representative of the law to do what he wants of me." He collapsed on a couch.

Shortly thereafter, the governess returned with a letter. The private detective unsealed it with a trembling hand. It was a summons from the police commissioner.

The police commissioner of the Ninth Division asks Monsieur Cocantin to present himself at his office without delay in order to discuss a matter of great concern.

"And the policeman?" asked Cocantin.

"He left," replied Madame Robbes.

"Left!" repeated the director of the Céléritas Agency. A light of hope glimmered inside Cocantin. "Perhaps I should flee?"

"Never!" bellowed the housekeeper furiously. "You shall not flee! You're a murderer! You told me yourself! I'm ashamed to be employed by you. If I have to, I'll drag you to the commissioner myself. I'll deliver you to justice. My conscience will be satisfied, and I'll have my picture in the newspapers."

"I'm lost," concluded Cocantin.

An hour later, flanked by his housekeeper who hadn't left his company for a second, the private detective stood in front of the police commissioner. To Cocantin's astonishment, the officials received him with great cordiality.

"Are you feeling well, Monsieur Cocantin?" asked the commissioner.

"Yes, Monsieur."

The housekeeper then interjected herself into the conversation.

"And I, Mélanie Robbes, an honest woman, brought him here. If you need to know anything..."

"This matter doesn't concern you, Madame," declared the commissioner authoritatively. "Sit down and be quiet."

The official had no desire to hear the tirade that nearly erupted from the lips of Madame Robbes. Cocantin wondered if the commissioner was seeking to entrap him.

"Did you cause a small boat with two people inside to explode?" asked the official.

"Yes, Commissioner."

"Here's a communiqué from the Ministry, said the official solemnly. Let me read it to you."

The Minister of the Interior orders the Commissioner of Police to investigate the antecedents of Monsieur Cocantin, recommended for a high distinction due to his destruction of a small boat of explosives that two spies intended to use against an iron bridge.

Cocantin clasped his hands together. "*Mon Dieu!* Is this possible?"

"You may choose your reward. You can receive either 1,000 francs or the medal of the *Ordre de Palmes Académiques.*"

"The medal!" said Cocantin. "My fellow duck hunters will be so impressed when they see my medal! Thank you, Commissioner. Justice has truly triumphed. Vice has been punished, and virtue rewarded."

Following the departure of Roger de Trémeuse, Favraux left with Kerjean for the sheltered retirement of Sainte-Madeleine. As for Judex, he returned to La Frondaie with Jacqueline and Jean. They were sitting happily one morning when a letter arrived from Robert Bianchini.

My dear friend,

My daughter Clara and I are traveling to America. The dear child claims that she shall never leave her father. Her soul, so long shrouded in darkness, awakens like the light of day as a child opening her eyes for the first time. How happy we are!

"Jacques," said Jacqueline fervently, "you have done good deeds."

Before her husband could reply. Jean jumped on the knees of his adopted father.

"Oh, Papa, promise Mama that you'll never leave us."

Judex hugged both the mother and child.

"Yes, I promise, my beloved."

In the distance, a church bell rang.

Bianchini congratulates Cocantin and Judex

The Continuity of Judex's Second Adventure

As with the novelization of the first *Judex* serial, there were several continuity glitches in the original French text that I took the liberty to correct. There were also some contradictions between the two novelizations. I fixed those errors as well.

There was the issue of how much time passed since Judex's first exploit. In the original French text, Dr. Howey asked Prosper Cocantin about Favraux's supposed death and indicated that two years had passed since that event. This conversation would imply a gap of two years between the two adventures. However, when Judex found the mysterious note exhorting him to resume his fight against crime, the vigilante noted that only a single year had passed. This interval of one year is later confirmed when Jacqueline recalled that she and her husband were married at the chapel in the Chateau de Joyeuse a year ago. Therefore, I altered the conversation between Howey and Cocantin to reflect a gap of only one year.

There were conflicting references to the exact month in which the main events of the novelization were set. When Roger confronted Primrose with her role in the theft of the propeller plans, there is a reference to "the June sun." When James Milton accused Belles-Mirettes of being involved in the burglary, the original French had him identify the night of the robbery as being July 10. Clearly one of these references should be corrected. Although July would be more consistent with the references to summer in the novel, I have opted for June, even though that month straddles both spring and summer. My reason is based on the following rationale:

The novel has to take place before the outbreak of the World War I, somewhere inside a 1911-14 framework. A careful reading of the text shows that the robbery of the propeller plans must have happened on a Sunday. Cocantin visited Baronne d'Apremont on a Tuesday, and the robbery happened two days earlier. In the early years of the 20th century, July 10 only fell on a Sunday on 1904 and 1909, which is much too early for Judex's second adventure. A date of Sunday, July 10 is therefore inappropriate. So I've altered the date of the robbery from July 10 to June 14, which fell on a Sunday in 1914.

World War I erupted on July 28, 1914. Considering that weeks passed between Howey's death and the epilogue, the novel would have to be set no later than 1913 if it took place in July. However, if the novel's main events transpired in June, then the novel could take place in 1914. The epilogue would have then happened in mid-July. Having Judex's canonical crime-fighting career conclude in 1914 gives a certain poignancy to his exploits. This fact was noted in Georges Franju's 1963 remake of *Judex*. Therefore, for artistic reasons, I chose June over July.

The French text was careless about the sequence of days. Cocantin found the sample of Primrose's handwriting in the Baronne's apartment on a Tuesday. The next day, Dr. Howey surprised Jean writing a letter to his grandfather. The original French had Jean telling Howey that it was Saturday. I changed this to Wednesday. This alteration is also justified by Cocantin's Sunday visit to La Belle Fathma four days later.

The original text had contradictory remarks regarding the amount of time that had transpired since the abduction of the Bianchini sisters. Sometimes, it was 16 years, but it was also given as 17 years. I consistently made it 16 years. There was a similar discrepancy involving the age of the younger sister. Primrose's age was initially given as 20 when she first appeared, but her age later became 17. I madeit consistently 17.

There are interesting questions raised about the servants of the Trémeuse family. In *Judex*, the Dowager Countess lived at the Chateau de la Ferté in the forest of Dreux. Her only companions were three old servants: a coachman, a valet and a cook. She also owned the Villa des Palmiers on the Mediterranean coast. Based on *The Return of Judex*, her estates also included the Chateau de Joyeuse between Mantes and Saint-Germain. Before the marriage of Jacques de Trémeuse, there

284

would have been additional servants at the Chateau de Joyeuse besides the trio at Chateau de la Ferté. These servants must have included the youthful Martine, described as being a long-time servant of the Trémeuse family, and Baptiste the chauffeur. Following the marriage of Jacques de Trémeuse, Martine and Baptiste would have transferred from the Chateau de Joyeuse to La Frondaie. Although Baptiste was born near Dreux, he clearly wasn't one of the three servants living with the Countess in the Chateau de la Ferté.

The Return of Judex states that Baptiste left the service of the Dowager Countess to become Judex's chauffeur after his marriage to Jacqueline. Baptiste was probably loaned by the Dowager Countess to her son Roger during the events of *Judex*. Roger had a chauffeur who helped him rescue Jean from the clutches of Diana Monti and Amaury de la Rochefontaine. This driver was probably the same man whom Judex employed to chase Amaury's car after that villainous aristocrat abducted Kerjean. The nameless chauffeur of *Judex* must have been Baptiste.

There were two times in *The Return of Judex* when a loyal chambermaid watched over Jacqueline. The first instance transpired at La Frondaie, and the servant was clearly Martine. The second was at the Chateau de Joyeuse, and the original text didn't identify her. I made both women Martine, and simply had the maid travel with the Trémeuse family from La Frondaie to the Chateau de Joyeuse.

The Return of Judex apparently resolved a contradiction revolving around the exact age of Jacqueline's son, Jean. The first novel, *Judex,* gave Jean's age contradictorily as four and a half and five. Since Jean was identified as being six one year later, the natural conclusion is that he was really five in *Judex*.

Dr. Howey diagnosed that Cocantin was suffering from a "hypersensitive hysterotomy." This is an elaborate joke on Cocantin's lack of medical knowledge. A hysterotomy is a surgical incision of the uterus. Perhaps this false diagnosis was intended to be a clue that Howey was really a criminal?

The French text left a big hole regarding the authorship of the anonymous letter exhorting Judex to resume his campaign to fight crime. Therefore, I added two possible theories explaining who its author was. It could have been Judex's absent mother, or the manipulative Dr. Howey. How Howey learned both Judex's real identity and the details of Favraux's fake death was never explained, so I inserted a plausible explanation involving Captain Martelli, a character from the first novel.

One contradiction in the original text is that Howey was able to compel Primrose to give him details about Judex's trip to the Basket-Maker's Cabin, but was unable to force Jacqueline to reveal her father's whereabouts. I rectified this by having Judex and Roger speculate that Howey exercised a stronger hypnotic control over Primrose than he did over Jacqueline.

There were a lot of unexplained things about Primrose's abduction near the Seine in the original French text. *N'a-qu'un-Chasse*'s knowledge of the conversation between Judex and his allies at the Chateau d'Arbois remained a mystery. I inserted a statement about Milton's footman being an agent of the evil mastermind. The French text also failed to elaborate on the whistle overheard by *N'a-qu'un-Chasse* and his two female accomplices, as well as the blinding flash that accompanied the appearance of Primrose's abductor. I briefly rationalized those two occurrences.

The French text first described Lutin, the Pony Detective, as a gift to Jean from Primrose. Later it claimed that her foster father, James Milton, bought Lutin for Jean. I resolved this contradiction by making Lutin a gift from both Miltons.

When Cocantin was ordered to retrieve Lutin, on the French text, Roger was sent on an unexplained mission. I had Judex order Roger to cable their ally in Paris (James Milton).

During Jean's abduction by a hypnotized Primrose, a chambermaid named Juliette couldn't be woken up. The original text not only gave no explanation for her deep sleep, but never mentioned whether she ever woke up. I corrected both those oversights by providing the explanation that Juliette was drugged. We first learned that the Secret Raiders were interested in Favraux when the banker spotted two of their members near his abode. Later, Baronne d'Apremont tricked Cocantin into revealing the banker's location. The French text failed to connect these two incidents. My version has the Baronne's superior citing the earlier investigation by the two agents during a telephone conversation.

There seemed to be a missing section from the scenes at *Le Boule d'Or* in the French text. First, Favraux and Kerjean deliberately passed some information to Madame Pingaud to trick the Secret Raiders, but the text never revealed what they told her. Second, the Baronne's chauffeur parked the car in the inn's garage, and then suddenly appeared in the dining room after driving the vehicle to Favraux's villa. I added a few lines of dialogue to paper over these discrepancies.

In the scenes at the house in the Rue Musset, the Baronne's chauffeur was named Justin. Presumably, he was the unnamed chauffeur who drove the Baronne to Fontainebleau to carry out the orders of *N'a-qu'un-Chasse* earlier in the novel. A character named Mimile later appeared to help in the failed ambush near the Chateau Rouge. Mimile was then the Baronne's chauffeur at *La Boule d'Or*. Either the Baronne replaced Mimile with Justin, or there was one chauffeur whose full name was Mimile Justin.

There was some sloppy continuity involving Belles-Mirettes's betrayal of *N'a-qu'un-Chasse* in the original text. The original version had the one-eyed mastermind only telling Belles-Mirettes that he would be at Domicile #4 for one night. Yet Belles-Mirettes told Judex that *N'a-qu'un-Chasse* expected her on the following evening. Therefore, I had to alter the text to have *N'a-qu'un-Chasse* tell his female agent that he would stay at Domicile #4 for more than one night. I also had to insert lines explaining Belles-Mirettes's inexplicable change from mourning clothes to her more familiar masculine garb during her captivity.

I also modified *N'a-qu'un-Chasse's* plan to blow up the Chateau de Joyeuse. In the original French, Baronne

287

d'Apremont was suppose to break into the house and plant the dynamite inside the house *before* the timer had been attached. Then she would open the window in order for her superior to get into the house. She would then go outside, and *N'a-qu'un-Chasse* (alias Dr. Howey) would enter the house and attach the timer to the dynamite, leaving before the bomb exploded. This scheme doesn't make sense. Why have two different people break separately into the house? Why assemble the bomb inside Judex's residence? It's more logical for *N'a-qu'un-Chasse* to attach the timer to the dynamite outside the Chateau, and then have the Baronne plant it and set the timer. My translation made that modification.

When Howey was at the inn, he saw from the window of the Baronne's room that Judex had planted a sentinel near the front of the building. The original text totally forgot about this unnamed sentinel after Howey and the Baronne escaped. My version briefly identified Baptiste as the sentinel.

The two novels contradicted themselves on two major points. *Judex* concluded with Jacques de Trémeuse telling Pierre Kerjean that he intended to resume his crusade against injustice once he returned from his honeymoon. There was no indication of this intention in the original text of the sequel. Jacques had now made a firm decision to retire from crime-fighting. I simply added a statement that he changed his mind once he returned from his honeymoon.

There was a major geographical contradiction between the two novels. In *Judex*, the mine discovered by Robert Bianchini to restore the Trémeuse fortune was in Africa. In the sequel, the mine was magically teleported to South America. I resolved this inconsistency by having Bianchini discovered two separate mines for the Trémeuse family.

There were two contradictions between the two novels that I didn't alter. In *Judex*, the address of Cocantin's Céléritas Agency was 135 Rue Milton, and its telephone number was Central 86-45. In *The Return of Judex*, the address is 52 Rue Milton, and the telephone number is Louvre 72-97. We can rationalize the discrepancy by speculating that Cocantin must have moved his office to a new location on the same street.

Cocantin's age was given as 40 in *Judex*. His age then should be 41 in *The Return of Judex*. However, Cocantin's remark about living as long as his grandfather's age of 98 implied that the sleuth was 38. The detective said that he had 60 more years of life. Probably Cocantin rounded up his 57 remaining years to 60.

Although it was never mentioned in the text, Robert Bianchini's wife, Rosita, may have been South American. The Bianchinis may have made their home in Chile. The South American mine managed by Bianchini was in a place called Santa Juana. A Chilean municipality is named Santa Juana. According to my friend, Julián Puga, Santa Juana's main industries are cattle and agriculture. In real life, no mines exist there. There are mines in Santa Juana, Mexico, but that city is part of North America.

The mass poisoning of Judex's dogs is rather upsetting once you realize that the casualties must have included Vidocq the police dog, Maxime the poodle, an unnamed fox terrier and the 25 Vendean hounds from the earlier novel. In fact, the victims may have even included Flip and Bobby, the fox-terriers owned by Jean.

The penetration of the Trémeuse household by *N'a-qu'un-Chasse* parallels Judex's own undercover operations in the Favraux household in the first novel. Assuming the identity of Vallières, a Frenchman who had been living in the United States, Judex secured the position of Favraux's private secretary. Posing as Dr. Howey, an American expert on physical education, *N'a-qu'un-Chasse* secured the position of tutor to Jacques de Trémeuse's stepson.

There are many unanswered questions about *N'a-qu'un-Chasse*. The criminal was eventually revealed to be Carl Friedrichs, Robert Bianchini's treacherous secretary. Was this really the mastermind's true identity? Friedrichs could just be another false identity of this elusive criminal. Another mystery is whether there was a real Dr. Howey. Could *N'a-qu'un-*

289

Chasse have murdered a genuine Dr. Howey in the United States and then assumed his identity in France? There's also the matter of *N'a-qu'un-Chasse's* hypnotic powers. How did he gain them? There's also the criminal's strange notation of "B 45 X .9.1.22." What does it really mean? Is it a key to Howey's coded papers or something more?

What was *N'a-qu'un-Chasse's* real reason for seeking Favraux? Judex believed that the mastermind wanted to use Favraux to blackmail the Trémeuse family, but there's a hint of a totally different motive. At the chapel near the Chateau de Joyeuse, *N'a-qu'un-Chasse* claimed that Favraux knew an incredible secret worth a fortune. What was this secret?

Perhaps it is better that there are no definite answers to these questions. *N'a-qu'un-Chasse* is more compelling as a man of mystery. His origins appropriately remain shrouded in darkness.

There is one final matter. I noted in the introduction that Elsa Rhener was probably Baronne d'Apremont in the cinematic serial. Since the characters were distinct in the novelization, Elsa's final fate was unclear. It was hinted that *N'a-qu'un-Chasse* had murdered her, but that's only speculation. My own theory was that the real name of this supposedly Swiss woman was Elsa Lüchner. In order to hide from the Secret Raiders, she adopted the identity of a Scandinavian woman named Elsa Bergen. Under this alias, she became a governess to the Desroches family. Elsa Lüchner's activities in 1925 were described in Arthur Bernède's *Belphegor* (1927). The unabridged English edition of Bernède's novel, translated by Jean-Marc and Randy Lofficier, was published by Black Coat Press in 2012.

Rick Lai

A Chronology of the Canonical Judex Saga

1853. Birth of Pierre Kerjean.

1861. Birth of Julia Orsini.

1873. Birth of Prosper Kerjean.

1879. Birth of Baptiste, Judex's future chauffeur.

1881. Julia Orsini marries Pierre de Trémeuse.

1883. Birth of Jacques de Trémeuse, the son of Pierre and Julia de Trémeuse.

1884. Robert Bianchini begins his career as an engineer in the Western Hemisphere.

c.1884. Birth of Robert Kerjean (alias Baron Moralès), son of Pierre Kerjean.

1885. Birth of Roger de Trémeuse, the second son of Pierre and Julia de Trémeuse.

c.1885. Birth of Baronne d'Apremont.

1893. Pierre Kerjean is sentenced to 20 years in prison for fraud. Robert Bianchini marries his wife, Rosita. He discovers a mine in South America for Pierre de Trémeuse.

1894. Birth of Clara Bianchini (alias Belles-Mirettes), the daughter of Robert and Rosita Bianchini. A vagrant is found dangling from the Hanging Tree in the forest of Fontainebleau.

1897. Maurice-Ernest Favraux financially ruins Pierre de Trémeuse. Following Pierre's suicide, Julia de Trémeuse forces her two sons to swear an oath of vengeance against Favraux. Robert Bianchini restores the Trémeuse finances by discoveringa mine in Africa. Birth of Maria Bianchini (alias Primrose Milton), the second daughter of Robert and Rosita Bianchini.

1898. Rosita Bianchini is fatally murdered by Carl Friedrichs and Elsa Rhener. They abduct Clara and Maria Bianchini. Maria is abandoned in the forest of Fontainebleau where she is found by James Milton. Adopted by Milton, Maria is renamed Primrose. Robert Bianchini sells his interest to the South American and African mines to Julia de Trémeuse. Julia purchases the Chateau de la Ferté in the forest of Dreux.

1899. Elsa Rhener teaches Belles-Mirettes (Clara Bianchini) to steal.

1899-1913. As *N'a-qu'un-Chasse*, Carl Friedrichs organizes the Secret Raiders in the Western Hemisphere. At some point during this period, he establishes the false identity of Dr. Howey.

1908. Birth of Jean Aubry, the son of Jacques and Jacqueline Aubry, and the grandson of Maurice-Ernest Favraux.

c.1910. Jacques Aubry dies in an automobile accident in the United States.

1912. Under the false identity of Vallières, Jacques de Trémeuse (alias Judex) becomes Maurice-Ernest Favraux's secretary. Using the alias of Marie Verdier, Diana Monti becomes Jean Aubry's governess.

1913. Events of *Judex*.

1914. (June-Mid-July) Events of *The Return of Judex.*

1914. (July 28) Outbreak of World War I.

Rick Lai

Judex, Fritz Lang, and Dr. Mabuse

Perhaps the most famous fictional criminal in German popular culture is Dr. Mabuse. First created by Norbert Jacques in a novel, the sinister character became popularized in three films directed by Fritz Lang. A comparison of Lang's three films to Louis Feuillade's *La Nouvelle Mission de Judex* (1918) shows that the development of Dr. Mabuse owes a great debt to the French serial.

Fritz Lang was a great fan of Louis Feuillade. Lang's 1919 serial, *Die Spinnen (The Spiders),* was an attempt to create a German version of Feuillade's *Les Vampires (The Vampires,* 1915-16). Like its French predecessor, Lang's serial dealt with a gang of criminals whose most memorable member was a woman. Feuillade's initial success in the thriller genre had been the *Fantômas* films made during 1913-14. Just as Feuillade took a popular literary villain of French pulp fiction and transformed him into a cinematic success, Lang searched for a similar character in German crime fiction. When Lang discovered *Dr. Mabuse der Spieler (Dr. Mabuse the Gambler)* by Norbert Jacques, the director knew that he had found his Fantômas.

Jacques's novel began to be serialized in September 1921, and Lang's film version hit the theaters in April 1922. The screenplay of the film, co-written by Lang and Thea von Harbou, was very faithful to the novel, except in the conclusion. Whereas Jacques had Mabuse falling to his death during an exciting fight on an airplane, the film has an insane Mabuse apprehended by the Berlin police.

From the start, Mabuse was marketed like Fantômas. The poster for the 1922 film by Theo Matejkos with a gigantic Mabuse hovering over Berlin stemmed from the 1913 poster for the first *Fantômas* film in which the French criminal towered over Paris. Fantômas was a criminal genius who dominated the Paris underworld through a series of multiple identities. Similarly, Mabuse was a master of disguise lording over crime in Berlin.

What differentiates Mabuse from Fantômas is that the evil doctor has vast hypnotic abilities. The concept of a manipulative hypnotist has a long literary tradition which can be traced back to at least as early as Alexandre Dumas's *Joseph Balsamo* aka *Mémoires d'un médecin* (1846-48). Prior to the first Mabuse film, German movie audiences has been thrilled by the horrific mesmerist in *Das Cabinet des Dr. Caligari* (*The Cabinet of Dr. Caligari*, 1920). Therefore, there are ample sources for Jacques to get the idea of grating hypnotic abilities on a Fantômas-like mastermind. However, Louis Feuillade and screenwriter Arthur Bernède had already merged the Fantômas archetype with that of the evil hypnotist three years earlier.

After making popular films about French criminals, Feuillade decided to create a vigilante hero opposed to modern crime. The title character of *Judex* (1917) was a cloaked hero who at the very least anticipated the more famous crime fighter of American pulps and radio, The Shadow. For Judex's second serial, *La Nouvelle Mission de Judex* (1918), it became essential for Feuillade and Bernède to fashion a villain formidable enough to combat Judex. Their solution was the diabolical Dr. Howey, alias *N'a-qu'un-Chasse* (French slang for "Only Has One Eye"). While dominating the Paris underworld through a series of disguises, Howey established a reputation as an acclaimed American expert on physical education. Being invited into the homes of wealthy French patrons, Howey hypnotized members of their families to help him commit burglaries. Howey was not the true name of this master criminal. Instead of being an American, he was a German named Carl Friedrichs. This revelation was reflective of the anti-German prejudice stemming from World War I.

In both Jacques's novel and Lang's film, Mabuse primarily used hypnotism to browbeat opponents in gambling dens to lose substantial money to him in card games. Later he posed as a psychiatrist to successfully induce a patient into committing suicide. The mastermind would also unsuccessfully attempt to force a German state prosecutor to take his own life.

Whether Norbert Jacques based Dr. Mabuse on Dr. Howey can never be fully known. However, Lang's debt to Feuillade is very discernible. In his excellent *The Strange Case of Dr. Mabuse* (McFarland & Company, 2001), David Kalat documented how certain scenes from Feuillade's *Les Vampires* and the Fantômas movies were reworked into *Dr. Mabuse der Spieler*. Kalat's superb study didn't mention *La Nouvelle Mission de Judex* for understandable reasons. Since the serial no longer exists in its entirety, its access to film scholars is limited. Fortunately, Arthur Bernède's novelization of the screenplay can still be unearthed from used book dealers. My following comments are based on that novelization.

The influence of the second *Judex* serial on Fritz Lang became more noticeable in the second and third *Mabuse* film. In these two movies, Lang essentially hijacked the character from Norbert Jacques.

By 1930, Jacques had done very little with Mabuse. The author had resurrected the master criminal from a watery grave in a 1923 short story, "Dr. Mabuse auf dem Presseball" ("Dr. Mabuse at the Press Ball") only to have him arrested by German police. In the same year, Mabuse also appeared in a prequel to the original novel, *Ingenieur Mars*. In September 1930, Jacques tried to interest Lang into making a film based on a yet-to-be completed novel, *Mabuses Kolonie* ("Mabuse's Colony"). In the original novel, but not the film, Mabuse was committing his crimes with the ultimate goal of creating Etiopomar, a private kingdom in the Brazilian jungle. *Mabuses Kolonie* involved a deceased Mabuse leaving a last will and testament outlining the location of Etiopomar as well as Mabuse's plans for future crimes. Since Etiopomar didn't appear in the first Mabuse film, Lang rejected the idea that it should be the central focus of a sequel. However, Lang was fascinated by the idea that Mabuse would leave a blueprint for further crimes. The director collaborated with Thea von

Harbou, now his wife, on a screenplay with a totally different focus. Thus, *Das Testament des Dr. Mabuse* ("The Testament of Dr. Mabuse") was born. It would be released in 1933. Once Jacques authorized this sequel, he abandoned *Mabuses Kolonie* and wrote the novelization of Thea von Harbou's screenplay.

Das Testament des Dr. Mabuse had the mastermind confined in an asylum for his numerous crimes. Mabuse used his powers of mesmerism to gain control of the asylum director, Dr. Baum, in order to organize a new network of crime. Using Mabuse's name, Baum directed his criminal minions as a shadowy figure behind a curtain. Mabuse also wrote detailed records of all crimes that Baum should commit. Eventually Mabuse died from natural causes, but Baum continued to commit crimes in his name. At this point, the film adopted a degree of ambiguity. There were scenes where the ghost of Mabuse possessed Baum. However, it was unclear whether the episodes with Mabuse's evil spirit only occurred in Baum's imagination. Baum's downfall as a crime czar came to an end when one of his own men, Thomas Kent, turned against him. Although Kent had never seen the new Mabuse in the flesh, he was able to identify Baum by his voice.

The exposure of Baum as the new Mabuse resembles a key scene from Feuillade's *La Nouvelle Mission de Judex*. *N'a-qu'un-Chasse*'s fortunes changed radically when one of his female minions, Belles-Mirettes, changed her allegiance to Judex. Although she had only seen *N'a-qu'un-Chasse* disguised as a one-eyed man, she was able to identify him as Dr. Howey because she recognized his voice.

After Howey was exposed as a master criminal, Judex gained temporary possession of his house. Judex found detailed records of all crimes that Howey intended to commit in the future. This discovery foreshadows the central core concept of *Das Testament des Dr. Mabuse*. The premise of a blueprint for future crimes existed in the incomplete *Mabuses Kolonie*. If this idea was borrowed from Feuillade's serial, it would have been done by Jacques rather than Lang.

Lang may have gotten the inspiration for one of the most suspenseful sequences in *Das Testament des Dr. Mabuse* from *La Nouvelle Mission de Judex.* In one of the serial's chapters, Judex burglarized the home of a French baroness, Baronne d'Apremont, working for *N'a-qu'un-Chasse.* The baroness released metal barriers to trap Judex within a narrow space. Judex can blast open a wall of his prison chamber with a bomb in his possession. However, the blast would certainly kill him. Therefore, he had to shield himself in a large trunk in the room before setting the timer on his explosive.

When Kent's treachery became apparent to Baum in *Das Testament des Dr. Mabuse*, the master criminal trapped his ex-subordinate, as well as his fiancée, in a locked room with a time bomb. Kent skillfully recognized the bomb would probably punch an opening in the prison chamber. Therefore, he needed to find some way to shield both himself and his fiancée from the blast. He broke a water pipe. This causes the room to fill up with water which effectively acted as a protective cushion to the explosion.

When Lang fled Nazi Germany for America in 1933, he severed all connections with not only the character of Dr. Mabuse but also Thea von Harbou. After decades as a director in Hollywood, Lang returned to his homeland in 1958. Artur Brauner, a producer seeking to revive the film industry in West Germany, quickly hired Lang as a director. A third Mabuse film then became inevitable. With a screenplay that Lang co-wrote with Heinz Oskar Wuttig and Jan Fethge, this movie was released in 1960 as *Die Tausend Augen des Dr. Mabuse* (*The 1000 Eyes of Dr. Mabuse*).

In this film, we meet the third master criminal to assume the alias of Dr. Mabuse. In the chaos of Hitler's defeat, all the police records concerning the original master criminal had fallen into the hands of an admirer who then proceeded to brazenly copy his methods. This new Dr. Mabuse learned of the Hotel Luxor, a hotel that the Nazis had constructed in the last days of World War II. The establishment was secretly outfitted with television cameras and other devices in order to act as a center of espionage. The new Mabuse gained control of the Hotel Luxor, and used the hidden cameras on wealthy guests in order to provide intelligence for robberies. These cameras represent the "1000 eyes" of the title.

Mabuse adopted the identity of Peter Cornelius, a blind psychic. For a time, Mabuse as Cornelius tricked the police in believing that he had genuine powers of clairvoyance. Thus, the master criminal positioned himself to both give the authorities false information and learned intelligence from them.

The schemes of the new Mabuse unraveled when a female underling, Marion Menil, betrayed him. After her betrayal, Marion was severely wounded by a bullet to the chest. In the standard prints of the film, the impression was given that Marion survived an operation in the hospital. However, there supposedly is an extended version of the scene in which she died after the operation

Various parallels exist between Lang's third *Mabuse* film and Feuillade's second *Judex* serial. Prosper Cocantin, a bungling private detective, aided Judex in his investigation. Baronne d'Apremont tricked Cocantin into revealing important information by pretending to be a psychic called La Belle Fathma. The false identity of the treacherous baroness may have been the inspiration for Mabuse's alter ego of Peter Cornelius.

Besides her similarities to Thomas Kent from *Das Testament des Dr. Mabuse*. Belles-Mirettes, the woman who betrayed *N'a-qu'un-Chasse*, also resembled Marion Menil. Like Marion, Belles-Mirettes was shot in the chest after she turned against her criminal superior.

The concept of mass surveillance from the third *Mabuse* film also had its precedent in the *Judex* serials. In the first serial, Judex had a base underneath the ruins of a fortress called the Chateau Rouge. The vigilante hero abducted a corrupt banker and placed him in a prison in the Chateau Rouge. The cell was monitored by an early form of television. By the second serial, Judex had a network of television screens that allowed him to monitor multiple cells under the Chateau

Rouge. Judex imprisoned three agents of *N'a-qu'un-Chasse* in these cells.

N'a-qu'un-Chasse masqueraded as a one-eyed man. He boasted that, although he had only one eye, he could see all. By contrast, the third Mabuse posed as a blind man and was the secret master of "1000 eyes."

Further *Mabuse* films would be made by other directors. David Kalat noted that all of them have a recurring theme. The Mabuse figure engineers his own defeat. This was also true of Mabuse's predecessor, *N'a-qu'un-Chasse*. Feuillade's villain was blown up by his own explosive device.

There was a certain irony in the first *Mabuse* film made after Lang left the series. Produced by Brauner and directed by Harald Reinl, *Im Stahlnetz des Dr. Mabuse* (English title: *The Return of Dr. Mabuse*, 1961), Mabuse briefly wore a black hat and cloak. Although this costume may have been inspired by The Shadow, Mabuse was technically dressing up like Judex.

Rick Lai

SF & FANTASY

Léon Gozlan. *The Vampire of the Val-de-Grâce*
G.L. Gick. *Harry Dickson and the Werewolf of Rutherford Grange*
Edmond Haraucourt. *Illusions of Immortality*
Nathalie Henneberg. *The Green Gods*
V. Hugo, P. Foucher & P. Meurice. *The Hunchback of Notre-Dame*
Romain d'Huissier. *Hexagon: Dark Matter*
Michel Jeury. *Chronolysis*
Gustave Kahn. *The Tale of Gold and Silence*
Gérard Klein. *The Mote in Time's Eye*
Fernand Kolney. *Love in 5000 Years*
Louis-Guillaume de La Follie. *The Unpretentious Philosopher*
Jean de La Hire. *Enter the Nyctalope; The Nyctalope on Mars; The Nyctalope vs. Lucifer; The Nyctalope Steps In; Night of the Nyctalope*
Etienne-Léon de Lamothe-Langon. *The Virgin Vampire*
André Laurie. *Spiridon*
Gabriel de Lautrec. *The Vengeance of the Oval Portrait*
Alain le Drimeur. *The Future City*
Georges Le Faure & Henri de Graffigny. *The Extraordinary Adventures of a Russian Scientist Across the Solar System* (2 vols.)
Gustave Le Rouge. *The Vampires of Mars; The Dominion of the World* (w/Gustave Guitton) (4 vols.)
Jules Lermina. *Mysteryville; Panic in Paris; To-Ho and the Gold Destroyers; The Secret of Zippelius*
Jean-Marc & Randy Lofficier. *Edgar Allan Poe on Mars; The Katrina Protocol; Pacifica; Robonocchio; Tales of the Shadowmen 1-9*
Xavier Mauméjean. *The League of Heroes*
Joseph Méry. *The Tower of Destiny*
Hippolyte Mettais. *The Year 5865*
Louise Michel. *The Human Microbes; The New World*
Tony Moilin. *Paris in the Year 2000*
José Moselli. *Illa's End*
John-Antoine Nau. *Enemy Force*
Marie Nizet. *Captain Vampire*
C. Nodier, A. Beraud & Toussaint-Merle. *Frankenstein*
Henri de Parville. *An Inhabitant of the Planet Mars*
Gaston de Pawlowski. *Journey to the Land of the 4th Dimension*
Georges Pellerin. *The World in 2000 Years*
Ernest Pérochon. *The Frenetic People*
Pierre Pelot. *The Child Who Walked on the Sky*
J. Polidori, C. Nodier, E. Scribe. *Lord Ruthven the Vampire*
P.-A. Ponson du Terrail. *The Vampire and the Devil's Son*

Henri de Régnier. *A Surfeit of Mirrors*

Maurice Renard. *The Blue Peril; Doctor Lerne; The Doctored Man; A Man Among the Microbes; The Master of Light*

Jean Richepin. *The Wing; The Crazy Corner*

Albert Robida. *The Adventures of Saturnin Farandoul; The Clock of the Centuries; Chalet in the Sky*

J.-H. Rosny Aîné. *Helgvor of the Blue River; The Givreuse Enigma; The Mysterious Force; The Navigators of Space; Vamireh; The World of the Variants; The Young Vampire*

Marcel Rouff. *Journey to the Inverted World*

Han Ryner. *The Superhumans*

Brian Stableford. *The New Faust at the Tragicomique; The Empire of the Necromancers (The Shadow of Frankenstein; Frankenstein and the Vampire Countess; Frankenstein in London); Sherlock Holmes & The Vampires of Eternity; The Stones of Camelot; The Wayward Muse.* (anthologist) *The Germans on Venus; News from the Moon; The Supreme Progress; The World Above the World; Nemoville; Investigations of the Future*

Jacques Spitz. *The Eye of Purgatory*

Kurt Steiner. *Ortog*

Eugène Thébault. *Radio-Terror*

C.-F. Tiphaigne de La Roche. *Amilec*

Théo Varlet. *The Golden Rock. The Xenobiotic Invasion; Timeslip Troopers* (w/André Blandin); *The Martian Epic* (w/Octave Joncquel)

Paul Vibert. *The Mysterious Fluid*

Villiers de l'Isle-Adam. *The Scaffold; The Vampire Soul*

Philippe Ward. *Artahe*

Philippe Ward & Sylvie Miller. *The Song of Montségur*

MYSTERIES & THRILLERS

M. Allain & P. Souvestre. *The Daughter of Fantômas*

A. Anicet-Bourgeois, Lucien Dabril. *Rocambole*

A. Bernède. *Belphegor*; *Judex* (w/Louis Feuillade); *The Return of Judex* (w/Louis Feuillade)

A. Bisson & G. Livet. *Nick Carter vs. Fantômas*

V. Darlay & H. de Gorsse. *Arsène Lupin vs. Sherlock Holmes: The Stage Play*

Séamas Duffy. *Sherlock Holmes in Paris*

Paul Féval. *Gentlemen of the Night; John Devil; The Black Coats ('Salem Street; The Invisible Weapon; The Parisian Jungle; The*

Companions of the Treasure; Heart of Steel; The Cadet Gang; The Sword-Swallower)
Emile Gaboriau. *Monsieur Lecoq*
Goron & Emile Gautier. *Spawn of the Penitentiary*
Steve Leadley. *Sherlock Holmes: The Circle of Blood*
Maurice Leblanc. *Arsène Lupin vs. Countess Cagliostro; Arsène Lupin vs. Sherlock Holmes (The Blonde Phantom; The Hollow Needle); The Many Faces of Arsène Lupin*
Gaston Leroux. *Chéri-Bibi; The Phantom of the Opera; Rouletabille & the Mystery of the Yellow Room; Rouletabille at Krupp's*
Richard Marsh. *The Complete Adventures of Judith Lee*
William Patrick Maynard. *The Terror of Fu Manchu; The Destiny of Fu Manchu*
Frank J. Morlock. *Sherlock Holmes: The Grand Horizontals; Sherlock Holmes vs Jack the Ripper*
Antonin Reschal. *The Adventures of Miss Boston*
P. de Wattyne & Y. Walter. *Sherlock Holmes vs. Fantômas*
David White. *Fantômas in America*

SCREENPLAYS

Mike Baron. *The Iron Triangle*
Emma Bull & Will Shetterly. *Nightspeeder; War for the Oaks*
Gerry Conway & Roy Thomas. *Doc Dynamo*
Steve Englehart. *Majorca*
James Hudnall. *The Devastator*
Jean-Marc & Randy Lofficier. *Royal Flush*
J.-M. & R. Lofficier & Marc Agapit. *Despair*
J.-M. & R. Lofficier & Joël Houssin. *City*
Andrew Paquette. *Peripheral Vision*
Robert L. Robinson, Jr. *Judex*
R. Thomas, J. Hendler & L. Sprague de Camp. *Rivers of Time*

NON-FICTION

Stephen R. Bissette. *Blur 1-5. Green Mountain Cinema 1; Teen Angels*
Win Scott Eckert. *Crossovers* (2 vols.)
Jean-Marc & Randy Lofficier. *Shadowmen* (2 vols.)
Randy Lofficier. *Over Here*

ART BOOKS

Jean-Pierre Normand. *Science Fiction Illustrations*
Raven Okeefe. *Raven's L'il Critters; Rave's Faves*
Randy Lofficier & Raven Okeefe. *If Your Possum Go Daylight...*
Daniele Serra. *Illusions*

HEXAGON COMICS

Franco Frescura & Luciano Bernasconi. *Wampus*
Franco Frescura & Giorgio Trevisan. *CLASH*
L. Bernasconi, J.-M. Lofficier & Juan Roncagliolo Berger. *Phenix*
Claude Legrand, J.-M. Lofficier & L. Bernasconi. *Kabur*
Franco Oneta. *Zembla*
L. Buffolente, Lofficier & J.-J. Dzialowski. *Strangers: Homicron*
Danilo Grossi. *Strangers: Jaydee*
Claude Legrand & Luciano Bernasconi. *Strangers: Starlock*

www.ingramcontent.com/pod-product-compliance
Lightning Source LLC
Chambersburg PA
CBHW030343020726
47493CB00003B/670